George B. Smith

William I. and the German Empire

A Biographical and Historical Sketch

George B. Smith

William I. and the German Empire
A Biographical and Historical Sketch

ISBN/EAN: 9783337169329

Printed in Europe, USA, Canada, Australia, Japan

Cover: Foto ©Andreas Hilbeck / pixelio.de

More available books at **www.hansebooks.com**

AND THE

GERMAN EMPIRE

A Biographical and Historical Sketch

BY

G. BARNETT SMITH,

AUTHOR OF "POETS AND NOVELISTS," "LIFE OF HER MAJESTY
THE QUEEN," "THE BIOGRAPHY OF MR. GLADSTONE,"
ETC. ETC.

NEW AND CHEAPER EDITION

REVISED AND BROUGHT DOWN TO DATE

LONDON

SAMPSON LOW, MARSTON, SEARLE, & RIVINGTON

LIMITED

St. Dunstan's House

FETTER LANE, FLEET STREET, E.C.

1888

PREFACE TO THE NEW EDITION.

Since the ensuing work was written, that event to which Europe had long looked forward with apprehension has occurred. The Emperor William has died full of years and honours. As Berlin is now the acknowledged centre of European politics, such a change naturally excites the profoundest interest in other capitals. But in Germany there is reason to hope that it will bring no accession to the war fever, as it must have done if the Emperor's death had occurred during the work of reconstruction. German unity is now an acknowledged fact, and the German races have been successfully consolidated into one great nationality. This gives hope for the future; and the testament of the dead and the programme of the living Emperor alike constitute a policy of peace which affords a tranquillising prospect for the European continent. Of the great Emperor William it may well be said that he rests from his labours while his works do follow him.

G. B. S.

March 13th, 1888.

PREFACE TO THE FIRST EDITION.

THE Emperor William is not only in himself a vigorous and striking personality, but he is the embodiment of that great German Power which is now the first factor in European politics. He is thus invested with a double interest, individual and national. In tracing his singularly fortunate and dramatic career in the following pages, I have therefore sought to combine with the personal narrative some account, first, of the Prussian Kingdom and people, and secondly, of the foundation and consolidation of the new German Empire. My information has been gathered from a variety of sources, as I have acknowledged in the body of the work. In the Appendix I have given a collection of Statistics from recent returns, which furnish a bird's eye view of the extent, growth, and present position of Germany. I have thus endeavoured to give a triple aspect to this sketch—the biographical, the social and progressive, and the historical; and I shall be glad if in consequence it be found to possess a more than ephemeral value.

G. B. S.

CONTENTS.

CHAPTER X.

CHAPTER XI.

CHAPTER XII.

CHAPTER XIII.

CHAPTER XIV.

CHAPTER XV.

APPENDIX.

WILLIAM I. AND THE GERMAN EMPIRE.

CHAPTER I.

THE EMPEROR'S BIRTH AND ANCESTRY.

CARLYLE has deified the greatest of all the Kings of Prussia in a work whose literary vigour and intensity stand confessed. With a breadth and skill suggestive of the effects of Rembrandt in art, he has painted a graphic and enduring portrait of the redoubtable Frederick, and one which no German writer has been able to rival. Whether the Prussian monarch was worthy of all the laudation of his English biographer is a debateable point. Carlyle's judgment was to some extent led captive because he saw in Frederick the last of the great kings; but others will continue to hold that this mighty conqueror was but a composite god after all—that if he was in part pure gold, he had feet of clay, and that the line once applied to a wholly different personage, 'the wisest, greatest, meanest of mankind' is equally applicable to Frederick the Great.

This sketch of the life of the German Emperor opens with some references to his illustrious ancestor, because there are not only points of similarity in their characters, but equally dramatic surprises in their respective careers. The Emperor William has not those literary gifts for which Frederick was distinguished, and which curiously enough led the latter to become an ardent admirer of French thought as exemplified in Voltaire and Maupertuis; but he has many of the same personal qualities. The simplicity of his habits, his unostentatious demeanour, his strong understanding, his energy, and his personal courage, had all their counterparts in Frederick. The earlier ruler, moreover, witnessed during his life such an extension of Prussia as cannot be paralleled, except by the extension of the German nation in the time of the Emperor William. A century only separates the two

B

men, but it is one of the most momentous centuries in the history of the human race.

A rapid historical glance over this century as affecting Prussia, gives us at the same time the personal history of the Emperor William's immediate progenitors. Frederick the Great, who had few of the higher aspirations of humanity, and whose love of everything French was in striking contrast to the Francophobia prevalent amongst so many of his countrymen in our own day, led two distinct lives. He was the man of letters and the man of action. In the former capacity he wrote a series of memoirs and histories which would have gained him some note had they not been the productions of a king. As a man of action and a soldier, he was swift, alert, judicious, and far-seeing, and he succeeded in building up one of the most powerful states of modern Europe. Dying in 1786, he left a splendid legacy to his successor and nephew, Frederick William II. But once more was observed that frequent occurrence in history, of talent being succeeded by incompetency, and strength by vacillation. The new monarch undertook wars which he was unable to carry through, and soon impoverished the well-filled Prussian treasury, turning the magnificent inheritance of seventy million thalers which existed on his accession to a deficit of twenty-two million thalers, which negative legacy was the only thing he bequeathed to his unfortunate subjects. But not content with running down the prestige of the kingdom without, this king incurred great unpopularity at home by muzzling the press, introducing oppressive legislative enactments, and in imitating our own Charles II. by lavishing his resources upon mistresses and favourites. Yet at the same time the domains of Prussia received an accession of 46,000 square miles of territory during his reign by purchase and inheritance, and by that renewed infamy the second partition of Poland in 1793.

In 1797 Frederick William II. was gathered to his fathers —where it would have been well if he had been gathered long before—and great hopes were entertained of his son, Frederick William III., the father of the subject of our biography. Immediately upon his accession, he dismissed the idle and vicious favourites of his predecessor, and made a tour of the provinces of the kingdom, accompanied by his noble and beautiful young queen, Louisa of Mecklenburg-Strelitz. The King desired to improve the condition of his subjects, and to raise the financial status of Prussia, and for some time honestly worked for these objects. Could he have looked into the horoscope of the future, and seen something of the sad misfortunes which awaited him in the course of only a few years, his courage might have been stimulated to action to avert these impending calamities; but with that fatal weakness which has beset so many of the House of Brandenburg at critical moments, his will failed him, and he was unable to grapple with the difficulties of his position. While the great European struggle with France was in progress, the King of Prussia endeavoured to maintain an attitude of neutrality, which made him unpopular with the other German princes. At length he concluded an alliance with France, which at first promised well, as it brought him the territories of Hildesheim, Paderborn, and Münster; but the veil was soon lifted upon the treacherous character of Napoleon, and in 1805 Frederick William was compelled to enter into a compact with Russia, whose object was to drive Napoleon out of Germany. By another turn in the diplomatic wheel, however, Prussia agreed to the designs of France, and consented to receive the electorate of Hanover, which naturally meant war with England. European complications became so threatening and unavoidable in 1806, that in response to the calls of his Queen and people, Frederick William declared war against France. The result was that by Napoleon's victories at Jena, Eylau, and Friedland, the kingdom of Prussia was practically crumpled up. By the Treaty of Tilsit the King lost the greater part of his dominions. Queen Louisa vainly endeavoured to procure some modification of the humiliating conditions of peace; and Napoleon's unmanly and insulting treatment of the hapless Queen is a serious stigma upon a character pretty well studded with heartless and offensive blots of this kind. The Prussians had to submit to the indignity of a French occupation of Berlin for three years. Then the King lost his high-minded and chivalrous Queen. For some time Frederick William was a tool in the hands of Napoleon; but his spirit was not subdued, and his unremitting efforts at this period of his life to reorganize his enfeebled government by self-sacrifices of every kind, endeared him greatly to his

people. He not only effected reforms of great moment in
the administration, but established the University of Berlin.
The sun of Napoleon now began to set, and after the battle of
Leipsic, in which the allies were signally victorious, Prussia
regained almost all her former possessions. Her bearing
at Waterloo raised her prestige still higher. Frederick
William accompanied the allies to Paris, and signed the
treaty of peace. Now that the power of Napoleon was
utterly destroyed, the King of Prussia began to devote
himself to internal reforms. His best and greatest achieve-
ment was the formation of the great commercial league
known as the Zollverein, which organized the German
customs and duties upon one uniform basis. But while he
sought to encourage trade and manufactures, Frederick
William remained a despot towards his people. He solemnly
promised them a constitution, but repudiated his promise;
and it was only too manifest that he dreaded the progress of
Liberal principles. Into political and religious questions
generally he carried the old spirit of absolutism as opposed
to the spirit of enlightened constitutionalism. Dying in
1840, the King left behind him, in the shape of a document
addressed to his eldest son, a virtual condemnation of some
of his own principles. 'Beware,' he said, 'of the love of
innovation, now so general; beware of impracticable theories,
so many of which are now in vogue; but, at the same time,
*beware of an almost equally fatal, obstinate predilection for
what is old*; for it is only by avoiding these two shoals that
really useful changes proceed.' Then he indicated what to a
large extent has been the policy of Prussia since his death:
'The army is now in a remarkably good condition; since its
reorganization it has fulfilled my expectations; as in war,
so also in peace. May it never lose sight of its high destiny, but may the country likewise never forget what it
owes to it. Do not neglect to provide for, as far as lies in
your power, concord among all the European powers; but,
above all, may Prussia, Russia, and Austria, never separate
from each other. Their union is to be regarded as the
keystone of the great European alliance.'

The Prince Royal having closed the eyes of his father in
death, was greeted by the Emperor of Russia, his brother-in-
law—who was also present in the death-chamber of the
King—as Frederick William IV. The new monarch had

received an unusually extensive and liberal education, and literature and the fine arts exercised a strong fascination over him all through his career. His reign opened with the concession of many minor reforms, but the hopes which the Prussians had built upon a larger and fuller liberty were doomed to be disappointed. Mr. Lowe observes, in his *Life of Prince Bismarck*, that the King ' had not been three months on the throne, when he bluntly told his subjects that he deemed a constitution unsuited to their wants, and meant to stick to the Zemstvo-like system still in force. What was worse, there was no reasoning with a sovereign, who, as the Prince Consort of England fairly judged him, adopted mere subjective feelings and opinions as the motive principle of his actions and was as a " reed shaken by the wind." The truth is that Frederick William IV., an accomplished and amiable gentleman in many respects, was born to be a professor of the fine arts, or a teacher of rhetoric; but it was a cruel freak of nature to make him a king of any kind whatever. Of all modern monarchs, he most resembled James I. of England ; but while not a bit less tenacious than the Stuart of the Divine-right doctrine, the Hohenzollern was even much more addicted to theology and the pedantry of the schools. Strauss, the acute author of the *Life of Jesus*, was one of those who satirized his crying frailties in this respect in a pamphlet entitled " Julian the Apostate ; or, the Romanticist on the throne of the Cæsars." Frederick William IV., did not, it is true, like James I., tremble at the sight of a drawn sword; but he had few soldierly instincts or sympathies, and therefore the army, that mainstay of an absolute monarch, soon came to return with interest the indifference of its chief. On the other hand, the King hated his bureaucracy, that other pillar of the Prussian State, for its rationalistic bent, and was in turn scorned by it for his ardent orthodoxy. The cruel disappointment, too, of all their dearest hopes had cooled the loyalty of the great mass of the people.'

So, although the King was in some respects well-intentioned, and was of a chivalrous nature, he committed grave mistakes, and became embroiled with his subjects in such a manner as to endanger the stability of his throne. He was also vacillating in his foreign policy. Having encouraged the Duchies of Holstein and Schleswig in their revolt against

Denmark, and sent troops to assist them, without rhyme or reason he abandoned their cause. Then, taking umbrage at the revolutionary character of the Frankfort Diet, he refused to accept the imperial crown which it offered him, though a united Germany had been the dream of his life. One writer, nevertheless, declares concerning this episode, that history has not on record a finer instance of self-sacrifice than the refusal of Frederick William to take advantage of the national passion for the purposes of his own ambition, and to ride on the wave of that enthusiasm, which he himself felt more than anyone, towards the prize of the Imperial Crown of Germany. Though it was the object of all his thoughts, that the German race should be united into one mighty monarchy, he felt that the primary title to sway that sceptre abode with the house of Hapsburg. So when the deputation from the Frankfort Assembly called upon him to offer him the crown of Charles V., he replied that he could not accept the offer unless it were confirmed by those whose rights as sovereign princes would be affected by it. His younger brother, the present Emperor, held slightly different views as to the natural supremacy of the Hapsburgs over the Hohenzollerns, though he too at first declined to take the title of Emperor.

In 1847 Frederick William published a patent convoking all the Provincial States in an assembly in Berlin, and creating a House of Lords. But Europe was soon in the throes of a revolution, which spread to the Prussian capital. This popular movement was at first resolutely opposed by the King; but when the people persisted in demanding the removal of the troops from the capital, and the populace stormed the arsenal, and seized on the palace of the King's brother—who was then very obnoxious to the Liberals—his Majesty was compelled to accede to their wishes. He found that he could only restore tranquillity to the capital by calling back the popular leaders to power, and publishing an amnesty. A futile war of constitutional assemblies ensued; constitutions were framed and abandoned; and when the revolutionary spirit had died away, the advanced members of the Assembly of 1848 were prosecuted and harshly treated. The religious and aristocratic parties regained their former ascendency at court, and political and religious liberty, as well as the freedom of the press, were largely curtailed. It is not surprising that under these circumstances the King became more unpopular than ever. His life was twice attempted—once in 1847 by a dismissed burgomaster named Tschech, and again in 1850 by an insane discharged soldier named Sefeloge. Nor was the King's name regarded with much favour abroad during the time of the Crimean War. Though pressed to declare himself on one side or the other, he wavered to such an extent as to offend both Russia and the Allies, and ultimately he took no part with either.

The fact was, there was little of the man of action in Frederick William IV. He found more pleasure in the pursuit of literature and the arts, and at his Court were to be met some of the finest spirits of the age—Schelling and Tieck, Cornelius and Mendelssohn. In course of time the burden of the crown and the cares of State became too much for him. His health had suffered greatly during the critical period of 1847–48, and early in 1852 an affection of the brain became manifest. For some years he struggled on, but in 1857 he was struck down by an attack of apoplexy, from which he never recovered. It became apparent in the following year that a Regency must be established. The King had married, in 1823, Elizabeth Louisa, daughter of the King of Bavaria, but as there was no issue, and, consequently, no son to appoint in the sovereign's place, the King's brother and heir presumptive to the throne, the present Emperor, was appointed Regent.

I must now trace the Emperor William's life up to the present juncture. William I., King of Prussia and Emperor of Germany, was the second son of Frederick William, Crown Prince of Prussia, and of Princess Louisa of Mecklenburg-Strelitz, to whom reference has already been made. He was born on the 22nd of March, 1797, in the Palace at Berlin, then occupied by his father, and situate between the old palace of Frederick the Great, and the new palace, 37, Under the Linden, now and for many years back occupied by the Emperor-King. At his baptism he received the names of Friedrich Ludvig Wilhelm. Amongst his numerous sponsors were the Emperor and Empress of Russia, the Prince and Princess of Orange, and the Landgraves of Hesse-Cassel and Hesse-Darmstadt. Only a few months after the Prince's birth, his father succeeded to the throne of Prussia. The times were very grave, and the young Prince grew up under the gloom engendered by the disastrous defeat of Jena, and the overshadowing power of Napoleon. It is curious to read that Prince William, who has lived to enter upon his tenth decade, was in his infancy a very delicate child, and that he was reared with difficulty. The care of him was entirely entrusted to persons of the gentler sex, and after a few years he repaid their watchfulness and assiduity. When only five years of age, he was present, with his mother, at a public ceremony in the Town Hall of Cocln, a division of Berlin. At Christmas, 1803, he donned the uniform of the Rudorf regiment, subsequently known as the Zieten regiment, which has since attained a still wider celebrity as the 'Red Hussars.'

As is the custom with Prussian princes, the youthful William was early made familiar by personal experience with service in the army. Speaking of the Prince's formal presentation to the Queen in his new uniform, a recent writer, in a brief sketch of the German Monarch, states that 'the Emperor still retains a lively remembrance of it, as well as of the keen delight he experienced at being permitted for the first time to wear uniform. The uniform itself was even gayer then than it is now—scarlet dolman slashed with silver, white facings, dark blue and gold pelisse, fur busby and white plume, boots and breeches.' This fine 'arrangement' in scarlet and white, and blue and gold, delighted the boy's heart, as did also the uniform of the Towarzcy Regiment—the predecessors of the famous Uhlans—which was presented to him a year later. From the age of seven, he was instructed in military exercises.

As regards his secular studies, he was at one time under the charge of Privy Councillor Dellbrück, who was succeeded by Professor Reimann. In the science of war he had the benefit of the tuition of Generals Von Scharnhorst and Von Knesebeck. 'Von Scharnhorst was one of the earliest and most sedulous advocates of the system of National Defence, the fundamental principle of which is compulsory man service, or, as its German appellation (*Allgemeinewehrpflicht*) more correctly describes it, " a common obligation to take up arms." He doubtless imbued his august pupil with his own convictions; for Prince William, when he became a member of the Army Reorganization Commission upon attaining his majority, energetically supported the adoption of the above principle into the Prussian army. His instructor in law was the celebrated international jurist, De Savigny; and he took lessons for nearly a year from Rauch—the sculptor of the famous statue of Frederick the Great—and from Schenkel, Berlin's greatest architect, in the plastic arts. As his taste for music, if he had any, was so latent as to be altogether undiscoverable, his judicious parents spared him the *peine forte et dure* of an apprenticeship to counter-point, thorough bass, and five-finger exercises.'

Prussia was soon at war with Buonaparte. The celebrated Rahel von Warnhagen repeatedly heard the lieutenants of the Guards in Berlin and Potsdam, boasting, with as much flippancy as infatuation : ' With the Austrians, it may have been easy work for Napoleon ; but just let him attack us Prussians, and he is sure to get more than he bargained for.' This was but another example of pride going before a fall, as the event proved. In 1806 the troops marched out of Berlin, and amongst those who watched them from the windows of the Palace was the youthful Prince William. Queen Louisa followed her husband to the headquarters of the Prussian army, and the young princes were left alone in Berlin. After the disastrous battle of Jena they were conveyed to Schwedt. At this place they were shortly joined by their mother, who burst into tears upon first greeting them. Some historians state that Her Majesty addressed her children in the following words, and as they were certainly used by the Queen at this time, the context would seem to show that they must have been spoken to the young Princes :—' You see my tears ; I am weeping for the destruction of our army. It has not satisfied the expectation of the King. In one day an edifice has been destroyed which will take great men two centuries to rebuild. Prussia, its army, and its traditional glory are things of the past. Ah ! my children, you are not yet of that age when you can fully comprehend the great calamity that has befallen us. But after my death, and when you recall this unfortunate hour, do not content yourselves with merely shedding tears. Act ! Unite your powers ! Perhaps the guardian angel of Prussia will watch over you. Liberate your people from the disgrace and degradation they will have to endure. Conquer France and retrieve the glory of your ancestors, as your great-grandfather did at Fehrbellin, when he defeated the Swedes. Be men, and strive to be great generals. If you have not that ambition, then you are unworthy to be the descendants of Frederick the Great.' This high-souled Queen was indeed worthy to have brave sons.

The Royal family now moved about from place to place, and in January, 1807, we find them at Königsberg, where the King also came for a few days. On the 1st of the above month Prince William entered the army. He was three months under the usual age of ten years, but he received his commission from his father, and within a year got his first promotion. His first two commissions were in fact dated respectively January 1st, and December 24th, 1807. He had evidently by this time greatly improved in health, as he went through all the drills, parades, and reviews customary with the First Guards. Of his character we have this glimpse, in a letter written on his eleventh birthday by his mother to the Grand Duke of Mecklenburg-Strelitz: 'Our son William—permit me, venerable grandpapa, to introduce your grandchildren to you in regular order—will turn out, unless I be much mistaken, like his father; simple, honest, and intelligent. He resembles him most of all, but will not, I fancy, be so handsome.' One who was qualified to judge, while echoing to the full the maternal praises of the Prince, affirms that he turned out to be handsomer than any of the Hohenzollerns, alive or dead.

On the termination of the war, the fatal treaty of Tilsit was signed. Prussia not only lost all her possessions between the Rhine and the Elbe, with the Old March and Magdeburg, but also the greater part of Poland. From the acquisitions between the Rhine and the Elbe, Napoleon formed the new Kingdom of Westphalia for his brother Jerome; out of the Polish provinces, the Grand Duchy of Warsaw, for the King of Saxony; and by way of insulting while spoliating the King of Prussia, the instrument of peace expressly stated that the restoration of the other conquered countries, especially of the marches on the right side of the Elbe, of Silesia, Pomerania, old East Prussia, and West Prussia, was 'made *only out of respect for His Majesty the Emperor of Russia.'*

It was a painful time of sorrow and privation for the fallen family at Königsberg. The Royal table was with difficulty supplied with the meanest food, and the King was so embarrassed for money that he had to send the golden dinner-service of Frederick the Great to the mint. Yet the sons bore everything with a brave heart, and Prince William set himself to study the works of his great-uncle, the famous warrior-philosopher. In consequence of the proximity of the French, the Royal family removed from Königsberg to Memel; and at this place the Queen, who was almost prostrate from mental and physical suffering, was attacked by typhus fever. But the enemy still came on, and this courageous woman insisted on leaving Memel, though it was winter and the weather was very inclement: 'I would rather render myself to God,' said the Queen, 'than fall into the hands of those men.' Her children also were ill, for the Crown Prince had been attacked with scarlet fever, and Prince William suffered at the same time from nervous fever. There was scarcely a gleam of hope anywhere, and the Queen wrote to her father, 'All is over with us, if not for ever, at least for the present. My hope is gone. We have slept too long under the laurels of Frederick the Great.'

At length the foreign occupation of Berlin ceased, and the French left the city. The Prussian Royal family returned thither on Christmas Eve, 1809, Prince William entering the capital with his parents by the Bernau gate. Time had brought, outwardly, at least, a spirit of partial resignation, for Queen Louisa, in writing to Madame Von Berg, had said: 'I do not complain to live in the years of misfortune; it will, I trust, chasten both me and my family.' Nevertheless, deep down in her heart was a feeling of despair and of hopeless grief. The King, too, was so depressed that he wanted to resign, feeling that God was working against him. In 1810, however, he was called upon to sustain the bitterest trial of all—his beloved wife was stricken down with a fatal illness. Some time before, she had thus written to her father with prophetic insight concerning the future of Napoleon and her own life: 'I do not believe that the Emperor Napoleon Buonaparte is firm and secure on his throne, brilliant as it is, at this moment. Truth and justice alone stand firm and secure; yet he is only politic, that is to say, worldly-wise, not acting in obedience to eternal laws, but according to circumstances such as he finds them. Besides this, he sullies his rule with many acts of injustice. He does not mean honestly to the good cause and to mankind. In his unbounded ambition he cares only for self, and for his own personal interest. At the same time, he knows no moderation in anything; and he who is not able to restrain himself must lose his balance and fall. I firmly believe in a God, and consequently in a moral order of the world, which I do not see realized in an ascendency of brute force. I therefore hope that the present evil times will be followed by better ones. It is quite evident that all that has been done, and is doing, is not to be permanent, nor to be considered as the best state of things, but a state of transition to a happier goal. This goal, however, seems to lie far off; we shall probably not see it reached, but die in the meanwhile. God's will be done!'

Waterloo avenged Prussia, and Napoleon fell never to rise again; but the already dying Queen did not live to see the re-creation of her country. She died at the castle of Hohenzieritz, on the 19th of July, 1810, in the thirty-fifth year of her age. She passed away peacefully in the presence of the King and of her sister, the Princess of Solms. On examination, the physicians found a polypus at her heart; it was grief for the fatherland that had killed her. When her beloved Magdeburg was lost, she had exclaimed, 'that if she could lay open her heart, the name of that city would be found written upon it in indelible characters.' The King was crushed by this overwhelming sorrow. Days before his consort's death he had cried out in anguish: 'Oh, if she were not mine she would live, but as she is mine she is sure to die!' The strong man fainted when he told his children of their irreparable loss, and the grief of the young Princes was touching to behold.

When Napoleon heard of the death of the Queen whom he had insulted, he remarked: 'The King has lost his best minister.' But her spirit lived on, and began to infuse itself into the people. Liberation was approaching, though for the present Europe could only realize that God's hand was heavy upon the Prussian nation and its Sovereign.

CHAPTER II.

FROM YOUTH TO MANHOOD.

PRUSSIA soon began her work of preparation for another struggle with the French Colossus. And the King, who had now only his country and his children to think of, rose up after his paroxysms of grief were over, and strained his eyes not without hope into the future. The whole nation was in a state of expectancy, awaiting the development of events which should again lift the Prussian standard from the dust. Amongst others who were hoping to be of service to the fatherland, and who were training themselves accordingly, was Prince William, now thirteen years of age. One of his tutors, in describing his Royal pupil as he appeared at this time, wrote: ‘At thirteen I found Prince William possessed of a sharp, practical understanding, a remarkable love of order, and a talent for drawing. He had a firm will, and a singularly earnest mind for his age.’ The Prince received constant instruction in strategy, field-planning, fortification, and in military history. Under the direction of Major Von Pirch he went through his military duties with infantry, cavalry, artillery, and engineers. That he was specially skilled in engineering is proved from a piece of field-work, whose whole details of construction he directed in 1811, when he was not yet fourteen years of age.

Prince William was appointed First Lieutenant on the 15th of May, 1812, and Captain on the ensuing 30th of October. He was now attached to his father's staff, and went to Frankfort-on-the-Main, where he took command of his company of the Guards. On the 22nd of January, 1813, the King left Berlin, and set out for Breslau. He was accompanied by his children, and in his train were two famous men, Scharnhorst and Blücher, who both did much for the salvation of their country. There was an animated scene at Breslau, the windows of all the houses being filled with spectators; the streets were thronged with marching troops, cannon, powder-waggons, and vehicles laden with arms of every description. The place was like a human sea, and every one felt that a new era was dawning. Frederick William issued a proclamation on the 3rd of February, calling upon the young men of the country voluntarily to arm for the protection of the Fatherland. Although it was not distinctly affirmed that the war was to be conducted against the French oppressor, all true hearts understood the Royal proclamation, and hailed the expected deliverance of Germany. At Kalisch, on the 27th, a treaty of alliance was concluded with Russia, and the Emperor Alexander visited the King and the Prussian princes at Breslau.

War against France was formally declared on the 27th of March, and before the close of the year, Napoleon found, to his cost, that the Prussia he had despised had mobilized a new army, and one as hopeful in spirit as it was strong in numbers. Scharnhorst had done his work of organization splendidly, and a cry went forth from thousands of Prussian lips for the expulsion of the French from German soil. Much to his chagrin, Prince William was not allowed to take part in the first campaign, chiefly owing to his delicate health. He was therefore not present at the battle of Gross-Görschen, where the Prussian foot-guards suffered severely. When promotions were granted, and the young Prince received his commission as First Lieutenant, he said to his father, 'How can I feel worthy of it? I who have been sitting by the fireside while my regiment has been marching through the fire.' The King replied, 'It was I who ordered it, and you shall lose nothing by my commands.' But after the power of Napoleon was first broken at Leipsic, and in response to repeated entreaties, the King granted permission to his impatient son to join the army. Accordingly, on the first day of the new year, 1814, the Prince crossed the Rhine at Mannheim, in the staff of his father. The allied army was commanded by Prince Schwarzenburg. It was on French territory, at Bar-sur-Aube, on the 27th of February, that Prince William received his 'baptism of fire,' and in this case there appears to have been no doubt either as to the martial ardour or courage of the recipient. 'Under his father's eye,' we read in one account of the engagement, 'he charged the French with the Pskow Cuirassiers, riding on their right wing; and as he was returning at an easy trot from that charge, in which the Russian horsemen suffered terribly, his father, the King, noticing an infantry regiment some distance off, heavily engaged with the enemy, turned to him and said, " Ride back and find out what regiment that is, and to what corps all those wounded belong." Turning his horse, Prince William drove in his spurs, and dashed back into the thick of the fray. The regiment (Kaluga Infantry) was clustered on the crest of a slope covered with vines, and was exchanging a murderous fire with a body of French Tirailleurs occupying the opposite slopes. Officers and men were falling fast, as Prince William rode up to the Colonel, and, saluting as though on parade, made the inquiries he had been ordered to make with perfect coolness. As soon as he had obtained all the desired details, he rode off at a canter, and, joining the King, verbally reported what he had learnt. His Majesty uttered no word of approval, or even of acknowledgment, though the whole Royal staff was pressing round the gallant lad in delighted admiration.' But the honours which deservedly followed the young soldier's brave conduct were not long delayed. The Emperor of Russia conferred upon Prince William the Cross of St. George, a much-prized distinction, and on the 10th of March the King of Prussia showed that he had not forgotten his son's services, by bestowing upon him the Iron Cross, a decoration more highly-valued by Prussian soldiers than any other. On receiving the Iron Cross, Prince William said to his brother, the Crown Prince, ' Now I begin to understand why Colonel von Luck shook hands with me so warmly the other day, after I had made my report, and why all the other staff officers smiled so significantly.' But if the King had been sparing of his son's praise on the field, he despatched a glowing report to the home circle at Berlin, and the Prince's sister, Charlotte, afterwards Empress of Russia, sent her brother a letter of congratulation, in which she remarked, ' that all his sisters looked with pride on their brother William.'

The war went all in favour of the Allies, and on the 31st of March, 1814, the King of Prussia and the Emperor of Russia made their triumphal entry into the French capital. Prince William accompanied his father, who took up his quarters at the Hôtel Villeroi in the Rue de Bourbon. The Prince had now been promoted to the rank of major for gallantry in the field. Frederick William remained in Paris for upwards of two months, and then, early in June, he came with the Emperor Alexander upon a visit to England, at the pressing invitation of the Prince Regent. They remained from the 7th to the 23rd of June, and there was little else but feasting and lionizing during the whole of that period.

The King of Prussia and his two sons excited deep interest, but the greatest English honours were undoubtedly paid to bluff old Blücher. He was obliged to have recourse to even more stratagems than he had employed in the field to evade the myriad practical displays of enthusiasm of which he was the object. But he was mightily pleased with the British metropolis. 'No, indeed,' he said, 'there is no city in the world like London.' When the University of Oxford made the King and the Emperor doctors, they also included Metternich and Blücher in the honours. Blücher characteristically remarked, 'You ought to make Gneisenau apothecary, for he has worked the pills for me: we two always go together.' The blunt marshal had a contempt for diplomatists, whom he described as 'those rascally quill-drivers.' When peace was about to be signed, he told them to do their share of the work, adding, 'Ye will have to answer before God and man if our work is in vain, and has to be done over again.' He was just the sort of warrior to captivate British tars and soldiers. When he left England, 300,000 people collected to greet him at Portsmouth; two sailors danced a hornpipe on the top of his carriage, and, on reaching his hotel, the gallant marshal drained a formidable and foaming tankard of beer 'To the health of the English nation.'

If Paris and London were so enthusiastic, it may be imagined what Berlin was like when the victorious King entered it in August, accompanied by his sons and followed by his brave generals and army. The scene has never faded from the recollection of the German monarch, who then took part in it with no small share of pride and rejoicing.

Early in the year 1815 Prince William was confirmed in the Royal Chapel at Charlottenburg. Not long afterwards Europe was again startled from its security by the intelligence that Napoleon had left Elba, and was once more in the field. Blücher's first exclamation on hearing the news was, 'Well, here is a pretty kettle of fish!' He then called on the English Ambassador, and, 'swore that, if he caught the rascal (Buonaparte), he would have him shot without any further ceremony.' The Allies were soon ready to engage their old foe, and Prince William, at the head of a battalion of Fusiliers of the First Regiment of the Guard, was about to cross the French frontier, when news of the glorious victory of Waterloo arrived. Once more the allied sovereigns entered Paris, and on this occasion the Emperors of Russia and Austria and the King of Prussia concluded that famous compact known in history as the Holy Alliance.

A durable peace now ensued for Europe, and Prussia began the task of consolidating her power, under the direction of the King, assisted by the celebrated Stein, who occupied a position at this time equivalent to that now held by Bismarck. Both were master-spirits in the art of construction and reorganization; and what Stein did for the State, Gneisenau and Scharnhorst did for the army. While this work was in progress, Prince William was not idle. In 1817 he was promoted to the rank of Colonel, and took command of the First Battalion of the 1st Foot Guards. He was also elevated to the rank of a Privy Councillor. Accompanying his sister Charlotte to St. Petersburg, where she was to espouse the Czarewitch Nicholas, he held the crown over her head during the marriage ceremony (according to Russian custom), when the wedding took place on the 13th of July. The Prince was advanced to the rank of a Major-General on attaining his majority in 1818, and, so great was the King's confidence in him, that, during His Majesty's lengthened visit to Russia shortly afterwards, he was entrusted with the charge of the whole Prussian Military Department.

The Prince's life from this time forward was a very active one. In addition to tours of military inspection made throughout the Prussian provinces, he was sent on frequent professional missions to Austria, Italy, Russia, Belgium, Switzerland, &c. He was advanced to the rank of Lieut.-General, commanding a *Corps d'Armée*, and he took an active part in the work of the reorganization of the army. We obtain a pleasant glimpse of him in 1820 in the letters of Baron Bunsen. The King of Prussia and two of his sons, Prince William and Prince Charles, paid a visit to Rome in that year. The King himself was conducted by Niebuhr round the Eternal City, while Bunsen took charge of the two Princes. 'They are both very observant and intelligent,' writes Bunsen, 'the one twenty-three, the other twenty years of age, and at the same time patterns of engaging and yet dignified demeanour. Prince William, the elder of the two, is of a serious and manly character, which one cannot behold and perceive without feeling heartily devoted to him, and in all sincerity to hold him in high esteem.' On the accession of Czar Nicholas to the throne of Russia in December, 1825, Prince William was deputed to bear his father's congratulations to the Emperor and Empress, the latter being the King's daughter.

The Prince did not escape the tender passion, and we hear of a bitter disappointment in love which for some years drove from his mind all thoughts of matrimony; but, being on a visit to the Court of Saxe-Weimar in 1828, on the occasion of the betrothal of his brother, Prince Charles, to the Princess Mary, he saw for the first time the Princess Augusta, a handsome and cultivated girl of sixteen. She made a great impression upon him, just as he did amongst the frequenters of the Court, for Baron von Gagern wrote: 'Prince William presents before all the most noble and most striking figure of the Court, at once simple, brave, jovial, and gallant, yet dignified in his bearing. He is much drawn by the attractions of the Princess Augusta.' The betrothal of the Prince and Princess followed in February, 1829, and the wedding ceremony was celebrated on the 11th of June ensuing, in the Royal Palace at Berlin. Amongst the magnificent entertainments in honour of the occasion was a tourney called 'The Spell of the White Rose.' The bridegroom in silver armour held the lists in honour of his bride. The Prince's elder brother and the Emperor of Russia were present, and these three illustrious personages, who were all of imposing stature, were affirmed to be the three handsomest gentlemen of their day. On the 18th of October, 1831, the Princess William gave birth to the present Crown Prince of Prussia, who received the names of Frederick William Nicholas Charles.

The King of Prussia had four sons. The eldest, the Crown Prince, married Elizabeth of Bavaria, a Roman Catholic, who did not change her religion; Prince William, as stated above, married Augusta of Weimar, who became the King's favourite daughter-in-law; Prince Charles married in 1827 Mary of Weimar; and Prince Albrecht married in 1830 Marianne, Princess of the Netherlands, from whom he was at first separated and in 1849 divorced. His Majesty had also three daughters: Charlotte Alexandra, the eldest, married in 1817 the Emperor Nicholas of Russia; the next, Alexandrina, married in 1822 the Hereditary Grand Duke of

Schwerin; and Louisa, the youngest, married in 1825 Prince Frederick of the Netherlands. When the last of his daughters, and one specially beloved for her likeness to her mother, left the King, his loneliness was very great. After fifteen years of widowhood, being then in his fifty-fifth year, Frederick William married the Countess Augusta Harrach, a lady twenty-four years of age, whom he had met when drinking the waters at Töplitz. It was a morganatic marriage, and proved a very happy one. The King raised his bride to the rank of Princess of Liegnitz and Countess of Hohenzollern.

In 1834 Prince William commanded a military deputation despatched by the King of Prussia to honour the unveiling of a monument to the deceased Emperor Alexander in St. Petersburg. A few months later, at a Prussian Court ball, the Prince was much struck by two youths of lofty stature, who were introduced to him by the Master of the Ceremonies, and he pleasantly remarked, 'Well, it seems that Justice now-a-days recruits her youngsters in conformity to the Guards' standard!' The youths were lawyers practising in the Berlin Courts, and the taller of the two was none other than Otto Augustus Leopold von Bismarck. This was the first glimpse which Kaiser and Chancellor had of each other.

Frederick William III. had a tinge of superstition in his nature, and he had long entertained the conviction, and often given expression to it, that he should die in 1840. During his stay in Paris, in 1815, he had visited the notorious soothsayer, Mademoiselle Lenormand. It is stated that she prophesied the death of Napoleon to take place in 1821, and that of the King of Prussia in 1840. As the former prophecy—if it were really made, and it would seem to have been so from the King's attitude—actually came true, he could never shake off the feeling that the second would likewise. And indeed, at three o'clock in the afternoon of Whitsunday, the 7th of June, 1840, a day which had thus proved fatal to three of the rulers of Prussia—Frederick William III. breathed his last in the palace of Berlin, beneath whose windows had assembled a large crowd of the middle and lower classes.

Not long before the monarch's death, an incident occurred which testified to the strength of the military passion in the King's breast—a passion which was certainly transmitted to his second son. As the King lay ill upon his couch, the bands of the various Guard regiments marched past the palace playing patriotic tunes with great gusto. Prince William, in subsequently reporting the day's proceedings to his father, apologized for the strength of the music, hoping that it had not distressed the sufferer. 'I liked it very well,' replied the King, 'it did not disturb me in the least. I was able to distinguish each company and squadron as they went by. I hope they followed one another in proper numerical order.' The Prince having set his mind at rest on this point, his Majesty added, 'I only saw the parade for a moment. Everything was as it should have been.'

On the accession to the throne of his brother, Frederick William IV., Prince William became heir presumptive, and assumed, according to custom, the title of Prince of Prussia.

CHAPTER III.

PRINCE OF PRUSSIA.

THE new King was not long in discovering that conflicting elements were at work in Prussia. The spirit of freedom had touched most European peoples, and its influence was felt to some extent already in Germany. The nation had formed high expectations of Frederick William IV., and was looking forward to sweeping Constitutional reforms. These hopes were doomed to be disappointed. The King reverted to the old policy of the Prussian sovereigns, and became enamoured as were his predecessors of absolutist ideas. For two years he pursued a course of dubiety and indecision, and in 1842 crossed over to England for a change of scene, leaving the Prince of Prussia as Regent during his absence.

In 1844 Prince William had an important interview with Baron Bunsen at Berlin, in reference to the impending Constitutional struggle. 'The Prince spoke with me more than an hour,' says Bunsen; 'in the first place about England, then on the great question—the Constitution. I told him all that I had said to the King of facts that I had witnessed. Upon his question, what my opinion was? I requested time for consideration, as I had come hither to learn and to hear; but so much I could perceive and openly declare, that it would be impossible longer to govern with Provincial Assemblies *alone,*—it was as if the solar system should be furnished with centrifugal powers only. The Prince stated to me his own position relative to the great question, and to the King, with a clearness, precision, self-command, and openness which delighted me! He is quite like his father; throughout a noble-minded Prince of Brandenburg—of that house which has created Prussia.'

In July, 1844, the Prince of Prussia visited England, with Bunsen as his guide. He was received by the Queen and Prince Albert at Windsor on the 31st of August. 'I like him very much,' Her Majesty writes the same day. 'He is extremely amiable, agreeable, and sensible; cheerful and easy to get on with.' A later entry in her diary records: 'He is very amusing, sensible, and frank. On all public questions he spoke most freely, mildly, and judiciously, and I think would make a steadier and safer king than the present. He was in ecstasy with the park and the trees, as he is with everything in England.' The Prussian Ambassador also stated that the Prince 'took an affection for England—admired her greatness, which he perceives to be a consequence of her political and religious institutions.' But Sir Theodore Martin, in his *Life of the Prince Consort,* observes: 'The cry throughout Europe at this time was for Constitutional government upon the English model; but the Prince seems to have felt that a Constitution like ours, which had grown up with the growth of the nation, and owed its form, as well as its stability, to the fact that it was in harmony with the national culture and life and habits, was not a thing to be applied to the other nations of Europe, where none of the conditions were the same.' We further read that a very cordial and intimate relation was established between Prince Albert and the Prince of Prussia during this visit. 'Frank and sincere as both were by nature, and both watching with anxious interest the aspect of affairs on the Continent, which was already prophetic of coming storms, this was only to be expected. The friendship was cemented by personal intercourse during four subsequent visits of the Prince of Prussia to England in 1848, 1850, 1853, and 1856, and came to a happy climax in the marriage by which the reigning families of Prussia and England became united in 1858.'

When 1848, the dread year of revolution, came, it found the King of Prussia in the throes of discord and conflict with the people. Berlin consequently felt the force of the popular upheaval. While the King was by no means to be pitied, his brother, Prince William, incurred undeserved odium. 'Calumniated by his countrymen, forsaken by his friends, temporarily sacrificed upon the altar of expediency by his brother (for whom he entertained a personal affection as sincere as his loyalty towards his Sovereign was perfect), actually banished from his native land, in the service of which his whole life had been spent—how profitably and efficaciously subsequent events triumphantly proved—the Prince of Prussia was, for several months, a wretched, disappointed, all but broken-spirited man. But though compelled to retreat before the storm that swept over Prussia, and well-nigh uprooted the Monarchy to which he was heir-apparent, he never lost courage, or sacrificed an iota of his personal dignity. He took no notice of the accusations raised against him, nor of their later refutation, which was complete.' Amongst other charges levelled at him, it was said that he had commanded the slaughter of the people on the occasion of the first *émeute* in Berlin on the 13th of March, and that he was responsible for the ill-treatment of the prisoners taken by the troops during the disturbances of the 18th. Yet it was shown that four days before the first of the disturbances in the capital occurred, the Prince had ceased to be in command of the division of Guards garrisoning Berlin and Potsdam, and therefore could not have given the orders to the soldiery. He had been appointed to the General Governorship of the Rhine Provinces and Westphalia on the 9th of March, and had taken leave of his fellow-officers of the Guards. The officers of his staff, moreover, solemnly averred that, during the six days of his sojourn in Berlin, while the revolution was raging, he categorically refused to give any order whatever, even on the most pressing occasion, and always replied, 'I have no orders to give.'

But mobs never argue, and rightly or wrongly the insurgents of Berlin had imbibed the idea that the Prince of Prussia was even more reactionary than the King. They attacked his house, breaking the windows, and the Prince's life was in jeopardy. His friends besought him to leave

Berlin until the excitement had calmed down; but he resolutely declined to do so, except under an express decree issued by the King. There was nothing for it but for Frederick William to issue such a decree; and the Prince, who declined to quit Berlin so long as his flight might be construed into an act of fear, reluctantly left his native land for a time. Taking a steamer at Hamburg, he arrived in London on the 27th of March. All kinds of calumnies were still propagated against him, and long after he had taken up his abode in London the report was current in Berlin that he was on his way back from Warsaw with a Russian army to put down the national movement. Affairs in the Prussian capital became more settled when the King yielded to some of the demands of the democracy. His Majesty withdrew the troops from Berlin, the obnoxious Ministry went out of office, and a Parliamentary Government was promised, while the King agreed to place himself at the head of the movement for the unity of Germany.

On reaching London the Prince of Prussia took up his residence in the house of the Prussian Ambassador, the Chevalier Bunsen. The following breakfast scene is related by Bunsen: 'F. had fetched an armchair and placed it in the centre of one side of the table; but the Prince put it away himself, and took another, saying: "One ought to be humble now, for thrones are shaking;" then I sat on one side of him, and he desired Frances to take her place on the other. He related everything that came to his knowledge of the late awful transactions; and, let reports be what they may, I cannot believe that he has had any share in occasioning the carnage that has taken place, but conclude that the general opinion condemning him has been the result of party spirit, and of long-settled notions as to what was likely to be his advice and opinion.'

So great was the public excitement, however, that Prince Albert, writing on the 30th of March to Baron Stockmar, said: 'We cannot let the Prince of Prussia come now. He has made enemies because he is dreaded; but he is noble and honourable, and wholly devoted to the new movement for Germany. He looks at the business with the frank integrity of the soldier, and will stand gallantly by the post which has been entrusted to him.' During his stay in England, the Prince studied carefully the British Constitution and our mode of government, and wherever he went he attracted admiration by his frank and manly bearing, and the uprightness and sincerity of his character. Although the Queen was not able to receive him as a State visitor, she saw him on more than one occasion, and he had also frequent interviews with Prince Albert, and with the leading statesmen of the day—Peel, Palmerston, and Russell. The Duke of Wellington showed his feeling for the Prince by arraying himself in the full uniform of a Prussian General, and calling upon his Royal Highness at the Prussian Ambassador's. The Prince afterwards spent a week with the Duke at Strathfieldsaye.

While in England, an opportunity was afforded the Prince of Prussia to make known his views on the question of Constitutional reforms and the reconstruction of Germany. Herr Dallmann, the historian, had prepared a paper entitled, 'A Draft Constitution for Prussia;' and this was read by the Prince, who found it substantially in accord with his own views. He wrote to Dallmann, to the effect that the principles upon which the proposed new Constitution was based, would ultimately bring about the unity of Germany. With regard to the Constitution of the Upper Chamber, however, he held that it would be impossible for the Sovereigns of Germany to sit at the same council-board with their subjects, as they would be in danger of being overruled in the discussion of public affairs. He would prefer to see all members of the Royal house installed in a separate chamber of princes, with which the King could hold communication before any important question was submitted to Parliament. He also dissented from the proposition that regular officers and staff-officers in the Landwehr should be nominated by the Sovereign, preferring that the selection of generals to command the German army should rest with the King, while the selection of all other officers should be the prerogative of the minor States. Bunsen asked, as a commentary upon the Prince's letter, 'Is the Prince an Absolutist or a Reactionist? That he is always open-minded and honest nobody ever denied, not even his greatest enemies, whenever they were writing or speaking with any knowledge of the man.' The Prince of Prussia remained in England till the close of the month of May, when he returned to Berlin. Queen Victoria, writing to the King of the Belgians, remarked : 'He was very sad at going. May God protect him ; he is very noble-minded and honest, and most cruelly wronged. He seemed to have great confidence in Albert, who cheered him, and gave him always the best advice.' To Madame Bunsen the Prince said on parting: 'In no other place or country could he have passed so well the period of distress and anxiety which he had gone through as here, having so much to interest and occupy his mind, both in the country and in the nation.'

That the Prince of Prussia's political views had undergone some modification during his visit to England is clearly apparent from the following letter, written by him from Brussels on the 30th of May, to King Frederick William : 'I beg respectfully to inform your Majesty that, in accordance with the commands imparted to me, I have quitted London, and am at present on the Continent. I deem this a most opportune moment for giving renewed expression to the sentiments, already well-known to your Majesty, with which I return to my native country. I venture to hope that the free institutions, to found which still more firmly your Majesty has convoked the representatives of the people, will with God's gracious aid become more and more developed to the benefit of Prussia. I will devote all my powers sincerely and faithfully to this development, and look forward to the time when I shall accord to the Constitution, about to be promulgated after conscientious consultation between your Majesty and your people, such recognition as shall be prescribed to the Heir-Apparent by constitutional charter.'

Nor is this the only evidence that he had resolved upon accepting the new situation. Replying to an address presented to him soon after his return to Prussia, by the civil and military authorities at Wesel, he thus spoke: 'A clear conscience alone has enabled me to live through what has recently befallen me, and with a clear conscience I return to my fatherland. I have all the time hoped that the day of truth would dawn. At last it has dawned. Meanwhile much has been changed in our country. The King has willed that it should be so : the King's will is sacred to me; I am the first of his subjects, and adhere to these new conditions with all my heart; but justice, order, and law must govern, not anarchy—against this last I will strive with my whole might. That is my calling in life.' Upon the principles here enunciated, he had been elected a Deputy for the District of Wirsitz to the first National Assembly. When he entered the House of Representatives for the first time, his appearance was the signal for loud cheering on the part of the Right, who rose to greet him, while the party of the Left kept their seats. The Speaker having announced that 'the member for Wirsitz desired to speak on a personal matter,' the Prince rose and delivered a short but straightforward speech. He affirmed his readiness to devote his powers honestly and conscientiously to the maintenance of a constitutional Government, now that the King had thought fit to adopt that form of rule; and he expressed the hope that the old Prussian motto would continue to guide the Legislative Body, 'With God, for King and Fatherland!' Then he left the Chamber amid a storm of cheers from the Conservatives, and sounds of disapprobation from the Radicals.

The constitutional question again led to an insurrection, the seat of which was this time in Baden. It may be explained that the revolutionary movement of the previous year had compelled the German princes to sanction the election of a National Assembly, or general congress of representatives of the German people. The Assembly met at Frankfort in 1849, and selected the Archduke John of Austria, as Vicar of the Empire, to administer the affairs of the German nation generally. Prussia resented this choice. The Assembly next elected the King of Prussia hereditary Emperor of the Germans. Frederick William declined the Imperial Crown, as we saw in a previous chapter, because it was offered him by the people, and not by the princes. He was angry with the deputies for their previous conduct, and he now began to adhere more and more to those Absolutist ideas which the people fondly hoped had been abandoned. The draft of an Imperial Federal Constitution was promulgated by Prussia, Hanover, and Saxony, but Austria and Bavaria refused to join in it.

Popular disaffection arose in the Grand Duchy of Baden, and the crisis soon became acute. Provisional National Committees were formed in Baden itself, and also in the Palatinate, and the Bavarian Government declared the Palatinate to be in a state of insurrection. Prussia thereupon assisted the Confederated German States in putting down the revolution. The King appointed Prince William Commander-in-Chief of the army of operation in Baden and the Palatinate. He set out for the scene of action on the 10th of June, and as he was approaching Kreuznach from Mainz, he was fired at from the roadside. The Prince escaped uninjured, but the bullet intended for him wounded the leader and postillion of the second carriage. The assailant was captured, and put on trial for his life at Mainz, but the jury, which was anti-monarchical in its sentiments, acquitted him.

The Prince of Prussia proclaimed the whole of the Grand Duchy of Baden to be in a state of war, and declared that all offenders against military law should be brought to a court-martial, and visited, if thought necessary, with capital punishment. The insurgents, who were commanded by a Pole named Mieroslawski, sustained several severe defeats, and the rising was effectually quelled. At the close of his brief but decisive campaign the Prince of Prussia received the orders *Pour la Mérite*, Grand Cross of Philip the Valorous, Grand Cross of Maximilian Joseph, and Grand Cross of Charles Frederick. Saxony, as well as Baden, felt the wave of disaffection, and a rebellion broke out at Dresden. Obstinate conflicts between the people and the military took place in the streets, but ultimately the revolt was quelled.

Meanwhile, the constitutional discussions at Berlin continued, and it was not until early in the year 1850 that success crowned the efforts to come to some understanding between King and people. At length after months of difficulty and disquietude, a new Constitution was published, on the 2nd of February. This instrument defined the powers of King and Parliament and the duties of the Ministers of the Crown. Although many modifications were subsequently made, it formed the basis of the Constitution as now by law established. A Representative Chamber—as well as a House of Peers—was provided for, and a great advance was made in the direction of universal suffrage. It was true that outside of the Kingdom there was still cause for anxiety. Austria was chagrined at the alliance between Prussia, Hanover, and Saxony, which had resulted in the new German Constitution, and at one time war seemed imminent; but the difficulties were satisfactorily adjusted, and the treaty of Olmütz was concluded.

Returning to the personal thread of our narrative,—for his

services in the pacification of Baden, the Prince of Prussia was appointed to the governorships of Rhineland and West-phalia. In 1850 he was despatched on a mission to St. Petersburg, and from thence he journeyed direct to London, in order to be present at the christening of Prince Arthur, one of whose sponsors he had consented to be. Another visit was paid to this country in 1853, when the Prince was present at the naval and military reviews at Spithead and Chobham respectively; and on leaving England he proceeded to Vienna upon an inspecting mission connected with the Austrian contingent of the Federal army. In 1854 he was appointed Colonel-General of Infantry, advanced to the rank of Field-Marshal, and nominated governor of the Federal fortress of Mayence. This same year the Prince celebrated his silver wedding, and gave his consent to the betrothal of his only son Prince Frederick William—now Crown Prince of Germany—to the Princess Royal of Great Britain. Lord Palmerston considered that such a union would unquestionably be to the interests of the two countries immediately concerned, and of Europe in general. In her *Journal*, the Queen gives the following interesting account of the betrothal, under date September 29th, 1855: 'Our dear Victoria was this day engaged to Prince Frederick William of Prussia, who had been on a visit to us since the 14th. He had already spoken to us, on the 20th, of his wishes; but we were uncertain, on account of her extreme youth, whether he should speak to her himself, or wait till he came back again. However, we felt it was better he should do so, and during our ride up *Craig-na-Ban* this afternoon, he picked a piece of white heather (the emblem of "good luck") which he gave to her; and this enabled him to make an allusion to his hopes and wishes as they rode down *Glen Dirnoch*, which led to this happy conclusion.' Prince Albert wrote to Stockmar: 'Prince Fritz William left us yesterday. Vicky has indeed behaved quite admirably, as well during the closer explanation on Saturday, as in the self-command which she displayed subsequently and at the parting. She manifested towards Fritz and ourselves the most child-like simplicity and candour and the best feeling. The young people are ardently in love with one another, and the purity, innocence, and unselfishness of the young man have been on his part equally touching.' The Queen and Prince Albert were anxious to keep the engagement secret for a time, but knowledge of it oozed out, and the *Times* published an article referring to 'the projected alliance in language as little considerate to the feelings of the Sovereign and her husband, or of the young people themselves, as it was insulting to the Prussian King and nation, and indeed, to all Germany.' Sir Theodore Martin affirms, in his *Life of the Prince Consort*, that the article was one of the worst of a series by which the leading journal had done its best to make England detested throughout Germany.

The Crimean War had just broken out, and the relations between England and Prussia were of none too cordial a character, in consequence of the uncertain policy of the Prussian Court. The young Prince Frederick William and his father were strongly opposed to the principles of the party at Berlin, which had done its best to prostrate Prussia at the feet of the Emperor of Russia. We learn from the work from which we have just quoted that the dominant influence of Russian counsels was made clearly apparent by the dismissal from the Prussian King's service of all the men—Bunsen, General Bonin and others—who had made themselves obnoxious to the Czar by their known antagonism to his policy in Turkey. These changes were effected by the King without communication with the Crown Prince, his brother, to whom they were so distasteful, that he left Berlin for Baden-Baden, urging the necessities of his health as a reason. The King of Prussia, who still professed the warmest friendship for England, felt that some explanation of his conduct was needed, and in a very lengthy letter to the Queen he endeavoured to justify his proceedings. Her Majesty, however, had felt his conduct deeply, and in the course of a trenchant reply, she said to the King: 'If such men as these—a loving brother among them, a Prince noble and chivalrous to the core, and nearest to the throne—have felt themselves constrained to part from you at a momentous crisis, this is *a serious symptom*, which may well give your Majesty occasion to take counsel with yourself, and to test with anxious care whether the hidden source of evils, past and present, may not perhaps be found in your Majesty's views.'

But in addition to interposing other difficulties in the way of the Allies, King Frederick William, acting in concert with the Princes of the minor kingdoms of Germany, did his utmost to paralyze the action of Austria, which had shown a disposition to take an active part on the side of the Western Powers. While negotiations between France, England, and Austria were going forward, Prussia formally declared that, if Austria should enter the field against Russia, she would consider herself absolved from the conditions of the defensive and offensive treaty which subsisted between Austria and herself. As soon as this became known, the indignation roused against Prussia both in France and England, was so great, that Prince Albert considered it expedient to call the attention of the Prince of Prussia to the serious alienation between the countries likely to ensue from Prussia's perseverance in this line of policy. But nothing was done—Prussia adhered to her foolish course, and France and England, with the aid of Victor Emmanuel, were left to engage the gigantic power of Russia, and they succeeded ultimately in crushing her designs in the East; but had the German Powers cordially supported the Allies, the Crimean War would happily have been brief and decisive.

The Prince of Prussia presided in 1855 over the Military Commission, which decided upon the adoption of the needle-gun throughout the Prussian army. On the 1st of January, in the succeeding year, he celebrated his fifty years of military service, when the King conferred upon him the command of the 7th Hussars, and gave him a sword of honour. The officers of the army, by whom the Prince was held in high esteem, presented him with a massive silver shield, and the veteran old warriors gave him a magnificent silver helmet. The Queen of England, moreover, sent him the insignia of the Bath, by the hands of the gallant Sir Colin Campbell.

While the Prince of Prussia was at Baden in 1857, he became acquainted with his future antagonist, Napoleon III. In the following autumn King Frederick William had a paralytic stroke, upon which softening of the brain supervened. He did not recover, and being the victim of a second stroke in October, on the 23rd of that month the Prince of Prussia, by royal decree issued from Sans Souci, was entrusted with the administration of the government for a period of three months. As the condition of the Sovereign became manifestly hopeless, the Prince was periodically confirmed in his office, but these provisional arrangements never extended beyond the time of three months originally fixed, until, as we shall see in the ensuing chapter, he became permanent Regent.

The Princess Royal of Great Britain was married to Prince Frederick William of Prussia on the 25th of January, 1858. The Prince of Prussia came over for the ceremony, which took place in the Chapel Royal, St. James's. When the fair English girl went out to the land of her adoption, never had a Princess been received by the Prussians with as much enthusiasm as she. And their first impressions of her have only been confirmed and strengthened by the good and noble life she has since led amongst the people.

In the month of August following the marriage, Queen Victoria and the Prince Consort went over to Germany to visit their daughter. At Aix-la-Chapelle the Royal travellers were received by the Prince of Prussia, who was their companion for the rest of the journey to Babelsburg. Dusseldorf, Potsdam, Herrenhausen, Madgeburg, Berlin, and other places were visited. At the small station of Wildpark, near Potsdam, the Queen and Prince found their daughter waiting for them, and embraces and tears of joy followed. The Royal party were magnificently entertained during their stay by the Prince of Prussia and the Court circle, but they took up their residence at the house of their son-in-law and daughter. After a stay of nearly seven weeks in Germany, her Majesty and the Prince Consort returned to England with feelings of rejoicing over the happiness of their eldest child, and of thankfulness for the cordial understanding which existed between the courts of St. James's and Berlin.

CHAPTER IV.

THE PRINCE AS REGENT.

So long as the Prince of Prussia remained provisional Regent only, the members of the Berlin cabinet were independent of his authority; and, as on many questions of policy they were by no means agreed, a good deal of friction ensued. Eventually, an end was put to a situation which the Prince felt to be irksome, for, on the 7th of October, 1858, he was formally appointed to the Regency with full powers. The

King's decree ran that the Prince should act as Regent 'until the moment the King should be again able to fulfil the duties of his Royal functions.'

The Crown Prince assumed office on the 8th, and issued a series of orders in the official journal, indicating a policy in which the Constitution would be respected, and measures of useful reform promoted to meet the wants of the time. A meeting of the Prussian Chambers was convoked for the 20th of October, and on that day the Regent addressed them in a speech of much gravity, delivered with deep emotion. Having referred to the sad condition of the King, taking God to witness that his prayers never ceased for his brother's recovery, the Crown Prince went on to say :—

'I have taken upon myself the heavy load and responsibility of the Regency, and I have the firm will to continue to perform what the Constitution and the laws exact from me. I expect no less from you, gentlemen. Special messages will submit to you in the sitting of the two united Chambers the documents relating to the Regency, and, on your request, every explanation which may be useful will be given to you. Gentlemen, the more serious the times are, in consequence of the illness of our King, the higher must we exalt the flag of Prussia by the conscientious fulfilment of our duty, and by remaining united by a bond of mutual confidence. I conclude this solemn act by that shout which formerly so joyously responded through this Chamber—"Long live the King!"'

A joint committee of the two Chambers was elected, which agreed upon a report recommending the Chambers to declare the Regency necessary. This report was adopted without dissentient voices by the Chambers, and on the 26th of October, the Regent, after thanking them for their unanimity, took the oath required by the constitution in the *Weisse Saal*, or White Hall of the Palace, in the presence of the members of both Houses.

The policy of the new ruler of Prussia was foreshadowed in a formal address by the Prince. On the questions of religion and education, the Regent thus expressed himself: 'In religion there had been many abuses, and both churches would be strenuously opposed if religion again were to be used as a political cloak. The Evangelical Church had returned to an orthodoxy which was not in harmony with her principles, and that orthodoxy had placed the greatest bar on Evangelical union. The Catholic Church had her rights constitutionally confirmed, but encroachments could no longer be suffered. The education of the State would be so devised that Prussia would be foremost in the intelligence of the world.' As to the all-important question of the Prussian army, the Regent observed: 'The army has created the greatness of Prussia, though both the army and the State suffered severely at one time from neglect. The war of emancipation has proved the capabilities of the Prussian arms, but the victories of the past must not dazzle us to blindly overlook the defects of the present. There are many things requiring alteration which money and time will effect. It would be a grave mistake to be satisfied with merely a cheap army reorganization, which could never realize the expectation of the country at a critical moment. Prussia should be respected, and to that end it was imperative that a powerful army should be maintained, so that when the supreme moment came, she could throw her full weight in the scale.' With regard to Prussia's relations with other Powers, the Prince said: 'The world must learn to know that Prussia is always ready to protect her rights. A firm and, if necessary, energetic policy, developed with caution and prudence, will procure for Prussia that political respect and power which it would be impossible for her to gain by force of arms alone.'

The Prince of Prussia's appointment as Regent was hailed with great satisfaction in England, and especially by the Prince Consort, who looked forward to the substitution of a liberal policy for the reactionary system under which Prussia had long been suffering.

The fall of the Manteuffel Ministry, which represented the old aristocratic party in Prussia, was a necessary consequence of the change in the supreme direction of affairs. At first, indeed, Baron Manteuffel declined to resign, but his ministry was at an end when the Prince Regent sent him an official announcement to the effect that he had summoned the Prince of Hohenzollern to Berlin, and charged him with the formation of a ministry. Prince Hohenzollern-Sigmaringen was a relative of the Royal family of Prussia, and was a lieut.-general in the army. He became head of the Ministry without a portfolio. Baron Schleinitz was appointed Foreign Minister; Herr Patow, Minister of Finance; Herr Flottwell,

Minister of the Interior; General von Bonin, Minister of War; Herr Bethmann-Hollweg, Minister of Public Instruction; Herr von Massow, Minister of the Household; and Herr von Auerswald, a member of the Cabinet without office. All these names gave 'a strong guarantee for the infusion of a sounder and more liberal spirit into the future government of the country, while the appointment as Minister of War of General von Bonin, who had made himself obnoxious to the late government by his anti-Russian policy, was hailed as an indication that the foreign policy of the country would no longer be unduly controlled by influence from St. Petersburg.'

The Prince Consort was so delighted with these appointments that on the 9th of November he thus wrote from Windsor Castle to the Prince of Prussia: 'Let me from my heart of hearts wish you joy of the brilliant solution of the second part of your great and difficult task. Your Ministry is, indeed, one of honourable men; it will command respect both abroad and at home, and you will, and rightly, be applauded for the calm and resolute way in which you have managed to effect what justice and the best interests of your country seemed to you to enjoin. You will have had to encounter hostility from without as well as struggles within your own soul, and I can quite understand how much the conflict must have cost you. Still, at the same time, in your own convictions you doubtless found much to cheer and strengthen you, and the growth in self-reliance, of which you speak to me as the result of the success that has attended the line you took up in the affair of the Regency, cannot fail to be further augmented by this second success. Prince Hohenzollern has acted nobly and patriotically in undertaking the post of President of the Ministry, and you will have a true, a staunch, and an active friend in him.'

Baron Stockmar was on a visit to Berlin at this time, and he was much impressed by the character of the Prince Regent, and the injustice which had been done him in some quarters. 'I have had an opportunity,' he wrote to Prince Albert, 'of gaining a clearer insight into his nature, and found that he deserves much more regard, esteem, and confidence than the majority of the people about him have given him. On one occasion, when he expounded to me his views as to the policy of Prussia in regard to a neighbouring

State, I found them so sound, so simple, so sincere and honourable, that I kissed his hand.'

The Prince of Prussia's statement to his new Ministry, in Council assembled, set forth his domestic and foreign policy in the clearest manner, and one which augured well for the future of Germany, and also of Europe. Yet he had a difficult task in reconciling the demands of the aristocratic party on the one hand, and those of the democrats on the other. But the Prince's guiding principle was that there could be no just conflict of interests between Sovereign and subjects, and he had demonstrated his faith in the nation by insisting that his Ministry should in no way interfere with the elections to the Chambers. The result of those elections gave an overwhelming majority to the Liberals, so that the Prince was amply justified in his trust of the people.

Before the Italian War of 1859 broke out, the Prince of Prussia was anxious to know the views of England on the complications which had arisen, especially as France had made direct advances to Prussia, with the view of inducing her to hold aloof from Austria in any eventuality. In an able memorandum addressed to the Prince Consort, the Regent said: ' The pretext for a war in Italy is to be the form of government of the different States. But the true cause is Sardinia's desire for aggrandizement. And Governments which are not concerned with the matter are asked to take part in it. Where is the statute of international law to be found, that teaches us to wage war against a State because we do not like its form of government? Or are we compelled to aid the unjustifiable desire for aggrandizement of one State at the cost of another?

'There is also another reason which will drive Napoleon into war, viz., his opinion that a Napoléonide must break through the Treaties of 1815 whenever an opportunity for doing so arises. To this there is a simple answer, that all the other Governments are called upon to ensure the maintenance of these treaties. If France be perfectly convinced of this, she will think twice before going to war. But, on the other hand, Austria must also be exhorted to desist from taking any provoking steps in Italy. "Whoever provokes war wantonly will not easily find allies!" This is a standing phrase of mine with foreign diplomatists here; it expresses my firm conviction.

'Now the question arises for Prussia: What is she to do if France assists Italy in a conflict with Austria? Public opinion has for the last four weeks expressed itself throughout Germany in such a decided manner against France in case of such an emergency, that one cannot shut one's eyes to the fact. And herewith Prussia's line of action would seem to be clearly marked out; for the wars of the Revolution have shown us that, should the French arms be victorious, they would soon be turned against Germany and Prussia, if they had remained neutral and had quietly looked on at all the disasters of Austria.

'But what would be our position if England should declare in favour of France, and thereby of Italy, in such a war? And further, what are we to do, if Russia should threaten to join such an Anglo-French alliance? Would not such an alliance force a neutrality (though an armed one) upon Germany and Prussia? On the other hand, suppose that England and Russia should remain neutral, and Austria be victorious against the Franco-Italian alliance, while Germany and therefore Prussia remained idle spectators, what would be the position of Prussia? How are we to escape the dangers of such alternatives? This question I put to you.'

The Prince Consort, in a reply which was approved by Lord Derby and Lord Malmesbury, enforced upon the Prince Regent the importance of trusting, not to arrangements with other Powers, but to a frank and cordial understanding and sympathy with his own people. At the same time it was the one main essential thing for Prussia's safety and strength that her language should be loud and firm.

The war was eventually circumscribed between France, Italy, and Austria; Prussia and England remaining neutral. But Prussia placed her army on a war footing, and in closing the session of the Chambers on the 14th of May, the Prince Regent thus alluded to the position that the country would maintain in the conflict which had then commenced— 'Prussia is determined to maintain the basis of European public right, and the balance of power in Europe. It is Prussia's right and duty to stand up for the security, the protection, and the national interests of Germany, and she will not resign the assertion of these her prerogatives. Prussia expects that all the German Confederate Powers will stand firmly by her side in the fulfilment of that mission, and trusts that her readiness to defend the common Father-land will merit their confidence.' After the war had pro-gressed for some time to the disadvantage of Austria, it was brought to a conclusion by the Peace of Villafranca.

The army reforms which the Prince carried out during his Regency were most thorough in character. They were strongly opposed by the Legislative body, but the Regent insisted on carrying them through, feeling convinced that they were necessary for the future glory and safety of the country. The old general-service law of 1814 was rigidly enforced, and 60,000 instead of 40,000 men were called out annually for exercise. Not long after he came to the throne, four new regiments of guards, thirty-two of infantry, ten of cavalry, and five of artillery had been created; the chasseur and engineers' companies were strengthened; the artillery was reorganized, and the military train, as well as three new military academies and a non-commissioned officers' school, were all added to the existing army institutions of Prussia, thus giving her a martial strength which drew upon her the eyes of Europe.

One of the German Emperor's biographers forcibly ob-serves that 'the Prince Regent, as soon as he came into power, hastened to prepare his people for the long series of struggles which he foresaw to be inevitable, if Prussia were destined, under his guidance, to achieve her mission in Europe, viz., to take, and keep in such sort that it might never escape her, the leadership of Germany. To this end he drew the whole vigorous youth of the nation into the ranks of the army, and revived that warlike tone in Prussian feeling that had almost died out since the war of eman-cipation. This martial temper, once aroused, smoothed many difficulties from Prince William's path, after his accession to the throne, and may with truth be said to have ignited the enthusiasm which, blown into a flame by Prussia's first successes in the field, burnt brightly and more brightly throughout the momentous period of transition inaugurated by the campaign of 1864, until, in the spring of 1866, it suddenly burst into a furious blaze, and, annihilating all that stood in its way, swept along with awful might, an irresistible torrent of roaring fire that consumed Prussia's "favourite foes" and Germany's ancient fetters in one grand and terrible conflagration.'

The Congress of German Princes held at Baden-Baden in 1860, strengthened Prince William in his resolve to push onward the work of the reorganization of the army. He was very solicitous for the future, and observed to his fellow-potentates : 'I consider it my duty to guard Germany and protect her frontiers, nor will I be deterred in the execution of this, even though my apprehensions are not shared by my allies.'

When the provinces of Savoy and Nice were annexed to France in 1860, the Prince Regent of Prussia addressed a memorandum on the subject, dated Berlin, March 4th, to the Prince Consort. He denied that the annexation was in any way justified, and added : 'No one is more interested in the question than Prussia and Germany, because of the left bank of the Rhine, which corresponds exactly to what the *versants des Alpes*, as a geographical protective line would be, in the event of an invasion by the Alpine passes. In this point of view we are therefore more interested, and bound to speak out against schemes of annexation of this kind, than all the other great Powers, so that an approval of them may not at some future day be cited against us as a precedent, and that you, too, may not by acquiescence now, have to take part some day in forcing upon us a surrender of the left bank of the Rhine. Another point to which Prussia could not assent is that of the recognition of non-intervention as a principle. . . . In Italy the sovereigns have on their side rights secured to them by treaty, and all that the people desire is reasonable reforms, which unhappily the sovereigns have failed to grant at the right time. But they have not on their side any covenanted rights to such reforms. At the same time the probability is, that the failure of these sovereigns to grant reforms at the right time will result in their being deposed. Oh, that this example might open the eyes of many a German sovereign ! But, so far from its doing so, they grow blinder and blinder.' The far-seeing anticipations in this letter were destined to be realized in the South of Europe. Meanwhile, the cession of Savoy and Nice to France, having been decided upon, the Prince Consort wrote to Baron Stockmar : 'Russia gives her silent assent ; Austria intimates her delight that Sardinia is to have justice meted out to her according to her own code ; Prussia is, as usual, timorous and undecided ; and so one of the most perilous arrangements is brought about which

Europe, and Prussia in particular, could by possibility have had to face!'

Venetia almost immediately afterwards became a subject of anxiety, it being apprehended that Sardinia, in order to regain it, unless restrained by France, would be impelled forward by the impetus which the national movement in Italy had received from the successes of the insurgents and the Garibaldian army in Sicily. Diplomatists were most anxious that Austria should not be forced into the field by an attack on Venetia, because that would certainly have involved other Powers in the conflict. The action of Prussia and Germany, therefore, became a matter of the gravest interest. The Emperor of Austria and the Prince Regent of Prussia met at Töplitz on the 25th of July, and the wildest speculations were soon afloat as to what had occurred. The British Government, however, were speedily made acquainted with the exact facts, through a letter addressed by Prince William on the 29th to the Prince Consort. From this it appeared that there had been no written or even verbal engagement, but only a thorough discussion and communication of ideas. While the Emperor of Austria was anxious that Prussia and Germany should act in common in case of a common danger, he (the Emperor) had not the least intention of acting aggressively, and he proved to be right in his conjecture that there would be no attack upon Venetia that year.

Another meeting of Sovereigns, on the 22nd of October, gave rise to all kinds of rumours throughout Europe. The Emperors of Russia and Austria, and the Prince Regent of Prussia, foregathered at Warsaw. Francis II., the despot of the Two Sicilies, fondly hoped that the result would be to put down the movement for Italian freedom, but, in this, happily, he was disappointed. Other conjectures asserted that there was a coalition of the northern Powers to secure a revision of the Treaty of Paris of 1856, to guarantee Austria from attack in Venetia or Hungary, and even to effect the isolation of England from the other European Powers. Again Prince William wrote to the Prince Consort, and assured him that the reports above referred to, as to what had taken place at Warsaw, were mere fables. It was agreed between Prussia and Austria, with regard to the subjects of conference which might be fitly settled in a congress, that England must be previously informed of everything before decisions were taken. The Prince Regent declared that there was no mention of a treaty, nor of a revival of the Holy Alliance. 'The Sovereigns were unanimous in their conviction of the danger arising out of the ambiguous policy of the Emperor Napoleon, and of the necessity of demanding guarantees from him in order to preserve the peace of Europe, to uphold the shaken foundations of public law, and to arrest the progress of a general revolution.'

Prussia, however, did not relish England's recent policy in Italy, and she was especially angry with Lord John Russell's despatch strongly approving of the means by which Italian freedom was being secured. Then the *Times* was engaged at this period in incessant attacks upon Prussia, and everything Prussian, so that a feeling of irritation was set up between England and Prussia, which did not die away until a considerable period had elapsed.

While the Prince Regent was thus engaged in international diplomacy, that event occurred in Berlin which raised him to the actual sovereignty of the kingdom. On the 2nd of January, 1861, Frederick William IV. expired at the palace of Sans Souci. The Princess Frederick William (now Crown Princess of Germany) had been suddenly summoned, on New Year's eve, to the death-bed of the King, and in a letter which she wrote to Queen Victoria, she described the last sad hours of the amiable and talented man, whose last days had been passed in intellectual gloom. His Majesty was interred in the Friedenskirche at Potsdam, on the 7th of January. 'Immediately behind the coffin came the royal standard, borne by General Wrangel, and followed by the King, leading the Queen Dowager. Her visible emotion was shared by every member of the Royal family, and by the throng of kings and princes, who had come to pay the last honours to one whose political faults were at that moment buried in the recollection of his kind heart and distinguished gifts.'

The King is dead! Long live the King! Prussia had lost one sovereign, but in William I. she had gained a monarch stronger in will than most of her previous rulers, and one who was destined to lift the Prussian people and the German race to such a pinnacle of greatness as they had never hitherto achieved.

CHAPTER V.

KING OF PRUSSIA.

KING WILLIAM marked his accession to the throne by the publication of an amnesty for political offences, and this was accepted as a good augury by the Liberals. Their anticipations of constitutional reforms, however, were not destined to be realized, for his Majesty soon manifested his intention of consolidating the throne and strengthening the army, rather than launching forth upon a career associated with popular progress.

The Queen of England created the King of Prussia a Knight of the Garter, and Lord Breadalbane, at the head of a special mission, went over to Berlin with the insignia. The ceremony of the investiture took place on the 6th of March, amid circumstances of great state and splendour, in the White Saloon of the Palace at Berlin. The King thus wrote to the Prince Consort a few days afterwards: 'A thousand hearty thanks for the welcome lines with which you greeted me as a new brother of the Order through Lord Breadalbane, whom I was delighted to see on this festive and to me most gratifying errand. I cannot sufficiently express to you how happy the Queen has made me by the grant of the ancient and noble Order, to possess which is a real distinction. To you also I must express my thanks, as I cannot help thinking you have not been without some share in prompting her Majesty's determination. We have given the ceremonial as much state and solemnity as we could, and this was no more than the Queen's gracious act demanded. We flatter ourselves with the hope that those who formed your mission have been thoroughly satisfied. I share your hope that this event may prove a new bond of friendship between us and our respective countries.'

On the 14th of July the startling news was telegraphed to the English Court from Baden-Baden, that an attempt had been made to assassinate King William, by a young Leipzig student named Oscar Becker. His Majesty was taking an early morning walk in the *Allée* of Lichtenthal, when he met a young man, who appeared to manifest great satisfaction in seeing the most popular of German sovereigns —a satisfaction which he exhibited by taking off his hat and bowing several times. The King presently met Count Flemming, and continued his walk in conversation with that nobleman. Soon afterwards a firearm was discharged close behind, and the King felt that he was struck by a bullet. Happily the missile first encountered the collar of the King's coat, which it penetrated, and then his cravat; and by these its force was so much deadened that it inflicted no more than a severe contusion on the left side of his Majesty's neck. The wound did not bleed, but the King was for a short time stunned. Two shots were fired, according to one account. The assassin was immediately seized by the bystanders, and proved to be the same person who had shortly before saluted the King with such apparent cordiality. On the ground was found a pistol which had recently been discharged.

Becker was a young man, twenty-two years of age, and came of a respectable family. At his lodgings, a second pistol was found. On his examination, the accused freely admitted that he had gone to Baden with the express design of killing the King, not because he had any hatred of kings in general, and still less of King William, whom on the contrary he greatly loved, but because he considered that his Majesty stood in the way of the unity of Germany, which would be promoted by cutting him off. He was tried at Bruchsal, and the proceedings were somewhat singular. Becker now denied all his previous statements. He asked why he should seek to kill King William, knowing that his son would be unable to do more for German unity? He denied that he had any intention of killing the King; and asserted that his sole motive was to alarm him, and so to cause a commotion in Germany, and then to kill himself. For this purpose he said he had loaded one pistol with powder only, which he intended to fire at the King, and the other with powder and ball, with which he intended to kill himself. He declared that when he found that the King was wounded he was utterly astonished, and could only account for the catastrophe by supposing either that he had taken with him from his lodgings the wrong pistol, or that he had, in his confusion of mind, loaded the same pistol first with powder and then with powder and ball.

The prisoner at first treated the matter very lightly; afterwards he began to sob and faint, and then to exhibit excitement. He was a foolish youth, of weak mind, excited by the idea of the unity of Germany, but without any definite understanding of what it meant, how it was to be brought about, or what its consequences might be. He was found guilty, but as the execution of one who was only an imbecile would have given importance to a senseless and abortive act, he was placed in confinement. 'It is most extraordinary,' wrote Lord Palmerston to the Queen respecting the attempted assassination, 'that such an attempt should have been made, as it can scarcely be imagined that the King of Prussia can have a personal or political enemy in the world.'

The King of Prussia visited the Emperor Napoleon at Compiègne on the 6th of October, and as the interviews of sovereigns always give rise to speculation, it was said of this meeting that its object was a close alliance between France and Prussia, with a detachment from England. The visit, however, was merely one of courtesy, in return for that paid by the Emperor of the French at Baden-Baden. Some of the journals, nevertheless, asserted that the old question of rectifying the French frontier as settled in 1815 had been discussed by the two monarchs. Sir Theodore Martin observes respecting the interview: 'The King of Prussia left Compiègne with a grateful consciousness of the admirable good taste and feeling shown by the Emperor in forbearing to entangle him in disagreeable discussions, not only upon this subject, but upon any of the other European problems which were at that moment waiting for solution. It was almost a matter of course that very varied accounts, some of them sufficiently disquieting, of what had passed at Compiègne should reach the English Government; but thanks to the same frank spirit, which, through the medium of the Prince Consort, had possessed them of the truth as to the interviews at Baden-Baden, at Töplitz, and at Warsaw, they were early made aware of the fact that nothing had occurred of the slightest significance in a political point of view.

A magnificent spectacle was witnessed on the 18th of October, 1861, in the Church of the Castle of Königsberg. The coronation of King William, an act which had been opposed by many leading men, took place amid great pomp. There had been no coronation in Prussia for one hundred and sixty years. Since the time of Frederick I., the provinces and guilds had paid their homage to each successive sovereign by deputation shortly after his accession; and the Royal economists who occupied, one after another, the Prussian throne, had forborne from saddling their treasuries with coronation expenses, laying out in public works the sums thus saved to the exchequer. But the King deemed that, as his brother had, by granting a constitution to Prussia, parted with some of his hereditary privileges and Royal prerogatives, it would be highly desirable to impress the fact upon the Prussian people that kingship was not esteemed by its new representative as a mere honorary office, but as a great and momentous charge and a solemn responsibility, with all but unlimited functional powers.

The spirit in which the King viewed the ceremony may be gathered from what he said in addressing the members of the Prussian Chambers the day before his coronation: 'The Rulers of Prussia receive their crown from God. This is the signification of the expression, "King, by the grace of God," and therein lies the sanctity of the Crown, which is inviolable.' So King William placed the crown upon his own head. After this, the most notable feature of the ceremony, it is interesting to read of another incident, which is thus described in a letter written by Lord Clarendon from Berlin, to Queen Victoria: 'Everything was conducted with the most perfect order—the service not too long, the vocal music enchanting; but the great attraction of the ceremony was the manner in which the Princess Royal did homage to the King. Lord Clarendon is at a loss for words to describe to your Majesty the exquisite grace and the intense emotion with which her Royal Highness gave effect to her feelings on the occasion. Many, and older as well as younger men than Lord Clarendon, who had not his interest in the Princess Royal, were quite as unable as himself to repress their emotion at that which was so touching, because so unaffected and sincere.' The Crown Princess herself, in writing to her mother, said: 'I should like to be able to describe yesterday's ceremony to you, but I cannot find words to tell you how fine and how touching it was. It really was a magnificent sight. The King looked so very handsome, and so noble with the crown on; it seemed to suit him so exactly. The Queen, too, looked beautiful, and did all she had to do with such perfect grace, and looked so *vornehm* (distinguished). The moment when the King put the crown on the Queen's head was very touching. I think there was hardly a dry eye in the church.'

But the King's enunciation of the Divine Right of Kings, and his further announcement that he entered into no obligation to regard the Diet as a Parliament, gave rise to much solicitude in England. The Prince Consort wrote to Baron Stockmar : 'The speeches of the King of Prussia at Königsberg have produced a bad impression here, and the theory of the Divine Right of Kings (apart from being an absurdity in itself, and exploded here for the last two hundred years) is suitable neither to the position and vocation of Prussia, nor to those of the King. The difficulty of establishing united action between Prussia and England has been again infinitely augmented by this royal programme.'

A curious and amusing accident occurred at King William's coronation. It appears that all the flags and standards of the Prussian army had been brought to Königsberg, and set up provisionally in a room, the door of which faced the entrance to the King's apartments in the Schloss. As soon as their temporary adjustment had been completed, on the day before the ceremony, the room was vacated and the doors were locked, to prevent any unauthorised persons from meddling with the standards. A loud crash was suddenly heard within the room, and when the doors were opened it was found that the gigantic stand of colours had fallen to the ground, carrying with it all the emblematic honours of the army. The King smiled when he was informed of the circumstance, and said, 'Let the flags be set up again, and in the throne room itself this time. Perhaps it will be as well to say nothing about the accident, which, if they knew of it, might make a great many worthy people unnecessarily uncomfortable.' The incident was kept secret for some years, but when at length the knowledge of it oozed out, there were certain superstitious persons who declared it to be prophetic of the King's ultimate downfall.

When the session of the Prussian Chambers was opened in January, 1862, the Deputies were addressed by the King, who, in a lengthy speech, reviewed the condition of public affairs. He congratulated them on the satisfactory state of the country and of the national finances, and announced a modification in the law concerning the obligation of military service. The constitutional movement in the Electorate of Hesse was then the all-engrossing topic, and his Majesty said that the efforts of the Government were being directed towards the re-establishment of the constitution of 1831, with the modification of articles contrary to the federal laws. A vehement debate on the subject took place subsequently in the Chamber of Deputies. It was the object of the Liberal party to induce the Prussian Government to interfere and compel the Elector of Hesse to re-establish the constitution of 1831, which had been suppressed by the armed intervention of Austria in 1852. A resolution binding the Government to interfere was carried by a majority of 241 to 58, and Prussia, in conjunction with other German States, addressed a note to Austria on the subject.

The Prussian Ministry and the Lower Chamber being at variance, the King abruptly dissolved the Chambers on the 11th of March, and appealed to the constituencies. The ground of the quarrel was this. The Chambers, being strongly opposed to any increase of the army, and wishing instead to reduce its numbers, demanded that the Ministry should submit the Budget for consideration, item by item; this the Ministry refused, alleging that the state of Europe rendered such a measure inexpedient. A resolution was carried against the Government by 171 votes to 143, and the Ministry resigned. The King declined to accept their resignation, and dissolved the Chambers instead. But the Cabinet fell to pieces on the retirement of three of its most Liberal members, and a new one was formed under Prince Hohenlohe. The King issued a proclamation to the people on the 20th of March, to the effect that he should maintain the constitution and the rights of the crown, and that the weakening of the crown would be greatly injurious to the Fatherland. As touching foreign policy he should maintain without change the course he had hitherto pursued. In a second proclamation his Majesty stated that while he would consent to any savings which might be provisionally effected in the military budget, he must positively repeat his former declarations that in the department of the military administration there could be no reductions which would endanger the strength and effectiveness of the army.

The elections went strongly against the Ministry, and the King was greatly exasperated. Instead of opening the Diet in person, he deputed the Prime Minister to take his place. But, notwithstanding that the royal mouthpiece insisted upon the army reorganization measures being carried, the Chamber of Deputies voted an address to the King, in which they called upon him to grant, amongst other concessions, a reduction of taxation, and to interfere in the affairs of Hesse-Cassel.

Matters had now come to a dead lock, and it is said that when the Ministry informed the King that it was impossible to carry on the Government in the face of the opposition of the Chamber, his Majesty exclaimed, 'If you still find it impossible to pass the Reorganization Bill through the Chamber, tell me where I can find the man with courage enough to uphold it in defiance of the Deputies.'

The man with the iron hand was soon forthcoming, and it proved to be none other than Herr von Bismarck, who in the course of the next generation was to become the most prominent figure in Europe. Otto von Bismarck-Schönhausen came of a noble family. He was born at Schönhausen, in one of the Elbe provinces, in 1815. At a very early period he showed a firmness of character more than ordinary. Having passed the studies prescribed for young men of his position, and adopted the profession of the law, he entered the army and served the allotted period. After that preliminary school of training, this descendant of blue-blooded Pomeranian squires was appointed member of the Diet of Saxe, and there became conspicuous for his vigorous and persistent denunciation of democracy and constitutionalism. In 1848 he maintained an expectant attitude, watching the revolutionary storm as it swept by. In 1851, when the popular movements had been crushed, and the democratic elements broken up, Bismarck entered the diplomatic service. He was appointed to the Frankfort Legation, at that critical time one of the most important which a German statesman could occupy. He had not long held this position before he came to the conclusion that Austria was the deadly antagonist of Prussia, and that sooner or later there must be a struggle for the ascendency in Germany. Even in his efforts for the common Fatherland there was always present the desire to elevate the House of Hohenzollern, at the expense, and to the humiliation of the House of Hapsburg. In 1852 he was sent to Vienna, where he successfully exerted his influence in driving Austria away from junction with the Zollverein. There had been nothing since the peace of 1815 which so helped forward the unity of Germany under the supremacy of Prussia as this great commercial convention. In 1859 Bismarck was appointed to the Embassy at St. Petersburg, and three years later he was transferred to Paris, where he was favourably received. He went over to London on a visit, and was introduced, amongst other personages, to Mr. Disraeli, who, however, regarded Bismarck's views upon the regeneration of Germany as the 'mere moonshine of a German baron.' But these views were realized to the full, and there were few of Bismarck's contemporaries in 1862 who had the remotest idea of his resolute nature, and that indomitable will which, in militarism and politics, is the synonym for genius.

Such was the man who was recalled from France to become the Parliament-tamer of Berlin. While enjoying the scenery of the Pyrenees in the middle of September, the future German Chancellor was overtaken by a telegram from King William summoning him to Berlin. With all haste Bismarck obeyed the summons, and arrived in Berlin on the 19th of September. 'Who in Heaven's name is Herr von Bismarck, that he should be placed in such a high station?' Such, says Mr. Lowe, was the question which most people in Prussia began to ask. The reply of the Liberal press was, '*Bismarck—c'est le coup d'état*,' and he was greeted with a storm of abuse, receiving such epithets as 'a swaggering Junker,' 'a hollow braggart,' 'a Napoleon-worshipper,' and 'a town uprooter.' Junkerism, it may be mentioned, was the term applied to the reactionary Conservative landed gentry, who were the deadly enemies of reform.

Bismarck soon put himself in evidence, and King William only smiled over the great unpopularity of his new Prime Minister. The monarch had perfect confidence in the man of his choice, and it is said that when a Russian princess complimented the King upon an improvement in his looks, he pointed to Bismarck and said, '*Voilà mon médecin*'— 'there is my physician.'

Into the conflict with the Chambers the new minister threw himself with energy and spirit. There was no shrinking in him from the strongest measures when he considered them to be necessary. Only a few days after his accession to power, when speaking in the Budget Committee, he said : 'It is not by speechifying and majorities that the great questions of the time will have to be decided—that was the mistake made in 1848 and 1849—but by *blood and iron.*' This now historic phrase represented the policy upon which Bismarck meant to proceed both in the treatment of constitutional questions and in the unification of Germany. The circumstances which followed his accession to power led to a comparison between 'demented Bismarck and his ditto King, and Strafford and Charles I. *versus* our Long Parliament.' But Carlyle pointed out that the issues between King William and his Diet were very different; they were 'as like as Monmouth to Macedon, and no liker.' No fair standard of comparison could be instituted between Parliamentary life in England and that in the less free States of the Continent.

'Bismarck,' says a writer whom I have just quoted, 'had the conviction of a Luther, and, like a Luther, nothing could daunt or shake him.' But there is all the difference in the world between a Luther strongly denouncing the crying evils of a corrupt church, and a Bismarck riding rough-shod over the representatives of the Prussian people. 'In the Chamber debates Bismarck was contemptuous but never angry, cutting and sarcastic without being coarse; and his social accomplishments gave him a great advantage over his opponents, in whom over-education contrasted strongly with underbreeding. He was as cool under Parliamentary fire as the Duke of Wellington ever was under a hail of bullets; and when the doctrinaires and the professors, who were the curse of the Chamber, were thundering against him about tyranny, revolution, impeachment, and all the rest of it, he would calmly sit down before them to write a chatty letter to his wife, or to thank his sister for a present of sausages and black puddings.' But the spirit of opposition in both parties soon degenerated into a habit of aggression, and from quarrelling about the constitution they began to wrangle about the rules of debate. Yet it must be said that the Ministers of whom Bismarck was chief were more tyrannical in spirit, and paid less regard to the authority of the Speaker, than any other members of the Prussian Diet.

In the closing days of September the Chamber passed a vote adverse to the Government, whereupon Bismarck informed the Deputies that the Chamber, having rejected the charges for reorganizing the army, included by Government in the Budget for 1862, the Ministry must presume that the House would adopt a similar course with regard to the new items in the Budget for 1863. The King, therefore, had authorized him to withdraw the Budget for 1863; but it would be laid before the House in the following session, 'with a bill supporting as a vital condition the reorganization of the army.' At the instigation of Ministers, a vote was procured in the Upper Chamber annulling the proceedings of the Deputies. This the Lower House resented, and the session was closed by a message from the King. Bismarck read the message, which stated, without any circumlocution, that 'the Budget for the year 1862, as decreed by the Lower Chamber, having been rejected by the Upper Chamber on the ground of insufficiency, the Government of his Majesty is under the necessity of carrying out the Budget as it was originally laid before the Lower House, without taking cognizance of the conditions prescribed by the Constitution.'

This extremely arbitrary act must have spread dismay amongst the Deputies, pointing, as they no doubt felt it did, to a policy of future repression of the rights and liberties of the people. The King's action was equivalent to saying that taxes would be levied and the government carried on independently of Parliament; and, indeed, for the remainder of the year this was the state of things. The views of the King on this momentous question were specifically formulated in his answer to an address drawn up and submitted to him by various deputations from the country. After recapitulating the course pursued by the Chamber of Deputies, his Majesty said: 'I wish to preserve the Constitution intact to my people; but it is my indispensable mission, and my firm will also, to maintain intact the Crown inherited from my ancestors and its constitutional rights. This is necessary for the interests of my people. But to do this, or for the defence of the blessings I have already alluded to, a well-organized army is requisite, and not a self-styled national army, which ought, as a Prussian has not blushed to say, to stand behind the Parliament. I am firmly resolved not to sacrifice anything more of my hereditary rights. Say so to those who have delegated you. You now know, you now have heard my view of things. Let every one of you propagate them and support them in extended spheres. If this is done, matters will improve; for Almighty God has always watched over Prussia. He will continue to protect us. Is not Prussia's motto, " With God, for the king and the country"?'

The constitutional struggle was renewed in 1863. The session of the Chambers was opened on the 14th of January, when Bismarck, as President of the Council, read the King's speech. This document reaffirmed the Royal policy of the previous year. The Government had acted as its own Chancellor of the Exchequer and Parliament, but promised that, as soon as the accounts had been finally balanced, it would move for the retrospective approbation of both Houses of Parliament for the expenses incurred. The speech also intimated that the position of Prussia relatively to the Federal Diet must be taken into consideration. During the debate on the Address in the Chamber of Deputies, Bismarck made a speech which caused intense dissatisfaction amongst the members. 'Your decisions,' he said, 'are only to regulate the Budget as regards its total amount and its details. If you are to have the right to demand of the King the dismissal of ministers who do not enjoy your confidence; if, by your decisions with regard to the expenditure, you are to have the right to do away with the army reorganization; if you had the right (as you constitutionally have it not, though claiming it in this Address) to control the relations between the executive power and its functionaries; if you had all these rights—you would be *de facto* in possession of the complete power of government in this country. On the basis of these demands this Address reposes. By it the Royal House of Hohenzollern is required to abdicate its constitutional rights of government in favour of the majority of this House.'

A storm of contradiction here drowned the speaker's voice, and the President rang his bell. Bismarck, resuming, said, 'It is the same thing in another form. You declare the Constitution violated so soon as the Crown and the Upper House do not do your will. You know as well as any one in Prussia that the Ministry acts in the name and according to the commands of his Majesty. The Prussian Ministry is in this respect quite different from the English. The latter, call it what you will, is only the Ministry of the Parliament, but we are the Ministers of the King.' The President of the

Council proceeded to say that theoretically it was undeniable that the Chamber had the right to reject the whole Budget, and thereby bring about the dismissal of all functionaries, the abandonment of the army reorganization, and many other things besides. But such a theory was incompatible with practice, and practically the like had not yet happened. 'We closed the last session in the hope that you would return hither in a more conciliatory mood than that in which you departed. The Government have made great concessions; it is now your turn to make concessions, and, unless you do so, we shall have difficulty in terminating the conflict.'

But, instead of making concessions, the Deputies carried—by 255 to 68 votes—an Address to the King, in which they severely commented upon the unconstitutional mode in which the government was conducted. Amongst other things, the Address said: 'Since last session Ministers have carried on the public administration against the Constitution and without a legal Budget. The supreme right of the representatives of the people has thereby been attacked. The country has been alarmed and has stood by its representatives. Abuses of the power of the Government are now taking place just as in the sad years preceding the Regency. Your Majesty recently declared that nobody should doubt your intention of maintaining the Constitution; but the Constitution has already been violated by the Ministers. Our position imposes on us the most urgent duty of solemnly declaring that peace at home and power abroad can only be restored by the return of the Government to a constitutional state of things.'

The King was exceedingly wroth when he heard what had been done, and refused to receive the deputation appointed to carry up the Address. But he communicated a reply to the President of the Chamber, which was read in the House. His Majesty emphatically affirmed that the Government had not been guilty of violating the Constitution. With respect to the Budget, the Deputies had altered it until it became impracticable; and the Upper Chamber, in the exercise of its constitutional right, rejected it. It was rather a transgression of the constitutional powers of the Chamber of Deputies that that body persisted in regarding its one-sided decisions concerning the grant or refusal of the State expenditure as definitely binding on the Government. On the question of the right of the representatives of the people to grant expenditure, the King said: 'I also recognize that right, and will observe and guard it so far as it is founded on the Constitution. But I must call the attention of the House to the fact that, according to the Constitution, the members of both Houses of the Diet represent the whole people, and the Budget can be established only by law—to wit, by a resolution agreed to by both Chambers, and approved by me. If such agreement was not to be brought about, it was the duty of the Government, until such time as it should be arrived at, to carry on the administration without interruption. It would have acted unjustifiably if it had not done so.'

This was carrying the constitutional war into the enemy's camp; but although the voice was the voice of the King, the hand which wrote these lines was the hand of Bismarck. In conclusion the King observed: 'After I have, for a year past, proved, by a diminution of nearly four millions in the sums demanded from the people, as well as by ready acquiescence in the practical wishes of its representatives, that my sole aim is to bring about a termination of the opposition which the measures of my Government have encountered, as well in great things as in small, I expect that the Chamber of Deputies will no longer disregard these proofs of a conciliatory disposition, and I now call upon it to testify on its part its desire to meet my patriotic and paternal views in such a manner as to render possible that work of agreement which is a necessity of my heart—of my heart, whose only desire is to promote the welfare of the Prussian nation, and to maintain for the country the position assigned to it by a glorious history, through the faithful union of King and people.'

A thoroughly Ministerial address was brought before the two Chambers, and the Upper House proved itself conveniently subservient. Out of a total of 240 members 144 absented themselves, and when the Address was put the remaining 96 supporters of the Government carried it 'unanimously.' The King in his reply said 'it did his heart good' to receive so loyal an address, and the Government was emboldened to abide firmly by the view which it had taken up.

The Polish question now intervened. Russian Poland was during the whole of this year the theatre of a great patriotic revolt. It was carried out with Mieroslawski's assistance, and had the sanction of Mazzini. The resources of Russia were taxed to the uttermost before the insurrection could be subdued; but her usually cruel and terribly repressive policy prevailed. Some exciting debates took place in the Prussian Chamber on the relations of Prussia towards Russia and Poland. An intense feeling of indignation had been roused throughout Europe in consequence of a report that the Prussian Government had entered into a convention with Russia to surrender to her the fugitive Poles who sought refuge in Prussia, and to permit Russian troops to enter her territory for the purpose of seizing them. During a debate in the Lower Chamber on the 26th of February, Bismarck declared that the statements made with respect to the agreement with Russia were incorrect; but he refused to explain what the agreement was. According to contemporary reports, his speech was remarkable for the bold insolence with which he treated the Chamber and the authority of the Vice-President. Bismarck began by denouncing the successive interpellations with respect to the Prusso-Russian convention; and then referring to a suggestion by Deputy Unruh, that if the measures taken by the Government for the security of Prussian frontiers and interests were to lead to external complications, the means for the defence of the country should be refused to the King, he asked, 'Is not that saying to the foreigner, "Come hither; the moment is favourable?"' The speaker was here interrupted by loud exclamations and contradictions; but after he had proceeded again for a short time, the President told him that his language had nothing whatever to do with the question before the Chamber.

Bismarck then became very angry, and said in his supercilious way: 'I am not subject to the disciplinary influence of the Chamber. My only superior is his Majesty the King, and I have yet to learn that any legal or constitutional enactment has placed me under the discipline of the President of this House.'

Vice-President Behrend: 'I have not deprived the Minister-President of the word, nor could I do so consistently with the Constitution. But, according to the regulations of this House, its President exercises disciplinary power so far as its four walls extend (*loud applause*), and that power will I exert.'

Von Bismarck: 'I do not speak here in virtue of your regulations, but in that of the authority deputed to me by the King. On the ground of the paragraph of the Constitution, which prescribes that the Ministers must be allowed to speak, and must be heard as often as they demand it'—(*interruption*)—'you have no right to interrupt me. I must mark that view as an erroneous one, which the Government does not share. I was saying, then, the same Deputy Von Unruh who, in 1848, indelibly associated his name with the refusal of taxes'—(violent commotion arose in the Chamber, with cries of 'It is scandalous!' 'adjourn!' The President rang his bell continuously).

The Vice-President threatened to adjourn, but ultimately Bismarck was allowed to conclude. This little scene throws a side-light upon the manner in which constitutional questions were debated between the Ministers and the Chamber. On the present occasion the Chamber of Deputies adopted, by 246 to 57 votes, a resolution 'That the interest of Prussia requires that the Government, in face of the insurrection which has broken out in Poland, should not assist or favour either of the contending parties, or allow armed persons to touch the Prussian soil without at the same time disarming them.'

Another unseemly episode occurred on the 11th of May, when Bismarck behaved in so aggressive a manner, that he was peremptorily ordered by the President to be silent. This was a little too much for the Minister, who was high in the favour of his Sovereign; so in a few days he brought down 'a most high message from his Majesty the King to read to the House.' This document was really a scolding for the Deputies. It was signed by the King and countersigned by the Ministers, and it denounced the claim of the President of the Chamber of Deputies ' to subject our Ministers to disciplinary power, and to impose silence upon them.' An Address, in reply to this message, was drawn up and carried. It was presented to the King, who in his reply reasserted the privilege of Ministers, and thus marked his disapprobation of the course pursued by the Chamber. ' My Ministers possess my confidence; their official acts have been done with my consent, and I thank them for their care to oppose the anti-constitutional attempt of the House to extend its power. By the co-operation which the House declares that it refuses to my Government, I can only understand that co-operation to which the House is entitled by the Constitution; any other can neither be claimed by it, nor has been asked for by my Government. In presence of such a refusal, the real meaning of which, moreover, is made by the whole contents and tone of the Address, as well as by the demeanour of the House during the last four months, a further continuation of the present session can lead to no result. Neither as regards domestic affairs, nor with respect to foreign relations, would it be favourable to the interests of the country.'

Bismarck was accordingly despatched to close the session of the Chambers, and this was done on the 27th of May, in the White Hall of the Palace. The Speech from the Throne, which was read by the Minister, recited that the Chamber of Deputies had placed itself in direct opposition to the Government, and, notwithstanding the answer of the King, had remained in a position adverse to an understanding. By its debates upon foreign politics the Chamber had endeavoured to paralyse the influence of the Government, and had thereby increased the excitement prevalent in the provinces bordering upon Poland. It had accepted misrepresentations of the opponents of Prussia, and aroused apprehensions of external dangers and entanglement in war, for which the existing relations to foreign Powers gave no well-founded cause. In its recent Address, moreover, the Chamber had altogether refused its co-operation with the Government. This rendered the close of its deliberations unavoidably necessary. The Government reserved to itself the power of determining the manner in which the unsettled financial measures should be brought to a conclusion, and hoped to come to a future understanding with the representatives of the people.

The Bismarck Ministry proceeded to further high-handed measures, and on the 1st of June a Royal decree was issued authorizing the suppression of newspapers 'which persistently exhibited tendencies dangerous to the welfare of the State'—thus striking at the Liberal press—and the exclusion altogether of foreign journals for the same cause.

The conduct of the Sovereign and his Ministers led to a temporary estrangement between King William and his son, the Crown Prince, whose views were shared by his wife, our

Princess Royal. On the 31st of May, the Crown Prince addressed a letter to his father, which showed how keenly sensible the heir-apparent was of the unconstitutional course which his Royal parent was pursuing. The Prince thus wrote: 'Expressions you lately made use of in my presence regarding the possibility of forcing your measures upon the country oblige me to speak out on the subject. On dismissing the Auerswald Cabinet you told me that, being more Liberal than yourself, I had now got an opportunity for enacting the usual part of a Crown Prince, and throwing difficulties in the way of your Government. At that time I promised you to keep back and maintain silence, and offer no opposition. Intending to keep my promise, as I do, I yet feel it my duty to speak to you in private. I beseech you, my dearest father, not to invade the law in the way you hinted. Nobody is more fully aware than myself that to you an oath is a sacred thing, and not to be trifled with. But the position of a Sovereign in regard to his Ministers is sometimes very difficult. Skilled as they are in the lawyer's art, and expert at interpretation, they know how to represent a measure as fair and necessary, and by degrees to force a Sovereign into a path very different from that he intended to tread.'

Not very pleasant reading this, either for King or Minister. One can see the former twisting his moustachios in a paternal rage as he reads his son's virtual condemnation of Ministers, and justification of the course pursued by the representatives of the people. But there must be a reply, of course, so the King wrote: 'You say you do not intend to offer any opposition. You must not have been cautious, then. Opposition speeches of yours have got abroad and found their way to me. You have now an occasion for making amends by expressing yourself in a different way, by slighting the Progressists and courting the Conservatives. The decree of June 1, besides being in consonance with the Charter, and more particularly with clause 63, will be laid before the Landtag. The decree, so far from being the enormity you say, ought to have been introduced in the shape of a bill, even under the late Liberal Cabinet; for it was on this condition only I sanctioned the law protecting printing offices against the supervision and interference of the police.'

But the breach between the King and the Crown Prince widened. On the 3rd of June the latter lodged a formal protest against the decree affecting the press. It was addressed to Bismarck, with a request that he would communicate it to the Cabinet. The Prince thus strongly expressed himself: 'I deem the proceedings of the Cabinet to be both illegal and injurious to the State and the dynasty. I declare the measure to have been taken without my wishing and knowing it, and I protest against any inferences and ascriptions to be possibly based upon my relation to the Council of State.' On the following day the Prince wrote again to the King, stating emphatically that the Charter had been evaded and set aside in the case of the decree on the press. At Dantzic, moreover, where he arrived on the 5th of June on a tour of military inspection, he returned an answer to an address from the municipality, the tone of which greatly offended the King. His Majesty wrote to his son, and demanded a disavowal of sentiments which he assumed must have been falsely reported. If not, and they were repeated, he threatened to recall him to Berlin and deprive him of his military command.

The Prince thus courageously replied: 'The address I delivered at Dantzic is the result of calm reflection. I long owed it to my conscience and my position, to profess, in the face of the world, an opinion the truth of which has forced itself upon me more fully from day to day. The hope only of being able after all to avoid placing myself in opposition to you stifled the monitions of my internal voice. But now, ignoring my different views, the Ministry have taken a step imperilling my future and that of my children. I shall make as courageous a stand for my future as you, my dear father, are making for your own. I cannot retract anything I have said. All I can do is to keep quiet. Should you wish me to do so, I hereby lay at your feet my commission in the army and my seat in the Council of State. I beg you to appoint me a place of residence, or to permit me to select one myself, either in Prussia or abroad. If I am not allowed to speak my mind, I must naturally wish to dissever myself entirely from the sphere of politics.'

Ultimately the storm blew over, though not until it had greatly disturbed the Royal Household and the Court, for the Crown Prince had his sympathizers as well as the King.

A Royal decree was published on the fourth of September, dissolving the Prussian Chambers. The Ministry regarded the situation as hopeless, knowing that the Deputies would never cease to oppose their arbitrary and unconstitutional measures. So they made a report to the King, upon which his Majesty promptly acted.

The new Chambers met in December, and the Liberal party was as strong as ever; but circumstances occurred which seemed to open up a prospect of reconciliation between the Deputies and the Government. The death of the King of Denmark raised the question of the right of succession to the Duchies of Schleswig and Holstein. The Prussian Liberals enthusiastically espoused the cause of the Prince of Augustenburg, in opposition to that of Christian IX., the present King of Denmark.

We shall presently trace the course of the Schleswig-Holstein difficulty, but in the meantime it may be stated that an Address to King William was drawn up in the Chamber of Deputies, the object of which was to set aside the Treaty of London entered into in May, 1852, with respect to the succession to the Danish Crown, and to compel the Prussian Government to recognize the Prince of Augustenburg as Duke of Schleswig-Holstein. Now the Government had applied for a loan in order to be prepared for the possible necessity of war arising out of the complications in the Schleswig-Holstein question, but they refused to adopt the extreme course of withdrawing from a treaty which the King of Prussia had solemnly signed in 1852, and the Chamber was unwilling to grant the loan, except upon that condition. The Committee on the loan agreed to the Address by a majority of sixteen to five votes. The dissentients were anxious to refuse the ministerial demand altogether. Bismarck hinted that a refusal of the loan by the Chamber would facilitate the course of the Government on other questions besides that of Schleswig-Holstein—which was intended as a threat to intimidate the members into submission by holding over their heads the probability of a prorogation or dissolution of the Chamber. Notwithstanding the threat, however, the proposal for the loan was ultimately rejected by the Chamber.

In the struggle which now ensued between the gallant little state of Denmark and the powerful kingdom of Prussia, the sympathies of England were enlisted on the side of the weaker Power. It was felt that she had right on her side, and it was felt also that the antiquated pretensions which German jurists had raked up from the dust of her libraries were merely a cover to conceal the real object of Prussia, which was to obtain the strong harbour of Kiel as a port in which some German navy of the future might ride at anchor.

The Danish Monarchy—as we find from historical facts and statistics published at the time of this new struggle—consisted of the Kingdom of Denmark Proper and the Duchies of Schleswig, Holstein, and Lauenburg. The Kingdom of Denmark and Schleswig formed together the original Danish realm, whilst Holstein and Lauenburg were German territories which had been acquired since, and were known as the German Duchies of the King of Denmark, by right of which he sat as a member of the Germanic Confederation. The Duchy of Schleswig, or South Jutland, covered 3,530 English square miles, with 409,907 inhabitants, who belonged to three different nationalities, Danish, Frisian, and German, more than half being Danes. Schleswig was originally a part of the Danish province of Jutland, but in the year 1232 it was detached and became a fief of the Danish Crown. In 1459 it escheated to the Crown, but was maintained as a separate fief, and was soon afterwards divided between the three principal branches of the House of Oldenburg. King Frederick IV. obtained guarantees from England, France, and other powers for the quiet possession of the duchy in future times. The whole duchy was reincorporated into the Crown, and once more made an integral and inseparable part of the Danish State,—first by letters patent of August 22, 1721, and subsequently by the homage of the inhabitants.

The Duchy of Holstein comprised 3,280 English square miles, with 544,419 inhabitants of purely German nationality. Though a fief of the German Empire until 1806, it had been in connection with Denmark ever since 1460, when it was acquired by King Christian I., on the occasion of the reversion of Schleswig, the last Duke having possessed also Holstein. As in the case of Schleswig, so the descendants of Christian I. divided Holstein amongst themselves; the Royal branch obtaining the Glückstadt division, the Gottorp

branch the Kiel division, and the Sönderburg branch the
Plöen division. The Danish kings, however, bought back
the Plöen division, and regained in 1773 the Kiel division by
a treaty of exchange with the then reigning Duke of Gottorp,
who afterwards ascended the Russian throne. When the
German Empire was dissolved Holstein was declared allodial,
and became united to the body politic of the Danish Monarchy
by letters patent of Sept. 9, 1806. The Duchy of Lauenburg, which contained 402 English square miles, with 50,147
inhabitants, was acquired in 1815, and was 'for ever incorporated into the Danish Monarchy,' by letters patent of
Dec. 6, 1815, and the homage of the estates Oct. 2, 1816.

It is important to note that the Act of Incorporation of
1721, by which the Duchy of Schleswig was made an integral
part of the Danish kingdom, established the succession for
that duchy according to the Royal law of Denmark.
Nothing could be clearer or more emphatic than this new
oath of allegiance for Schleswig, taken by the then Duke of
Augustenburg and Schleswig :—'I therefore promise *and
engage for myself, my heirs and successors*, by these presents,
and in virtue of them, that I and they will acknowledge and
hold your Royal Majesty of Denmark, Norway, &c., as our
only Sovereign Lord, will be to you and your Royal hereditary
successors in the Government *secundum tenorem legis regiæ*,
true, faithful and obedient. So help me God and His Holy
Word.'

With so long a possession of these duchies on the part of
Denmark, and with so clear a title, how arose the dispute
which was to wrench the duchies from the Danish Crown?
The quarrel began in 1848, when an insurrectionary party
in the Danish Monarchy, known as the Schleswig-Holstein
party, appealed to Germany for aid in establishing the union
of the two Duchies of Holstein and Schleswig, with a separate
constitutional existence from the rest of the monarchy. The
insurrection was fostered by Germany, and after a prolonged
struggle the Peace of Berlin of July 2, 1850, was signed, by
which Germany withdrew from the war, and agreed to
pacify the Duchy of Holstein. Notwithstanding the conclusion of the peace, however, the points in dispute remained
open. At the request of Denmark, German troops marched
into Holstein, and occupied the duchy. But when the
country had been pacified, Germany refused to withdraw her

troops, and to reinstate the King of Denmark in his full sovereign authority in Holstein and Lauenburg, the two duchies which constituted the only German federal territories embraced in the Danish Monarchy. Germany insisted upon assurances as to the future government of the territories, and the conditions for reinstating the King of Denmark in his full sovereign authority formed the subject of the diplomatic correspondence of 1851-2. On the 28th of January, 1852, the King of Denmark issued a proclamation containing the entire constitutional programme of the Danish Government, and embracing also certain points agreed upon with Austria and Prussia. The Germanic Diet accepted the proclamation as satisfactory in respect to the constitutional regulation of the positions of the federal territories embraced in the Danish Monarchy.

The dispute between Denmark and Germany was now regarded as settled, and the King of Denmark was reinstated in his full sovereign authority, both in Holstein and Lauenburg. The Rigsraad, or Council of the Realm, a general Legislative Assembly for the whole monarchy, was constituted in 1855, and to this assembly, numbering 80 members, Denmark Proper contributed 47 representatives; Schleswig, 13; Holstein, 18; and Lauenburg, 2. In 1858, however, the Constitution of 1855 was abrogated as regarded Holstein and Lauenburg, with the result that these duchies were put out of all constitutional union with the other parts of the Danish Monarchy. They were once more placed under the absolute authority of the Sovereign, with Assemblies having jurisdiction over local affairs. But difficulties arose owing to the pretensions of the Holstein Assembly, and these were temporarily adjusted by the mediation of Great Britain. Prussia and Austria declared themselves satisfied if Denmark would, for the present, confine the contributions of Holstein towards the general expenditure of the monarchy to the sums fixed by the normal budget of 1856.

A very important step was taken by the Danish Government on the 30th of March, 1863. An ordinance or proclamation was issued, endeavouring to meet the requirements of the Diet in respect to placing the Assembly of Holstein on an equal footing with the Rigsraad for Denmark Proper and Schleswig. It was decreed that no law should be valid in Holstein which had not obtained the sanction of the Assembly of that Duchy, and that no expenditure beyond the sums fixed by the normal budget of 1856 should be defrayed by Holstein, without the previous approval of the Holstein Assembly. And the Danish Government even agreed to abolish this limitation of the financial jurisdiction of the Holstein estates, if it should be objected to by the Germanic Diet. This ordinance had momentous consequences. Although Denmark had thus given every evidence of her desire to act fairly by the Duchies, Germany was dissatisfied. She asserted that the proclamation was a violation of Federal rights, and that the Danish Government had torn in pieces the treaties of 1852. The Germanic Diet, by two decrees, demanded the repeal of the ordinance of March 30, under threat of ' a process of execution.' The Diet, in its decrees, did not confine itself to the affairs of Holstein and Lauenburg, but expressly included the Danish crown-land Schleswig, the alleged ground being a violation by Denmark of the agreements of 1851-2.

Thus the whole subject of dispute was again opened up. Denmark asserted her rights, and received the sympathy of Sweden. Germany showed a spirit of aggression by wanting to compel the separation of Schleswig from all connection with Denmark Proper in respect of common affairs; and unfortunately certain proposals which had been made by the English Foreign Secretary in September, 1862, were used as an additional pretext by Germany for her interference.

Europe was startled, on the 15th of November, by the announcement of the sudden death of the King of Denmark. His successor, Prince Christian, the father of the Princess of Wales, ascended the Danish throne as King Christian IX., but on the following day there appeared a proclamation of Frederick, Prince or Duke of Augustenburg, who—as his father had abdicated his claims—insisted on his right to be recognized as the Duke of Schleswig-Holstein. Strange to say, the father of this claimant to the Duchies, had, on the 30th of December, 1852, signed a renunciation in which he said, ' *We promise for us and our family, by our princely word and honour*, not to undertake anything whereby the tranquillity of his Majesty's dominions and lands might be disturbed, nor in any way to counteract the resolutions which his Majesty might have taken, or in future take, in reference to the arrangement of the succession to all the lands now united under his Majesty's sceptre, or to the eventual organization of the monarchy.' The Duke, moreover, had accepted from the Danish Government a sum of 3,500,000 dollars in compensation for the surrender of his claims. The Prussians, anxious to find some excuse for their interference, alleged that the money paid under this very clear compact was compensation merely for the loss of property, and not for the surrender of seignorial rights ; but, owing to the part which the Duke of Augustenburg took in the rebellion of 1848, his whole estates became legally forfeited. Besides, there could be no two readings of his undertaking not to disturb the right of succession ' to all the lands then united under his Majesty's sceptre.' As King Frederick VII. was the last of his line, and had no issue, the Great Powers, in conjunction with the Crown of Denmark, had provided for the eventual succession to the throne by a solemn treaty. By this instrument, known as the Treaty of London, of May, 1852, the succession was secured by Christian IX., whose queen would, according to the *lex regia*, have been entitled, on the death of Frederick VII., to reign over Denmark Proper and Schleswig, but she ceded her rights to her husband. Touching Holstein-Gottorp, the legal heir to that duchy, after the Sovereigns of Denmark, was the Emperor of Russia, but in June, 1851, he ceded his rights of inheritance to the present dynasty. The Treaty of London provided that Prince Christian of Schleswig-Holstein-Sönderburg-Glücksburg, married to Louise, only daughter of the Landgravine of Hesse-Cassel, and named by King Frederick VII. as his successor, should be recognized by them, on the decease of Frederick, as King of Denmark. By the articles of the above treaty, the rights and reciprocal obligations of the King of Denmark and the Germanic Confederation concerning the Duchies of Holstein and Lauenburg established by the Federal Act of 1815, and the Federal right existing at the time of the treaty, were declared not to be altered by the said treaty. King Christian issued on the 6th of December, a proclamation to the inhabitants of Holstein, in which he stated that his claims had been recognized by the Powers, and that if necessary armed force would be employed in putting down any insurrectionary movements which had for their object the dismemberment of the Danish Monarchy. But the Frankfort Diet met, and

resolved to administer government in the Duchies of
Holstein and Lauenburg, without reference to the disputed
right of succession. Federal Commissioners were appointed,
and the Danish Government was summoned to withdraw
its troops from the Duchies within seven days. Austria,
Prussia, and Saxony further supplied soldiers to be in
readiness to enter Holstein, in case resistance should be made
by the Danes, and hostilities begin. The Prince of Augustenburg addressed a letter in support of his claims to the
Emperor of the French, who, in a cautious reply, and one
conceived in a waiting spirit, expressed the hope that the
Prince's claims might be investigated by the German Diet,
and that its decisions might be submitted to the Powers
represented in the Convention of London.

When the Federal Commissioners entered Holstein they
were warmly greeted by the inhabitants, who were very
hostile to the Danish rule. The Prince of Augustenburg
made his appearance about the same time at Kiel, and was
welcomed with enthusiasm as the rightful Duke of Schleswig-
Holstein. Several of the German States, flagrantly setting
aside the Treaty of London which they had signed, now
strenuously opposed the Danish right of succession. Meanwhile the Government of Copenhagen withdrew the Proclamation of the 30th of March, which had been made the
ostensible ground of Federal interference; and the British
Government endeavoured, but in vain, to induce the King to
procure the repeal of the Constitution of November, by
which the Germans alleged that Schleswig had, contrary to
good faith, been incorporated with Denmark Proper. The
year therefore closed with the Constitution of November in
full force, and the Danish and German troops confronting
each other on the opposite banks of the Eider, waiting for
the signal which should inaugurate the conflict.

Concurrently with the Schleswig-Holstein imbroglio,
difficulties arose in connection with the Germanic Confederation. A congress of German sovereigns and princes met
at Frankfort in the month of August to discuss a project for
the reformation of the Bund. It was the Emperor of Austria
who took the initiative, and he invited the other German
potentates to deliberate with him upon a scheme of
reform. The Emperor of Austria had a personal interview
at Gastein with the King of Prussia, and tried to induce

F

him to attend, but the King declined. Bismarck was also strongly against the scheme. However, nearly the whole of the other kingdoms, principalities, and free towns of Germany accepted the invitation, and Frankfort became the scene of such a gathering of kings and princes as had rarely been witnessed in Europe.

The Emperor Francis Joseph opened the proceedings, and the Congress, disappointed at the non-representation of Prussia, sent the King a collective invitation by the hands of the King of Saxony. His Majesty declined this second invitation as decidedly as he had done the first, and Bismarck waxed extremely angry. 'I was so nervous and excited,' he afterwards said, 'when the King of Saxony came, that I could scarcely stand on my legs, and in closing the door of the adjutant's room I tore off the latch.' Writing to his wife, he remarked, 'I cannot leave the King on account of all this Frankfort "windbaggery."' In his introductory address to the Congress, the Emperor of Austria thus indicated his proposed plan of reform: 'Being of opinion that the sphere of action of the Bund shall be enlarged, I propose that the Executive power shall be placed in the hands of a Directory, which shall have a Federal Council at its side. We require the periodical meeting of an assembly of deputies which shall have full power to participate in the legislation and in the control of the finances of the Bund. I propose that there shall be periodical meetings of the German Princes. By the introduction of an independent Federal Court a satisfactory guarantee is given for the proper administration of justice in Germany. In all these matters the principle of the equality of the several independent states will, as strictly as possible, be upheld. At the same time, due regard must be paid to their political influence and to the number of their inhabitants, in order that an effective executive power and a general representation in the Bund may be inseparably united.'

The Emperor could not conceal his chagrin, however, that King William had declined his invitation. The same feeling thus found expression in the collective answer of the other sovereigns and princes to the speech of the Emperor as read by the King of Bavaria: 'I deeply share with your Majesty, and certainly all our dear confederates share it with me, the regret that we cannot yet salute his Majesty the King of

Prussia among us. Let me firmly hope that at our next meeting this strong ring will complete the great chain of German power and grandeur.'

There were thirty-five states in the German Confederation, and the only princes who had declined to take part in the Congress, were the King of Prussia, whose contingent to the Federal Army was 79,484 men, and the Prince of Lippe-Detmold, whose contingent was 691.

Yet another effort was made to overcome the scruples of the King of Prussia, in an autograph letter from the Emperor Francis Joseph. King William, writing from Baden-Baden on the 20th of August, replied as follows to this latest invitation: 'In my letter of the 4th inst. I expressed to your Majesty my readiness to co-operate in an improvement of the Federal Constitution, in accordance with the age, and, at the same time expressed the conviction that, if the intended aim was to be reached, such a work could not be commenced by a meeting of sovereigns without harmonious preparatory discussions; and on this account I regret to be obliged to decline your Majesty's invitation to be present at the meeting at Frankfort on the 16th inst.

'If I unwillingly repeat my declination of the invitation which in its form is so honourable to me, my conviction is still the same as that expressed in my explanation of the 4th inst.; and I retain it the rather as I have yet received no official information of the basis of the propositions. The information which has reached me by other means only strengthens me in the view to fix my determination only when, by business-like deliberations on the matter by my Council, the proposed changes in the Federal Constitution may be harmoniously discussed in their relations to the just power of Prussia and to the just interests of the nation. I owe it to my country and the cause of Germany to give no explanations which may bind me to my federal allies, before such discussion has taken place. Without such, however, my participation in the discussions would be impracticable. This consideration will not restrain me from giving the same consideration to any communication which my federal allies may transmit to me, which I have always devoted to the development of the general interests of the country.'

The King of Prussia was not to be caught, and Bismarck, in giving to the representative of Prussia at the Frankfort Diet the reasons why his Majesty declined to take part in the Congress, wrote, *inter alia*: 'Your Excellency will receive from the Ministry at Berlin the more detailed development of the views of the Government of the King upon our own plans of reform, and the actual propositions of Austria. For the moment, I restrict myself to declaring that these last, as we think, do not correspond to the position to which the Prussian Monarchy has a right, nor to the legitimate interests of the German people. Prussia would be renouncing the position which her power and her history have made for her among the whole of the European nations, and would risk making the forces of the country serve for purposes alien to the interests of the country, and for the determination of which we could not exercise the degree of influence and control to which we can with justice pretend.'

The Prussian King and his Minister saw that the time was rapidly approaching which must decide the question of supremacy in Germany. The Emperor of Austria was regarded by many of the German princes as their natural head, but Herr Von Bismarck took a very different view, and would not countenance any step which might seem to give a secondary position to Prussia. The rights of his country were not to be maintained or extended by a mere palaver like that at Frankfort. The Minister had other ends in view which would have been defeated had the Prussian eagle once but had its claws clipped by the Frankfort Congress. So Francis Joseph was left to ruminate over the new position he had created in German diplomacy. The Congress passed a great many articles and resolutions, but Bismarck knew that the sword was capable of cutting through any such paper settlements of German interests.

CHAPTER VI.

THE WAR WITH DENMARK.

WHEN the year 1864 opened there was still some hope that war might be averted. England sympathized strongly with Denmark in regard to her difficulties with Prussia. Besides the natural feeling of interest and admiration she felt for a minor Power, which was in all but mortal conflict with a greater, England was moved by the fear that 'the dismemberment of the Danish monarchy might lead to an undue and dangerous predominance of Prussia on the Baltic.' Moreover, there was a third consideration with Englishmen, and a strong one, albeit one only of national sentiment and affection. The Princess of Wales, the wife of our heir apparent, was a daughter of the King of Denmark, and she had already won all British hearts by her beauty, her gentle nature, and her winning manners. When, rightly or wrongly, the idea gained ground that her father was being unjustly treated by Prussia, the feelings of British sympathy with the Danish Sovereign were still further strengthened.

The Prince of Augustenburg had been received at Kiel by the Commissioners who administered the Federal Government in Holstein; and Denmark, acting under the advice of the British Government, withdrew from a province which she had neither the legal right to defend against the representatives of the Diet, nor the physical power to hold. It was matter of regret with many statesmen that Denmark did not act as judiciously in respect to Schleswig, by evacuating that duchy and accepting the comparatively moderate terms which were still offered by the Great Powers. Austria and Germany, which in January were denounced by the German Liberals as enemies to the national cause, still recognized the rights of Christian IX. to the entire Danish monarchy, under the treaty of 1852. But demanding from Denmark the immediate repeal of the common constitution of the kingdom of Schleswig, they proposed to the Diet that in case of refusal the duchy should be occupied as a guarantee for the required concession.

To the wonder of Europe, Austria and Prussia, notwithstanding their antagonistic interests, were now to be seen moving in concert in the Schleswig-Holstein question. The minor German States, acting under the guidance of the Saxon Minister, Baron Beust, clamoured for immediate war, and, for the first time since the creation of the confederacy, they outvoted Prussia and Austria in the Diet. This vote decided the two Great Powers upon asserting their political supremacy in Germany, and their united forces were speedily concentrated on the frontier of Schleswig. The troops crossed the Eider on the last day of January, and after a few skirmishes, the Danish soldiers evacuated the line of the

Dannewerke, falling back upon the fortified position of Düppel, opposite the island of Alsen. The Austrian generals next proceeded to occupy the northern portion of Schleswig, and a part of Jutland; while the Prussians, assisted by an Austrian contingent, laid siege to Düppel.

Meanwhile the King of Prussia and Bismarck were fighting the Chamber of Deputies on the question of the supplies rendered necessary by the military movements undertaken by Prussia. As the Chamber persisted in its refusal to pass the bill which authorized the loan, the King peremptorily closed the session on the 25th of January. The Chamber had taken up a strong position in its previous conflicts with the King and the Ministry, but now it laid itself open to animadversion, inasmuch as while it urged upon the Government an armed interference in the affairs of the Duchies of Schleswig and Holstein, it persistently denied the Government the means of carrying on its operations. The King's speech to the Deputies contained the following passages:—

'While the Upper House has expressed, in an address to the King, its confiding readiness to support the Crown in this serious question, the required consent to a loan has been refused by the Chamber of Deputies, and even the grant of those supplies has been withheld which Prussia, as a member of the German Confederation, is undoubtedly bound to contribute. . . . The inimical character of these resolutions, in which is expressed an endeavour to subject the foreign policy of the Government to unconstitutional coercion, is heightened by resolutions by which the majority of the House of Representatives side beforehand against the Prussian fatherland on the supposition, arbitrarily raised by them, of warlike complications between Prussia and other German States. Such conduct on the part of the House of Representatives can only act in a pernicious manner on the strengthening and development of our constitutional condition, and we must for the present renounce hopes of an understanding. The Government of his Majesty must, however, consider itself bound, under all circumstances, to maintain with all its power, and in the full exercise of the royal rights, the preservation of the State, and the welfare and honour of Prussia. It is still firmly convinced that it will find sufficient and increasing support in the patriotic sentiments of the country.'

Public opinion was divided upon the legal rights of Denmark, in regard to the two duchies Schleswig and Holstein. While it all surged in favour of Denmark, as regarded the former, the popular feeling in Holstein was almost unanimously in favour of Germany. A deputation from that duchy presented an address to the Federal Diet, in which, after stating that their fathers knew how to preserve German rights and German manners, German truth and German feeling, against all attacks, and that the people had risen as one man to offer homage to the Duke of Augustenburg as their rightful Sovereign, they called for justice to be done. The Danes, however, denied that there was any such thing as a Schleswig-Holstein crown, or even a Schleswig-Holstein State. In the Upper House at Copenhagen, Bishop Monrad, the President of the Council, elicited loud cheers when he said, ' The programme which we have to follow, simply, clearly, and without evasion is this—not to allow a single German soldier to pass the Eider, without offering the best resistance in our power, and to use every effort to expel from Schleswig all who shall venture to intrude.'

In acting thus confidently, Denmark relied upon the support of the Western Powers, believing that England and France would interfere to prevent the violation of the Treaty of London of 1852, to which they were parties, and which covenanted to secure to the Danish Crown all the dominions which then belonged to it. The Danes furthermore relied upon the strength of their fortifications called the Danne-werke, on the north side of the Eider. Field-Marshal von Wrangel commanded the Prussian forces which were assembled at Kiel, and on the 1st of February they marched out of the town and crossed the Schleswig frontier, occupying Gottorp, while the Danish troops retired at their approach. General de Meza commanded the Danish army, and he was summoned by Wrangel to evacuate the town of Schleswig, to which his answer simply was that he had orders to defend it. A severe conflict took place on the 2nd of February between the Danes and Germans, near Missunde, on the Schlei, upon which General de Meza had retired with the first division of his army. Unable to contend with the superior forces of the Germans, the Danes retreated northwards. Schleswig was evacuated, the Austrians occupied Flensburg, and the Prussians pushed on towards Düppel.

Indignation at the abandonment of the Dannewerke broke out in Copenhagen, and the Commander-in-Chief was deprived of his post. De Meza, however, with his greatly inferior forces, had no other option, and the Danish Rigsdag passed a vote of thanks to the army for the gallant spirit it had displayed in the unequal struggle. On the 7th of February, General Von Wrangel issued a proclamation, in which he announced that Austrian and Prussian commissioners would administer the civil government of Schleswig, and ordered that the German language should be thenceforth used in all branches of the administration. But the smaller States of the Federal Diet now became dissatisfied with the mode in which Austria and Prussia were superseding the authority of the Diet in their conduct of the campaign. These Powers, nevertheless, took little notice of the protests made against their action.

The Danish army now concentrated itself at Fredericia, a fortress on the confines of Schleswig and Jutland, Düppel—opposite to Alsen—and in the little island of Alsen itself, which was held by 12,000 men. The siege of Düppel was undertaken by the Prussians, who brought all the resources of modern artillery against it. Line after line of the Danish defence was gradually taken, and on the 18th of April the last remaining bastions were stormed, and the Prussians became masters of the place. Fredericia was then abandoned by the Danes. The conduct of the Prussians in Jutland was most arbitrary and oppressive. Von Wrangel issued a proclamation in which he imposed a forced contribution upon the province of £96,000, 'in compensation for the damage to property caused to Prussian as well as to other German subjects by ships and cargoes captured by the Danes.' From the small town of Viborg, containing a population of less than 5000, a Prussian general demanded the immediate delivery of 19,600 lbs. of bread, 30,000 lbs. of oats, 380 lbs. of roasted coffee, 2700 lbs. of rice, 380 bottles of wine, 1200 bottles of brandy, 3000 cigars, 1300 lbs. of tobacco, 25,000 lbs. of hay, and 11,000 lbs. of straw. This requisition was followed up by others equally exorbitant. In a naval engagement off Heligoland, the Danes for the first time gained an advantage over their opponents.

England now endeavoured to avert the further prosecution of the war by a conference of the Great Powers. Together with Denmark, she took her stand upon the provisions of the treaty of 1852; but Prussia at once threw that treaty to the winds, alleging that war had abrogated it, and that she was no longer bound by it. Austria was not quite so emphatic in her declarations, and the Federal Diet, after considerable difficulty, agreed to send a representative to the conference. The first meeting took place in London on the 25th of April, and on strong representations being made by England, France, Russia, and Sweden, it was agreed that hostilities should be suspended from the 12th of May to the 12th of June. In the meantime Denmark was to raise her blockades. The plenipotentiaries of Austria and Prussia were asked to explain why their governments had occupied a large portion of the Danish territory, and what their future intentions were; and the answer was given that the treaty of 1852 was no longer in force. The conference failed to come to an understanding upon the points in dispute, but a prolongation of the armistice was arranged, and it was agreed to continue the suspension of hostilities until the 26th of June. Proposals were then made by England as to the boundary-line which was to separate Denmark from the duchies, but the Danish and German plenipotentiaries hopelessly disagreed upon this point, and the labours of the conference consequently came to an end with an abortive result.

A new cabinet was formed at Copenhagen, and in opening the session of the Rigsraad on the 25th of June, the King expressed a hope that the sympathy of England would grow into active support. A few days afterwards hostilities were renewed. The Prussians crossed over to Alsen, and after a sharp engagement the Danish troops which came up were compelled to retreat with a loss in killed and wounded of nearly 3000 men. In the following month a quarrel arose between the Federal and Prussian troops, and the forcible occupation of Rendsburg by the latter led to much bad blood. The affair blew over after a strong resolution passed by the Saxon chambers.

The struggle with Denmark practically concluded with the capture of Alsen and the abandonment of Fredericia. As the Danes were left alone to pursue a very unequal war, they were at length compelled to yield and make overtures for a peace. Negotiations were accordingly opened at Vienna, between the plenipotentiaries of Austria, Prussia, and Denmark, for the purpose of settling the preliminaries between those Powers. On the 1st of August these preliminaries of peace were signed: by them the King of Denmark renounced all his rights to the Duchies of Schleswig, Holstein, and Lauenburg, in favour of the King of Prussia and the Emperor of Austria, engaging also to recognize any arrangements those Powers might make in respect to the duchies. The frontier dispute was settled by mutual concessions. Debts contracted on account of the Danish monarchy were to be divided between the Kingdom of Denmark upon the one hand, and the ceded duchies upon the other, in proportion to the population of the two parts. But the loan contracted in England by the Danish Government in the month of December, 1863, was to remain at the charge of the Kingdom of Denmark; and the repayment of the war expenses incurred by the Allied Powers was to be undertaken by the duchies. A treaty of peace, upon the basis thus laid down, was ultimately signed at Vienna on the 1st of October.

Bismarck, having now obtained all he wanted, wrote a very cool note to the Prussian Minister in London, to the effect that he hoped the British Government would not refuse to recognize the moderation and placability which had been displayed by the two German powers, Austria and Prussia. They did not wish, he said, to dismember the ancient and venerable Danish monarchy, but to bring about a separation from it of parts with which a further union had become impossible through the force of circumstances and events. The Danish monarchy had received no wounds which could not be healed.

This view of the crippling of Denmark was a little too cynical for the British Government; and as England was directly challenged for her opinion, Earl Russell gave expression to the grave dissatisfaction of his Government at the course pursued by the German Powers. His lordship wrote: 'Her Majesty's Government would have preferred a total silence, instead of the task of commenting on the conditions of peace. Challenged, however, by Herr Von Bismarck's invitation to admit the moderation and forbearance of the great German Governments, Her Majesty's Government feel bound not to disguise their own sentiments upon these matters. Her Majesty's Government have, indeed, from time to time, as events took place, repeatedly declared their opinion that the aggression of Austria and Prussia upon Denmark was unjust, and that the war as waged by Germany against Denmark had not for its groundwork either that justice or that necessity which are the only bases on which war ought to be undertaken. Considering the war, therefore, to have been wholly unnecessary on the part of Germany, they deeply lament that the advantages acquired by successful hostilities should have been used by Austria and Prussia to dismember the Danish monarchy, which it was the object of the treaty of 1852 to preserve entire. . . . If it is said that force has decided this question, and that the superiority of the arms of Austria and Prussia over those of Denmark was incontestable, the assertion must be admitted. But in that case it is out of place to claim credit for equity and moderation.'

Immediately after her victorious contest with Denmark, Prussia began to treat the smaller States of the German Diet with superciliousness and hauteur. They soon found that in egging on Prussia and Austria to the very uneven conflict with Denmark, they had been making a rod for their own backs.

Bismarck addressed a note, on the 13th of December, to the Prussian Ambassador at Munich, in which he openly manifested his contempt for any resolution which the Federal Diet might pass in opposition to the alleged rights and interests of Prussia.

The man of iron had triumphed, and Denmark had been the first to feel the weight of his oppressive hand. It was with sadness and deep emotion that the King of Denmark received a deputation who conveyed a farewell address from the inhabitants of Schleswig. 'You have told me,' said his Majesty, with pathos and simple dignity in his reply, ' how bitterly you grieve to be separated from Denmark and the Danish Royal House, and I pray you to believe that it has also been most painful to me to be placed under the necessity of relinquishing the ancient Danish crown land of Schleswig, united for centuries with Denmark. Of all the cares and sorrows which have been heaped upon me during my brief rule, nothing has more depressed my mind, nothing weighed more deeply upon my heart, than the separation from the brave, faithful, and loyal Schleswigers, who have, upon so many difficult occasions, constantly given the most brilliant proofs of fidelity and devotion to Denmark and the Danish Royal House, and who have cherished no dearer or more zealous wish than to remain united with the kingdom under my sceptre. But, my friends, we must all bow to the will of Providence, and I will pray to the Almighty that He may give both to you and to me the requisite strength and endurance to bear the bitter pangs of separation. I thank you heartily for your presence at this place, and will consider it as an additional proof of your devotion to me and the Danish Royal House. My best wishes for your future welfare will always be with you. May God preserve and bless you all!'

Though nothing could reconcile the King to the loss of his beloved provinces, the Danish Royal House may well regard with pride—and find some solace therein—the fact that it has provided a King for Greece, and that the illustrious unions which its princesses have formed have given to Russia an Empress and to England its future Queen.

CHAPTER VII.

THE STRUGGLE WITH AUSTRIA.

For some time the relations between the two great German Powers, Austria and Prussia, were to remain of a friendly character. The Emperor Francis Joseph gave many proofs of his esteem and friendship for his royal brother of Prussia, and he decorated Bismarck with the order of St. Stephen. The Prussian Minister had already received from King William the coveted order of the Black Eagle, and not long afterwards he was created a Count.

On the meeting of the Prussian Chambers in January, 1865, Count Bismarck, in the debate on the speech from the throne, evolved further ideas upon constitutional questions which must have alarmed the Deputies. Constitutional rule he declared to be based on a compromise, especially in Prussia, where there were side by side three estates with equal powers. The Chamber of Deputies, by its resolution of September, 1862, had abandoned the path of compromise, and the existing Government, on its entry into office, had found a conflict already in progress. 'The Chamber of Deputies,' observed the Minister, 'asks that this conflict should be ended by an alteration of the present organization of the army. This is impossible. As regards foreign policy, a premature statement of the intentions of the Government in reference to pending questions is also impossible. I can only state that the interests of the country will be maintained. The blood of our soldiers will not have been shed in vain. The public Press and the Chamber of Deputies have reproached the Government with having entered into an alliance with Austria. On this question the future will throw a clearer light.'

But the Ministerial oracle was dumb as regarded any further revelations. The Government was secretly working, but declined to unfold its plans. The Chamber of Deputies could only see a solution of the conflict with the King and his Ministers by a formal acknowledgment on the part of the Government of the constitutional right of the Chamber to vote the Budget, and an assurance that the military expenses of the country should be diminished as much as possible. The Minister of the Interior nevertheless replied that the King would not yield a single iota on the question of military reform, and the House must, therefore, select another test of the extent of its constitutional power—namely, its right to vote the Budget. But the Upper House was staunch to the throne, and the King thanked it in warm terms for its loyal address. He attributed the success of the army to the fact that all its triumphs had been carried through and effected upon the one basis of the fear of God. As for those representatives with whom the Ministry was at loggerheads, he practically said: 'I shall try to make peace with them; but, if I cannot, then I shall do without them.'

But the Deputies might well view the condition of the public finances with alarm, seeing that the Budget had increased since 1849 from 94,000,000 to 151,000,000 thalers, while the population had only risen from 16,300,000 to 19,500,000 in the same period. The yield from the income-tax alone had gone up from 20,500,000 to 32,000,000 thalers.

Bismarck now brought in a bill for the increase of the

navy, and he was anxious for the Prussian Diet to declare that the acquisition of the port of Kiel was necessary. He was looking ahead, and, when questioned as to whether Austria would be compensated in the event of an increase of the power of Prussia in the duchies, he would not commit himself beyond saying that no proposal had either been made or accepted by which the rights of Prussia would be violated or her destinies influenced for a long period to come. As the Minister remained reticent, the Chamber continued hostile, and passed a resolution, declining to grant any loans to the Ministry, which had practically set aside the right of voting the Budget. Bismarck had claimed during the debate that Kiel and the entire duchies were owned by Prussia. He admitted that they were owned in common with the Kaiser, but affirmed that the share which Prussia had in the property would never be abandoned except on condition of Kiel Harbour being handed over to her for good. No votes of the Schleswig-Holstein estates, no proclamations of the Pretenders would drive Prussia from the duchies; she would stick to her programme, defending the justice and the necessity of it to the last man.

Yet the Lower House not only refused a loan, it rejected also the bill brought in to legalize the increase of the army. Again the King closed the Chambers, Bismarck dissolving them in his name on the 17th of June. As he could not get a Budget from the Chamber, King William now resolved to become his own Budget-maker, and to act as though a representative constitution did not exist. A Royal decree was issued, in which his Majesty said: 'Not having succeeded in coming to an understanding with the Diet upon the bill for the Budget of the year 1865, I order, in accordance with the Report of the Ministry of State, dated the 4th of July, inst., that the estimate returned herewith, showing the expected revenue and expenditure for the current year, shall serve as a regulation for the administration of the finances. I hereby at the same time place at the disposal of the Minister of Marine a sum not exceeding 500,000 thalers for the construction of heavy cast steel guns for the fleet, and the Ministers of Marine and Finance will have to account to me for the employment of this sum at the end of the year.'

A further stage in German affairs was marked on the 14th of August, when an important convention between Prussia and Austria was signed at Gastein, by the respective Ministers of the two countries, Bismarck and Count Blome. The convention was afterwards signed at Salzburg by the King of Prussia and the Emperor of Austria. It began by declaring that 'their Majesties, the King of Prussia and the Emperor of Austria, having become convinced that the co-dominion hitherto existing in the countries ceded by Denmark through the treaty of peace of the 30th of October, 1864, leads to inconveniences which endanger, at the same time, the good understanding between their governments and also the interests of their duchies; their Majesties have, therefore, come to the determination no longer to exercise in common the rights accruing to them from article 3 of the above-mentioned treaty, but to divide geographically the exercise of the same until further agreement.' So, by the Gastein Treaty, the sovereignty of Schleswig now virtually centred in Prussia, and that of Holstein in Austria; while, in consideration of the payment of two-and-a-half millions of Danish dollars, the Emperor Francis Joseph ceded to King William all his rights of co-proprietorship in the Duchy of Lauenburg.

But this mutual arrangement, while pleasant enough to the two monarchs, drew forth strong protests from the Cabinets of Paris and London. M. Drouyn de Lhuys, the French Minister for Foreign Affairs, wrote: 'Upon what principle does the Austro-Prussian combination rest? We regret to find no other foundation for it than force, no other justification than the reciprocal convenience of the co-sharers. This is a mode of dealing to which the Europe of to-day has become unaccustomed, and precedents for it must be sought for in the darkest ages of history. Violence and conquest pervert the notion of right and the conscience of nations.' In almost identical terms, Earl Russell likewise wrote: 'All rights, old or new, whether based upon a solemn agreement between sovereigns or on the clear and precise expression of the popular will, have been trodden under foot by the Gastein Convention, and the authority of force is the sole power which has been consulted and recognized. Violence and conquest, such are the only bases upon which the dividing Powers have established their Convention. Her Majesty's Government greatly deplores the disregard thus manifested for the principles of public law and the legitimate claim that a people may raise to be heard when their destiny is called into question.'

When the Frankfort Diet assembled on the 24th of August, the Prussian and Austrian representatives laid before the Diet copies of the convention. But the smaller German States condemned the treaty, for it overthrew all the grounds on which the war with Denmark had been undertaken, while the only result of the spoliation of the northern kingdom was the aggrandizement of Prussia. Accordingly, a committee of delegates from the minor German States which met at Frankfort, issued a circular in which they affirmed that by the Gastein Convention the Governments of Austria and Prussia had violated in the most flagrant manner the clearest principles of right, and especially that of the duchies to settle their own future. The document further stated that the measures which it foresaw must follow the Convention, would, in addition to shaking the sentiment of right of the German people, probably annihilate for years the material and moral prosperity of the duchies, freed from the Danish yoke by German blood.

General von Manteuffel was appointed Prussian Governor of Schleswig, and he issued a proclamation in which he made the following large assumptions on behalf of Prussia: 'By the Gastein Convention you are transferred to a separate administration under the authority of the King of Prussia. Government by Prussia signifies justice, public order, and the advancement of the general prosperity. In assuming the Government, I promise to regard your interests, and expect obedience to his Majesty's commands.' Field-Marshal von Gablenz, the new Austrian Governor of Holstein, adopted a different tone. 'Holding aloof,' he said, 'from the exercise of any decided policy, I am inspired solely by the desire of remaining a stranger to all party intrigues, of striving incessantly to develop the prosperity of the country, and, strengthened by the confidence of the population, of meeting the justly founded wishes of the people.'

The King of Prussia now assumed, by Royal proclamation, the title of Duke of Lauenburg. Shortly afterwards an important document was published—to wit, the decision of a Commission which had been appointed by the Prussian

Government to investigate the question of the legal rights involved in the dispute relative to the Duchies. The Commission, which included the Prussian Crown lawyers, reported that the King of Denmark was the rightful Sovereign of the 'entirety' of the Duchies of Schleswig, Holstein, Sonderburg, and Glücksburg, and that the only pretence of title on the part of Prussia and Austria to those provinces, was the cession of them by the treaty of October, 1864, which had been extorted from King Christian IX. at the point of the sword. Further, that the claim of Prince Frederick of Augustenburg was barred by the renunciation made by his father 'for himself and his heirs' in December, 1852. This was equivalent to saying that the only title of Prussia and Austria was derived from the right of conquest, because they had been victorious in a war unjustly provoked by themselves. The allies were not only thus condemned by the public opinion of Europe, but by a judicial body composed of Germans, whose decision was above suspicion.

With the permission of King William, in October Bismarck had an interview with the Emperor Napoleon at Biarritz. The latter did not know what to make of his visitor, and asked Prosper Mérimée if he was mad. But subsequently, in his *Letters to an Unknown*, Mérimée said, 'Bismarck has quite won me; as, indeed, he also captivated Napoleon himself by his frankness and the charm of his manners. But politically the interview appears to have led to nothing definite.

The Prussian Government did not go the right way to conciliate the people by forcibly interfering to prevent a banquet announced to be given by the citizens of Cologne to the Liberal members of the Chambers. When the session opened on the 17th of January, 1866, Herr von Grabow, President of the Lower House, condemned this incident, and added that the Deputies were still waiting in vain for a settlement from Ministers of educational, trade, district, and principal affairs, based upon Liberal principles. The administration of the State was altogether devoid of Liberal principles, proof of which was afforded by the measures taken against Liberal newspapers, associations, and meetings, and Liberal officials and citizens.

The Lower House boldly continued its opposition to the Ministry, and in February it voted by a large majority that the union of the Duchy of Lauenburg to the Crown of

Prussia should not take place until it had been approved of by both the Chambers. This hostile and courageous attitude greatly displeased the King, and the session was abruptly closed on the 23rd of February, after an existence of only six weeks. Before the Chambers adjourned, Herr Gneist caustically and eloquently reviewed the history of the dispute between the Government and the Deputies, and observed, 'Let us hear no more of compromise. What we require is an atonement for the offence given to the public conscience—an atonement for the violation of the laws of this people.'

King William indicated his opinion of any interference with his sovereign rights in Schleswig, by issuing a proclamation which declared that any Schleswiger signing an address or delivering a speech in favour of the Duke of Augustenburg would thenceforth be liable to be imprisoned for a period varying from three months to five years, while the actual attempt to abolish the Austro-Prussian sovereignty over the duchies, and hand over the country to any of the rival pretenders, rendered the offender liable to a penalty of from five to ten years' hard labour. What would such patriots as Pym and Hampden have done if they had been handed over without their consent to a new ruler, and had been forbidden even to discuss the supposed title and claims of their new sovereign ?

Great events were impending that soon overshadowed the differences between King and Deputies. As in the case of individuals, Powers which have worked together for a common object are sure to quarrel in the long run, especially if their enterprises have been unjustifiable. Prussia and Austria, the whilom bosom friends, began to upbraid each other, the ostensible cause of the dispute being the occupation of the Duchies of Schleswig and Holstein. Beneath the surface, however, was the deep-seated rivalry between the two Powers, each of which aspired to be master in Germany. As they were in the constant habit of giving checks to each other, much irritation ensued. Nor was Prussia alone causing concern to Austria; Italy was anxious to come to hostilities with the latter Power, and made active warlike preparations for a contest which she resolved should not long be delayed. Seeing what was before her in the Italian quarter, Austria increased her armaments, whereupon Prussia took umbrage at her proceedings, and asserted that the increase in the military strength of Austria was really a menace against herself.

Count Bismarck now set to work in earnest, glad to get a pretext of any kind for falling out with Austria. He was resolved upon the exaltation of Prussia at any cost. In March the Berlin Government sent a circular despatch to the minor German States, pointing out the necessity of their coming to an immediate decision as to which of the two Powers they would side with in the struggle which the armaments going on in Austria seemed to render imminent. 'It is urgent for Prussia to know if, and to what extent, she may rely upon assistance in case she should be attacked by Austria, or forced into war by unmistakable menaces.' It was Bismarck's lot frequently to get the worst of the logic, and some of the States now replied by referring him to the 11th clause of the Federal Act, by which war between German Governments, members of the Bund, was prohibited, and a pacific mode of settling disputes was provided. The Bavarian Government plainly said that any Federal State which declared war against another Federal State must be considered as having violated the Federal Constitution. The upshot was, that seventeen out of the thirty-three States which formed the Bund seceded from it; and all the minor northern States, with the exception of the elder house of Reuss, took the part of Prussia.

But Bismarck went on his way, and scored a strong point by making a secret treaty of alliance with Italy, according to which the two countries agreed to engage in war with Austria, though each on its own account. It did not seem a very manly way of fighting an enemy this—one to cripple her in a certain quarter, and the other to keep her engaged in another. Allies fighting for a common cause is a different thing. But Italy engaged to declare war against Austria as soon as Prussia should have either declared war or committed an act of hostility. Prussia, on her part, agreed to continue the war until the mainland of Venetia, with the exception of the fortresses and the city of Venice, either was in the hands of the Italians, or until Austria declared herself ready to cede it voluntarily; and King Victor Emmanuel promised, on his part, not to lay down his arms until the Prussians should be in full and legal possession of the Elbe duchies.

Now ensued a long correspondence between the Governments of Austria and Prussia, each endeavouring to lay the blame upon the other of making hostile preparations in anticipation of a conflict, and each calling upon the other to disarm. We find the Emperor Francis Joseph expressing his sincere satisfaction at the announcement that Prussia had agreed to a simultaneous disarmament of the two Powers; but as Italy was preparing for an attack upon Venetia, of course Austria must look after herself in that quarter. To this Count Bismarck replied that Austria must disarm altogether, and that there was no ground for saying that Italy meditated an unprovoked attack upon the Empire, which was an astounding assertion in view of the provisions of the secret treaty between Prussia and Italy.

The Austrian Emperor rejoined by issuing orders for placing the whole army upon a war footing, and for concentrating a portion of it on the Bohemian and Silesian frontiers. At the same time Count Mensdorff wrote to the Austrian Minister at Berlin to the effect, that it was ridiculous to say Italy meditated no attack upon Austria, when the forcible detachment of a part of the Austrian territory was the already announced programme of the Florence Government. If Austria was not to be allowed to make preparations for warding off this attack, then she must consider the negotiations for a simultaneous disarmament on the part of Prussia on the one side, and of Austria on the other, as being at an end. Austria had given solemn assurances, both at Berlin and at Frankfort, and Prussia could therefore have no reason to apprehend aggression on her part, while Germany could have no cause to fear that she would disturb the peace of the German Confederation. 'In Berlin,' said Count Mensdorff, 'it cannot be unknown that we have not only to provide for the integrity of our own Empire, but also to protect the territory of the German Bund against an aggressive movement on the part of Italy; and we therefore may and must, in the interests of Germany, seriously ask of Prussia whether she thinks the demand that the frontiers of Germany shall be left unguarded, compatible with the duties of a German Power.'

Bismarck was careful not to answer this question; but his policy had become very apparent a few days before, when a peremptory demand was made by the Prussian Government upon the Saxon Government to give an account of the reasons why the Saxon army had been strengthened; and they were told that if the armaments were not at once discontinued, the Berlin Cabinet would take such measures as might appear to be necessary. But by way of reply to this threat, on the 5th of May a motion was made in the Federal Diet at Frankfort by the representative of Saxony. that the Bund, 'in accordance with Article XI. of the Act of Confederation, do summon Prussia to give a formal declaration that her intentions are of a pacific nature;' and this was carried by a majority of ten votes to five.

Meanwhile a startling incident occurred at Berlin, which diverted for a moment the attention of Prussians from foreign affairs, while it at the same time testified to the feeling of hatred with which Count Bismarck was regarded by a portion of his own countrymen. On the afternoon of the 7th of May, as the First Minister was returning to his own residence from the Palace, and was passing down the central avenue of the Linden, two shots were fired at him. Bismarck turned round and grasped the wrist of the assassin with one hand, and his throat with the other; but his assailant, though a very young man, struggled desperately, and managed to fire off three more bullets from a six-chambered revolver, two of which actually grazed the Minister's breast and shoulder. Notwithstanding a momentary feeling of weakness, Bismarck held on to his antagonist, and gripped him as in a vice; and as a battalion of the Guards was by this time marching down the Linden, he handed him over to the soldiers, by whom he was taken off to prison. Bismarck went home and wrote an account of the affair to the King. Then he entered the drawing-room, where several guests had assembled for dinner, and very calmly confided to his wife the intelligence, 'They have shot at me, my child; but don't fear; there is no harm done. Let us now go in to dinner.' The family doctor afterwards declared that the Minister had been saved only by a miracle. The King came to offer his congratulations, and the day closed with popular rejoicings.

The youth who made the attempt proved to be one Ferdinand Cohen, twenty-two years of age. He was the stepson of Karl Blind, a political exile from Baden, residing in London, and now well known in the literary circles of the metropolis. Cohen, who had adopted the name of Blind, was a youth of good education. He had espoused Republican principles, and journeyed from South Germany to Berlin with the set purpose of removing a man who was 'universally denounced as the oppressor of Prussian liberties, and the diabolic disturber of German peace.'

Young Blind was executed, which from the Minister's point of view was perhaps not the wisest thing to do; for Bismarck many years afterwards (May 9, 1884) complained in the Reichstag that the dead body of his would-be assassin 'became the object of a cult; that ladies of considerable name, whose husbands enjoyed a certain reputation in the scientific world, crowned it with laurels and flowers, and that this was tolerated by the police—the mass of the ordinary officials, perhaps even some of the higher ones, being rather on his side.' By way of correcting certain erroneous inferences from the Chancellor's statement, however, Herr Karl Blind thus wrote to the *Times* concerning his adopted son: 'The nobility of his character, and the patriotic nature of the motives which carried him away to the deed, were universally acknowledged at the time, even by political adversaries. His death was made the theme of a eulogistic poem by Marie Kurz, the wife of Hermann Kurz. His portrait, crowned with oak-leaves, was worn by many militiamen in the south on their helmets when they were called out for the war. With Nihilist ideas he had nothing whatever to do. His object was to prevent what the Imperial Chancellor in recent years himself has twice designated as a "war between brethren." I hold a number of letters of warmest sympathy, written in the days of deepest grief and sorrow, to my wife and myself, by men of political standing in Germany, of the moderate National Liberal, as well as of the Progressist and Democratic parties.'

Returning to the historical thread of our narrative, 'when the two giant brothers (Austria and Prussia) began to feel for their swords and shake their gauntleted fists at each other, Napoleon III., like another Iago feigning horror at the brawl between Cassio and Roderigo, made a show of proposing that they should submit their quarrel to a European congress at Paris—a proposal which, though accepted by Prussia, was virtually rejected by her rival; but he had previously plied Bismarck with offers of an alliance against

Austria, whereof the main objects were the cession of the Duchies to Prussia, of Venetia to Italy, and of more than the left bank of the Rhine to France.' And as a comment upon modern sovereigns and their diplomatic wiles, it may be stated that while Napoleon was tempting Bismarck with offers of an alliance against Austria, he was at the same time secretly treating with Francis Joseph for the cession of Venetia in return for Silesia—'the province most proudly prized by Prussian king and people.'

General Gablenz, the Austrian Governor of Holstein, convoked an assembly of the States, to meet on the 11th of June; but other events of moment intervened. The Prussian troops in Schleswig crossed the frontier on the 7th of May, to assert the right of Prussia to a joint occupation of the duchy; and as the Austrians were not in sufficient force to offer any effectual resistance, they retired from Holstein. The Prussian Governor of Schleswig, General Manteuffel, then issued a proclamation to the inhabitants of Holstein, in which he declared that the Provisional Government established there in September, 1865, was abolished, and appointed a Prussian President for the administration of the affairs of both the duchies—Schleswig and Holstein.

In vain did Austria protest against these acts, and accuse Prussia of a violation of the Gastein Convention. The Frankfort Diet passed a resolution, that the military commission should watch that the ordinary Federal contingents in Federal garrisons should not be exceeded, the object being to prevent Prussia from reinforcing her proportion of the garrison in the important fortress of Mayence. The representative of Prussia, by way of retort, then announced in the Diet, that she would consider the imperative requirements of her self-preservation as more important than her relations to a Confederation which, in its opposition to the supreme Federal laws, did not add to the security of the members of the Confederation, but rather endangered it.

It was at this juncture that the other Great Powers of Europe endeavoured to avert the outbreak of hostilities by a conference; and England, France, and Russia invited Austria, Prussia, and Italy, and the German Diet, to send representatives to meet in Paris and settle the terms of peace. Prussia, Italy, and the Diet accepted this invitation, but Austria made it a condition to her assent, that the negotiations should exclude all pretensions on the part of any one of the Powers to obtain an aggrandizement of territory. This stipulation obviously pointed to the claim of Prussia upon the two Duchies of Schleswig and Holstein, which she was not now in the least likely to abandon; so the French Emperor declared that it was useless for the Powers to meet, and the proposed Conference fell through. Two persons, Napoleon and Bismarck, were delighted with this abortive result. Prussia had agreed to the Conference with reluctance, and when the despatch announcing the failure of the Congress was brought to Bismarck, he exclaimed, '*Vive le Roi!*'

King William himself was much averse to this war in the outset. He was not only personally attached to the Emperor of Austria, but he did not like to be the first to break through the old German traditions. Those religious scruples, moreover, which have moved him at many stages in his history, intervened to make him shrink from incurring the responsibility of a European war. Then, protests and addresses poured in from all quarters, invoking a curse upon that Power which should be the first to cause a deadly strife between brethren. But Bismarck's iron will overcame all obstacles, and within six or seven days from the failure of the project for a Conference, Prussia withdrew from the Germanic Confederation, and by that step virtually declared war against Austria.

The two great German Powers now made active preparations for meeting in the field. The Frankfort Diet decreed, on the 14th of June, that the forces of the different States, members of the Bund, should be mobilized. What Prussia did is thus paraphrased in graphic language by Mr. Lowe, in his *Life of Prince Bismarck:* '"Look here, you ravenous and unreliable hawks," said Bismarck, on the day after the Prussian eagle had escaped from the discordant aviary at Frankfort; "look here, you Kings of Saxony and Hanover, and you also, Elector of Hesse Cassel! Your geographical facilities for dealing Prussia an open or secret blow are too great for us to remain in a day's doubt about your intentions. Therefore declare unto us before midnight your readiness to disarm and to accept our reform schemes, in return for our guarantee of your territorial and sovereign integrity, or—your blood be upon your own heads!"

'What were a Catholic and literary King John ruled by a diplomatic Dugald Dalgetty of a Beust, and a poor old blind King George boastful of his ancient lineage, and a whimsical tyrant of an Elector of Hesse, to say to a terribly imperative summons of this kind? All three returned equivocal answers tantamount to "No!"—and in less than two days their capitals were in the grip of Prussian troops, the two kings fugitive from their dominions, and the Elector on his way to Stettin as a State prisoner! Never had there been such prompt and splendid action since Frederick the Great, suspecting the designs of the Saxons, marched on Dresden and seized the proofs of their conspiracy with his foes; or since Nelson sailed to Copenhagen and disabled the Danish fleet from serving the Corsican robber against the Mistress of the Seas.'

Prince Frederick Charles, who commanded the Prussian troops in Saxony, upon entering that kingdom, issued from Görlitz a proclamation to the inhabitants, in which he said: 'We are not at war with the people and country of Saxony, but only with the Government, which, by its inveterate hostility, has forced us to take up arms.' Hesse-Cassel was overrun without any opposition. The Prussian force was divided into three main armies. Prince Frederick Charles commanded in Saxony and Bohemia, the Crown Prince operated in Silesia, and General Herwarth commanded the third army, called the army of the Elbe.

In Von Moltke Prussia now found the first strategist in Europe, as she had already found the first diplomatist in Bismarck. 'The confidence with which Bismarck had spoken and acted was to a great extent the result of his complete trust in the capability of the Prussian army, and of the soldier who was its mind and brain, to make good his actions and his words; and now he drew back and watched, while Hellmuth von Moltke set all the wondrous machinery in harmonious motion by a gentle pressure of his finger, and while he pored over his map in the office of the Grand General Staff at Berlin, as at a pensive game of chess, and moved his military pawns by touch of electric wire. Never before had war been waged in this way; never had any method of waging war been more swiftly, more surprisingly successful.' Nevertheless, at the opening of the campaign, there were not wanting those in Europe who thought that Austria might emerge victorious from the struggle.

The Emperor of Austria issued a war manifesto to his people on the 17th of June. Beginning with a review of the course of events which led up to the brink of hostilities, he explained why he was compelled to draw the sword. 'While engaged in a work of peace, which was undertaken for the purpose of laying the foundation for a Constitution which should augment the unity and power of the Empire, and at the same time secure to my several countries and peoples free internal development, my duties as a sovereign have obliged me to place my whole army under arms. On the frontiers of my empire, in the south and in the north, stand the armies of two enemies who have allied with the intention of breaking the power of Austria as a great European State. To neither of those enemies have I given cause for war. I call on an Omniscient God to bear witness that I have always considered it my first, my most sacred duty, to do all in my power to secure for my peoples the blessings of peace.'

'One of the hostile Powers,' continued the Emperor, referring to Italy, 'requires no excuse. Having a longing to deprive me of parts of my Empire, a favourable opportunity is for him a sufficient cause for going to war. The negotiations with Prussia in respect to the Elbe duchies clearly proved that a settlement of the question in a way compatible with the dignity of Austria, and with the rights and interests of Germany and the duchies, could not be brought about, as Prussia was violent and intent on conquest. The negotiations were therefore broken off, the whole affair was referred to the Bund, and at the same time the legal representatives of Holstein were convoked.

'The danger of war induced the three Powers—France, England, and Russia—to invite my Government to participate in general conferences, the object of which was to be the maintenance of peace. My Government, in accordance with my views, and, if possible, to secure the blessing of peace for my peoples, did not refuse to share in the conferences, but made their acceptance dependent on the confirmation of the supposition that the public law of Europe and the existing treaties were to form the basis of the attempt at mediation, and that the Powers represented would not seek to uphold special interests which could be prejudicial to the balance of power in Europe, and to the rights of Austria. The fact that the attempt to mediate failed because these natural suppositions were made, is a proof that the conferences could not have led to the maintenance of peace. Recent events clearly prove that Prussia substitutes open violence for right and justice.'

This able and now historic document next recapitulated the facts connected with the withdrawal of Prussia from the German Bund, and her employment of force against those sovereigns who had faithfully discharged their Federal duties. The Emperor's manifesto thus concluded: 'The most pernicious of wars—a war of Germans against Germans—has become inevitable, and I now summon before the tribunal of history—before the tribunal of an eternal and all-powerful God—those persons who have brought it about, and make them responsible for the misfortunes which may fall on individuals, families, districts, and countries. . . . We shall not be alone in the struggle which is about to take place. The princes and peoples of Germany know that liberty and independence are menaced by a Power which listens but to the dictates of egotism, and is under the influence of an ungovernable craving after aggrandizement; and they also know that in Austria they have an upholder of the freedom, power, and integrity of the whole of the German Fatherland. We and our German brethren have taken up arms in defence of the most precious rights of nations. We have been forced so to do, and we neither can nor will disarm until the internal development of my Empire and of the German States, which are allied with it, has been secured, and also their power and influence in Europe. My hopes are not based on unity of purpose—on power alone. I confide in an Almighty and a just God, whom my house from its very foundation has faithfully served—a God who never forsakes those who righteously put their trust in Him. To Him I pray for assistance and success, and I call on my peoples to join me in that prayer.'

If Prussia had her Moltke, Austria had her Benedek, a brilliant and an experienced soldier, and a man of high reputation. He was appointed Commander-in-chief of the Austrian army of the North, and distributed his forces along the frontier that separates Moravia from Saxony and Silesia. But his plans were differently laid from those of the Prussian strategist. Not anticipating the rapid movements of the enemy, General Benedek hoped to encounter his foes in detail, and to cut them off as they penetrated the passes and entered the Austrian territory at separate points. General von Moltke, on the contrary, had so constructed his plans that the three great German armies were all to converge upon a given point, which they actually did; so that masterly strategy, aided by the terribly-destructive power of the new needle-gun, wrought havoc amongst the Austrians, and ultimately brought the war to an end in an incredibly short space of time. Days sufficed for military movements which, in past times, would have required months to execute.

Prince Frederick Charles established himself with the First Prussian Army on the 22nd of June at Hirschfeld, a village near the frontier town of Zittau, which guards the passes leading from Friedland in Bohemia to Lusatia in Saxony. From this place he issued a proclamation, and on the following day the First Prussian Army crossed the Bohemian frontier in two columns, one marching by way of Görlitz, and the other by Zittau. Several small skirmishes with the enemy took place, and on the 28th there was a severe battle at Münchengrätz. The Austrians, who were reinforced by the Saxons, fought well, but were finally driven back upon Gitschin. The Prussians still pressed them, and took up their position on the high ground in front of the town.

Meanwhile the Second Prussian Army, under the command of the Crown Prince, by a strategic movement, which completely deceived the Austrians, suddenly made its appearance at Nachod and Trautenau in Bohemia, having passed without opposition the frontier at Reinerz and Landshut. The mountain defile leading to Nachod was occupied by the Austrians, but, after a short skirmish, they abandoned it on the 27th of June. The advance-guard of the Prussians, however, whose leading columns were under the command of General Steinmetz, was soon afterwards engaged by a strong Austrian force, and for the moment compelled to retreat; but the Crown Prince came to Steinmetz's aid, and, after a hotly-contested battle, the Austrians were ultimately defeated with a loss of 4000 men. A second sanguinary battle was fought on the same day between the armies of the Crown Prince and the Austrian Field-Marshal Gablenz at Trautenau, when the soldiers of Francis Joseph were again defeated. The Prussians pushed forward as far as Skalitz, of which town they took possession. All through the contest the Prussian Generals understood each other's plans, which were carried out to a nicety; but the course pursued by the Austrians was full of mistakes and strategic blunders. Archduke Leopold, for example, is said to have disobeyed the positive orders of his Commander-in-Chief, General Benedek, which were that he was not on any account to attack the Prussians when he confronted them at Skalitz, but to retire slowly until he could meet with more support. Benedek's object was to draw the enemy from their strong position on the rising ground above Skalitz, and to enable the Archduke to occupy the ridge opposite, the Prussians being thus inveigled into the valley beneath. But the Archduke, by some strange piece of infatuation, completely traversed these orders, and attacked the Prussians on the heights. The result was that he was driven back and pursued by the Prussians, who seized upon a formidable and advantageous position, from which subsequently they could not be dislodged. The Prussians were now very jubilant, and on the 1st of July the Crown Prince issued a general order, in which he recalled the successive incidents of the short but brilliant campaign.

The Third Prussian Army, that of the Elbe, under General Herwarth, after engaging the enemy near Turnau, and driving him back, effected a junction with the First Army under Prince Frederick Charles. This was near the town of Gitschin. Benedek, therefore, ordered Count Clam Gallas, with the First Austrian *Corps d'Armée*, to hold Gitschin while he himself took up a position at Dubenitz, in order to meet the army of the Crown Prince as it debouched from the passage of the Elbe. But Clam Gallas, also against his orders, it is stated, attacked the Prussians, with the result that he was driven out of his position, while the enemy captured Gitschin. General Benedek now found his left flank exposed, and ordered his army to fall back in the direction of Königgrätz. The *Times'* correspondent, describing this new and perilous situation, wrote: 'Benedek, who had taken up a strong position with his centre near Dubenec, his left towards Miletin, and his right covered by the river and by Josephstadt, found himself in the twinkling of an eye placed in a position of the greatest danger. His left was "in the air." The Prussians were not only on his left, but in his rear; and at the same time another great army was marching to effect its junction with them where he was altogether exposed. He instantly wheeled back his left and centre, and then, retiring his right, took up a line at Königgrätz at right angles to the line he had occupied to the west of Josephstadt.' But so serious was his danger, and so distrustful was Benedek of the *moral* of his troops, that, before the great battle was fought, he telegraphed to the Emperor of Austria, 'Sire, you must make peace!'

Peace was not made, and there was soon such a shock of arms as the battle-grounds of Europe have rarely witnessed. The King of Prussia entered Gitschin on the 2nd of July, and, on receiving a deputation from the authorities of the town, he thus addressed them : 'I carry on no war against your nation, but only against the armies opposed to me. If, however, the inhabitants will commit acts of hostility against my troops without any cause, I shall be forced to make reprisals. My troops are not savage hordes, and require simply the supplies necessary for subsistence. It must be your care to give them no cause for just complaint. Tell the inhabitants that I have not come to make war upon peaceable citizens, but to defend the honour of Prussia against insult.'

On the following day, the 3rd of July, was fought the great battle of Königgrätz, as it was called by the Prussians, or Sadowa, as it was called by the Austrians. King William was received with wonderful enthusiasm by his troops, and he thus spoke of his reception in a letter to Queen Augusta : ' The rejoicing which broke out here ' (he was at Langenhof on the Königgrätzer Chaussée) ' when the Guards caught sight of me is simply indescribable. The officers seized my hands to kiss them, which, for once in a way, I was obliged to permit, and so it went on all the time under fire, from one body of troops to another, ever forwards! and everywhere hurrahs without end!'

The disposition of the Prussian army was as follows : The First Army, under Prince Frederick Charles, formed the centre; the Elbe Army, under General Herwarth, the right; and the Second Army, under the Crown Prince, the left wing. The 7th Division marched in front of the First Army, through Goritz, Czerknitz, and Sadowa, to effect a junction with the right wing of the Crown Prince. The 8th Division marched upon Milowitz, being destined to advance upon Königgrätz. The Second Army Corps was to operate against Donalitz, south of Sadowa. The Third Army Corps formed the reserve of the centre. The Elbe Army pushed forward from Smidar towards Nechanitz. The army of the Crown Prince was directed to march from Königinhof in a straight line upon Königgrätz. The Austrian army was drawn up on a range of low hills between Smiritz and Nechanitz, and extended over a length of about nine miles, the centre occupying a hill on which was the village of Chlum or Klum, distinguished by a clump of trees. This was the key of the Austrian position. The Prussian army consisted of 256,000 men, and against this General Benedek had nominally an army of 225,000 men; but as a large deduction must be made for the baggage guards, the various escorts, the garrisons of Josephstadt and Königgrätz, the sick, and those tired by marching, and the killed, wounded, and prisoners in recent actions—he had not more than 190,000 or 195,000 soldiers actually at his command.

The King of Prussia had determined to give his army a day's rest on the 3rd, intending to begin the supreme struggle on the 4th; but at midnight of the 2nd of July, a Prussian reconnaissance revealed the fact, that the Austrians were preparing to attack. Accordingly a council was held between the King, Moltke, Bismarck, and Von Roon, and it was decided to begin the attack with the dawn of day. The Prussian cavalry and horse artillery accordingly began to move at seven in the morning, and the Austrian guns opened upon them from a battery near the village of Sadowa. The battle which ensued has been described by many skilful writers, but from the accounts furnished by the correspondents of the *Times* we select one or two passages as being best descriptive of the crucial features of this memorable engagement. The military correspondent, who was present with the Prussians at the battle, wrote:

'It was ten o'clock when Prince Frederick Charles sent General Stulnapl to order the attack on Sadowa, Dohilnitz, and Mokrowens. The columns advanced, covered by skirmishers, and reached the river bank without much loss; but from there they had to fight every inch of their way. The Austrian infantry held the bridges and villages in force, and fired fast upon them as they approached. The Prussians could advance but slowly along the narrow ways and against the defences of the houses, and the volleys sweeping through the ranks seemed to tear the soldiers down. The Prussians fired much more quickly than their opponents, but they could not see to take their aim ; the houses, trees, and smoke from the Austrian discharges, shrouded the villages. Sheltered by this. the Austrian Jägers fired blindly where they could tell by hearing that the attacking columns were, and the shots told tremendously on the Prussians in their close formations ; but the latter improved their positions, although slowly, and by dint of sheer courage and perseverance, for they lost men at every yard of their advance, and in some places almost paved the way with wounded. Then, to help the infantry, the Prussian artillery turned its fire, regardless of the enemy's batteries, on the villages, and made tremendous havoc amongst the houses. Mokrowens and Dohilnitz both caught fire. and the shells fell quickly and with fearful effect among the defenders of the flaming hamlets ; the Austrian guns also. played upon the attacking infantry, but at this time these were sheltered from their fire by the houses and trees between.

' In and around the villages the fighting continued for nearly an hour; then the Austrian infantry who had been there, driven out by a rush of the Prussians, retired, but only a little way up the slope into a line with their batteries. The wood above Sadowa was strongly held, and that between Sadowa and Benatek, teeming with riflemen, stood to bar the way of the 7th Division. But General Fransky, who commands this division, was not to be easily stopped, and he sent his infantry at the wood, and turned his artillery on the Austrian batteries. The 7th Division began firing into the trees, but found they could not make any impression, for the defenders were concealed, and musketry fire was useless against them. Then Fransky let them go, and they dashed in with the bayonet. The Austrians would not retire, but waited for the struggle ; and in the wood above Benatek was fought out one of the fiercest combats which the war has seen. The 27th Prussian regiment went in nearly 3000 strong, with 90 officers, and came out on the further side with only two officers and between 300 and 400 men standing ; all the rest were killed or wounded. The other regiments of the division also suffered much, but not in the same proportion ; but the wood was carried. The Austrian line

was now driven in on both flanks, but its commander formed
a new line of battle a little higher up the hill, round Lipa,
still holding the wood which lies above Sadowa.'

Meanwhile, General Herwarth was fighting a desperate
battle with the Saxon troops at Nechanitz, a village seven
miles from Sadowa. Courageously did the Saxons meet the
foe, but they were slowly driven backwards upon the main
body of the Austrian army. The Prussians now endeavoured
to carry the wood above the villages of Sadowa and Dohilnitz,
a very important strategical point, but the Austrian batteries
played upon them with murderous effect. The whole battle
line of the Prussians could gain no more ground, and was
obliged to fight hard to retain the position it had won. At
one time it seemed as if it would be lost, for guns had been
dismounted by the Austrian fire, and in the wooded ground
the needle-gun had no fair field, and the infantry fight was
very equal. Herwarth, too, seemed checked upon the right.
The smoke of his musketry and artillery, which had hitherto
been pushing forward steadily, stood still for a time.
Fransky's men, cut to pieces, could not be sent forward to
attack the Sadowa wood, for they would have exposed themselves to be taken in rear by the artillery on the right of the
Austrian line formed in front of Lipa. All the artillery was
engaged except eight batteries, and these had to be retained
in case of a reverse, for at one time the firing in the Sadowa
wood, and of the Prussian artillery on the slope, seemed
almost as if drawing back towards Bistritz. The First Army
was certainly checked in its advance, if not actually being
pushed back.

The chances of victory were now exactly even for both
armies, and the moment was critical. The Prussian Generals
were waiting uneasily for the Crown Prince, and the position
reminded the *Times* correspondent of the closing hours of
the battle of Waterloo, when the Duke of Wellington so
anxiously awaited the coming of Blücher. But at half-past
one in the afternoon the army of the Crown Prince emerged
into view, and at once engaged the Austrian right. The
Austrians failed to carry the village of Klum, and now found
themselves exposed to a cross fire. What followed is thus
described : 'Suddenly a spattering of musketry breaks out of
the trees and houses of Klum right down on the Austrian
gunners, and on the columns of infantry drawn up on the

slopes below. The gunners fall on all sides—their horses are disabled—the firing increases in intensity—the Prussians press on over the plateau : this is an awful catastrophe—two columns of Austrians are led against the village ; but they cannot stand the fire, and after three attempts to carry it retreat, leaving the hill-side covered with the fallen. It is a terrible moment. The Prussians see their advantage ; they here enter into the very centre of the position. In vain the staff-officers fly to the reserves, and hasten to call back some of the artillery from the front. The dark blue regiments multiply on all sides, and from their edges roll perpetually sparkling musketry. Their guns hurry up, and from the slope take both the Austrians on the extreme right and the reserves in flank. They spread away to the woods near the Prague road, and fire into the rear of the Austrian gunners.

'The lines of dark blue which came in sight from the right teemed from the vales below as if the earth yielded them. They filled the whole background of the awful picture, of which Klum was the centre. They pressed down on the left of the Prague road. In square, in column, deployed, or wheeling hither and thither—everywhere pouring in showers of deadly precision—penetrating the whole line of the Austrians—still they could not force their stubborn enemy to fly. On all sides they met brave but unfortunate men ready to die if they could do no more. At the side of the Prague road the fight went on with incredible vehemence. The Austrians had still an immense force of artillery ; and although its concentrated fire swept the ground before it, its effect was lost in some degree by reason of the rising ground above, and at last by its divergence to so many points to answer the enemy's cannon. Chesta and Visa were now burning, so that from right to left the flames of ten villages, and the flashes of guns and musketry, contended with the sun, that pierced the clouds for the honour of illuminating the seas of steel and the fields of carnage. It was three o'clock. The efforts of the Austrians to occupy Klum and free their centre had failed ; their right was driven down in a helpless mass towards Königgrätz, quivering and palpitating as shot and shell tore through it. "*Alles ist verloren !* " Artillery still thundered with a force and violence which might have led a stranger to such scenes to think no enemy could withstand it. The Austrian cavalry still hung like white thunder-clouds on the flanks, and threatened the front of the Prussians, keeping them in square and solid columns. But already the trains were steaming away from Königgrätz, placing the Elbe and Adler between them and the enemy.'

Thus was won for Prussia the great battle of Sadowa, or Königgrätz, which was to have an important effect in aggrandizing one great State engaged at the expense of the other, and to make King William the paramount German Sovereign. Many interesting anecdotes are related of the bearing of the King of Prussia and his Generals during the deadly conflict. Writing to his wife after the battle, Bismarck said: 'On the 3rd the King exposed himself to danger all day, and it was very fortunate that I was with him, for all the cautionings of others were of no effect. No one would have ventured to speak as I permitted myself to do the last time, and with success, too, when a whole mass of ten troopers and fifteen horses of the 6th Regiment of Cuirassiers lay wallowing in their blood close to us, and the shells whirred in unpleasant proximity to the King. The worst, fortunately, did not go off. Still, I would rather it be so than that he should err on the side of caution. He was very enthusiastic about his troops, and rightly so, and did not appear to notice the shells that were whirring and bursting around him. He was just as quiet and comfortable as on the Kreuzberg (parade-ground at Berlin), and kept on finding battalions which he wanted to thank and say good-evening to, until we were once more under fire.'

A writer in the *Deutsche Revue* for October, 1884, recalled a very interesting and characteristic incident of Sadowa: ' At a critical point in the battle Bismarck met Moltke, and offered him a cigar. The strategist carefully selected the best weed in the Chancellor's case, and the latter took comfort, thinking to himself that if the General was still calm enough to make a choice of this kind, things could not be going so very bad with them after all.' Moltke, however, was just the man to be perfectly immovable and impassive when other men would be tremulous with excitement and shaking with fear.

Again, in the course of conversation on one occasion, Bismarck thus spoke of the demeanour of King William on this memorable day: 'The attention of the King was wholly fixed on the progress of the battle, and he paid not the slightest heed to the shells that were whizzing thickly around him. To my repeated request that his Majesty might not so carelessly expose himself to so murderous a fire, he only answered: "The Commander-in-Chief must be where he ought to be." Later on, at the village of Lipa, when the King in person had ordered the cavalry to advance, and the shells were again falling round him, I ventured to renew my request, saying, "If your Majesty will take no care of your own person, have pity at least on your (poor) Minister-President, from whom your faithful Prussian people will again demand their King; and in the name of that people I entreat you to leave this dangerous spot." Then the King gave me his hand, with a " Well, then, Bismarck, let us ride on a little." So saying, his Majesty wheeled his black mare, and put her into as easy a canter as if he had been riding down the Linden to the Thiergarten. But for all that I felt very uneasy about him; and so, edging up with my dark chestnut to Sadowa' (the name given to the King's mare after the battle) 'I gave her a good (sly) kick from behind with the point of my boot; she made a bound forward, and the King looked round in astonishment. I think he saw what I had done, but he said nothing.'

After the victory of Skalitz, the King had despatched an *aide-de-camp* to the Crown Prince's head-quarters with the order *Pour le Mérite* for his Royal Highness, as a recognition of his important services. So rapid were the movements of the Prince's army, however, that the decoration could not reach its destination before the battle of Sadowa. On the evening of that day the King met his brave son near the village of Streselitz, and after clasping him fondly in his arms, the King took the collar of the order from his own neck and flung it round that of his son. Both were unable to speak from emotion, and the King thus wrote concerning the incident: 'At last I came upon Fritz, with his staff. What a moment, after all we had gone through, and upon the evening of such a day! I gave him the order *Pour le Mérite* with my own hands, so that the tears ran down his cheeks—for he had never received my telegram announcing the conferment. It was, therefore a complete surprise.'

The battle of Sadowa cost Prussia 10,000 men in killed

and wounded; but Austria lost 40,000 men, including 18,000 prisoners, 11 standards, and 174 guns. When he saw how the day had gone, General Benedek exclaimed, 'I have lost all except, alas! my life.'

As a result of this sanguinary engagement, General von Gablenz was sent from the Austrian lines to the Prussian head-quarters to propose an armistice. But the enemy decisively rejected this proposition, and the whole of the Prussian forces proceeded to advance, the army of Prince Frederick Charles making for Brünn, the capital of Moravia. The Crown Prince moved on Olmütz, and General Herwarth, with the army of the Elbe, went westward in the direction of Iglau. The Emperor of Austria superseded General Benedek in his command, and appointed the Archduke Albert, who was then at the head of the Austrian army in Venetia, Commander-in-Chief of the Army of the North. This was a severe blow to Benedek, upon whom the hand of fate weighed heavily. He had been more unfortunate than culpable, and the officers under him had committed serious blunders in defiance of his express orders. The rank and file of the Austrians had fought splendidly.

Francis Joseph was in terrible straits, and saw that something must be done. His army in the north had been beaten by the Prussians, and could not recover itself, and his dominions were threatened with complete ruin. Add to this, that the second large portion of his armies was engaged in another critical struggle, that of endeavouring to hold Venetia against the Italians. It was at this juncture that the wily French monarch, Napoleon III., stepped in. He had done not a little, as we have seen, in the way of making overtures to both Prussia and Austria on previous occasions, and he now offered himself as arbitrator between them. Francis Joseph, in the hope of putting a stop to the Italian war, ceded Venetia to France, to be held in trust for Italy. This step would of course enable the Emperor of Austria to release his troops south of the Tyrol, and to despatch them against the Prussian forces which were marching onwards upon Vienna. Napoleon telegraphed to the King of Prussia, offering his mediation and proposing an armistice; and his offer being accepted, an armistice of five days was arranged, to begin from the 22nd of July.

But we must now go back a little, and glance at other

ramifications of this brief but brilliant campaign against Austria and her supporters. As soon as war was declared the Hanoverian army was placed on a stronger footing, and it began its march from Göttingen against the Prussian forces. On the 27th of June the Hanoverians were attacked at Merschelen, on the left bank of the Unstrut. They fought gallantly, and claimed the victory, as they repulsed the enemy, though they were too much exhausted to follow up their success. But on the following day they were surrounded by a vastly superior force, and, finding themselves cut off on all sides, were compelled to capitulate. On giving an undertaking not to serve against Prussia during the remainder of the campaign, they were treated with all the honours of war.

The Emperor of Austria, after the defeat of Sadowa, issued this manifesto to his 'faithful peoples' of the Kingdom of Hungary: 'The hand of Providence weighs heavily upon us. In the conflict into which I have been drawn, not voluntarily, but through the force of circumstances, every human calculation has been frustrated, save only the confidence I placed in the heroic bravery of my valiant army. The more grievous are the heavy losses by which the ranks of those brave men have been smitten; and my paternal heart feels the bitterness of that grief with all the families affected. To put an end to the unequal contest—to gain time and opportunity to fill up the voids occasioned by the campaign—and to concentrate my forces against the hostile troops occupying the northern portion of my Empire, I have consented, with great sacrifices, to negotiations for the conclusion of an armistice.

'I now turn confidently to the faithful peoples of my Kingdom of Hungary, and to that readiness to make sacrifices so repeatedly displayed in arduous times. The united exertions of my entire Empire must be set in motion, that the conclusion of the wished-for peace may be secured upon fair conditions. It is my profound belief that the warlike sons of Hungary, actuated by the feeling of hereditary fidelity, will voluntarily hasten under my banners, to the assistance of their kindred, and for the protection of their country, also immediately threatened by the events of war. Rally, therefore, in force to the defence of the invaded Empire! Be worthy sons of your valiant forefathers, whose heroic deeds gained never-fading wreaths of laurel for the glory of the Hungarian name.'

Three days later the Emperor issued another manifesto, in which, after referring to the heavy misfortune that had befallen the Army of the North, he announced that he had accepted Napoleon's offer of mediation. 'I am prepared to make peace upon honourable conditions, in order to put an end to the bloodshed and ravages of war. But I will never sanction a treaty of peace by which the fundamental conditions of Austria's position as a Great Power would be shaken. Sooner than that should be the case, I am resolved to carry on the war to the utmost extremity, and in this I am sure of my peoples' approval.'

The Diet of Frankfort had become practically extinct owing to recent events, and on the 16th of July the Prussians occupied the city (from which the Bund had departed), and heavily requisitioned the inhabitants. The First Prussian Army entered Brünn, the capital of Moravia, on the 12th of July. The Crown Prince, with the Second Army, marched southwards, and the Army of the Elbe, by the morning of the 14th, was only about fifty miles from Vienna. Notwithstanding the negotiations for an armistice, on the 22nd of July, owing to some misunderstanding, an engagement took place between the troops of Prince Frederick Charles and the Austrians, in which the latter were once more severely worsted. This was the battle of Blumenau. With the object of capturing Presburg, General Fransky requested permission from Prince Frederick Charles to attack Blumenau. This was granted, and Fransky, with three Prussian divisions, set to work. The Austrians were surrounded, and the fighting became desperate. The combat was still progressing furiously when an Austrian officer appeared with a flag of truce. Firing ceased on both sides, and the Austrians were then able to realize the deadly peril in which they were placed, for the Prussians had taken them in front and in rear. This was the last engagement of the campaign, and the armistice averted another scene of terrible slaughter. After a good deal of difficulty the corps under Benedek, and various other Austrian corps, reached positions of security on the Danube. The Emperor directed an immense entrenched camp to be constructed completely surrounding Vienna on the north side of the Danube, and the bulk of the army assembled at a short distance from the capital.

But these and other precautions in view of the prosecution of the war happily proved unnecessary. Peace preliminaries between Austria and Prussia were signed at Nikolsburg on the 26th of July. Bismarck once more re-constructed the map of Germany, and Europe was anxious to know what would become of Saxony under the new arrangement. As Mr. Lowe observes, Bismarck ' was finally moved from his firm resolve to annex the Kingdom of Saxony, whose stubborn and intriguing opposition (under its Prime Minister, Herr von Beust) to his reform schemes had been one of the main causes of the war. But on the subject of Saxony, which had bled so freely for him on the field of Königgrätz, Francis Joseph was, or pretended to be, quite inexorable; and his protestations were supported by the Emperor of the French, who had been personally implored by Beust to stand up for the King of Saxony in his hour of stress, as the King of Saxony, alone of all the German Princes, had stood by the Great Napoleon after his collapse at Leipzig—a prayer with which Napoleon the Little was all the more willing to comply, as, under the mask of magnanimity, he would thus be able to thwart the ambitions and disquieting schemes of successful Prussia. As a matter of fact, Saxony was less essential to the territorial perfection of Prussia than Hanover and Hesse; and Bismarck wisely deemed it not worth the while to provoke a renewal of the conflict for the sake of this kingdom, provided its accession to the new confederation of the North were secured. Rather, however, than yield on the latter point, he threatened to break off the peace negotiations; and thus a compromise was effected which saved the sovereign integrity of Saxony, but yet defeated her desire of throwing in her fate with the States of the South, under—in all probability—a French protectorate.'

The treaty was definitively signed at Prague on the 23rd of August. Apart from the question of Saxony, the territorial gains of Prussia under the treaty were very great. Before the war broke out, the Kingdom of Prussia consisted of the following nine provinces: Eastern Prussia, Western Prussia, The Grand Duchy of Posen or Polish Prussia, Silesia, Brandenburg, Pomerania, Saxon Prussia,

Westphalia, and Rhenish Prussia. The Treaty of Prague brought the following accessions to these territories: Hanover, Hesse-Cassel, Nassau, Hesse-Homburg, that part of Hesse-Darmstadt which lies to the north of the Maine, and the little principality of Hohenzollern, described as the cradle of the Prussian Royal House. The Duchies of Schleswig, Holstein, and Lauenburg had been previously annexed.

The last act in connection with the war was the exchange of prisoners between Austria and Prussia on the 27th of August. Some idea of the strength of the forces engaged in the conflict may be gathered from the extraordinary facts of this exchange. There were released on the Prussian side 523 Austrian officers, and 35,036 rank and file, while about 13,000 Austrian prisoners were still left behind in the Prussian hospitals. Austria only released 7 Prussian officers, and 450 non-commissioned officers and men; while about 120, severely wounded, remained behind in Austrian hands. The proportion of Austrians given up to Prussians was 83 to 1. Altogether, the loss of the Austrians, in killed, wounded, prisoners, and missing, was computed at about 90,000, and that of the Prussians at 21,989.

Well might the King of Prussia and Count Bismarck congratulate themselves upon the results of the Bohemian campaign. But there was still important work before them —not in the battle field, but in the Prussian Chambers. If the Prussian power was to be consolidated, it must be by the support of the people, and the strengthening of home interests. Much blood had been shed, and it was for the King and the nation to see that it had not been shed in vain.

CHAPTER VIII.

AN INTERREGNUM OF PEACE.

AMID feelings of deep thankfulness and rejoicing in Berlin, the new session of the Prussian Chambers was opened by the King, in person, on the 5th of August. His Majesty was now more popular than ever with the people at large, and also with a considerable proportion of the Deputies. 'The speech from the throne,' wrote an English

correspondent, who was present at the inaugural ceremony,
' did not disappoint the expectations raised by the promising
state of politics. The King, who entered with the Crown
Prince and other Princes of the House, received the pregnant
manuscript from the hands of his Premier, and read it aloud
with a firm and sonorous voice. His Majesty began by
thanking God for the victory accorded to his arms. He
hoped that the results of the campaign would redound to the
permanent benefit of the country, and pave the way for the
attainment of the national objects of Germany. Then
passing to domestic affairs, he briefly commented upon the
constitutional controversy that had been going on before the
war, and accounting for the irregular military expenditure,
by a reference to the necessities of the time, asked for a Bill
of Indemnity. His Majesty's words—sober and unpretending
as ever—were received with loud applause. As the royal
speech, so the attitude of the House: business-like, and
without the slightest tinge of an elation which might have
been pardonable in the first flush of a brilliant success.'

The passages in the King's speech relating to the Bill
of Indemnity and the constitutional questions at issue
between the Government and the Chambers, ran as follows:
' An agreement with the representatives of the country, as
to the settlement of the Budget, has not been able to be
effected in the last few years. The State outlay incurred
during this period is, therefore, destitute of that legal basis
which, as I again acknowledge, the Budget can alone receive
through the law. Article 99 of the Constitution ordains it
annually to be agreed upon by my Government and the
two Houses of the Diet. Although my Government has,
nevertheless, carried on the Budget for several years without
this legal basis, this has only been done after conscientious
examination, and in the conviction, in accordance with duty,
that the conduct of a settled administration, the fulfilment of
legal obligations towards public creditors and officials, the
maintenance of the army and of the State establishments,
were questions vital to the interests of the State, and that
the course adopted, therefore, became one of those inevitable
necessities which, in the interest of the country, a Government cannot and must not hesitate to adopt.

' I trust that recent events will in so far contribute to effect
the indispensable understanding, that an indemnity for

having carried on the administration without a law regulating the Budget—application for which will be made to the representatives—will readily be granted to my Government, and the hitherto existing conflict be therewith finally, and the more securely, brought to a conclusion; as it may be expected that the political position of the Fatherland will admit an extension of the frontiers of the State, and the establishment of a united Federal army under the leadership of Prussia, the costs of which will be borne in equal proportion by all members of the confederation.'

The whole tone and spirit of this address were in striking contrast to the messages which the irate monarch had been previously accustomed to send down to the Chambers by the hand of his iron-willed Minister. The King now spoke with every consideration for constitutional principles, and his speech from many points of view disarmed criticism. Moreover, it is not so easy for men to fight against success, and the victorious King and an exalted Prussia formed an imposing spectacle which even recalcitrant Deputies could not resist. The Royal speech, however, gave great umbrage to the French Emperor. It made no allusion to his mediation, nor any reference to Italy. There was a vague mention of the King's 'few but faithful allies,' and that was all.

A Bill was brought forward for the incorporation of Hanover, Electoral Hesse, Nassau, and Frankfort with the Prussian Dominions, and after a discussion as to the date of its operation it became law. Next, a Bill of Indemnity, to save the Government from the consequences of having acted in violation of the law by collecting taxes which had not been voted by the Chambers, was introduced. It passed the Lower Chamber by the large majority of 230 against 75 votes, and in the Upper House was accepted unanimously. In the Chamber of Deputies, Count Eulenberg, Minister of the Interior, stated that by the adoption of the Bill the Government would be morally compelled to act in a friendly spirit towards the House. The indemnity was not an armistice with the Government; its adoption would be the preliminary to a real and lasting peace. Count Bismarck no doubt laughed in his sleeve at these Ministerial assurances, for whenever occasion required it, as he or the Sovereign might think, the Government would have no scruple in again traversing the Constitution, Indemnity Bill or no Indemnity Bill notwithstanding. But for the time being he was delighted that the Legislative wheels moved so easily. All went exactly as he would have it to go.

Nor did Bismarck and the other directors of the war go without reward in the shape of substantial current coin of the realm. Bismarck was not only made a Major-General, but received a money gift amounting to £60,000, English sterling; General Roon, the War Minister, received £45,000, and Generals Moltke, Steinmetz, Vogel, Von Falckenstein, and Herwarth von Bittenfeld, £30,000 each.

On the day when the Treaty of Prague was signed—though as yet he was unaware of that diplomatic act—Thomas Carlyle wrote to a friend: 'That Germany is to stand on her feet henceforth, and not be dismembered on the highway; but face all manner of Napoleons, and hungry, sponging dogs, with clear steel in her hands and an honest purpose in her heart—this seems to me the best news we or Europe have heard for the last forty years or more. May the heavens prosper it! Many thanks also for Bismarck's photograph; he has a Royal enough physiognomy, and I more and more believe him to be a highly considerable man: perhaps the nearest approach to a Cromwell that is possible in these poor times.'

When King William received an address from a Committee of the Lower House, he felt impelled to say something respecting the kings whose territories he had absorbed. 'Since the war,' remarked his Majesty, 'I have been obliged to dispossess certain sovereigns, and annex their territories. I was born the son of a King, and taught to respect hereditary rights. If, in the present instance, I have nevertheless profited by the fortune of war to extend my territory at the cost of other sovereigns, you will appreciate the imperative necessity of the step. We cannot permit hostile armies to be raised in our rear, or in localities intervening between our provinces. To preclude the recurrence of such an event was a duty imposed upon me by the law of self-preservation. I have acted for the good of the country, and I beg you to convey my sentiments to the House.'

This was excellent special pleading in its way, and the King no doubt felt that some justification was necessary for the annexations. But Hanover was unquestionably harshly treated. She naturally did not like the idea of being completely gobbled up by Prussia, and in September, a deputation of Hanoverians had an interview with King William in Berlin. They presented an address, in which the King was earnestly entreated to preserve the independence of Hanover. It was urged that it was particularly hard upon a Prince whose dynasty had been connected with the country for nearly a thousand years, to dethrone him simply because he took a different view of the Federal law from Prussia, which view ultimately compelled him to take up arms in its defence. But his Majesty was inexorable. He had resolved on cutting the claws of the eagle of Hanover. After reviewing the circumstances of the war, he plainly told the deputation that there was no hope for them. 'We have frankly said to each other what we think, and I prefer that, because it holds out a hope of a better understanding in future. The most careful consideration, which has been painful because of my relationship to the House of Hanover, imposes annexation upon me as a duty. I owe it to my country, to compensate it for the immense sacrifice it has made, and therefore I am bound to render impossible in the future any recurrence of danger from the hostile attitude of Hanover.' It is astonishing what arbitrary actions become reconcilable to conscience under the name of duty.

Prussia scored heavily all round in connection with this war and its after results. How Bismarck outwitted Napoleon is thus dramatically told by his biographer, from whom we have recently quoted:—

'Bismarck had left Berlin on the 30th of June, and on the 4th of August he returned with the King after an absence of little more than a month, with the draft of the Treaty of Prague, embodying the results of the war already referred to, in his pocket. Sitting in his cabinet two days after his arrival home, pondering proudly on the undreamt-of issue of the campaign and the jubilant acclamations which had greeted his return, he is aroused from his reverie by a knock at the door, and enter the Genius of Compensation in the shape of bland Monsieur Benedetti with the draft of a treaty in his hand.

'"*Ah, bon jour, votre Excellence*, how can I serve you?"

'"Well, to be brief, by restoring to France her Rhine frontier of 1814."

' " What ?   Your Excellency must be mad ! '

' " No, indeed. ' My pulse, as yours, doth temperately keep time and makes as healthful music.' The dynasty of my master were in danger if public opinion in France is not appeased by some such concession from Germany."

' " Tell your Imperial master that a war (against us) in certain eventualities would be a war with revolutionary means, and that, amid revolutionary dangers, the German dynasty would be sure to fare much better than that of the Emperor Napoleon."

' " No prevarication—Mayence, or an immediate declaration of war."

' " Very well, then, let there be war," said Bismarck, who knew that the Southern States had already agreed to sign secret treaties, conferring the command of their several armies on the King of Prussia in the event of a national struggle.

' And this, then, was the consideration which had induced Bismarck to let off the States of the South on such easy terms. At Nikolsburg he had put off French claims of compensation until after the conclusion of peace with Austria, and now he had devised means of defying them altogether. Now it was that Monsieur Benedetti bitterly experienced how bootless it is to shut the stable-door after the steed is stolen. He and his master had been completely duped.'

We shall have more of M. Benedetti anon. For the present it is ours to note how the King of Prussia and his minister consolidated the kingdom, and put themselves into a state of preparedness. In the first place a bill was introduced into the Prussian Chambers and carried through, which provided for the annexation of the Duchies of Holstein and Schleswig, ' except a portion to be agreed upon hereafter by a contract with the Grand Duke of Oldenburg.' The Prussian Constitution was to come into force in the specified districts on the 1st of October, 1867.

Berlin was alive with loyalty and excitement on the 20th of September, 1866, when the Prussian army made its triumphal entry into the city. The gallant and soldierly King rode first on horseback, and was accompanied by Count Bismarck and Generals Moltke, Roon, Voigtsretz, and Blumenthal. The correspondent of an English newspaper thus described the scene immediately before the brilliant cavalcade passed down the Linden : ' For my part I own I could spare but little attention for the King himself. A few yards further on there stood a group of horsemen. One was General von Roon, the Minister of War, another was General Moltke, the soldier to whom more than any single person the conduct and conception of the campaign are due. On the extreme right, in the white uniform of a major-general of Landwehr Cuirassiers, a broad-shouldered, short-necked man sat mounted on a brown bay mare. Very still and silent the rider sits, waiting patiently until the interview between the King and the civic authorities is concluded. The skin of his face is parchment-coloured, with dull leaden-hued blotches about the cheeks; the eyes are bloodless; the veins about the forehead are swollen; the great heavy helmet presses upon the wrinkled brows; the man looks as if he had risen from a sick-bed which he ought never to have left. That is Count Bismarck-Schönhausen, Prime Minister of Prussia. Yesterday he was said to be well-nigh dying; ugly rumours floated about the town; his doctors declared that rest, absolute rest, was the only remedy upon which they could base their hopes of his recovery. But to-day it was important that the Premier should show himself. The iron will, which had never swerved before any obstacle, was not to be daunted by physical pain or to be swayed by medical remonstrances. And so, to the astonishment of all those who knew how critical his state of health had been but a few hours before, Count Bismarck put on his uniform and rode out to-day to take his place in the royal *cortège*. Even now the man, who has made a united Germany a possibility, and has raised Prussia from the position of a second-rate Power to the highest rank among Continental empires, is but scantly honoured in his own country; and the cheers with which he was greeted were tame compared with those which welcomed the generals who had been the instruments of the work his brain had planned. But to those, I think, who looked at all beyond the excitement of the day—the true hero of that brilliant gathering was neither King nor Princes of the blood royal—generals nor soldiers, but the sallow, livid-looking statesman, who was there in spite of racking pain and doctors' advice and the commonest caution, in order that his work might be completed to the end.'

By way of marking the day with a white stone, an amnesty was proclaimed for all persons who had been convicted of high treason or other offences against the Crown, resistance to the State authorities, violation of public order, offences committed by the press in infringement of the Press Law of 1851, and for infractions of the ordinance of the 11th of March, 1851, regulating the right of public meetings.

A Bill for determining the mode of election to the new German Parliament was passed by the Chamber of Deputies; and when, during the debate, Count Bismarck was taunted with having made very little use of the late Prussian victories, he replied that history would explain concurrent events, when it would be found that the Prussian Government had made even a daring use of the victories gained by the army. The new constitutional measure provided that every Prussian, who had completed his twenty-fifth year, should be an elector, and that there should be one deputy for each 100,000 souls of the population as ascertained by the last census. Each deputy was to be elected for a distinct electoral district, and the right of election was to be exercised by personally depositing an unsigned voting-paper in a box to be provided for the purpose. Manhood suffrage was thus practically established, with the protection of the ballot. The Upper House adopted the new electoral law without alteration.

An important Treaty of Confederation was now entered into between the Governments of Prussia, Saxe-Weimar, Oldenburg, Brunswick, Sachsen-Altenburg, Sachsen-Coburg-Gotha, Anhalt, Schwartzburg-Sondershausen, Schwartzburg-Rudolstadt, Waldeck, Reuss (of the younger line), Lippe, Schaumburg-Lippe, Lübeck, Bremen, and Hamburg. These States embraced a population of about 2,000,000. Adding to this the 19,000,000 which constituted the Prussian monarchy before the war, with the 4,500,000 belonging to the annexed territories of Hanover, Electoral Hesse, Nassau, Frankfort, and the districts taken from Grand Ducal Hesse and Bavaria, the whole gave a population of about 25,000,000 for the Northern Confederacy. Bismarck's scheme was realized by the treaty, for it was agreed that a Confederate Constitution should be adopted by a German Parliament, and that the troops of the Confederates were to be under the supreme command of the King of Prussia. It was further mutually agreed to maintain the independence and integrity of the contracting States, and to guarantee the defence of their territories.

But while things were thus going well outside, the Finance Minister had some difficulty with the Lower Chamber. He asked for sixty million thalers, urging that a good many things remained to be settled, that Prussia must defend what she had acquired, and that she must always be able to take up arms for this purpose. 'The financial question is the chief point, and if the right moment be allowed to pass, the accomplishment of Prussia's aims may be deferred for years, and her very existence again endangered. Money must be at the disposal of the Government. We must have our hands upon our swords and our purses well filled!' The Deputies, however, would only vote forty million thalers, or two-thirds of the sum asked for, and with this the Government had to be content.

Count Bismarck made a very important speech in the Lower House in December, during a debate on the question of the union of the Duchies of Schleswig and Holstein with Prussia, and the cession of the northern part of Schleswig to Denmark. What was to be the attitude of Prussia if, on an appeal to the inhabitants, as proposed by France, they determined by a *plébiscite* in favour of such a re-annexation? The Minister pointed out that war with France was not to the interest of Prussia, who had little to gain even by beating her. The Emperor Napoleon himself wisely recognized the fact, that peace and mutual confidence should prevail between the two neighbouring nations. But to maintain such relations with France, a strong and independent Prussia was alone competent. If this truth were not admitted by all subjects of Napoleon III., it was a consolation to know that his Cabinet at least thought differently, and Prussia had to deal with his Cabinet only. 'Looking upon this vast country of Germany from the French point of view,' said Bismarck, 'the Emperor's Cabinet cannot but, tell themselves that to combine it again with Austria into one political whole, and make it a realm of 75,000,000 inhabitants, would be contrary to French interests. Even if France could make the Rhine her boundary, she would be no match for so formidable a Power, were it ever established beside her. To France it is an advantage that Austria does not participate any longer in our common Germanic institutions, and that a State whose interests conflict with her own in Italy and in the East, cannot henceforth constitutionally

I

rely upon our armed assistance in war. It is natural for France to prefer a neighbour of less overwhelming might, a neighbour in fact whom 35,000,000 or 38,000,000 of French are quite strong enough to ward off from their boundary, line in defensive war. If France justly appreciates her own interests, she will as little allow the power of Prussia as that of Austria to be swept away.'

There was a good deal of frank common sense in this presentment of the international relations of three of the leading European Powers towards each other; and for a time Napoleon felt the weight of Bismarck's arguments. The question also of the cession of Northern Schleswig was allowed to sleep for the present.

The King of Prussia closed the Legislature on the 9th of February, 1867, and in doing so thanked the Deputies for having brought his hopes to a fulfilment. By granting the indemnity for the financial administration carried on for several years without a Budget Law, they had held out the hand to a settlement of the dispute upon a matter of principle which had for years obstructed the co-operation of the Government with the representatives of the country. His Majesty recapitulated the many home blessings which had been secured during the expiring session. 'Assisted by agreement with the representatives of the country, my Government has been able to call into existence important facilities and improvements in all departments of public life. The preparatory steps towards abolishing the salt monopoly and the increase of judicial costs, the settlement of the relations of trading and innkeeping companies, the removal of the limitation of the rate of interest, the postal and commercial treaties, the conversion of the Pomeranian fiefs, the abolition of the Rhine navigation dues, the increase of the salaries of lower-class officials and of schoolmasters, together with the grant of the supplies for the construction and completion of important railways, will be hailed by large circles as grateful fruits of the session just completed.' So with a pat on the back from the head-master for being such good boys, and getting through their lessons, the Deputies were let out of school, and departed for their homes.

An imposing ceremony shortly afterwards took place in the throne-room of the Royal palace at Berlin, for on the

24th of February the first North German Parliament was opened by King William. The three hundred or so deputies of which this constituent assembly was composed had been returned from the various allied States, by universal suffrage. 'The walls of the time-honoured apartment,' wrote an English correspondent, 'looked down upon a gathering such as had never before been witnessed there. There met men from the Prussian frontier, where the winter lasts seven months, with the more fortunate sons of the Rhine, whose climate has little experience of northern rigours. The Schleswiger, a genuine descendant of the Saxon, preferring to this day the homely idiom of his race to the literary language of the common Fatherland, shook hands with a Frank from Coburg, whose ancestors, under Charlemagne, combated and converted to Christianity the tribes of the German North. The Thuringian and Hessian from the central parts of the country, after long years of separation, associated again with the Pomeranian from the Baltic, and the Frisian, the Anglo-Saxon brother of the Englishman, from the North Sea. With the exception of two, the various branches of the German national family were all represented in the Hall; and, though the absence of the missing ones was noted, and commented upon with regret, the hope of soon comprehending the Bavarians and Suabians in the goodly company beat strongly in many a loyal heart. When everything was ready, Count Bismarck, in his white cavalry uniform, repaired to the Royal apartment to inform the King that the first Parliament of the North German Confederacy was awaiting the Royal presence. Then the Royal train came into view, more solemn, more numerous, and more richly attired than any that has ever graced a similar display in Prussia.'

The King was elated in spirits, and his face glowed with pleasure as with manly and truly regal bearing he moved towards the throne. He was not only the acknowledged head of a powerful confederacy, but the Sovereign of a kingdom which had now taken first rank in Europe. In his speech to the 'illustrious, noble, and honoured gentlemen of the North German Confederation,' he began as he always did, by expressing his firm reliance upon Divine Providence, which had led Prussia by paths she neither chose nor foresaw. But as the Emperor of Austria claimed to have been led by the same guiding Hand, and he had been hopelessly beaten, it was obvious that both could not be the chosen children of Providence at this juncture. Perhaps King William would have adopted the opinion of the Great Napoleon, that 'God is always on the side of the big battalions.' He is more frequently, however, with those who are temporarily defeated and dispirited. However, be that as it may, the King of Prussia could certainly point to the astonishing success of the Prussian arms.

But while something had been gained, more yet remained to be striven for by Germany. His Majesty, consequently, thus indicated in the Royal speech the work which was still left to be achieved: 'The point of supreme importance at present is not to neglect the favourable moment for laying the foundation of the building; its more perfect completion can then safely remain entrusted to the subsequent combined co-operation of the German Sovereigns and races. The regulation of the national relations of the North German Confederation towards our brothers south of the Maine has been left by the Peace Treaties of last year to the voluntary agreement of both parties. Our hands will be openly and readily extended to bring about this understanding, as soon as the North German Confederation has advanced far enough in the settlement of its constitution, to be empowered to conclude treaties. The preservation of the Zollverein, the common promotion of trade, and a combined guarantee for the security of German territory, will form fundamental conditions of the understanding which it may be foreseen will be desired by both parties.

'As the direction of the German mind generally is turned towards peace and its labours, the Confederate Association of the German States will mainly assume a defensive character. The German movement of recent years has borne no hostile tendency towards our neighbours, no striving after conquest, but has arisen solely from the necessity of affording the broad domains, from the Alps to the sea, the essential conditions of political progress, which the march of development in former centuries has impeded. The German races unite only for defence, not for attack; and that their brotherhood is also regarded in this light by neighbouring nations is proved by the friendly attitude of the mightiest European states, which see Germany, without apprehension and envy, take possession of those same advantages of a great political commonwealth which they themselves have already enjoyed for centuries.

'It therefore now only depends upon us, upon our unity and our patriotism, to secure to the whole of Germany the guarantees of a future in which, free from the danger of again falling into dissension and weakness, she will be able to further, by her own decision, her constitutional development and prosperity, and to fulfil her peace-loving mission in the Council of Nations. I trust in God that posterity, looking back upon our common labours, will not say that the experience of former unsuccessful attempts has been useless to the German people; but that, on the other hand, our children will thankfully regard this Parliament as the commencement of the unity, freedom, and power of the Germans.

'Gentlemen, all Germany, even beyond the limits of our Confederation, anxiously awaits the decisions that may be arrived at here. May the dream of centuries, the yearning and striving of the latest generations, be realized by our common labours! In the name of all the allied Governments—in the name of Germany, I confidently call upon you to help us to carry out rapidly and safely the great national task. And may the blessing of God, upon which everything depends, accompany and promote the patriotic work!'

The Federal Assembly consisted of ten sections or parties, with the following distribution of strength: Conservatives, 59; Free Conservatives, 40; Centre, 27; Federal Constitutionalists, 18; National Liberals, 79; Free Unionists, 18; Radical Left, or Progressists, 19; Poles, 13; Danes, 2; and 'Savages' or Independents, 25; total, 297, which included deputies from the provinces annexed by Prussia. The balance of power was thus held by the National Liberals, a party which had sprung into being with the battle of Königgrätz. It was led by two men of marked ability, of whom Germany was destined to hear considerably more as time went on—Herr von Bennigsen, a country squire from Hanover, and Dr. Edward Lasker, a Jewish lawyer from Posen. Lasker had sat amongst the Radicals in the Prussian Chamber, but the striking events of 1866 had convinced him and many others that the best and truest course in the interests of Prussia, was to support the national policy of Count Bismarck. With the aid of the National Liberals, the objects of the Confederation progressed most satisfactorily.

A Bill was brought in to determine the constitution of the North German Confederation. This gave rise to prolonged debates, in the course of which Bismarck delivered an important speech, begging the deputies not to allow the lessons of six hundred years to remain ignored. It would be well, he urged, to take to heart the teachings inculcated by the abortive attempts to secure unity made at Frankfort and Erfurt. The failure of those attempts plunged Germany into a state of uncertainty and dissatisfaction; which lasted no less than sixteen years, and had to be terminated —as was manifest from the first—by some such catastrophe as that experienced in 1866.

But on the threshold of the deliberations, the Polish members of the united Parliament entered their protest against the incorporation of the former Polish territory into the North German Confederation. They were followed by other deputies, favourable to Denmark, who likewise brought forward a protest against the inclusion of North Schleswig. In reply to the Polish representatives, Bismarck asserted that the majority of the Prusso-Polish population were satisfied with their condition, especially the peasants, who had valiantly fought as Prussian soldiers against Denmark and Austria. It was only the nobility and clergy of Prussia who carried on political agitation. Then taking a firmer tone, the Minister added that the restoration of Poland was not to be thought of. Touching the Danish protest he said, 'The Emperor of Austria alone has the right, by virtue of the Austro-Prussian treaty, to require that a vote should be taken in North Schleswig to determine the future position of the Northern districts of that duchy. It is a matter of small importance for the power of the Prussian monarchy whether a few Schleswigers who speak Danish belong to Prussia or Denmark. The boundary line between the two countries will be drawn in conformity with the interests of Prussia. We do not intend to have to conquer Düppel afresh. The portion of Schleswig which will be ceded to Denmark will, at all events, be smaller than people in Copenhagen imagine; and before this cession is made, an understanding is necessary with Austria with reference to certain financial questions relating to the Duchies. The completion of the North German Confederation cannot wait for the settlement of these questions.'

This speech was Bismarckian all over. There is little consideration or none for smaller powers like Denmark, and every consideration for the interests of Prussia. So, when the deputies were discussing questions of taxation, military supplies, &c., he cut the matter short by saying, 'Let us not differ on trifles, when greater things are at stake. We cannot now have everything we want, but something may be gained. Assist Germany to vault into the saddle, and trust her to ride alone.' Bismarck attained his object; the North German Parliament framed its constitution, and in closing the session on the 17th of April, the King of Prussia congratulated the members on the patriotic earnestness with which they had accomplished their task.

His Majesty opened an extraordinary session of the Prussian Chambers on the 29th of April. The Royal speech noted, that the newly-formed confederation at present only included the States of North Germany, but an intimate national community would always unite them with the South German States. The firm relations which the Prussian Government concluded for offensive and defensive purposes with those States in the previous autumn, would have to be transferred to the enlarged North German commonwealth by special treaties. The object of the special session was the ratification by the Prussian Legislature of the new North German Constitution, and this having been achieved, the sittings were brought to a close on the 24th of June.

A very grave international question arose this year, which spread disquietude throughout almost the whole of Europe. This was known as the Luxemburg question. France was terribly chagrined by the long course of aggrandisement which had marked the fortunes of Prussia, and Napoleon had for some time been looking for a means of enriching France, and thus strengthening his own position with the people. He at last believed he had found this set-off in proposals for the cession of the Duchy of Luxemburg, with its strong fortress, to France. The Emperor considered that it would be a great thing if he could secure this formidable barrier on his north-eastern frontier. Luxemburg belonged to the King of Holland as Grand Duke, and it formed part of the German Federation which was broken up by the Prusso-Austrian war of 1866. The territory was guaranteed to the King of Holland in April, 1839, by a treaty concluded between Great Britain, Austria, France, Prussia, Russia, and the King of Holland as Grand Duke. The city of Luxemburg, as part of the German Confederation, had been garrisoned for some time past by Prussian troops; and the view now taken by Louis Napoleon was that the fortress would no longer be a merely defensive position for Germany, but, garrisoned as it was by Prussians, it would occupy an offensive position towards France.

The subject gave rise to many debates both in the French and North German Chambers. Count Bismarck, being questioned in the North German Parliament towards the close of March, said that it was necessary for Germany to take into account the just susceptibilities of France. Admitting that Luxemburg was an independent State, which the King of Holland could dispose of as he liked, and admitting also that the inhabitants of the duchy experienced a strong repugnance to being incorporated with Germany, he insisted upon the influence which the desire of maintaining pacific and friendly relations with its powerful neighbour must exercise upon the duchy.

The Emperor of the French had been greatly surprised by the publication of the secret treaties of alliance concluded in the preceding year between Prussia and the Southern States, and he now felt it high time to make a counter-move. This move was the taking over of Luxemburg by arrangement with the King of Holland. At first Bismarck inclined to favour the scheme, but it was only a diplomatic ruse to lead the French on: and when the question was discussed in the German Parliament, it led to a great explosion of patriotic wrath. 'Let France pause and consider her course before she acts,' exclaimed Herr Bennigsen. 'Germany seeks no war; but if France will not allow us to become a united country, we are ready to give her the most indubitable proof that the time of our domestic division is past, and that her attempts will be henceforth resisted by the entire nation.'

In reply to an interpellation on the Luxemburg question, in the Prussian Chambers on the 1st of April, Bismarck briefly recounted the course of the diplomatic negotiations. The Prussian Government, he observed, did not adopt the opinion, that an arrangement had been entered into between Holland and France; but it could not, on the other hand, assert that the contrary was the case. When asked by the King of Holland what course Prussia would adopt, in case His Majesty should in any way cede his rights over the Duchy, King William had declared that he would leave the responsibility of such a step to the King of Holland. Prussia would simply assure herself of the views entertained by the Powers which signed with her the Treaty of 1839, and by her Federal allies, as well as of the state of public opinion as represented by the North German Parliament. An offer on the part of Holland of her good offices to further negotiations between France and Prussia had been declined.

France now felt called upon to give her version of the negotiations, and in the *Corps Législatif* on the 8th of April, the Minister for Foreign Affairs, the Marquis de Moustier, announced that he had received orders from his Imperial master to acquaint the Chamber with the actual position of the Luxemburg difficulty. The explanation was briefly to the effect, that the French Government had always considered the matter from three points of view, namely, as connected with the free consent of Holland, the loyal examination of the Treaties by the great Powers, and the consultation of the wishes of the inhabitants by means of universal suffrage. France was quite ready to examine the question in concert with the great Powers, and she therefore believed that peace could not be disturbed.

This was a backing down on the part of the French Government. It really meant that France was not prepared for war; and amidst much that was tortuous and sinister in the Emperor's policy at this juncture, it was certainly to his credit that he saw it would be suicidal on the part of France to force on an immediate war with Germany. Consequently, it was agreed to hold a Conference in London for the settlement of the Luxemburg question. The Conference met on the 7th of May, when there were present representatives of the following Powers—England, France, Austria, Prussia, Russia, Holland, Italy, and Belgium. A Treaty was concluded on the 11th, by which Prussia agreed to withdraw her garrison from Luxemburg, and to dismantle the fortress;

while the Powers guaranteed the complete neutrality of the Grand Duchy under the crown of Holland. On the other hand, in consideration of the political or territorial loss sustained by Germany as the result of the neutralization, it was agreed that Luxemburg should continue to be a member of the Zollverein; and five years later a further bond of connection between it and the Fatherland was established, when the German Government acquired by treaty the administration of all the railways in the Grand Duchy. The treaty in connection with Luxemburg had a beneficial effect in many ways. It relieved France from the dangers attending a strong fortress upon her borders, and it gave to her northern frontier the guarantee of another neutralized State; while it secured to the King Grand Duke complete independence, and gave fresh pledges for the strengthening of good relations and for the maintenance of the peace of Europe. Of course France had not secured the great prize she had been striving for, the cession of the Duchy; but, failing that, it was certainly something to effect its complete neutralization.

The King of Prussia visited Paris in June, arriving in that city on the 5th with Counts Bismarck and Moltke. The King's nephew, the Emperor of Russia, was already there, and on the day after they had exchanged friendly greetings, an attempt was made to assassinate the Czar in the Bois de Boulogne by a young Pole, named Berezowski. Fortunately the attempt failed. There was a good deal of jubilant feeling between the visitors and their Parisian hosts, for it was a great festival of peace, signalized by the opening of the International Exhibition of Paris, a scheme which owed its origin to the French Emperor. The only distinguished potentate whose feelings were damped on the occasion was the Czar, and he naturally felt angry and chagrined that in a time of rejoicing, and while the guest of a foreign Sovereign, he should have been made the mark for an assassin's bullet.

The North German Parliament was opened by the King of Prussia on the 10th of September. It was the first Parliament assembled on the basis of the Federal Constitution. Money, military, marine, and commercial bills of various kinds were promised in the Royal speech. In the subsequent sittings of the Confederation, the question arose as to the entrance of South Germany into the North German Bund. Count Bismarck stated that no pressure whatever would be exercised upon the Southern States. If South Germany should give it to be understood that it was her wish to be excluded from the Bund, no Federal Government, he observed, would be so wanting in self-respect as to oppose such a wish. But Parliament would not desire to force him to abandon a certain necessary reserve on the subject, as such a course would probably conduce to bring about objects entirely opposed to those which he had in view.

The Northern Schleswig question again came up. Prompted by France, the Danish Cabinet asked the Berlin Government whether, in accordance with the Treaty of Prague, a *plébiscite* would now be taken in North Schleswig to determine its cession to Denmark or otherwise. Bismarck, who was always ready with a reply, pointed out that, before discussing the subject, Denmark must give Prussia guarantees for the protection of the German element in the ceded population, and agree to take over a proportionate share of the public debt of the Duchies. Denmark did not quite see this, and declined to push the matter further, so that Napoleon was again foiled in his efforts to discover some cause or other for international embroilment.

A good deal of ill-feeling was created in the diplomatic circles of Berlin, by the meeting of the French and Austrian Emperors at Salzburg, in August; Napoleon gave it out that his object was simply to pay a visit of condolence to the Emperor Francis Joseph in consequence of the sadly tragic death of his brother Maximilian in Mexico; but Bismarck did not accept this as exhaustive of the reasons for the Imperial meeting. So he indited a circular to the diplomatic agents of Prussia abroad, the tone of which was severely commented upon by the French press, and denounced as menacing and unfriendly towards France. He stated that the Prussian Government rejoiced that the domestic affairs of Germany had not been the object of political conversation at Salzburg. It had always been the aim of Germany to direct the stream of national development so as to fertilize, and not to destroy. They had avoided everything calculated to precipitate the national movement; had endeavoured, not to irritate, but to calm and quiet. It was therefore to be hoped that their efforts in this direction would be successful, if foreign Powers were as careful to avoid all which might lead the Germans to apprehend plans of possible foreign interference, and which in consequence might arouse in them a sense of violated dignity and independence. Consequently, in the interest of the peaceful development of her own affairs, Germany received with the most lively satisfaction the disavowal of any intention to interfere with her internal policy.

These references to possible foreign interference gave great annoyance to France, but the time was not yet ripe for a French march upon the Rhine.

King William opened the Prussian Chambers on the 15th of November, and in the course of his speech he thus alluded to the aspect of foreign affairs: 'The relations of my Government with foreign Powers have not undergone any change in consequence of the new conditions in which Prussia is placed in the midst of the North German Confederation. With the friendly character of those relations —the personal interviews with the majority of the reigning sovereigns in Germany and abroad, the opportunity for which was offered me last summer, perfectly harmonize. The peaceful object of the German movement is recognized and appreciated by all the Powers of Europe; and the peaceful endeavours of the rulers are supported by the wishes of the peoples, to whom the increasing development and amalgamation of moral and material interests make peace a necessity. The recent anxiety respecting a disturbance of peace in one part of Europe, where two great nations, both most amicably connected with us, appeared to be threatened by a serious complication, I may now look upon as having disappeared.'

Soon after the opening of the Session, Dr. Lasker brought forward a bill, the object of which was to protect members of the Legislature from being prosecuted before the legal tribunals for the opinions they might express in the Chambers. As this was really a bill to secure liberty of speech, and as two deputies, Herr Franzel and Herr Twesten, had been prosecuted and convicted for speeches they had made in the Chamber, Bismarck did not like to oppose the measure out and out. He deprecated the length to which the prosecutions had been carried, but reminded the House that the accusations launched against the Cabinet for consecutive years had been so exceedingly offensive as to become unendurable to any but the low, mean, and cowardly. There was a marked difference between a spoken and a written insult; oral accusations were quickly wafted away, but when printed they were communicated to millions, 'and he could not hinder their being cast up against him by any obscure scribbler who chose to do so.' He therefore proposed that the Deputies should be declared free to say what they liked, but that the reports in the public papers should be subject to the operation of the ordinary press laws.

Ultimately, the first reading of the proposed bill was carried by a majority of twenty-one votes.

Two of the Sovereigns whom the King of Prussia had dispossessed now began to give some trouble. From the pecuniary point of view, King William had behaved very handsomely to them. By way of compensating the King of Hanover for the loss of his crown, sixteen million thalers were voted to him out of the confiscated revenues of his kingdom, and the Elector of Hesse and the Duke of Nassau received the capital sum of eight and nine million thalers respectively. The Chamber opposed the grant to King George, but Bismarck threatened to resign if the indemnity were not voted, and the Deputies gave way. Then the King of Hanover, in his retirement near Vienna, began a series of active intrigues against Prussia. These did not long remain unknown to Bismarck, who was tolerably well aware of what was going forward in every Court in Europe. Yet in spite of this, Bismarck still supported the large indemnity to King George, assigning subsequently the following grounds for doing so: 'We were actuated by three several motives; in the first place, we wished to spare the feelings of his former subjects, who apprehended that the last of an ancient dynasty might be exposed to pecuniary difficulties; secondly, we wished to oblige those friendly Courts, England especially, who had addressed us in favour of the late Sovereign, and whom we had no wish to offend in a matter wherein our interests were not at stake; thirdly, we had been assured by some of those Courts, that though King George could not be prevailed upon to sign a formal act of abdication, still the acceptance of our money would make him feel "bound in honour" to desist from active intrigues.'

It soon became manifest, however, that the hope of King George's quietude was delusive. Whenever he had an opportunity he acted against the King of Prussia, and when war appeared probable, in consequence of the Luxemburg difficulty, a Hanoverian legion was formed for the purpose of fighting with France against Prussia. 'It was well known that King George was maintaining a treasonable correspondence with leading men in his late dominions. Through his agents he had enlisted some subjects of the King of Prussia, and caused others to desert. He had established journals to wage incessant war against the new order of things; he continued to support his legion in France, which cost him 300,000 thalers a year; a numerously-signed petition to the Emperor Napoleon, entreating him to liberate Hanover from the Prussian yoke, had been taken to Paris by a confidant of King George; and on the occasion of his silver wedding at Hietzing, about a fortnight after the Prussian Chamber sanctioned the indemnity treaties, he indulged in most inflammatory language to a crowd of his previous subjects, who, at His Majesty's cost, had made a pilgrimage to see him, and drink to the restoration of his kingdom.'

Under the circumstances, there was nothing for it but to impound the dethroned monarch's indemnity, and this King William proceeded to do. The same course was adopted towards the Elector of Hesse, who had likewise appealed to the rulers of Europe to win him back his throne. But as the indemnities were only sequestrated, and not yet actually confiscated, there was still opportunity for the King and the Elector to make their peace with Prussia, had they been inclined so to do. The dispossessed Sovereigns, however, proceeded to subsidize a number of journals, which attacked Prussia with singular malevolence, and endeavoured to precipitate a war between France and Germany. It was in relation to these newspapers that Bismarck said: 'There is nothing of the spy in my whole nature, but I think we shall deserve your thanks if we devote ourselves to the pursuit of wicked reptiles into their very holes, in order to see what they are about.' The means by which these journals were supported thus came to be known as the 'reptile fund.' But although the Prussian Minister felt compelled to act against King George, he was considerate towards the people of Hanover; and he proposed to the Chambers to grant to Hanover the interest on a capital of twelve million thalers as a provincial fund for the administration and support of certain local institutions. This proposal was changed to an annual grant of half a million, and in that form was adopted.

The Prussian Diet was closed by the King on the 29th of January, 1868. In his speech from the throne, His Majesty expressed his satisfaction that important measures had been passed, mainly by the joint action of the Government and the representatives of the country. He thanked both Chambers of the Diet for the readiness they had displayed in voting additional grants for the maintenance of the dignity of the Crown. The King then alluded to the measures which had been adopted to alleviate the distress in the province of East Prussia, and for the establishment of a provincial fund for Hanover. He also commended the unanimity of views displayed by the Chambers and the Government respecting the compensation treaties concluded with the former rulers of Hanover and Nassau.

The Reichstag, or Parliament of North Germany, was opened on the 22nd of March. The King announced that the re-organization of the postal service was in an advanced stage, and that postal conventions had been concluded with the South German States, with Austria, Luxemburg, Norway, and the United States of America. A treaty had also been concluded with the United States to define the nationality of emigrants between the two countries, and thus to prevent causes of misunderstanding between countries so closely united by commercial interests and bonds of relationship. In domestic matters many reforms had been conceded, while others were in progress. All through this year the Prussian Government expressed an earnest desire for the preservation of peace in Europe. It was engaged with many matters of internal policy, to which the warlike spirit was directly and strongly opposed. On the 15th of September King William himself, in answer to an address from the rector of the University of Kiel on the peace question, expressed himself satisfactorily and unequivocally: 'As to the hope you express,' he said, 'for the preservation of peace, no one can share it more sincerely than I do; for it is a painful necessity for a Sovereign, who is responsible before the

Almighty, to give the word for war. And yet there are circumstances in which a Prince neither can nor should avoid such responsibility. You yourselves have witnessed here, with your own eyes, evidence of the fact, that the necessity of a war may force itself upon a Prince as well as upon a nation. If there exists between us a link of confidence and friendliness, it is to war that we owe it. However, I do not see in all Europe any circumstance menacing peace, and I say so confidently, in order to tranquillize you.'

A new session of the Prussian Diet began on the 4th of November, and the King, in his opening speech, referred both to the subjects that would engage the attention of the Diet, and the various questions which had been satisfactorily adjusted since the last sittings. Many important benefits had been secured to Germany. By the conclusion of a revised Rhine Navigation Act, a new international agreement had been obtained for the traffic upon one of the most important of rivers. Further, there was no apprehension of a return of the distress which had grievously afflicted a portion of the Prussian provinces during the past winter—a result due to the excellent precautionary measures taken, and to the favourable harvest in every province of the monarchy.

The relations of the Prussian Government with foreign Powers were in every direction friendly and satisfactory. The events in the Western Peninsula of Europe gave some little cause for anxiety, but there was every confidence that the Spanish nation would succeed in finding in the independent formation of her national position a guarantee of her future prosperity and power. Something had been done towards realizing one of the dreams of civilization and humanity by the International Congress of Geneva, which had succeeded in completing and extending to the navies of the maritime Powers the principles already adopted for the amelioration of the wounded in war. Altogether, the sentiments of the Sovereigns of Europe and the desire of the nations for peace, gave ground for the belief, that the advancing development of the general welfare would not only suffer no immediate material disturbance, but would also be freed from those obstructing and paralyzing effects which had only too often been created by groundless fears, and taken advantage of by the enemies of peace and public order.

A personal episode relating to Baron Beust, the Austrian Prime Minister, caused some excitement in the Prussian Diet in December. For some time back the Austrian statesman had jealously watched the conduct and policy of his great Prussian rival. A severe attack having been made by one of the Prussian deputies upon Baron Beust, Count Bismarck rose and said: 'It is absolutely impossible for me to defend a foreign Minister without dilating on the policy of the State he serves—a task I do not feel called upon to perform at this moment with regard to the Chancellor of the Austro-Hungarian monarchy. Still, I may observe that I am ignorant of the existence of personal hostility to myself or this Government in—if I may call him so—my Austrian colleague. In former years I was on a friendly footing with him, and have no reason to suppose that a change has occurred. I should, therefore, deem myself bound to vindicate his conduct against what has fallen from a preceding speaker, had I not reasons for wishing to steer clear of the quicksands of international policy in to-day's debate. As to Austria's Liberalism, it consists in an army of 800,000 men, demanded and voted for a period of ten years, and some municipal arrangements introduced in Prussia fifty years ago. Even these Count Beust has taken care to render innocuous by a vigorous supervision on the part of the administrative authorities.' After delivering himself of these sneers, Bismarck concluded with a comparison which evoked much laughter: '*Au reste*, there is this similarity between Liberal Governments and the reigning beauties of the season, that the last out generally carries the day.'

An important constitutional change was resolved upon in this sitting of the Diet. The Chamber of Deputies adopted a resolution, requesting the Government to take steps for causing the Prussian Ministry for Foreign Affairs to be amalgamated by the year 1870 with a concentrated Foreign Office for the North German Confederation. Count Bismarck, rising during the debate, said that confidential negotiations with the Federal allies had convinced him that he would be able to lay the necessary bill on the subject before the North German Parliament at its next meeting.

There can be no question that the attitude of Austria at this juncture, and subsequently, did much to preserve the peace of Europe. With all our admiration for Bismarck as a strong man, we greatly doubt whether he would have adopted and maintained the same magnanimous attitude, had similar opportunities been placed within the grasp of Prussia after she had been humbled by a neighbouring Power. While Austria had lost her position in Germany, she still retained her sympathies towards her former Federal allies, though she would not side with Prussia in the Luxemburg difficulty. On the other hand, she did not attempt to profit by a war between France and Prussia, and her Government took care to prevent the Emperor Napoleon and the French Cabinet from expecting the co-operation of Austria in a conflict with Prussia. Impartial and neutral, her attitude, as we have observed, must have greatly contributed towards the maintenance of peace. Yet Austria had a difficult *rôle* to play, for she desired neither to exercise pressure upon Prussia to induce her to sacrifice German national interests, nor to lay herself open to the suspicion of confirming Prussia in her resistance, with a view of bringing about a conflict. She steered well between the international Scylla and Charybdis.

The year 1869 opened with a continuance of these peace prospects. The North German Parliament assembled on the 4th of March, and the King, in his speech from the throne, congratulated the Deputies on the unclouded state of Europe. A bill relative to the electoral law was promised, framed in accordance with Article 20 of the Constitution of the Confederation. It was intended to secure a uniform system of electoral procedure throughout the entire Confederation, and also to define the legal *status* of the Federal officials. The Budget of 1870 showed that an increase of the revenue was necessary. In regard to the postal arrangements between the Confederation and Foreign States, conventions had been concluded with the Netherlands, Italy, Sweden, and the Danubian Principalities. The organization of the Federal consular system was approaching completion. A consular convention concluded with Italy would regulate the respective powers of the consuls of both nations, thus ensuring uniformity in the conduct of the consular administration and the diplomatic representation abroad of North Germany. His Majesty observed that the first duty of the diplomatic agents abroad would be to secure the maintenance of peace between all nations who, like Germany, knew how to value its benefits. The fulfilment of that duty would be facilitated by the friendly terms existing between the North German Confederation and all Foreign Powers, and which were proved afresh by the peaceful solution of the difficulty that but lately threatened to disturb peace in the East. The negotiations and the result of the Paris Conference had proved the sincere endeavours of the European Powers to regard the blessings of peace as a valuable and common benefit, to be guarded by all as common property. Germany, having seen the success of this action, and having proved that it possessed both the will and the power to respect the independence of foreign States and to defend its own, was justified in trusting in the continuance of peace—to disturb which neither Foreign Governments had the intention, nor the enemies of order the power.

The Deputies got through their work amicably, and when they were dismissed on the 22nd of June, the Royal speech congratulated them on the completion of the first German conflict, which was a memorial both of German activity and sagacity. The unanimous co-operation of the Federal Governments with the national representatives in the common labouring for Germany's welfare, would—reiterated the King—with God's help, strengthen, as heretofore, the general confidence with which Germany, in fortifying herself at home, reckoned upon the preservation of peace abroad.

But although on matters of public policy generally there was a good understanding between the Prussian Government and the Deputies, the financial question continued to be discussed with great animosity. The agitation continued after the closing of Parliament, and gained in strength upon the retirement of Count Bismarck for the summer on the ground of ill-health. In his absence, the administration was entrusted to Count Eulenberg and Von Müller, who were regarded as uncompromising reactionists.

The Prussian Chambers met again on the 6th of October, and the King, who opened the session in person, said that an unavoidable deficit in the finances rendered an augmentation of the taxes necessary. 'The restoration and preservation of order in financial affairs is absolutely essential for the successful development of all the State institutions, and this cannot be delayed. The sacrifices demanded must not be eluded; the longer they are postponed, the more oppressive they will be for the country. Convinced that you share these views, I rely confidently upon your not refusing your assent to the propositions of my Government.' The King then announced that reforms would be introduced and the income tax remodelled, in order to secure a more efficient working of the law. The Eastern provinces would be placed on a basis of self-government, and new laws would be submitted with respect to public education. The speech concluded with an allusion to the success of the King's efforts to preserve peace and to maintain friendly relations with foreign Powers.

But the propositions concerning the taxes met with much opposition. The Finance Minister, Von der Heydt, finding that he was in danger of defeat, resigned, and was succeeded by Herr Camphausen, whose appointment strengthened the National Liberal element in Count Bismarck's Ministry. On October 30, the new Finance Minister explained his programme to the Diet, which he said was one to 'restore order in the administration of the finances, while the resources of the country should be spared as much as possible.' His proposed plan of consolidation, arranged to furnish means for covering a portion of the deficit, and to improve the method of paying the public debt, was passed by a large majority of the Diet in December. At the same time the Lower House adopted a resolution to extend the jurisdiction of the Federation over the entire civil law.

It is interesting to note that the national debt of Prussia, at the end of 1869, amounted to 442,639.372 thalers, 184,471,491 of which were, however, railway debts. It was computed that the interest and sinking fund for the payment of the principal would, in 1870, require 28,648,600 thalers; but 10,223,511 thalers of this sum belonged to the railways, and would be covered by their profits. Of the total national debt 377,925,827 thalers belonged to the old provinces; viz., 211,225,925 thalers State debt bearing interest, 133,061,000 thalers railway debt bearing interest, 2,553,902 thalers provincial debt bearing interest, 12,835,000 thalers interest-bearing notes, and 18,250,000 thalers bank-notes bearing no interest. The debts of the provinces united to the kingdom, in 1866, were as follows: Hanover, 21,096,291 thalers

Hesse, 15,249,950 thalers; Nassau, 20,158,755 thalers; Hesse-Homburg, 99,429 thalers; Frankfort, 7,754,171 thalers; and Schleswig-Holstein, 354,948 thalers. A large portion of these debts, however, was for railways, and would be covered by their profits.

Towards the close of the year two incidents occurred which were of considerable interest in relation to Protestant Prussia and its monarch. King William, regarding himself as the guardian of Protestantism, issued the following decree touching a day of special prayer for the Church: 'The great movements which in our age are making themselves felt in the religious life both of nations and individuals, and are pressing forward to a decision; and the tasks they impose on the Protestant Church of our country—are apparent to all, and admonish us to entreat the support of Almighty God. It is therefore my will that a day be set apart in the Protestant Churches of my country for special prayer, that God may pour out His blessing on the present important deliberations as to the constitution of our Church, and to implore Him to protect the Protestant Church from all dangers that threaten it; and, to strengthen the ties which unite its members to each other and to the Church universal, I have appointed the 10th of November, the birthday of Dr. Martin Luther, for this purpose, and hereby commission the Minister and the highest ecclesiastical authorities of Prussia to make the necessary arrangements.'

Early in the ensuing December, in receiving a deputation from the Brandenburg Synod, His Majesty said: 'I am much obliged to you for your kind and cordial wishes, and shall be happy to see you finish your work in peace. It is very necessary, indeed, that something should be done to quiet the excitement lately prevailing in matters ecclesiastical. The enemies of the Church are numerous in these days. In this I am not alluding to the Roman Catholics, but to those who have ceased to believe. What is to become of us if we have no faith in the Saviour, the Son of God? If He is not the Son of God, His commands, as coming from a man only, must be subject to criticism. What is to become of us in such a case? I can only repeat, that I wish to see you finish in peace the work in which you are engaged.'

At this time Rationalism was spreading rapidly on the one hand, while on the other the Pope was issuing a bull against heretics, and formulating the Infallibility policy which was shortly to see the light.

During the interregnum of European peace which was now drawing to a close, Prussia had been perfecting her military organization, and we cannot do better than close this chapter by detailing her war strength, as it existed in 1869. The Prussian *Military Gazette* stated that a million of soldiers could, at any moment, be placed under arms by a single telegram from Berlin. The Prussian troops consisted of 325 battalions of infantry, 268 squadrons of cavalry, 11 regiments of artillery, with 1146 guns, and 12 battalions of engineers, making in all 410,000 soldiers. The Federal contingents were of the following strength: Saxony, 29 battalions, 24 squadrons, 96 batteries, and 6 guns; Brunswick, 3 battalions, 4 squadrons, and 6 guns; Mecklenburg-Strelitz, 1 battalion; and Hesse Darmstadt, 10 battalions, 8 squadrons, 24 guns, and one battalion of engineers —total 53,000 men. But this force of 463,000 only represented the standing army of North Germany. In case of emergency, Prussia could also command the services of the troops of Baden, Würtemberg, and Bavaria, and immediately order a levy of her reserve, consisting of 120 battalions of infantry, 76 squadrons of cavalry, 240 guns, and 12 battalions of engineers; or an army of 143,000 men. Then there was an additional force of 200,000 men at her disposal for the occupation of towns and garrisons. Finally, the above numbers did not include the officers' military train, military labourers, nor special corps of any kind.

With regard to her navy also, Prussia had made great strides, and, whereas not long before she had no fleet worth speaking of, the Prussian navy was now second to none in the Baltic Sea. Russia was jealous of the facility and the rapidity with which she turned out vessel after vessel, obviously intending to make good her pretensions to supremacy in the Baltic, where hitherto Russia had ridden alone. In 1868 the Prussian and Russian fleets cruised together, but when Count Bismarck proposed to do the same in 1869, Russia indignantly refused. The *Goloss* of St. Petersburg thus gave vent to the feelings animating the Russian official mind: 'After seizing Kiel and the Bay of Jahde, Prussia has constructed in that bay the naval port of Keppens, and thus at once become a naval power and a dangerous rival to us in the Baltic. When the canal between the Baltic and the North Sea, the construction of which is already seriously contemplated at Berlin, is completed, the naval power of Prussia, which formerly only existed in the dreams of Prussian patriots, will become an accomplished fact.' The *Goloss* accused Prussia of false dealings in her relations with Russia, and added : 'Our commercial legislation has been such that, if the Prussian Minister of Commerce had been asked for his advice, he could not have invented anything more advantageous for Prussian interests. The sliding scale of the customs tariffs which have been recently abolished, and the obstacles created by our bureaucracy, have drawn nearly all our northern maritime commerce into Prussian harbours. The Crimean War and the construction of the railway communication between our western provinces and Königsberg have made that port the head-quarters of our northern trade. Moreover, the mercantile marine of North Germany increases yearly, while merchant ships under the Russian flag are scarcely ever seen on foreign waters.'

But the real sting of this remarkable article in the *Goloss* came in its closing sentence : 'If France does not think proper to put a stop to Prussian impetuosity, that Power will in a few years absorb the whole of Germany, or, in other words, become the arbiter of Europe.' Russia did not want to fight Prussia, and yet she wished to see her crippled because of her own interests. So, with a Mephistophelian smile, she threw out hints which she knew would make France wince and goad her into action perhaps. The very ideas so frankly expressed in the *Goloss* article had been flitting through the mind of Napoleon for several years back. He knew how rapidly Prussia was pushing to the front, and that even now she might almost be called the mistress of Europe. How long was this to continue, while the war party in France chafed under the inactivity and irresolution of the Emperor? It was destined to continue until just such time, and no longer, as Napoleon could find some good or bad pretext for war, and then the war flame was to burst out over Europe.

CHAPTER IX.

BEFORE reciting the circumstances which led to one of the greatest wars of the century, several matters affecting Prussian history during the first half of the year 1870 demand attention. Count Bismarck, who was almost overwhelmed by his Herculean labours, became on the 1st of January Foreign Minister, no longer of Prussia solely, but of the whole of the North German Confederation. As, in addition to this office, he also held the onerous post of Chancellor, two subordinates were appointed to assist him in the Chancellorship—Herr von Thile, who transacted the minor details in the department of Foreign Affairs, and Herr von Delbrück, who assumed charge of those in the Home Department.

The Federal Parliament was opened by the King on the 12th of February. His Majesty announced that the Assembly would be called upon to extend and complete the institutions which had been agreed upon by the separate governments of the Confederation. In particular he adverted to the new penal code, that was to establish a uniform system of criminal procedure throughout North Germany, thereby greatly advancing the work of national unity.

The question of the speedy admission of the Grand Duchy of Baden into the North German Bund was brought forward this session by the National Liberal party. Count Bismarck, whose views in favour of centralization were well known, caused considerable astonishment by opposing this measure. The opinion gained currency, that he was anxious for the moment not to give ground of offence to France. He wanted the provocation to come from that quarter. So he told the Deputies that the adhesion of Baden was not yet desirable, and would tend to retard the natural progress of the South German States if precipitately carried out. The North German Confederation would reserve to itself the right of designating a more favourable moment for the reception of the Duchy as one of its members. But while he thus abstained from any territorial extension of the Bund, he used all diligence to make sure of the ground already gained. For example, a measure was passed to assimilate weights and measures throughout North Germany in connection with the intended assimilation of the coinage, and a copyright law was also passed. Further, a general penal code for North Germany was adopted before the close of the session.

When the King of Prussia closed the Diet, he thankfully acknowledged the readiness shown by both Houses to assist the Government in its aims by the sanction of the proposed law of consolidation, which, he felt assured, would offer increased facilities for a more rapid amortization of the public debt. The Government had succeeded in establishing an equilibrium between the revenue and expenditure in the Budget for 1870, without being compelled to resort to onerous taxation. But the King expressed his grief and surprise that the comprehensive administrative reforms which had been submitted to the Diet for consideration and approval in the earlier part of the session had not been brought to a satisfactory conclusion—the more so, as the wants of the country imperatively demanded those reforms, especially that of a change of the mortgage system.

Upon the conclusion of the session, King William, accompanied by Bismarck, left Berlin for Ems, on a visit to the Emperor of Russia.

Internal difficulties now sprang up in Germany. An organization known as the Democratic Workmen's party, nicknamed the 'Honest' party, suddenly acquired prominence. It had its head-quarters at Stuttgart and Leipsic, and its main object was to break up Europe, and more especially Prussia and the North German Confederation, into a number of small communistic republics. Its leaders were Bebel, a master-turner, and Liebknecht, a journalist. Then there was the Progressive Workmen's party, formerly led by Schultze Delitsch, who was not a socialist, but now by Hirsch and Dunker. Strikes were advocated, and the English trades-unions held up to admiration. A third party, and the most advanced of all, was that of the German Socialists, followers of Ferdinand Lassalle. This organization sought to secure for the labourer a share in the profits of all commercial and industrial undertakings; and in order to obtain this, the Socialists demanded State assistance, encouraged strikes, denounced all indirect taxation, and assailed the capitalists. After Lassalle's death the party split up into three sections, each of which was hostile to the others, and to the world at large. These various parties caused the bureaus at Berlin no little trouble and solicitude.

But internal difficulties were soon to be overshadowed by events which were to draw upon France and Prussia the eyes of the whole civilized world. The close of June saw Europe in the enjoyment of profound peace, but there were subtle influences at work that were destined shortly to change the calm into a storm; to cause the death of thousands of brave men; and to blight and lay waste some of the most fertile, industrious, and prosperous provinces on the face of the earth. Yet, so late as the 30th of June, the Prime Minister of France, M. Émile Ollivier, officially declared in the Corps Législatif that peace was more secure than ever. The false security which this assurance gave rise to was soon dispelled. Within two or three days the political horizon was menaced by a dark war-cloud, and in the course of a fortnight war was formally declared, with the sequence of one of the bloodiest conflicts witnessed in modern history.

The ostensible causes of this war were wholly inadequate, and upon France lay the blame of provocation. The pretexts or grounds upon which she acted may be briefly stated. The Provisional Government of Spain, after several unsuccessful attempts to induce a foreign prince to accept the Spanish crown, resolved on the 4th of July to propose to the Cortes Prince Leopold of Hohenzollern-Sigmaringen as King of Spain. This news created great excitement in France, and suggestions of Bismarckian intrigues were rife, with an alleged design on the part of the Prussian monarch to plant a subservient relative on the southern frontier of France. On the 6th of July, two of the ministers, the Prime Minister and the Duc de Gramont, declared in the Corps Législatif that the candidacy of a Prince of the House of Hohenzollern, agreed upon without the knowledge of the French Government, would be injurious to the honour and the influence of the French nation. The Spanish Minister of Foreign Affairs hastened to assure France that the Prince was the free choice of the Spanish Government, and had been elected without previous negotiation with, or the co-operation of, any other European Power. France was profoundly indignant, however, and this explanation did not suffice. She demanded the formal withdrawal of the candidate, affirming that his occupancy of the Spanish throne was prejudicial to French interests.

King William was at Ems, and M. Benedetti, the French Ambassador to the North German Confederation, personally requested His Majesty, on the 9th, to forbid Prince Leopold's acceptance of the Spanish crown. The King declined, stating he had no right to give orders to a Prince of Hohenzollern who was of age. The King added that, beyond giving his personal sanction as head of the Hohenzollern family, he had had no hand in the candidature. After this interview the Prussian Government issued a circular despatch to its representatives in Germany to the effect, that the Government of Prussia had no part whatever in the selection of Prince Leopold to the Spanish crown. The Prince himself, seeing the dangers which threatened Europe, of his own motion sent in his resignation on the 12th of July.

Sanguine spirits now hoped that the difficulty would be got over, but they had reckoned without the war party in France. With singular recklessness and culpability, the Duc de Gramont notified the Prussian Ambassador in Paris, Baron von Werther, that France was not satisfied, and that the King of Prussia himself must write to the Emperor Napoleon, excusing himself for having personally sanctioned Prince Leopold's candidature, take a definite part in its present withdrawal, and promise that under no circumstances should that candidature be renewed. Count Bismarck declined to lay these new and humiliating claims of France before the King. Accordingly, on the 13th of July, M. Benedetti forced himself into the presence of the King in a public walk at Ems, and renewed the propositions in an imperious manner. The King, with great indignation, refused to listen to the demands of the Ambassador, and turned upon his heel. The Ambassador was further notified by one of the adjutants of His Majesty that he would not grant another audience upon the matter.

Next day Baron von Werther was recalled from Paris, and M. Benedetti from Ems. A mad war excitement now seized upon both nations, though there were not wanting far-seeing men among the French Left who inveighed against the injustice as well as the danger and impolicy of a war with Germany. King William returned to Berlin on the 15th, and was greeted with frantic enthusiasm. Addresses now poured in from all parts of Germany, and when the Federal Council of the North German Confederation met at Berlin, it unanimously recognized the necessity of energetically repelling 'the arrogance of France.' Orders were issued for the mobilization not only of the army of the North German Confederation, but also of the armies of those South German States which, according to treaty, were to be under the supreme command of the King of Prussia in the event of war. The South German States at once promised their aid, greatly to the surprise of France. In the French Corps Législatif, M. Émile Ollivier—speaking in the name of the Government—demanded the arming of the Garde Mobile, with a grant of 500,000,000 francs for the land army, and 16,000,000 for the navy, all of which demands were at once granted. The Senate also passed the desired credit, and on Sunday, the 18th, went to St. Cloud to congratulate the Emperor on the decision arrived at. The Paris populace was strangely excited. On the Boulevards crowds assembled, singing the *Marseillaise* and ' *Mourir pour la Patrie*,' and shouting ' *Vive la Guerre!*' '*À Berlin!*' and ' *À bas la Prusse!*'

Never did a nation rush so headlong upon its fate. Napoleon has been almost wholly blamed for the war, but, as he said after the crowning disaster of Sedan, he had no power to arrest the belligerent feeling. It is true the fever had seized upon the entire population, but the feeling ought never to have reached this height of frenzy; and it would not have done so but for the Emperor's previous policy. Alarmed by the progress of Prussia, he had long sought an opportunity for humbling her, and in the fateful summer of 1870, he rashly jumped to the conclusion that his destiny pointed him to Berlin.

CHAPTER X.

THE GREAT WAR WITH FRANCE.

There was little hope that the thunderbolts of war might be averted, but the English Government resolved to make a final effort. Our ambassador at Berlin, Lord Loftus, tendered an offer of mediation, but it was declined by Count Bismarck so long as France should not declare her readiness to accept the intervention of England. There was only one brief period when the French Ministry paused. It was when they found that there was no likelihood of Austria striking in on her own account, and avenging herself for the disaster of Sadowa. But the hesitation lasted only for a moment. The French people were bent upon war, quite as much so, it must be confessed, as the Emperor Napoleon himself. But French officialism was disgracefully at fault. When Marshal Lebœuf, the War Minister, was questioned by the Duc de Gramont, he replied, 'Ready? ay, more than ready!' The event proved that he spoke with fatal ignorance of the real state of things. And when the mobilization of the French army was undertaken, it brought to light grave facts which had not previously been suspected. The Duc de Gramont subsequently said, 'I could easily have avoided the war in twenty ways.' The Prussian Government afterwards published Napoleon's correspondence, found at St. Cloud, and it showed that the imposing regiments of the army of the Rhine were actually destitute of the most necessary commissariat appliances. Invaluable days were frittered away, and nothing was ready. The Prussians carried through their mobilization with their accustomed accuracy and despatch and the Governments of Bavaria, Würtemberg, and Baden unanimously sent in their adhesion to the cause of the King of Prussia.

With regard to weapons, the French had for some time been trying to find a rival to the formidable needle-gun of the Prussians, and they believed they had discovered it in the *chassepôt,* which was said to have given proof of its capacity to carry bullets to further ranges and to be more manageable by the holder, than the weapon which had won the campaign against Austria. Then the French had another powerful engine of death, the *mitrailleuse.* It was a small moveable cannon revolver, which could discharge from its various mouths between three and four hundred bullets in the space of one minute. With these weapons the French deemed themselves secure.

The French army was disposed in a slightly curved line from Strasburg to the frontier of Luxemburg, thus extending over about 150 miles of country. There were seven corps, in addition to the Imperial Guard. Macmahon was at Strasburg with the 1st corps ; De Failly with the 5th, near Saargemund ; Frossard with the 7th, opposite Saarbrück ; then came General l'Amirault, with the 4th corps ; and last on the line Bazaine with the 3rd corps, stationed at Sierck, to the north of Thionville. The 7th corps, under General Douay, occupied Belfort, in the Upper Rhine Department ; the Imperial Guard was at Metz, under Bourbaki ; and Canrobert commanded the 6th corps, or the army of reserve, at Châlons.

The formal declaration of war presented by France to Count Bismarck, rested upon the following basis : 1. The insult offered at Ems to M. Benedetti, the French Minister, and its approval by the Prussian Government. 2. The refusal of the King of Prussia to compel the withdrawal of Prince Leopold's name as a candidate for the Spanish throne ; and 3. The fact that the King persisted in giving the Prince liberty to accept the throne. As the Prince of Hohenzollern's candidature was no longer before Europe, the French were virtually rushing upon a terrible war because of a fancied insult to M. Benedetti by the King of Prussia.

Before the first blow was struck, yet one more attempt was made at mediation, the Pope writing an identical letter to King William and the Emperor Napoleon. The King of Prussia thus replied : 'Most august Pontiff, I am not surprised, but profoundly moved, at the touching words traced by your hand. They cause the voice of God and of peace to be heard. How could my heart refuse to listen to so powerful an appeal ? God witnesses that neither I nor my people devised or provoked war. Obeying the sacred duties which God imposes on sovereigns and nations, we take up the sword to defend the independence and honour of our country, ready to lay it down the moment those treasures are secure. If your Holiness could offer me, from him who so unexpectedly declared war, assurances of sincerely pacific dispositions, and guarantees against a similar attempt upon the peace and tranquillity of Europe, it certainly will not be I who will refuse to receive them from your venerable hands, united as I am with you in bonds of Christian charity and sincere friendship.' As Napoleon did not give the assurances demanded, the Pope's mediatorial offer fell through.

The French blundered in the very outset of the campaign. It had been the Emperor's intention to mass 150,000 men at Metz, 100,000 at Strasburg, and 50,000 at the camp at

Châlons. Then to unite the two armies of Metz and Strasburg, and at the head of 250,000 men to cross the Rhine at Maxau, leaving on his right the fortress of Rastadt. Next, the 50,000 men at Châlons, under the command of Canrobert, were to proceed to Metz to protect the rear of the army and guard the north-east frontier. Meanwhile the fleet, cruising in the Baltic, would have held a portion of the Prussian force in check, to guard against invasion from the coast. But these plans ignominiously broke down. Only 100,000 men were ready for the army of Metz; 40,000 only for that of Strasburg; Canrobert's corps was divided, and neither cavalry nor artillery were ready. When the Emperor ordered the missing regiments to be pushed on, the reply came that Algeria, Paris, and Lyons could not be left without garrisons. The French fleet, which was the only thing ready, sailed for the Baltic; but, as fortune or fate would have it, its services were not required.

The Germans took the initiative in the field, and were somewhat surprised that they should have been called upon to do so, as they expected to have been anticipated by the French. The King of Prussia arrived at Mayence on the 31st of July, accompanied by Generals Von Moltke and Von Roon. His Majesty assumed the style of Commander-in-Chief, though the real head and moving spirit of the German hosts was that great strategical genius—Von Moltke. The Prussian forces were distributed in three armies; the command of the first army, forming the right wing of the entire force, was assigned to General von Steinmetz; that of the second, or centre army, to Prince Frederick Charles, 'the Red Prince,' the King's nephew; and that of the third division, consisting of the armies of the south, to the Crown Prince. The whole of the three armies amounted in number to about 450,000 men.

The first decisive movement began on the 2nd of August, when the French corps of General Frossard, numbering about 30,000 men, advanced from St. Avold against Saarbrück. In view of the Emperor and the Prince Imperial it shelled the open town, and the Prussian advanced post retired. The French occupied the heights, but not the town itself, and Napoleon telegraphed to the Empress: 'Louis has received the baptism of fire. He displayed an admirable *sang froid*, and was in no way excited. He has preserved a ball which dropped close to him. There were soldiers who wept when they saw him so calm.'

More serious business was soon to follow. After a German success at Wissemburg, in which General Abel Donay was killed, the great battle of Wörth was fought on the 6th of August. The Crown Prince was on his way towards the passes of the Vosges, when Marshal Macmahon intercepted his advance, taking up a strong position west of Wörth. He had not, however, got his forces together in full strength, and before he could do so he was attacked by the Crown Prince's superior divisions. For fifteen hours the ground was desperately contested; but although the French were reinforced by Failly's corps, they were ultimately defeated. Their loss in killed and wounded was estimated at 10,000, and amongst the dead were Generals Colson and Raoul. Two eagles, thirty cannons, six mitrailleuses, 360,000 francs, and 8000 prisoners fell into the hands of the Germans. The German loss was about 4000 in killed and wounded. Out of Macmahon's army corps of 40,000 men, only 5000 were at length able to retrace their steps, broken and dispirited, towards Châlons. On the same day as the battle of Wörth, a desperate fight occurred on the heights of Spicheren, near Saarbrück, between the advanced Guard of the 1st German Army, under General Göben, and the left wing of the French, under General Frossard. The French position was again strong, and the conflict went on for hours. General Steinmetz and Prince Frederick Charles came on the field towards the last, and the French were beaten back to Forbach, where they again made a gallant stand; but in vain. The Germans took 2500 prisoners, and a vast quantity of war material.

Disguise it how the French might, their army of invasion had been beaten at all points. Paris had been buoyed up by false telegrams, one report actually announcing a great victory, with the capture of 25,000 prisoners, including the Crown Prince himself. When the truth became known, the rage and disappointment of the people found vent in loud execrations; and these feelings were not allayed by the following telegram from the Emperor: 'Marshal Macmahon has lost a battle. General Frossard, on the Saar, has been compelled to fall back. The retreat is being effected in good order. *Tout peut se rétablir.*' But how was all to be put right?

The entire French army now fell back, and Macmahon, closely pursued by the Germans, retreated precipitately upon Nancy and Metz. Other corps followed his example, until the French occupied a new position along the line of the Moselle. Meanwhile, Paris was greatly moved. A proclamation issued by the Empress Eugénie, who had been appointed Regent, left no room to doubt that the French had suffered serious reverses. Paris was declared in a state of siege; the Chambers immediately assembled, and a new Cabinet was appointed, with Count Palikao as President. The Senate and the Corps Législatif agreed to an increase in the army, and a reorganization of the National Guard; it was resolved to push on the war vigorously, and the war credit was raised to 1,000,000,000 francs. Marshal Bazaine was appointed to the supreme conduct of the war, in place of Leboeuf; nothing was said of the Emperor, and the command of the forces of Paris was entrusted to General Trochu, who, singularly enough, three years before, had lifted up his voice alone against the ill-prepared condition of the French army, and whose warning was now rapidly being verified.

The German armies speedily effected a change of front to the right. The King of Prussia moved his head-quarters on the 11th of August, establishing himself across the frontier at St. Avold. On leaving Saarbrück he addressed the following proclamation in French to the French people: ‘We, William, King of Prussia, make known the following to the inhabitants of the French territories occupied by the German armies. The Emperor Napoleon having made, by land and by sea, an attack on the German nation, which desired and still desires to live in peace with the French people, I have assumed the command of the German armies to repel this aggression, and I have been led by military circumstances to cross the frontiers of France. I am waging war against soldiers, not against French citizens. The latter consequently will continue to enjoy security for their persons and property so long as they themselves shall not by hostile attempts against the German troops deprive me of the right of according them my protection. By special arrangements which will be duly made known to the public, the Generals commanding the different corps will determine the measures to be taken towards the communes or individuals that

L

may place themselves in opposition to the usages of war. They will, in like manner, regulate all that concerns the requisitions which may be deemed necessary for the wants of the troops, and they will fix the rate of exchange between French and German currencies, in order to facilitate the individual transactions between the troops and the inhabitants.'

The French now continued to retreat, and it was the object of Napoleon to fall back across the Meuse in the neighbourhood of Verdun, and to form at Châlons a junction with Macmahon and the new corps, thus being able to oppose the further advance of the Germans by an army of more than 300,000 men. The German generals regarded it as a matter of supreme importance to prevent the concentration of the French at Châlons, and to that end to cut off the retreat of Bazaine. Accordingly, on the 14th of August, the German vanguard, belonging to the army of Steinmetz, came up with the three corps of Decaen, Frossard, and L'Amirault, near Courcelles, and a sharp contest ensued. Both sides fought well and equally claimed the victory, but in the end the Germans were the gainers; for the French retired into Metz and the Prussians remained on the field of battle. Next day the army of the Moselle, under the command of Bazaine, left Metz, accompanied by the Emperor and the Prince Imperial, in order to retreat by way of Verdun to Châlons. On the 16th, as their presence had become an obstruction to the army, Napoleon and his son left the troops, and started alone in a carriage upon the route to Châlons. They narrowly escaped being captured by the Prussians on the way, but at length reached their destination.

On the 16th King William's head-quarters were fixed at Pont à Mousson, between Metz and Nancy. It was now the object of the Prussians to cut off the retreat of the French army on Verdun and Châlons. Several sanguinary engagements ensued, but they all ended to the advantage of the Prussians. On the day above-named, Tuesday the 16th, a number of French divisions, with the Imperial Guard, were stopped on their march westwards near Mars-la-Tour by General Von Alvesleben with three Army Corps, subsequently reinforced by Prince Frederick Charles and another corps, and were driven back towards Metz after a battle lasting twelve hours. The French made another stand at Gravelotte on the 18th, but were again completely defeated. On this occasion the King of Prussia commanded his troops in person. These two battles were desperately contested. Gravelotte was the bloodiest battle of the whole campaign. The French had 112,000 men in action and reserve, with 540 guns; the Germans had 211,000 men with 822 guns. Against this vastly superior force of the Germans the French had the advantage of position, but it was not sufficient against such overwhelming odds. The Germans suffered even worse than the enemy, for their loss amounted to one-seventh of the effective strength, and that of the French to one-eighth. Bismarck complained that the jealousy of some of the Prussian leaders was the cause of his side losing many of their men. Between the 14th and 18th of August, the French lost in killed, wounded, and prisoners, 50,000 men. The German losses were likewise terribly severe. At Mars-la-Tour they amounted to 17,000; and at Gravelotte to a higher number still. Some regiments were completely decimated. The wife of a Prussian officer wrote, ' The first regiment of Dragoon Guards went first under fire, and were so slaughtered that only 120 men were left; the 2nd Dragoons were taken to make up the number of the 1st, and were in their turn cut down. The very flower of the Prussian nobility has perished. Our friends and familiar faces that we had met every year in society are all dead, and there is the saddest desolation.' This fearful havoc was caused by the French infantry, which had masked a line of mitrailleurs and concealed them from the advancing Prussians, opening out when charged, and thus leaving the foe exposed to the fire of the machines. Amongst the killed was Prince Salm-Salm, who was with the Emperor Maximilian in Mexico. The result of these fiercely contested engagements was that henceforth Bazaine's army was effectually sealed up in Metz; it had entirely lost communication both with Paris and Macmahon.

Late at night on the 18th of August, Bismarck penned this telegram to Queen Augusta, at the dictation of the King: ' The French army in a very strong position westward of Metz, attacked, completely beaten after a battle of nine hours, cut off from its communication with Paris, and hurled back on Metz.'

Dr. Busch gives the following graphic recital from Count

Bismarck's own lips of his experiences on that awful day: 'The whole day I had nothing to eat but the soldiers' bread and fat bacon. Now we found some eggs—five or six—the others must have theirs boiled; but I like them uncooked, so I got a couple of them, and broke them on the pommel of my sword, and was much refreshed. When it got light, I took the first warm food I had tasted for six-and-thirty hours; it was only pea-sausage soup, which General Goeben gave me, but it tasted quite excellent. . . . I had sent my horse to water, and stood in the dusk near a battery, which was firing. The French were silent, but when we thought their artillery was disabled, they were only concentrating their guns and mitrailleuses for a last great push. Suddenly they began quite a fearful fire, with shells and suchlike—an incessant cracking and rolling, whizzing and screaming in the air. We were separated from the King, who had been sent back by Roon. I stayed by the battery, and thought to myself, "if we have to retreat, put yourself on the first gun-carriage you can find." We now expected that the French infantry would support the attack, when they might have taken me prisoner, unless the artillery carried me away with them. But the attack failed, and at last the horses returned, and I set off back to the King. We had gone out of the rain into the gutter, for where we had ridden to, the shells were falling thick, whereas before they had passed over our heads. Next morning we saw the deep holes they had ploughed in the ground.

'The King had to go back farther, as I told him to do, after the officers had made representations to me. It was now night. The King said he was hungry, and what could he have to eat? There was plenty to drink—wine and bad rum from a sutler—but not a morsel to eat but dry bread. At last, in the village, we got a few cutlets, just enough for the King, but not for anyone else, so I had to find out something for myself. His Majesty wanted to sleep in the carriage, among dead horses and badly-wounded men. He afterwards found accommodation in a little public-house. The Chancellor had to look out somewhere else. The heir of one of the greatest German potentates (the young Hereditary Grand Duke of Mecklenburg) kept watch by our common carriage, that nothing should be stolen, and (General) Sheridan and I set off to find a sleeping place. We came to a house which was still burning, and that was too hot. I asked at another—"full of wounded soldiers." In a third, also full of the wounded. In a fourth, just the same, but I was not to be denied this time. I looked up and saw a window which was dark. "What have you got up there?" I asked.—"More wounded soldiers."—"That we shall see for ourselves." I went up and found three empty beds, with good and apparently fairly clean straw mattresses. Here we took up our night quarters, and I slept capitally.'

Once more the Germans showed their great superiority in all that concerns the strategical aspects of war. They even carried on the conflict with still greater vigour and aggressiveness than ever. Barrack huts were rapidly constructed round Metz, for which even doors and windows from the neighbouring villages were called into requisition as material. A telegraph was carried round the whole of the investing camp, and a railroad formed at a little distance from the works, to connect the lines of operations. All the officers were provided with maps of the country, on which the minutest details were carefully set down, even to the marking of trees, hedges, and watercourses. Meanwhile, since the battles of Wissembourg and Wörth, the Crown Prince had received large reinforcements, and he now detached his Baden contingent to besiege Strasbourg, while some of his Bavarian troops proceeded to besiege Phalsbourg and other fortresses of the Vosges. The Prince himself, with his main army, marched westwards across Lorraine, took the town of Nancy without resistance, and crossed the Moselle; then he turned northwards and had joined the direct road from Metz to Verdun, at the time the armies of Steinmetz and Frederick Charles were occupied in pushing Bazaine back into Metz. These two armies were now left to beleaguer Metz, under the command of the Red Prince, Steinmetz being removed from his leadership on the ground, as alleged, that he was too prodigal of life in conducting his military operations.

The campaign which followed may soon be narrated, the details being gathered from the accounts of the special correspondents published at the time. The Crown Prince marched towards Châlons, and King William, following his movements, had his head-quarters at Bar-le-Duc on the 24th of August. But the French camp at Châlons had broken up three days before, and Macmahon, with 180,000 men, had begun what proved to be his fatal movement through Rheims to the north-east. His object was to join hands with Bazaine, and thus bring the united armies down on the rear of the Crown Prince, cutting him off from his communications with Prince Frederick Charles and also with Germany, or else compelling him to retreat hastily, in fear of such a contingency. This Macmahon is said to have done in opposition to the Emperor's wish, but in compliance with the orders of the Paris Regency.

These movements exactly suited Von Moltke, and fell in with the great strategical ruse he had practised upon the French. He had purposely encouraged the idea that the bulk of the German army was marching straight on Paris, and that a comparatively insignificant force only was left with Prince Frederick Charles before Metz. But Frederick Charles's army was already so strongly entrenched round Metz, that it was able to spare the 4th and 12th North German Corps and Prussian Guard to take shape as a 4th Army, 80,000 strong, which was confided to the command of the Crown Prince of Saxony, and designated the Army of the Meuse. This army now marched westward, to block the passage of the French down the valley of the Meuse, and to join the forces of the Crown Prince. As soon as he learnt of Macmahon's north-easterly march, the Crown Prince also struck northwards to Grand Pré and Varennes. There was thus a race between the two armies, and the Germans again gained the advantage, owing to the bad organisation of their enemies. Macmahon lost several valuable days at Bethel as the result of commissariat difficulties. An important engagement took place at Beaumont on the 29th, when the French were surprised by two Prussian and a Bavarian corps, and driven into Mouzon; and at Carignan, on the following day, they were again defeated, the Prussians entering the place and taking 23 guns and 3000 prisoners.

Owing to masterly strategy, by the evening of the 31st the German armies had concentrated round Sedan. Macmahon was almost completely surrounded by an iron circle. Twelve hours' fighting had taken place, with the result that the French army, baffled and diminished, had been forced to take shelter under the walls. Macmahon was wounded, and surrendered the chief command to General Ducrot; but soon after General de Wimpffen arrived on the battle-field with an order from the Minister of War, appointing him commander-in-chief in case any accident should befall Marshal Macmahon. On September 1st, when the French were retreating on all sides, Wimpffen proposed to Napoleon, who in a fit of gloom and desperation had exposed himself recklessly in the thickest of the fight, to concentrate a large force in order to break through the enemy's lines at Carignan, and to save him from being made a prisoner; but the Emperor refused to sacrifice the troops to save himself. Wimpffen, who recoiled at the idea of capitulation, then asked to resign, but this also Napoleon would not permit. Soon after five o'clock a French colonel left Sedan with a white flag. Firing suddenly ceased, and the news of the proposed capitulation, with the presence of Napoleon in the surrendering army, flashed like lightning through the German ranks. Frantic shouts rent the air: 'Victory, victory! the Emperor is there!'

King William meanwhile had sent Lieut.-Colonel Bronsart to Sedan to demand an unconditional surrender. The Emperor, in return, sent his adjutant, General Reille, to the King with the following letter: 'My brother, since I have not been vouchsafed to meet death in the midst of my troops, I lay my sword at the feet of your Majesty.' The King said before opening the letter, 'But I demand as a first condition that the army lay down its arms;' then after a few minutes' conversation, he thus replied to the fallen sovereign: 'My brother, I accept your sword, and ask you to appoint some one with whom the negotiations concerning the capitulation of your army may be conducted.' Moltke as military and Bismarck as political commissioner, afterwards met Wimpffen at Donchery. Moltke demanded an unconditional surrender of the fortress and the whole army, but offered to liberate all generals and officers on their giving a written pledge not to take up arms again in the course of the war, nor to act in any other manner against the interests of Germany. Wimpffen declared that sooner than sign such a capitulation he would blow up himself and the fortress. To which the saturnine Moltke responded, 'Very well, then, if the capitulation be not signed by nine o'clock to-morrow morning the bombardment will begin anew.'

Early on the morning of September 2nd, the Emperor Napoleon left Sedan with the hope of getting more lenient conditions from King William; but Bismarck the astute waylaid him at Donchery and took him into a small house, where they discussed the capitulation. Moltke soon arrived, and was requested by Napoleon to present his wishes to the King. His Majesty, however, would only ratify the terms of capitulation as proposed by Moltke, and declined to see Napoleon until after the conclusion of the capitulation. Wimpffen was at last obliged to yield, and the capitulation was signed by him and Moltke.

The first act in the Franco-Prussian drama was thus played out. Never had so dramatic a day dawned upon either of the sovereigns who formed its most conspicuous figures. For one, there was a still greater height of glory than any he had yet attained; for the other, there was the loss of everything except life. The events which immediately culminated in the surrender of Sedan, as well as the particulars of the surrender itself, were very graphically described in a letter written by King William himself to Queen Augusta at Berlin. No other account gives a better description of the events than this, and as it is also deeply interesting from the personal point of view, we shall give it entire. The letter, dated Vendresse, South of Sedan, September 3rd, is as follows: 'You will have learned through my three telegrams the whole extent of the great historical event which has just taken place. It is like a dream, even when one has seen it unroll itself hour by hour; but when I consider that after one great successful war I could not expect anything more glorious during my reign, and that I now see this act follow, destined to be famous in the history of the world, I bow before God, who alone has chosen my army and allies to carry it into execution, and has chosen us as the instruments of His will. It is only in this sense that I can conceive this work, and in all humility praise God's guidance and grace. I will now give you a picture of the battle and its results in a compressed form. On the evening of the 31st and the morning of the 1st, the army had reached its appointed positions round Sedan. The Bavarians held the left wing, near Bazeilles, on the Meuse; next them the Saxons, towards Moncelle and Daigny; the Guards still marching towards Givonne, the 5th and 11th Corps towards St. Menges and Fleigneux. As the Meuse here makes a sharp bend, no corps had been posted from St. Menges to Donchery; but at the latter place there were Wurtemburgers, who covered the rear against sallies from Mézières. Count Stolberg's cavalry division was in the plain of Donchery as right wing; the rest of the Bavarians were in the front towards Sedan.

'Notwithstanding a thick fog, the battle began at Bazeilles early in the morning, and a sharp action developed itself by degrees, in which it was necessary to take house by house. It lasted nearly all day, and Schöler's Erfurt division (Reserve 4th Corps) was obliged to assist. It was at eight o'clock, when I reached the front before Sedan, that the great battle commenced. A hot artillery action now began at all points. It lasted for hours, and during it we gradually gained ground. As the above-named villages were taken, very deep and wooded ravines made the advance of the infantry more difficult, and favoured the defence. The villages of Illy and Floing were taken, and the fiery circle drew gradually closer round Sedan. It was a grand sight from our position on a commanding height behind the above-mentioned battery, when we looked to the front beyond Pont Torey. The violent resistance of the enemy began to slacken by degrees, which we could see by the broken battalions that were hurriedly retreating from the woods and villages. The cavalry endeavoured to attack several battalions of our 5th Corps, and the latter behaved admirably. The cavalry galloped through the interval between the battalions, and then returned the same way. This was repeated three times, so that the ground was covered with corpses and horses, all of which we could see very well from our position. I have not been able to learn the number of this brave regiment, as the retreat of the enemy was in many places a flight. The infantry, cavalry, and artillery rushed in a crowd into the town and its immediate environs, but no sign was given that the enemy contemplated extricating himself from his desperate situation by capitulation. No other course was left than to bombard the town with the heavy battery. In twenty minutes the town was burning in several places, which, with the numerous burning villages over the whole field, produced a terrible impression.

'I accordingly ordered the firing to cease, and sent Lieut.-Colonel von Bronsart, of the general staff, with a flag of truce, to demand the capitulation of the army and the fortress. He was met by a Bavarian officer, who reported to me that a French *parlementaire* had announced himself at the gate. Colonel von Bronsart was admitted, and on his asking for the Commander-in-Chief, he was unexpectedly introduced into the presence of the Emperor, who wished to give him a letter for myself. When the Emperor asked what his message was, and received the answer, " to demand the surrender of the army and fortress," he replied that on this subject he must apply to General de Wimpffen, who had undertaken the command in place of the wounded General Macmahon, and that he would now send his Adjutant-General, Reille, with the letter to myself.

'It was seven o'clock when Reille and Bronsart came to me, the latter a little in advance; and it was first through him that I learnt with certainty the presence of the Emperor. You may imagine the impression which this made upon all of us, but particularly on myself. Reille sprang from his horse, and gave me the letter of the Emperor, adding that he had no other orders. Before I opened the letter, I said to him, " But I demand, as the first condition, that the army lay down its arms." The letter begins thus—" *N'ayant pas pu mourir à la tête de mes troupes, je dépose mon épée à votre Majesté,*" leaving all the rest to me. My answer was that I deplored the manner of our meeting, and begged that a plenipotentiary might be sent, with whom we might conclude the capitulation. After I had given the letter to General Reille, I spoke a few words with him as an old acquaintance, and so this act ended. I gave Moltke powers to negotiate, and directed Bismarck to remain behind in case political questions should arise. I then rode to my carriage and drove here, greeted everywhere along the road with the loud hurrahs of the trains that were marching up and singing the National Hymn. It was deeply touching. Candles were lighted everywhere, so that we were driven through an improvised illumination. I arrived here at eleven o'clock, and drank with those about me to the prosperity of an army which had accomplished such feats.

'As on the morning of the 2nd I received no news from Moltke respecting negotiations for the capitulation, which were to take place in Donchery, I drove to the battle-field, according to agreement, at eight o'clock, and met Moltke, who was coming to obtain my consent to the proposed capitulation. He told me at the same time that the Emperor had left Sedan at five o'clock in the morning, and had come to Donchery, as he wished to speak with me. There was a château and park in the neighbourhood, and I chose that place for our meeting. At ten o'clock I reached the height before Sedan. Moltke and Bismarck appeared at twelve o'clock with the capitulation duly signed. At one o'clock I started again with Fritz (the Crown Prince), and, escorted by the cavalry and staff, I alighted before the château, where the Emperor came to meet me. The visit lasted a quarter of an hour. We were both much moved at seeing each other again under such circumstances. What my feelings were—I had seen Napoleon only three years before at the summit of his power—is more than I can describe. After this meeting, from half-past two to half-past seven o'clock, I rode past the whole army before Sedan. The reception given me by the troops, the meeting with the Guards, now decimated—all these are things which I cannot describe to-day. I was much touched by so many proofs of love and devotion. Now, farewell! A heart deeply moved at the conclusion of such a letter.—WILHELM.'

The devotional and religious element in King William's communication to his wife, which extended even to his telegrams, caused much comment, generally of a good-humoured, rallying kind, in the French and English journals. The following quatrain was an amusing parody upon his characteristic telegrams :—

> ' By will Divine, my dear Augusta,
> We've had another awful buster ;
> Ten thousand Frenchmen sent below—
> Praise God from whom all blessings flow.'

Yet there can be no doubt that the King was perfectly sincere in his expressions of gratitude to Almighty God. He holds strongly to the Lutheran faith ; and it has been his custom, even from his youth, to trace the hand of the Divine in all the great and varied incidents of his career.

The interview between the two sovereigns took place at the beautiful château of Bellevue, near Fresnoy, a few miles from Sedan. It is stated that the King and his Imperial captive retired into a conservatory leading from one of the saloons, and had a few minutes' earnest conversation, after which the Emperor spoke to the Crown Prince, and expressed his sense of King William's kind and courteous manner. Napoleon's great anxiety seemed to be not to be exhibited to his own soldiers. On leaving, his course was altered, so as to avoid Sedan; but, on the other hand, this exposed him to the painful humiliation of passing through the lines of the Prussian army. 'He was depressed,' wrote the King to Queen Augusta at Berlin, 'but dignified in his bearing, and resigned.' The Emperor had assigned to him as a residence the château of Wilhelmshöhe, near Cassel, a palace formerly belonging to the Electors of Hesse-Cassel. On the way thither he had an interview with Prince Pierre Bonaparte at Jemelle. A small crowd gathered at Liége to see the deposed Sovereign; but they maintained perfect silence. Napoleon himself was very calm, and smoked a cigarette.

By the capitulation of Sedan, about 83,000 men, inclusive of 4000 officers and over 50 generals, fell into the hands of the Germans. In the battles around Sedan, 25,000 men had been previously made prisoners, together with 25,000 more at the battle of Beaumont. There were also 44,000 wounded. The Germans captured, in addition, 70 mitrailleuses, 400 cannon, 10,000 horses, and an immense amount of ammunition. The French prisoners were interned in the several German States.

Rendered desperate by his position, Bazaine made a sortie from Metz at the very time the battle of Sedan was in progress. He endeavoured to break through the forces of Generals Mantenffel and Kummer, and was at first successful, expelling the Germans from several villages. But the arrival of the 9th German Army Corps and the 28th Brigade of Infantry enabled the Germans to re-establish themselves. They recaptured the lost positions, and drove the French back into the fortress.

The news of the surrender at Sedan caused intense excitement and agitation in Paris. Crowds of people assembled on the Boulevards shouting '*Vive la République!*' The Corps Législatif was hastily called together, and the Emperor was deposed. The National Guard and the Mobiles entered the

Palace of the Tuileries. The Empress was prevailed upon to make her escape by a back door of the palace to the house of an American dentist, Mr. Evans, by whom she was escorted to Trouville, and consigned to the charge of an English gentleman, Sir John Burgoyne, who was just about to sail for England in his yacht. The vengeance of the Paris mob wreaked itself upon everything bearing the Napoleonic name or being in any way connected with the fallen dynasty. The Imperial correspondence in the bureau at the Tuileries was seized, and subsequently published. It proved that official corruption had long lain at the base of the Imperial *régime*, and this system, becoming at length absolutely indispensable, had 'culminated in an utter negligence or betrayal of duty, truth, and honour by the very marshals and ministers whom Napoleon most trusted.'

The people clamoured for the continuance of the war. Gambetta and the Republican leaders assembled at the Hôtel de Ville, and constituted themselves a provisional Government. General Trochu was elected President and Commander-in-Chief of the Military forces, and the Government included Jules Favre, Minister of Foreign Affairs, Gambetta, Crémieux, Simon, Kératry, Arago, and others. The new Government decreed the dissolution of the Corps Législatif, and the suppression of the Senate. The Republic was proclaimed at Lyons, Bordeaux, Marseilles, and other provincial cities, and was everywhere enthusiastically welcomed.

Thus perished the Second Empire, which only a few months before had seemed stable and impregnable. With the supreme disaster at Sedan, Napoleon's sun set for ever. Nothing more dramatic has been seen in modern history, and even his bitterest foes felt pity and compassion for the fallen Emperor. A broken-hearted man, the rest of his life was doomed to be passed in physical suffering and mental anguish. The lesson taught by the career of the great Napoleon, of the mutability of human power and grandeur, had again been enforced by that of his relative, who, far from being Bonaparte's equal in genius, had aspired to something like his ambitious *rôle* of the arbiter of Europe.

— — — — — —

CHAPTER XI.

FROM SEDAN TO PARIS.

THOSE who regarded the war as the Emperor's war hoped it would conclude with the collapse of the Napoleonic dynasty, but the first manifesto of Jules Favre soon demonstrated that the French nation meant to reconquer its position if possible. On the other hand, in England and neutral States generally, there were many who thought that the Germans should have made overtures for peace, remaining content with an ample money indemnity for the sacrifices they had incurred in repelling the Imperial invader. But in reply to the French circular, Bismarck issued a counter manifesto to the foreign representatives of Germany, in which he stated that the demand for an armistice without any guarantees for the German conditions of peace could be founded only on the erroneous supposition that they were either indifferent to the interests of Germany, or assumed that she lacked military and political judgment. So long as France remained in possession of Strasburg and Metz, so long was its offensive power strategically stronger than Germany's defensive power, in all that concerned German territory on the left bank of the Rhine. Strasburg in the possession of France was always a gate wide open for attack on South Germany; whereas in the hands of Germany, Strasburg and Metz would obtain a defensive character.

Bismarck was never lacking in reasons when he desired to obtain possession of territory or fortresses. He wanted now Strasburg and Metz for Germany, and the French were determined he should not have them. We can hardly blame them for this, for although the onus of war in the outset rested upon the French, it was scarcely to be marvelled at from their point of view that they should resist spoliation and dismemberment.

Accordingly, both parties again took up the sword. France had still considerable numerical strength left. On the 13th of September General Trochu was able to review from 200,000 to 300,000 men of the National Guard and Mobiles. In addition there were in the provinces about 190,000 men. But undoubtedly the best and only compact army was that shut up in Metz with Bazaine. It was nearly

300,000 strong, and the French hoped every day to hear that it had succeeded in breaking through the Prussian lines. For some reason or other its leader had retired from the active command, which was now in the hands of Canrobert.

The Crown Prince's army set forward on its march to Paris, and on the 5th of September King William made his entry into Rheims. On the 14th his head-quarters were at Château Thierry, and on the 20th at Ferrières. After fighting several successful engagements, by the 19th the Germans had completely invested Paris. The besieging troops numbered from 200,000 to 230,000 men. Jules Favre desired an armistice in order to convoke a Constituent Assembly which could speak in the name of the people ; but as Bismarck demanded by way of preliminary the cession of Toul, Verdun, and Strasburg, and as the French Minister had said 'not an inch of our territory, not a stone of our fortresses,' the proposition fell through. M. Thiers now made a voluntary tour of visits to the Courts of London, St. Petersburg, Vienna, and Florence, in the hope of inducing the several governments to use their efforts to bring about at least a pause in the operations of the war ; but his diplomatic mission proved unsuccessful.

Paris was now cut off from the rest of the world, and the beautiful city was put in a state of preparation for the expected bombardment. Some courageous persons who wished to leave did so by means of balloons, which were also used as a method of communication with the provinces. Meanwhile many events were transpiring away from Paris, which caused deep regret and uneasiness in the French mind. Laon surrendered to the Germans on the 9th of September, Toul was taken on the 23rd, and on the 28th Strasburg capitulated, after being besieged for seven weeks. The rare and valuable old library of Strasburg was unfortunately destroyed. The districts of Lorraine and Alsace had now been entirely conquered, and were placed under the rule of German governors.

On the 1st of October nearly a sixth part of the French soil was held by the invaders, whose numbers reached 650,000. Troops which had recently been engaged in besieging Strasburg and Toul were now despatched to invest Belfort, Schlettstadt, Neu Brisach, and Soissons. The King of Prussia moved his head-quarters to Versailles on the 5th. As he drove with a military escort into the famed quarters of the Lewises, he was regarded with mingled feelings of anger and curiosity by the French. Some, as they gazed, described him as that 'old William,' and after acknowledging that he was a handsome man, added with the truly national shrug, 'Nevertheless, I should have been very well content not to see the good King of Prussia at Versailles.' Amongst all the Princes and Generals who followed in the train of His Majesty, none excited so much interest as Moltke and Bismarck, the two pillars of his fortunes. The bombardment of Paris, which had been expected for some time, did not begin, so that the magnificent city was saved from the ravages of shot and shell; the Germans had resolved to reduce it by famine instead of by fire. Outside the German lines there was a good deal of guerilla warfare, French peasants in some instances causing great provocation, which led to severe measures against the population on the part of the Germans. The reprisals, however, were in many instances cruel and indefensible.

The French Provisional Government was established at Tours; Gambetta, who was now the chief moving spirit of the people, left beleaguered Paris on the 7th of October by means of a balloon. This novel mode of conveyance narrowly escaped being riddled by the Prussian needle-guns, and subsequently it had a mishap near Amiens. The courageous amateur aëronaut, however, landed on *terra firma* with only a few bruises, and pushed on to Tours. His energy and activity infused into both Government and people new feelings of hopefulness. Gambetta became virtual Dictator of the nation, and his administration of the country and vigorous direction of the military operations excited universal admiration. Amongst others to whom he gave an important command was Garibaldi, but this appointment was far from pleasing to the Catholic party. In the second week of October, the French Army of the Loire was defeated by the 1st Bavarian corps under General Von der Tann. The Germans entered Orleans, and exacted from the Mayor a contribution of one million francs, which Bishop Dupanloup in vain endeavoured to get reduced.

A greater disaster still was in store for the French, and one which filled the War Minister, Gambetta, and his compatriots with grief and indignation. Bazaine began to feel that it was hopeless to think of holding Metz, when the provisioning of 173,000 men was no longer a possibility. This was his own explanation of his extraordinary conduct; but he was openly accused of Imperialist intrigues, and of a desire to re-enact the part of General Monk. The French commander first offered through General Boyer to surrender his army, but not the fortress; but this was peremptorily refused.

Several fruitless efforts were now made to diminish the number of mouths to be fed by sending bodies of inhabitants to the Prussian lines, from which they were inexorably driven back again, and ultimately, on the 27th of October, the 'virgin fortress' of Lorraine surrendered. By this capitulation, three Marshals of the Empire—Bazaine, Lebœuf, and Canrobert—more than 6000 officers, 173,000 subalterns and private soldiers, 3000 guns, 53 eagles, and forty millions of francs in treasure, fell into the grasp of the victors. A capture of such magnitude was probably unexampled in the annals of war. Up to this time it was estimated that the whole number of French prisoners taken by the German armies amounted to no less than four Marshals, 140 Generals, 10,000 other officers, and 323,000 rank and file. The news of the capitulation excited the utmost rage and consternation inside the fortress. Some of the inhabitants wept like children, and others marched through the city inciting the people to fight in their own defence and to die rather than surrender. Cries were heard of ' Oh, poor Metz! once the proudest of cities. What a misfortune! What an unheard-of catastrophe! We have been sold. All is lost! France is betrayed.' When Bazaine passed through Ars, on his way to Wilhelmshöhe, in a close carriage, and escorted by soldiers, he was greeted by women of the village with exclamations of ' traitor!' ' coward!' 'thief!' &c., ' Where are our husbands whom you have betrayed? Give us back our children whom you have sold!' . They even broke the windows of the carriage, and the Marshal would have been lynched but for the intervention of the Prussians.

By the terms of the capitulation all French officers were allowed to retain their swords, and all who pledged themselves not to take up arms against Germany during the remainder of the war were exempted from captivity. When the Imperial Guard, the *élite* of the French army, marched out of Metz, and laid down their arms at Frascaty, they were received by the Prussian troops with respectful dignity, and not a note of exultation was heard. As soon as the surrender became known, it was said that no General would betray an army of 173,000 men to an army of 200,000, if he did not want to be betrayed. The officers had spent their time in Metz in discreditable amusements and luxury, leaving the soldiers to starve and grow mutinous.

Thus, in less than four months, the second great French army, which was to have marched on Berlin, capitulated to the enemy. For his brilliant services in connection with the siege of Metz, Prince Frederick Charles was promoted by King William to the dignity of Field Marshal, and the same rank was conferred upon the Crown Prince for the very important victories he had won. This military dignity—the highest known in Prussia—had never before been conferred upon a Prince of the House of Prussia, and altogether, during the 230 years of the existence of the royal House of Brandenburg-Prussia, only upon sixty-two persons. General Moltke, who had just completed his seventieth year, received the title of Count. King William also issued this address to the united German forces under his command:—'Soldiers of the Confederate Armies! when we took the field three months ago I expressed my confidence that God would be with our just cause. This confidence has been realized. I recall to you, Wörth, Saarbrück, and the bloody battles before Metz, Sedan, Beaumont, and Strasburg; each engagement was a victory for us. You are worthy of glory; you have maintained all the virtues which especially distinguish soldiers. By the capitulation of Metz the last army of the enemy is destroyed. I take advantage of this moment to express my thanks to all of you, from the general to the soldier. Whatever the future may still bring to us, I look forward to it with calmness, because I know that with such soldiers victory cannot fail.'

Gambetta charged Bazaine with treason in surrendering Metz; but the latter indignantly denied the charge, and said that he had held out until he could hold out no longer, in consequence of sickness and hunger, and because so many of his soldiers had been placed *hors de combat.* In Paris the Belleville Revolutionists demonstrated against the Government, but a *plébiscite* being taken of Paris on the 2nd of November, the Government were triumphantly supported by 557,996 votes against 62,638 dissentients.

It was fortunate for the Germans that Metz had fallen, for the troops round Paris were beginning to cry out for reinforcements. As 200,000 soldiers were now liberated, however, it became necessary both to strengthen the army before Paris, and to attack the concentrating forces of the enemy in other directions. Accordingly, Prince Frederick Charles and the Duke of Mecklenburg moved upon the capital; General Manteuffel, with the newly-constituted First Army, pushed westward through the defiles of the Argonne into Picardy, and three corps marched to the south of Paris, to reinforce Von der Tann and his Bavarians. The first real German reverse of the war took place on the 9th and 10th of November, when General d'Aurelle de Paladines defeated Von der Tann, with the loss of 10,000 prisoners at Coulmiers, near Orleans. The French General did not know what to do with his victory, however, and he allowed the enemy to be strongly reinforced. Then on the 28th he vehemently attacked the left wing of Prince Frederick Charles at Beaune la Rolande, but was signally repulsed. The Germans, through the indecision of D'Aurelle, more than recovered their lost ground. On the 4th of December the Red Prince fell upon D'Aurelle's forces, and after severe fighting the Germans entered Orleans at midnight, the French being then in full retreat.

Gambetta threatened to bring D'Aurelle before a military tribunal. But the General had been only in command of a 'scratch' army, and he was determined not to capitulate to the Germans. He now resigned his command, and the War Minister appointed General Chanzy to succeed him with the western portion of the divided army, while General Bourbaki rallied the eastern portion at Bourges. The victory of Coulmiers had filled the capital with hope, and on the 29th of November the Second Army of Paris, under General Ducrot, began its offensive movements by a feigned sortie in the direction of L'Hay and Choisy le Roi. The real attack was opened on the following morning, when Ducrot advanced on the right bank of the Seine, near its juncture with the Marne. The French took the villages of Brie, Champigny, and Villiers, but after a terrible amount of desperate fighting they were driven from these, and Ducrot retired under the walls of Paris. Meanwhile Prince Frederick Charles pushed on in the direction of Tours, and the Duke of Mecklenburg encountered General Chanzy, who managed for the most part to hold his own. The Provisional Government, being now insecure at Tours, moved to Bordeaux.

Count Moltke having informed the Governor of Paris of the fall of Orleans, a special meeting of Ministers was called. Some were in favour of making overtures for peace, but General Trochu, by his eloquence and enthusiasm, influenced the council to decide unanimously on the continuance of the war. He affirmed that Paris could hold out until help came from the provinces, and that victories might follow reverses. It was hoped that General Faidherbe would soon be able to relieve the capital, but he was engaged near Amiens with General Manteuffel's army. A severe battle was fought at Pont de Noyelle on the 29th of December, and both sides claimed the victory; but, so far from being able to help the beleaguered Parisians, Faidherbe had his own hands full.

There was one other scene of operations, extending from the Vosges to the Jura, General Werder being in command of the Germans. A good deal of fighting took place, and a success achieved by Ricciotti Garibaldi at Châtillon made the invaders somewhat anxious as to their communications. General Garibaldi himself, with his army of volunteers, was at Autun, and, if he had no striking successes, he maintained his position. But in the course of November and December the Germans captured the following fortified places—Verdun, Neu Brisach, Thionville, La Fère, Phalsburg, and Montmédy. With these were taken 20,000 prisoners. The French, notwithstanding, were more resolute in defence of their soil than the enemy expected; and as the war must now be carried through at all costs, a new levy of German Landwehr, to the number of about 200,000 men, was demanded from Germany and despatched across the Rhine in the middle of December.

As Paris did not surrender, and a terrible frost had set in, the Germans at length resolved upon bombarding the city. Operations began on the 27th, when fire was opened from the powerful Krupp guns upon Mont Avron. The fort was soon silenced, and two days later the Germans occupied the position. The siege at once actively commenced, Lieutenant-General Von Kameke being appointed chief engineer by the German Commander-in-Chief. The besiegers were now in a favourable situation for the efficient bombardment of Forts Noisy, Rosny, and Nogent.

Such was the condition of things before Paris at the close of the year. We must now retrace our steps, and take up the historical thread of our narrative, as regards Germany, where we left it on the declaration of war. The King of Prussia issued a decree on the 19th of July, reviving the military order of the Iron Cross. It was to be bestowed without difference of rank or station, as a reward for merit gained either in actual conflict with the enemy, or at home in service connected with the defence of the honour and independence of the country. Another Royal decree related to the Voluntary Society for the care of the sick and wounded, together with the kindred brotherhoods of the knights of Malta and St. John. The French had their Central Committee in the Champs Elysées, and the English, though neutral in the war, rendered assistance to the sufferers in both armies out of the funds of the National Society for giving Aid to the Sick and Wounded in War. Queen Augusta and the Crown Princess assumed the head of the working institutions in Berlin, and superintended the preparation of material for the hospitals: and to commemorate the victory of Sedan, King William sent an order for the foundation of an invalid institution for the sick and wounded in war, to be called after his name. The 27th of July was observed as a general Fast Day throughout Prussia, to implore God's blessing on the German Army. The King thus characteristically expressed himself in a proclamation issued to his people: 'My conscience acquits me of having provoked this war, and I am certain of the righteousness of our cause in the sight of God. The struggle before us is serious, and it will demand heavy sacrifices from my people and from all Germany. But I go forth to it looking to the Omniscient God, and imploring His Almighty support. From my youth upwards I have learnt to believe that all depends upon the help of a gracious God. In Him is my trust, and I beg my people to rest in the same assurance.'

When the news of the fall of Sedan arrived in Berlin there was naturally a great popular demonstration. The statues of the national heroes on *Unter den Linden* were decorated with laurel leaves; the city was dressed in flags; and illuminations and fireworks closed the evening of the 3rd of September. Sunday, the 4th, was devoted to thanksgiving services, and on the 5th the Philharmonic Societies of Berlin serenaded the Queen with all the national songs in chorus. Luther's *Ein' feste Burg ist unser Gott*, the *Wacht am Rhein*, the *Deutsches Vaterland*, and 'God save the King,' were all sung with great spirit and energy. The victory had also another effect, for it hastened on the work of German unity which the French had hoped to destroy. King William received addresses from all parts recommending the immediate reunion of Northern and Southern Germany, as a measure which would make the nation free and strong, and enable it to bear with equanimity the ill-will of so many of its neighbours. Negotiations were now opened for the admission of Bavaria and Wurtemburg into the North German Bund, and many who were previously the bitter enemies of such a step now supported it.

But one incident to mar the unanimity of German feeling upon the war caused great excitement towards the close of September. Dr. Jacoby, and several other prominent leaders of the Democratic party in Prussia, were arrested for their violent opposition to the continuance of the war, and the annexation of Alsace and Lorraine. They thought that German ends should have been satisfied with the victory of Sedan and the fall of Napoleon, and gave vent to their opinions at a public meeting at Königsberg.

General Vogel von Falkenstein, military Governor of the Prussian provinces on the Baltic Sea, had the Democrats incarcerated in the fortress of Loetzeln; Dr. Jacoby protested against his arrest, and in a letter addressed to Count Bismarck demanded his release. The latter not only refused to interfere, but wrote a letter of approval to Von Falkenstein. The arrests created so much bad feeling, however, that the Government were compelled to abandon their high tone; and King William personally communicated to General von Falkenstein his desire for the removal of all obstacles for the holding of public meetings, and for the non-enforcement of all penalties attached thereto by the provisoes of martial law. His Majesty also ordered the immediate release of the prisoners already arrested for violating these laws.

Considerable difference of opinion undoubtedly existed in Germany as to the projected annexation of Alsace and Lorraine. The war party supported the annexation, alleging that the formidable military fortresses of Strasburg and Metz were necessary for the protection of the German frontier; others supported it because the inhabitants were German in race; a third party thought the cession of Strasburg alone ought to content Germany; while a fourth party objected to all annexation, as contrary to the wishes of the population concerned, and likely to lead to an enduring local hatred between nation and nation, besides being a source of embarrassment to Germany. Bismarck himself felt the difficulties attending the proposed annexation, and for a time he gave no indications as to the policy he should adopt. He had only as yet suggested part of the Prussian programme to the effect that France should cede Strasburg, Metz, and a strip of territory in connection with the latter citadel, so as to give it a communication with the German frontier. Moltke and the military authorities insisted upon this cession as being strategically necessary to the future safety of Germany against a sudden invasion like that of 1870. By way of making his position clear, Bismarck issued a circular on the 1st of October to the North German embassies and legations at Foreign Courts. Replying to Jules Favre's contention that Prussia would continue the war and reduce France to the condition of a second-rate Power, Bismarck said : ' The cession of Strasburg, Metz, and the adjacent territory, alluded to by me as part of our programme, involves the diminution of French territory by an area almost equal to that gained by Savoy and Nice; but the population of the territory we aspire to exceeds, it is true, that of Savoy and Nice by three quarters of a million. Now considering that France, according to the census of 1866, has 38,000,000 inhabitants, and with Algeria, which latterly supplies an essential portion of her army, even 42,000,000, it is clear that a loss of 750,000 will not affect the position of France in regard to other Powers; but, on the contrary, leaves this great empire in possession of the same abundant elements of power by which, in Oriental and Italian wars, it was capable of exercising so decisive an influence upon European destinies.'

There is no doubt that Bismarck rapidly educated the Germans to look for territorial acquisitions from France.

The internal reconstruction of Germany was meanwhile proceeding apace. Conventions were signed with Baden, whose military contingent became a direct portion of the Federal Army; with Hesse Darmstadt; and with Wurtemburg. Bavaria was allowed to retain her independent military administration; but the organization and formation of her army were to be in conformity with the rules governing the Federal Army.

The North German Parliament met on the 24th of November, and the King's speech (read in his absence) announced the new Constitution for a German Confederacy which had been agreed upon by the North German Confederation and the Grand Duchies of Baden and Hesse Darmstadt, and which had been unanimously adopted by the Federal Council. The agreements with Bavaria and Wurtemburg would also be brought forward for ratification. The Federal treaties were adopted, and on the 10th of December a bill determining the amendments of the Constitution necessitated by the introduction of the words ' Empire ' and ' Emperor ' was read three times and passed by 188 ayes to 6 noes. An address was also voted to the King. A war credit of 100 million thalers was carried by 178 to 8 votes; but during the debate Herr Liebknecht caused much excitement by declaring that the policy of the Government was in no way national, or the German Austrians would not have been shut out, and he asserted that the war was against Republicanism, as proved by Bismarck's undeniable negotiations with the ex-Empress of the French.

The King of Bavaria was the first potentate to suggest that the title of Emperor should be pressed upon King William. He wrote to the King of Saxony and the other German princes proposing that they should all urge on the King of Prussia to accept the reward of presidential rights in Germany together with the Imperial dignity. He also addressed King William himself on the subject, but the offer was in the outset declined.

However, a change was effected in the King's view, as was apparent from the reply made by His Majesty to the deputation which waited upon him at Versailles, on the 17th of December, from the North German Confederation. After thanking the deputation in his own name, and on behalf of the army and the country, the King said: 'The victorious German armies, among which you have sought me, have found in the self-sacrificing spirit of the country, in the loyal sympathy and ministering care of the people at home, and in its unanimity with the army, that encouragement which has supported them in the midst of battles and privations. The grant of the means for the continuation of the war which the Governments of the North German Confederation have asked for, in the session of the Diet that is just concluded, has given me a new proof that the nation is determined to exert all its energies to ensure that the great and painful sacrifices, which touch my heart as they do yours, shall not have been made in vain, and not to lay aside its arms until the German frontier shall have been secured against future attacks.

'The North German Diet, whose greetings and congratulations you bring me, has been called upon before its close to co-operate by its decision in the work of the unification of Germany; I feel grateful to it, for the readiness with which it has almost unanimously pronounced its assent to the treaties which will give an organic expression to the unity of the nation. The Diet, like the allied Governments, has assented to these treaties in the conviction that the common political life of the Germans will develop itself with the more beneficial results, inasmuch as the basis which has been obtained for it has been measured and offered by our South German allies of their own free choice, and in agreement with their own estimate of the national requirements. I hope that the representative assemblies of those States before which the treaties have still to be laid will follow the Government in the same path.

'The summons addressed to me by His Majesty the King of Bavaria for re-establishing the imperial dignity of the ancient German Empire has moved me deeply. You, gentlemen, request me in the name of the North German Diet, not to shrink from responding to this summons. I am glad to gather from your words the expression of the confidence and the wishes of the North German Diet; but you are aware that in this question, touching such high interests and grand recollections of the German nation, it is not my own feelings, nor even my own judgment, which can determine the decision.

'It is only in the unanimous voice of the German princes and free cities, and the corresponding wish of the German nation and its representatives, that I can recognize that call of Providence which I can obey, and trust in God's blessing. It will be a source of satisfaction to you, as well as to myself, to know that I have received intelligence from his Majesty the King of Bavaria that the assent of all the German princes and free cities is secured, and that the official ratification may be shortly expected.'

The new Constitution of Germany provided that the Emperor, as President of the German Bund, should have absolute power of declaring war when there might be danger of invasion, and of making peace under all circumstances. When there was no danger of invasion, the Emperor could only make war with the support of a majority in the Federal Council. Any proposed alteration in the Constitution could be vetoed if there were fourteen votes against it. The German armies in times of peace were to be under separate heads, the King of Bavaria having exclusive control over the Bavarian troops, but the Emperor over all others. The taxes of each State were still to be levied under their separate systems. The Diet, now to be called the German Parliament, was to be elected by a wide suffrage, the representation of every State being proportionate to its population. The Unionists regarded this Constitution as being very far short of the great national amalgamation which they desired; but it was ratified by the Legislatures of the separate German States.

A Russian Note, issued by Prince Gortschakoff in November, repudiated the treaty obligations of 1856, by which the Black Sea had been neutralized. It was at first thought that this pointed to a secret understanding with Prussia, but Mr. Odo Russell drew from Count Bismarck an assurance that he had no knowledge whatever of the document, and that he should be ready to accede to the proposal for a Conference. A second sensation was caused by a declaration on the part of Germany that the Federal Government no longer held itself bound to respect the neutrality of the Grand Duchy of Luxemburg in the execution of military operations. This was on the ground of the alleged violation of the duties of neutrality by the inhabitants of the Grand Duchy—a charge which was strenuously denied by the latter.

The people and the Luxemburg Chamber protested against the action of Germany, and a popular address to the Grand Duke, the King of Holland, was got up and signed by 43,773 persons in a few days. The Grand Duke was implored to save the country, and never to permit its destinies to be disposed of without a free vote of the population.

Another question which deeply affected Germany in 1870 was the promulgation of the doctrine of the Infallibility of the Pope. It was strongly opposed by Dr. Döllinger and others, who formed, in opposition to the decrees of the Œcumenical Council, a new party in the Church, called by the name of the Old Catholics. But while the Pope proclaimed himself infallible, the doctrine found him collaterally weaker from the terrestrial point of view, for his temporal sovereignty came to an end this year. King Victor Emmanuel entered Rome, and the Eternal City became the capital of Italy.

The year 1871 opened in gloom for the French, but with hopefulness on the part of the Germans that the war would soon be ended. On the first day of the new year there was enacted at Versailles, in the famous Hall of Mirrors, a scene which must have caused poignant anguish to every French heart. The victorious leader of the German hosts, King William of Prussia, gathered round him his companions in arms, who exchanged congratulations upon the downfall of French power and prestige. 'The apartments of the Royal palace,' wrote a correspondent, 'have been thrown open with something of royal pomp, and the Hohenzollerns have fairly taken possession of the quarters of the Bourbons. After a Lutheran service in the public chapel, with a splendid military band to assist, the King went over to the Gallerie des Glaces, where all the princes and officers were drawn up in a long line on one side, and where the King, after addressing to them a few words in a loud voice—words of thanks and of compliment on the great work of United Germany—wished them heartily a happy New Year.' The ceremonies of the day closed with a banquet, when the Duke of Baden, as the spokesman of the other German Princes, proposed the toast of ' King William the Victorious.'

But the work of the Germans outside Paris was not very easy. A force 220,000 strong had not only to invest a city with 500,000 fighting men and a vast circuit of forts, but to oppose the three armies of relief, which considerably outnumbered the detachments opposed to them in the north by Manteuffel, in the east by Werder, and in the west by the Duke of Mecklenburg and Von der Tann. Large draughts of men were being despatched from Germany, and the Germans themselves were now longing for the end of the war. Inside Paris, although good rations were given out, it was felt that a prolonged resistance was hopeless. The death rate was rapidly increasing, and now amounted to a total of 4000 per week. Even the favourite Trochu could no longer infuse courage into the inhabitants, and he was nonplussed what to do. On the 2nd of January Mézières capitulated with 2000 prisoners, but as a set-off against this the Garibaldians defeated a German column near Dijon. The battle of Bapaume was fought between the respective forces under Faidherbe and Manteuffel, but the result was indecisive. The French were checked, nevertheless, in their attempt to advance to the relief of Paris. From the 7th to the 10th engagements took place both in the east, where the French forces were under General Bourbaki, and in the south where they were commanded by General Chanzy, but the French suffered defeat in both instances. On the 12th General Chanzy was again defeated at Le Mans by Prince Frederick Charles and the Duke of Mecklenburg, and the Germans occupied Le Mans. Twice General Bourbaki attacked General Werder south of Belfort, but although the French fought with great obstinacy and gallantry they were repulsed. King William wrote to Von Werder as follows from Versailles: ‘Your heroic three days’ victorious defence of your position, in the rear of a besieged fortress, is one of the greatest feats of arms in all history. I express my royal thanks, my deepest acknowledgments, and bestow upon you the Grand Cross of the Red Eagle, with the sword, as a proof of this acknowledgment.—Your grateful King, Wilhelm.’

A sortie from Paris, on a larger scale than any hitherto attempted, was made on the 19th of January. General Trochu himself led this movement. No fewer than 100,000 men were engaged in it; but it was felt afterwards that had this army been divided into twenty corps of 5000 each, and had these corps been directed at the same moment against twenty points held by the Germans, a signal triumph might possibly have been secured. As it was, the immense masses only offered a mark for the German artillery. The French troops also were utterly wanting in steadiness and discipline. Thousands of men were butchered, and the French were driven back into Paris. The German loss in killed and wounded was estimated at 1300; that of the French at 6000 or more, besides prisoners. Trochu requested an armistice of forty-eight hours, but this was peremptorily refused by Moltke. On the same day as the sortie, General von Goeben drove back the advanced divisions of General Faidherbe's army from Beauvais to St. Quentin, so that the advance of the French relieving force was effectually checked on the north, south, and west. Longwy capitulated on the 25th, with 4000 prisoners and 200 guns.

The French were everywhere overmatched, and had troubles likewise of their own to contend with in Paris. The news of the various disasters to the French forces without Paris, and the failure of the sortie from the city itself, greatly exasperated the Red Republicans. There had been an *émeute* on the 22nd, and although the Government succeeded in quelling it, Generals Trochu and Le Flô had been compelled to resign as a sop to the public discontent. General Vinoy was appointed Governor of Paris, and General Clément Thomas Commandant of the National Guard. But the end was approaching; the week's death rate had risen to 4405; the rations of bread were reduced, and 8000 horses were sent to the shambles. An examination proved that the city was eight days nearer starvation than its rulers had calculated upon.

Capitulation had become a necessity, and on the 27th M. Jules Favre and General Beaufort went to Versailles to settle the terms with Count Bismarck. An armistice was arranged, and on the 29th of January the Emperor William telegraphed as follows to the Empress at Berlin :—

'Last night an armistice for three weeks was signed. The troops of the line and the Mobiles will be interned in Paris as prisoners of war. The Garde Nationale Sédentaire undertakes the preservation of order. We occupy all the forts. Paris remains invested. It will be allowed to procure provisions as soon as the arms have been delivered up. A Constituent Assembly will be summoned to meet at Bordeaux in a fortnight. The armies in the field retain possession of the respective tracts of country occupied by them, with neutral zones intervening. This is the first blessed reward of patriotism, heroism, and heavy sacrifices. I thank God for this fresh mercy. May peace soon follow!'

Jules Favre had many an earnest contention with Bismarck respecting the army, and at length the latter consented to allow 12,000 men under General Vinoy to retain their arms and serve as guardians of public order. The National Guard were also allowed to retain their arms, and act as a police force within the city. Paris was to pay a contribution of 200,000,000 francs within a fortnight. The forts were to be surrendered, and prisoners exchanged at once. The city was soon relieved with provisions, the Germans sending in large quantities, and the London Relief Committee also despatching consignments.

The news of the capitulation was received with great indignation at Bordeaux, and Gambetta, in an animated proclamation, declared that his policy was still the same, and that he was for war *à outrance.* The Paris Government condemned his action, however, and he resigned his post as War Minister after a sharp documentary conflict. New French elections were held, and the National Assembly was convened at Bordeaux.

With the surrender of Paris all active fighting ceased. On the 13th of February Garibaldi resigned his command of the Army of the Vosges, and on the same day Belfort surrendered with the honours of war, this being the last military operation of the great Franco-German War of 1870-71. Statistics recently compiled show that out of 33,101 officers and 1,113,254 rank and file of the German army who entered France, no fewer than 98,233 were killed or wounded. The French losses were considerably greater than those, and they were destined to be still further increased by internal dissensions and the sanguinary reign of the Commune.

CHAPTER XII.

KING WILLIAM BECOMES KAISER.

AFTER the consolidation of the North German States, followed by the great and glorious war with France, the King of Prussia could no longer contend against the unanimous feeling in favour of his assumption of the Imperial dignity. Accordingly, on the 18th of January, within the Hall of Mirrors in the palace of Versailles, he was proclaimed German Emperor in presence of all the princes associated with him, and surrounded by representatives of the different regiments. It was a grand and imposing spectacle, this coronation under the standards of the army before Paris. When the King entered the magnificent hall about noon, he walked with stately tread through the line of soldiers, himself as fine and upright a figure as any to be seen there.

Followed by his son, the Crown Prince, and the princes and generals of the Empire, he took up his place near the altar, and the group formed round him in a semicircle. The King wore a general's uniform, the Riband of the Black Eagle and a number of orders, and he carried his helmet in his hand. A chorale having been sung, the Court preacher, Dr. Rogge, read the Lord's Prayer and a Litany, to which the responses were sung by the band and by the princes and the congregation. The twenty-first Psalm followed, after which the reverend chaplain delivered a discourse founded on the words, ' Mene, Mene, Tekel, Upharsin,' and addressed to France. Then was sung a hymn, after which the Lord's Prayer was again read, and the religious service concluded with a German chorale.

Bismarck, without whose services there would have been no united Germany and no Emperor, then stood forward at the King's command, and read this proclamation : ' We, William, by God's grace King of Prussia, hereby announce that the German Princes and Free Towns having addressed to us a unanimous call to renew and undertake with the re-establishment of the German Empire the dignity of Emperor, which now for sixty years has been in abeyance, and the requisite provisions having been inserted in the Constitution of the German Confederation, we regard it as a duty we owe to the entire Fatherland to comply with this call of the united German Princes and Free Towns, and to accept the dignity of Emperor. Accordingly, we and our successors to the Crown of Prussia henceforth shall use the Imperial title in all the relations and affairs of the German Empire, and we hope to God that it may be vouchsafed to the German nation to lead the Fatherland on to a blessed future, under the auspices of its ancient splendour. We undertake the Imperial dignity conscious of the duty to protect with German loyalty the rights of the Empire and its members, to preserve peace, to maintain the independence of Germany, and to strengthen the power of the people. We accept it in the hope that it will be granted to the German people to enjoy in lasting peace the reward of the arduous and heroic struggles within boundaries which will give to the Fatherland that security against renewed French attacks which it has lacked for centuries. May God grant to us and to our successors to the Imperial Crown, that we may be the defenders of the German Empire at all times; not in martial conquests, but in works of peace in the sphere of national prosperity, freedom, and civilization.'

Officers and soldiers listened eagerly to the proclamation, given in the clearest tones by the Chancellor, and when the reading had ended, the Grand Duke of Baden advanced, and exclaimed in German in a loud voice, 'Long live the German Emperor William!' The whole of the distinguished assembly, numbering some six hundred souls, took up the cry as one man, and a military band stationed under the windows of the Salle struck up the Prussian National Anthem. Meanwhile, the reverberation of the French Artillery added another kind of impressiveness to the scene. The Emperor and the Crown Prince embraced each other thrice, and the German Princes paid homage to the former as the Kaiser. With this the ceremony concluded.

The Emperor William then received the deputations of officers from distant corps, and withdrew, accompanied by the Princes, Generals, and other illustrious personages. The deputations, with the rest of the guests, were entertained by the Emperor in the afternoon, previous to their leaving Versailles, at the Hôtel de France. An order of the day, addressed by his Majesty to the army, made mention that on this day, 'memorable for me and my house, I take, with the consent of the German Princes, and the adhesion of all the German people, in addition to my rank as King of Prussia, that of German Emperor. Your bravery and endurance, which I again recognize to the fullest extent, have hastened the work of the unification of Germany—a result which you have achieved by the expenditure of blood and lives. Let it always be remembered that the feeling of mutual friendship, bravery and obedience rendered the army great and victorious. Maintain this feeling; then will the Fatherland always regard you with pride as to-day, and you will always remain its strong arm.' The Upper House of the German Diet congratulated the King on his accession to the Imperial title. In his reply the Emperor said, 'May it be vouchsafed to me to lay for a united Germany the foundation stone of a glorious history, such as Prussia can show to-day after a period of seven hundred years.' The Emperor was anxious at all times to impress upon his subjects that this revival of the Empire was not merely a military revival; he wished it to be accompanied by signs of internal prosperity, and the progress of commerce and the industrial arts. But to the world at large the new Germany was an empire built up by the sword, and none knew better than its builders that the sword must ever be kept ready to be unsheathed if the empire was to be maintained with lasting strength.

There were great rejoicings in Berlin on the 27th of February over the acceptance of the peace preliminaries. These rejoicings were renewed on the 3rd of March, when the patriotic devotion of the Germans was made manifest, but with dignified moderation and a complete absence of electrical sentiment or enthusiasm. The crowd gathered in the streets of the Prussian capital was one of the most composed and orderly possible. There was no cheering, and no jokes of any kind were interchanged. 'Like regiments marching along in regular array, people moved from street to street, steadily, industriously, but without any outward sign of emotion. Only when the Crown Princess and the other Princesses drove along to inspect the charming sight was enthusiasm kindled, which vented itself in deep and continuous cheers.' While the French would have thronged the boulevards, the theatres, and the dancing gardens under similar circumstances, the Germans flocked to the churches, which were crowded with earnest worshippers.

The Treaty of Peace between France and Germany, concluded at Versailles on the 26th of February, was no doubt hard upon the former Power, though not so exacting as was at first feared. The negotiations were conducted in secret, and the plenipotentiaries on both sides were removed from all danger of outside pressure. The surrender of Metz was the great stumbling-block, and it was stoutly opposed by the French negotiators until they saw that continued resistance would imperil the cause of peace, and lead to the immediate resumption of hostilities. The only modification the Germans made in the original severity of their terms —though this was an important one—was the restitution of the fortress of Belfort, commanding the passes in the Vosges. This was conceded as an equivalent for permitting the German army to march through Paris. The principal conditions of the Treaty were the cession of Alsace and German Lorraine, and the payment of a war indemnity of five milliards of francs, being £200,000,000 in English money. It was considered that these demands were as great as Europe would allow, and that they were not unlikely to create a permanent feeling of hatred between the two countries— a foreboding which has unfortunately been realized. The boundary of the new frontier was described as commencing at the north-west portion of the Canton of Cattenom, towards the Grand Duchy of Luxemburg, tending southward to Rezonville, south-eastward to St. Marie, and again southward to the Swiss frontier by way of St. Maurice, Giromagny, and Delle. It was stipulated that the payment of one milliard of francs was to take place during 1871, and the remainder within three years from the ratification of the preliminaries. The third article provided for the gradual withdrawal of the German troops from France in proportion as the indemnity was paid or financial guarantees given. By a Convention subjoined to the Treaty it was provided that that part of the City of Paris in the interior of the enceinte comprehended between the Seine, the Rue de Faubourg St. Honoré, and the Avenue des Ternes, should be occupied by German troops, the number of which should not exceed 30,000 men. Access to that quarter was to be interdicted to the French troops, and to the armed National Guard, while the occupation lasted.

When the terms had been finally arranged, the Emperor William, ' with a deeply moved heart and with gratitude to God,' telegraphed at once the result to Berlin, while the French executive gave instructions to all the prefects, and recommended them to inform military commanders of the fact. M. Thiers, who had been appointed head of the executive power in France, brought forward the terms of the Treaty in the National Assembly at Bordeaux, but by the time he had read through the first article he was so

overpowered by his feelings, that he had to descend from the
tribune and leave the hall. The details of the Treaty were
then read by M. Barthélemy St. Hilaire. The terms of the
Treaty were ratified by 546 votes to 107, and a resolution was subsequently passed, amid loud cheers, deposing
Napoleon III. as the person ' responsible for all the misfortunes, the ruin, the invasion, and the dismemberment of
France.'

Great uneasiness prevailed respecting the projected entry
of the German troops into Paris. A cry of vengeance against
the Prussians arose in the Republican quarters, and it was
feared that serious disturbances would ensue. But a proclamation by M. Thiers, appealing to the patriotism and
self-restraint of the populace, and an order of the day by
General Vinoy to the army, exercised a tranquillizing effect.
It was resolved that the Bourse and the theatres should be
closed; that no newspapers should be issued; and that the
Germans should only find silence, emptiness, and mourning.
Every possible precaution was taken to avoid a conflict.

On the morning of the 1st of March, the German army, to
the number of 30,000, entered the French capital. The first
Uhlan appeared at the Arc de Triomphe about nine o'clock,
and he must have been surprised that he preserved a whole
skin. Then came the main body of the occupying troops,
the 6th and 11th Prussian corps, with about 11,000 Bavarians who had previously been reviewed by the Emperor at
Longchamps. The troops turned down the Avenue des
Champs Elysées, and proceeded in the direction of the Place
de la Concorde, their bands meanwhile playing the popular
Wacht am Rhein. The Duke of Coburg, General Blumenthal,
and their staffs rode at the head of the troops, followed by a
squadron of Bavarian Hussars, with bright pennons of blue
and white silk. Next came two batteries of Bavarian
artillery, and then rifles and infantry. The Leib regiment
attracted much attention. Its shattered companies were
only a quarter of their original strength, and the flag of the
regiment was hanging in ribbons from the stump of a broken
staff. The Arc de Triomphe was closed, so that the troops
could not march through. In passing by the closed arch, an
officer's horse slipped and fell, and a crowd pressed round the
dismounted rider. A comrade rode to his assistance amid
the hisses of the onlookers; one man was ridden over, and

two or three horsemen charged along the pavement. This scattered the mob, which from that moment looked on in profound silence. The Bavarians occupied an hour and a half in their march, and they were brought up by the Duke of Mecklenburg. Bismarck himself, calmly smoking a cigar, surveyed the scene for a short time, and then rode off to join the Emperor and the Crown Prince at Versailles.

The German soldiers began to leave Paris on the 3rd of March, and on that day the Emperor William telegraphed from Versailles to Berlin: 'I have just ratified the conclusion of peace, it having been accepted yesterday by the National Assembly in Bordeaux. Thus far is the great work complete, which by seven months' victorious battles has been achieved, thanks to the valour, devotion, and endurance of our incomparable army in all its parts, and the willing sacrifices of the whole Fatherland. The Lord of Hosts has everywhere visibly blessed our enterprises, and therefore by His mercy has permitted this honourable peace to be achieved. To Him be the honour; to the army and the Fatherland I render thanks from a heart deeply moved.' His Majesty's telegram was publicly read at Berlin amid salvoes of artillery and peals from the church bells. The city was illuminated, and an enthusiastic reception given to the Empress and Princesses.

The Prussian head-quarters at Versailles finally broke up on the 7th of March. The Emperor William remained for a few days at Baron Rothschild's château at Ferrières, but Count Bismarck returned straight to Germany. The Crown Prince reviewed the Northern Army at Rouen on the 12th, and then left for the Fatherland. The Crown Prince of Saxony was left in France at the head of the German army of occupation until a portion of the war indemnity had been paid. A grand public entry into Berlin was made on the 16th, when the Emperor, the Crown Prince, Prince Frederick Charles, and Count Moltke, with the whole of the head-quarters staff, proceeded from the railway station to the Palace amid enthusiastic acclamations.

The Emperor's seventy-fifth birthday was celebrated on the 22nd of March at Berlin with unusual splendour. A number of German Princes offered their congratulations in person, and the municipalities of Berlin, Breslau, and Charlottenburg presented addresses. At the close of his address the Burgomaster of Berlin said: 'The glorious sceptre of the Hohenstauffens is now transferred to the hand of the Hohenzollerns. We pray God to permit your Imperial and Royal Majesty long to enjoy the fruits of your exertions amid the love and reverence of the German people and the admiration of the world. May the German people be benefited for many years by the wisdom, firmness, and strength of him who has re-established the Empire! May the Emperor, who has extended our frontiers, and added fresh laurels to our banners, be destined alike to promote the blessings of peace, and to increase and develop our liberty, welfare, and culture. May God grant this!' After the Emperor had responded to the municipal addresses, the representatives of Austria, Spain, and Italy added their congratulations. The Emperor signalized the day by promotions amongst his most distinguished subjects. Bismarck was created a Prince; Moltke was made a Field Marshal and presented with the Order of the Iron Cross; Von Roon was raised to the rank of Count; and large dotations in land and money were subsequently accorded to these and other heroes of the war, as well as additional titles conferred upon the Princes of the Imperial House.

The first United German Parliament assembled on the 21st of March, and the session was one which caused an unusually severe strain upon Bismarck. The Ultramontane Deputies assumed a militant attitude and caused a great deal of trouble. The Emperor in his opening speech, after alluding to the accomplished work of German unity, proceeded to say: 'In former times, Germany, misled by the policy which its rulers adopted from foreign traditions, imbibed the seeds of decay through interference in the life of other nations. The new Empire takes its birth from the self-subsisting spirit of the people itself, which, never taking up arms except for defence, is steadfastly devoted to the works of peace. In its intercourse with foreign nations, Germany demands for her citizens no greater consideration than what justice and civilization involve, and uninfluenced by liking or disliking, leaves it to every nation to find its own way to unity, to every State to determine for itself the form of its constitution. We trust that the days of interference in the life of other nations will never, under any pretext or in any form, return.' This passage was a distinct intimation that Germany would not interfere on behalf of the Pope's temporal sovereignty. The Ultramontanes read it as such, and moved an amendment to the Address. Beaten upon this, they sought for other grounds on which to oppose the Government; but Bismarck proved too strong for them, though the prolonged conflict was harassing to the Chancellor.

The Bill for the Incorporation of Alsace and Lorraine was another question of a momentous and delicate character. Prince Bismarck knew that he must expect opposition, and by way of anticipating it, in a speech delivered on the 3rd of May, he made some important revelations. 'Ten months ago,' he observed, 'no one in Germany desired war, but all were determined, if it should be forced upon us, to carry it through, and to obtain guarantees against a recurrence of attacks by France. France, possessing Alsace, continually threatened Germany. On the 6th of August, 1866, the French Ambassador handed me an ultimatum demanding the cession of Mayence to France, and telling us, in the alternative, to expect an immediate declaration of war. It was only the illness of the Emperor Napoleon which then prevented its outbreak. During the late war neutral powers made mediatory proposals. In the first instance we were asked to content ourselves with the costs of the war, and the razing of a fortress. This did not satisfy us. It was necessary that the bulwark from which France could sally forth for attack should be pushed further back. Another proposal was to neutralize Alsace and Lorraine. But that neutral State would have possessed neither the power nor the will to preserve its neutrality in case of war. We were obliged to incorporate Alsace with the territory of Germany in order to ensure the peace of Europe. It is true the aversion of the population of Alsace and Lorraine is an obstacle to such a measure. Still, the population is thoroughly German, forming a sort of aristocracy in France by virtue of its noble and Teutonic qualities. We shall strive to win back to us this population, by means of Teutonic patience and love. We shall especially grant communal liberties. The Federal Council will carefully examine all amendments proposed by the Reichstag. Let us work together with mutual confidence.'

The Chancellor could not disguise the difficulties attending the incorporation, but with his usual indomitable spirit he resolved to overcome them. To do this he obtained permission to govern the annexed provinces as he chose, until the beginning of 1873 ; and he resolved to proceed by easy stages, gradually gaining the people over to look with complacency upon the German rule. The Bill for Incorporation was finally adopted with only two dissentient votes, and it was provided that the sole and supreme control of the two provinces should be vested in the Emperor of Germany and the Federal Council until the 1st of January, 1873, when the Constitution of the German Empire was to be introduced. This was a triumph for Prince Bismarck, as it practically meant the Government of Alsace and Lorraine by the German Chancellor.

The Poles once more demanded the separation of the Polish districts from the German Empire, a demand which drew a harsh and bitter speech from Bismarck. He told the Polish Deputies that they had no nationality, and that they had received no mandate either to represent the Polish people, or the Polish nationality. He did not share their fiction that the Polish rule was good or not bad. He could assure them that it was truly bad, and that therefore it would never return. The session ended with the Government as victorious in the Senate as it had been in the field.

Peace being now thoroughly assured between France and Germany, on the 16th of June the Prussian troops made their triumphal entry into Berlin, amid demonstrations of great joy. Business was suspended, and 200,000 strangers were reported to have arrived in the city. The body of troops which entered numbered about 42,000, consisting of the Prussian Royal Guards, and picked deputations from all the regiments of the German Federal and Allied Armies, infantry, cavalry, and artillery. Marshal von Wrangel, who was too old to take part in the war, led the cavalcade, and then came other generals and staff-officers. Next appeared the general officers who had served, like Falkenstein, as civil governors in the conquered territories ; and then rode the commanders of different army corps, and the illustrious men who commanded whole armies—the Duke of Mecklenburg, the Crown Prince of Saxony, and Field-Marshal Steinmetz. Generals Manteuffel, Werder, Von der Tann, and Goeben, who had also commanded armies, were among the party of general officers preceding.

Loud applause greeted the arrival of Bismarck, Moltke, and Roon, and this was deepened and intensified as soon as the Emperor emerged into view. He was in his field uniform, and rode his favourite dark bay war-horse. Close behind him rode the Field Marshals of the Royal House— the Imperial Crown Prince on a chestnut horse, and Prince Frederick Charles on a bright bay charger. A bevy of princes succeeded, guests of the Emperor, with their personal staff, glittering in varied uniforms, and making a gallant show. Lastly came the under officers of various German nationalities, bearing the spoils of war, the eagles and the colours. The Emperor, having received an address from the Burgomaster of Berlin, proceeded to inaugurate the equestrian war statue of his father, King Frederick William III., in a square at right angles with the Opera Platz. At night the whole city presented the appearance of an illuminated fairyland. A solemn thanksgiving service was celebrated in all the churches on the following Sunday.

There was an interchange of Imperial visits during the summer months of 1871 which attracted the attention of Europe. The Czar visited the Emperor William at Berlin in the first week of June, and a few days afterwards the Emperor went to Ems to meet the Czar. An interview between the Emperor William and the Emperor Francis Joseph took place at Ischl on the 11th of August. The ostensible reason for the conference was a settlement of the dispute respecting the repudiation of certain railway bonds by the Roumanian Government. But Bismarck had another object in view. Accompanying his Imperial master he desired to have a personal interview with the Austrian Chancellor Count Beust, to see whether a joint representation could not be made to the Italian Government for the amelioration of the Pope's position at Rome. The Old Catholic movement was in full force in Germany, and the Ultramontane element was very wroth with the Government on other grounds. Bismarck thought that by this little attention to the Pope matters might be somewhat smoothed over. Bismarck and Beust met at Gastein, but separated before the negotiations came to a definite issue.

The German and Austrian Emperors, however, with their

respective Chancellors, met again at Salzburg on the 6th of September. Europe wondered what these interviews meant, and all kinds of rumours were immediately set afloat. No formal league was concluded between the sovereigns, but the general results of the meeting became known, partly through Count Beust's circular to the diplomatic representatives of Austria, and partly through the statements of semi-official organs. From these it appeared that 'in the matter of the Roumanian railway bonds, the Austrian Government declined to act, alleging that it could not recognize the principle of State interposition to enforce the claims of private speculation, and had no desire to complicate its own relations with so near a neighbour as the Danubian Principality. With regard to the Pope, it was promised that Austrian influence should be exerted to further the course proposed by Bismarck. But the subject that probably lay nearer to the heart of both the negotiating parties than either of those just named, related to the rising tide of Socialism—the great revolutionary element which was threatening all fixed institutions in Europe, and of which the history of France had lately displayed so terrible a development. It is said that at this conference a resolution was taken to institute statistical inquiries on the same plan in both empires as to the nature, tendencies, and extent of the movement, to be followed up, if necessary, by a conference of special commissioners; also that it was agreed to sound the other principal Continental governments as to their willingness to take part in the investigation. For the rest, both interviews, that of Ischl and Gastein and that of Salzburg, resulted in a cordial understanding between the two Emperors and their chief ministers. Francis Joseph acquiesced in the position which the Prussian sovereign had taken as leader of Germany, and William the First engaged not to tamper with the German provinces of the Austrian Empire. When the potentates and statesmen on both sides met and compared ideas, it was to recognize that for both Powers there existed a common policy which it was their interest to pursue, and which the popular instinct in both nations had already sanctioned.'

The German Parliament met again at Berlin on the 16th of October. Public affairs wore a roseate hue, and the Emperor's speech was conceived in a gratulatory vein. His Majesty announced that the session would be short, and that the principal task before the Parliament was the regulation of the Imperial Budget. The existing transitional budget would be extended to the coming year; a gold coinage fitted for general circulation was to be established; and with regard to France, while relying upon a steady pacification and consolidation, the Government considered it practicable to permit the immediate evacuation of those departments which, according to the terms of peace, was to have occurred in the following May. Touching upon the relations between Germany, Russia, and Austria, the Emperor said : ' I rejoice to think that the interviews which I had this summer with the Sovereigns of these Empires—Sovereigns with whom I am personally on such intimate terms—will, by strengthening public confidence in a pacific future, materially contribute to secure it to Europe. The German Empire and the Austro-Hungarian Imperial State are, by their geographical situation and history, absolutely compelled to entertain friendly and neighbourly relations towards each other. The obliteration of the memory of a struggle forced upon us, much against our will, by the dissensions of a thousand years, will give sincere satisfaction to the whole German people.'

The controversy between the State and the Roman Catholic Church now passed into an acute stage ; Parliament had no sooner met, than a manifesto was addressed to the Emperor by the Archbishops of Cologne and Gnesen and eleven other prelates, complaining of various infractions of the agreement subsisting between the Romish Church and the Prussian State by the Ministry of Public Worship and Education, and especially in the case of the Gymnasium of Braunsberg, where the Government had kept a religious teacher in office despite his open adherence to Old Catholic doctrines. A flash of the Emperor's fiery but well-controlled temper burned in his reply. He told the bishops that he was surprised at their language, which was calculated to shake the confidence of his Catholic subjects ; and he was the more astonished, as the Pope had hitherto freely acknowledged the just treatment extended to the Church in Prussia. His Majesty denied that the Government had meddled with doctrinal controversies, or done more than its duty in seeking to avert the threatened conflict between Church and State. For himself, he could declare that whether his hopes of harmonious co-operation in promoting the interests of the new Empire were fulfilled or not, he would continue, as before, to grant to each community the fullest liberty consistent with the rights of others, and their equality before the law.

The religious freedom thus accorded to the Old Catholics was very distasteful to the Catholic bishops, who retired reproved and crestfallen from the Imperial presence. But a further blow to the intolerance and bigotry of the prelates and their co-religionists was shortly dealt in the Parliament itself. Von Lutz, the Bavarian Minister, brought in a Bill making it penal for clergymen to abuse their office by political agitation in the pulpit. Though the measure was general in character, and applied to the clergy of all denominations, it was specially aimed at the fanatical and aggressive Ultramontanes. In the Rhenish Provinces, Bavaria, and elsewhere, the Roman Catholic priesthood had been in the habit, during the elections, of delivering political sermons to their congregations, describing in pathetic terms the situation of the Pope, and urging their hearers to elect Ultramontane candidates, whom they represented as ready to assist the Holy Father in his struggle. The abuse of the clerical office and the pressure exercised upon the people became so great that legislation was necessary. Some of the Bavarian clergy had threatened to excommunicate all who circulated an official document issued by the Government on the Old Catholic question. Nothing could be said for the Ultramontanist practices, and the bill was carried by a large majority.

A new Imperial Coinage Bill passed into law in November, and a resolution was adopted for placing the civil and criminal law, and the judicial procedure and organization in the various Federal States, under the control of the Imperial Legislature. Although a Bill founded on this motion was passed by the Reichstag, it was rejected by the Federal Council on the ground that they had no right to sanction such fundamental changes without authority from the minor Parliaments. A very important measure carried this session, however, inaugurated a new arrangement regarding the immovable War Fund, which was demanded in the interests of German unity. Prussia had long maintained as one of her special institutions a war reserve fund of thirty million thalers; and as the result of the great political changes just accomplished, this arrangement was now to be extended to the whole empire. The War Treasury, instead of belonging to Prussia, was henceforth to be appropriated to the uses of all Germany; and it was to be raised from thirty to forty million thalers. It was curiously provided that this sum was to be deposited in gold and silver in the cellars of some citadel, and, lying torpid without yielding interest, to wait for the moment when the alarm of war should call it into service. There was a long discussion over this buried treasure, but the Government proposals were adopted in the end.

Socialism caused the rulers of Germany no small concern at this time. Bismarck knew that there was a good deal of discontent amongst the humbler classes, though in public he made light of the signs of this discontent. Herr Bebel, one of the Prussian deputies, gave utterance to the views of the Socialists in Parliament, and after remarking that what the Communists had done in Paris was but an outpost skirmish, which would be followed up some day by a great European battle, he said: ' War to the palaces, peace to the cottages, and death to luxurious idleness is, and ever will be, the watchword of the proletariat in all parts of the world.' Several strikes of workmen, notably in Berlin, occurred in the autumn; and, before the year closed, a meeting of working-men was convened in the capital by the Social Democratic Union. Its objects were—to protest against the petty remunerations given to the landwehr and reserves, as compared with the munificent grants made to the Generals and other officers; and to adopt some plan for greater industrial co-operation among Berlin working-men. The Union had always protested against the continuance of the war after Sedan, and condemned the annexation of Alsace and Lorraine, except with the assent of the inhabitants. It now passed a resolution condemning the retention of French prisoners in German fortresses, seeing that peace had been concluded. As a counter-balancing movement to that of the workmen, when the manufacturers assembled for their annual autumn meeting at Leipsic, they took into consideration the interests of the capitalists, and sought to contrive measures for overcoming the hostility of the workmen. Meanwhile, notwithstanding the complaints of the Socialists, the commercial condition of the Empire was most prosperous. The war had not sensibly interfered with business, and taxes yielded as much in 1870 and 1871 as in the preceding and less-disturbed years—a sure proof that the trade of the country was sound at heart. After the peace was concluded, commercial prosperity advanced 'by leaps and bounds,' and money was so plentiful that means could scarcely be found to employ it.

Financially, the German Empire presented a remarkable spectacle. Its great political reforms had been achieved without the imposition of additional burdens upon the people. Even in the year 1870, with the war in full force, the income from the Customs and Excise fully came up to the estimates. For 1872 the outlook was very encouraging. The Empire was presumed to spend in the coming year 110,500,000 thalers. This sum only represented the amount required for Federal purposes, and not the total of the German budgets. Then, in addition to the common outlay, there were the local budgets of the various States, computed at something like 260,000,000 thalers, making 370,500,000 thalers for the grand total of the German public expenditure. The Federal outlay of 110,500,000 thalers was covered by the Customs and certain indirect taxes permanently handed over to the Imperial Exchequer, as well as by the direct contributions of the various States. These various items amounted to about 78,000,000, so that there remained 32,500,000 thalers to be contributed by the treasuries of the various States.

The Prussian Diet was opened by the King on November 22, and in the speech from the throne he drew a broad line of demarcation between the jurisdiction of the German Reichstag and that of the Prussian Diet. While the maintenance of the national power and security, said his Majesty, belonged to the German Empire, it was for the Prussian representatives more thoroughly to devote themselves to the healthy development of the internal institutions. During this session Herr Camphausen, the Minister of Finance, carried through propositions for the use of the reserve funds of the public treasury in paying off the public debt, for increasing the salaries of the public teachers, for making liberal grants for the encouragement of art and science, and for making a considerable reduction in the public debt.

The year thus closed with happy omens both for Prussia and the newly-constituted Empire. Though there were some causes for internal solicitude, as is the case with all nations, the state of Germany in general was most satisfactory. As for the venerable Emperor himself, he had never been in better health or spirits. Physically, he could compete with the best of his subjects, as was proved in the month of December by his exploits in the Hanoverian forest of Göhrde, when with his own hand he brought down no fewer than twenty-one wild boars. Further, to increase his light-heartedness, and his sense of security over the future of Germany, he was well aware that in Bismarck and Moltke he had two buttresses which could not easily be shaken by adverse storms. The Empire was powerful, because peaceful, and it was advancing by rapid strides on the golden path of progress. Though, as we shall presently see, questions of moment were pressing forward for settlement, the German Government was quietly gathering strength to meet them.

CHAPTER XIII.

CONSOLIDATING THE EMPIRE.

THE German conflict with the Ultramontanes, of which there had been several premonitory symptoms, was waged with great vigour in 1872. The storm began in an unlooked-for and almost accidental manner. After transacting business one day with the Emperor, Bismarck went into the Prussian House of Deputies merely for a passing visit, when Dr. Windthorst, leader of the Catholic reactionary party, was on his legs. The Doctor made a speech complaining of the diminished advantages open to the Catholics in the State and in education; and his observations, which were of a very biting character, put the Chancellor into a fury.

Bismarck rose and delivered an impromptu reply, remarkable for its energy, its sarcasm, and its eloquence. It was received all through with continuous laughter and applause. A strange man for peace was this Windthorst, he intimated, whose own language displayed so total an absence of Christian gentleness. It was the tone and temper of the Centre party which made it impossible to give them a Catholic representative on the Ministerial Council. The head of that party had joined the Prussian body politic

with repugnance and ill-will, and he had never shown by
speech or action that he had overcome this repugnance, so
that it was doubtful even now whether the new formation
of the German Empire was pleasing or distasteful to him.
Passing from the personal to the general aspect of the
question, the Chancellor next made a dashing attack upon
the Clerical party, which afterwards led to great recriminations, followed by repressive legislation. 'When I
returned from France to devote myself to home affairs,' he
observed, ' the Clerical or Centre party, which had just been
formed, seemed to me a party whose policy was directed
against the predominance and unity of the State. I will
not conceal from you that the Government had hoped to
rely upon the assistance of the orthodox element in the
people. I thought it had a right to expect that they,
above all, would render unto Cæsar the things that are
Cæsar's. Instead of this we find ourselves systematically
withstood in the South, and most violently attacked in the
papers and in speeches destined for the instruction of the
lower classes. This conduct is the more extraordinary
inasmuch as the Pope and the Prussian bishops of the
Catholic Church, have repeatedly acknowledged the perfect
liberty their co-religionists enjoy under our institutions.
In their downright hostility, therefore, the Ultramontane
party cannot be actuated by dissatisfaction at the position
the Catholic Church holds, and indeed has long held among
us. Unfortunately we are at no loss to account for their
motives. When we find this party leaguing with Radicals
of every shade of persuasion—when we find them acting
in concert with men whose extreme politics make them
avowed enemies of the Prussian Constitutional Monarchy
and of the German Imperial Commonwealth—we need not
wonder at their drifting into persistent opposition, and
placing us in the painful position in which we now stand
with regard to them.'

The uncompromising views of the Government were not
long in bearing fruit. A School Inspection Bill was brought
forward in the House of Deputies, as the first definite move
on the part of the Ministry. This measure provided that
the supervision of all educational institutions, public and
private, should be entrusted to the State; that all officers
appointed as inspectors should be servants of the State,

and in no way responsible to the various religious denominations. The reception of the Bill was a curious one. The Catholics of course were strongly against it, but singularly enough the stiff orthodox Protestants united with the Ultramontanes, and the Poles were hostile to it on national grounds, viewing it as a step in the process of Germanizing the Polish provinces. Prince Bismarck could therefore only rely upon the Liberal party, but he had the support of Liberals of all shades of opinion.

The Court was very lukewarm about the measure, as both the King and the Queen were known to favour denominationalism, and the only supporter Bismarck had in the Royal circle was the Crown Prince. The Bill required careful piloting through the Chamber of Deputies. The Chancellor in the course of the debates again severely handled Windthorst, who had been rather growing personally in Court favour. Then, towards the close of a memorable speech, and one which had a great effect upon the House, Bismarck put forth his own *apologia*. 'The previous speaker,' he said, 'has reminded me of speeches I made twenty-three years ago—in the year 1849. I could simply dispose of this charge with the remark that in a space of twenty-three years—especially as they were the best years of a man's life—I have learned something, and that in my case I, at least, am not infallible! But I will go farther. Whatever professions I have made in regard to my Christian faith I now openly reiterate, and I will never hesitate to do so either at home or in public; but it is this very Christian faith which makes it my duty to the country where I was born, and where a high function has been entrusted to me, to protect it against all attacks. When the foundations of the State were attacked by barricades and the Republican party, I considered it my duty to stand at the breach; and if it should be attacked by other parties, whose duty it was and is rather to strengthen the State than to overthrow it, you will see me there at the breach also. Such is the conduct which Christianity and faith prescribe to me.' The speaker's vigorous pleading carried the Bill by a majority of 197 to 171.

Although the Emperor was not at first enthusiastic about this measure, he saw that its defeat would be a most damaging blow to the Government, and lead to a very unsettled state of affairs. He was consequently now anxious that it should become law. But if it passed the Deputies only by such a narrow margin of votes, what were its chances in the Upper House? Fortunately those chances were strengthened by the arrest of a youth of Polish descent on the charge of plotting and conspiring against the Chancellor. The case against him was trivial, but his examination revealed the important circumstance that he had been residing in the house of Canon de Kozmian, a Jesuit, and in the Canon's residence there were subsequently seized some important papers. When the School Inspection Bill came before the Upper House, Bismarck read out several passages from the confiscated correspondence, which were very damaging to Dr. Windthorst and Bishop Ketteler of Mayence, in regard to Ultramontane intrigues. The Chancellor went straight to the point in describing the aims and objects of the Roman Catholic party. He showed how utterly incompatible those aims were with the interests and policy of the new Empire, and then read the following extract from a despatch by one of his diplomatic representatives abroad: ' The revenge for which people are panting in France is being prepared for by getting up religious troubles in Germany. It is intended to cripple German unity by denominational discord, for which purpose the whole of the clergy are to be utilized under immediate orders from Rome. In connexion with the overthrow of German power, the Pope hopes to be able to re-establish his secular power in Italy.'

The Prince next made a strong appeal to the Conservative Opposition to support the Government. ' Nowhere has a government less interfered with the management of ecclesiastical concerns than in Prussia; nowhere have the two Christian denominations lived so long in such perfect concord. But we are now to be deprived of this invaluable boon, and must guard against our adversaries carrying out their charitable intention. One of our weapons of defence is the School Inspection Bill. Need I point out who our enemies are? While two Catholic Powers existed on our borders, each supposed to be stronger than Prussia, and more or less at the disposal of the Catholic Church, we were allowed to live in peace and quiet. Things changed after our victory of 1866, and the consequent ascendancy of the Protestant dynasty of Hohenzollern. And now that another Catholic Power has gone the same way, and we have acquired a might, which, with God's help, we mean to keep, our opponents are more embittered than ever, and make us the butt of their constant attacks.'

The Chancellor was again victorious. His arguments, personal, religious, and political, prevailed with the Upper House, and the Bill was carried by 125 votes to 76. This was a much more brilliant triumph than the one achieved in the Lower House, for Bismarck had far greater odds against him.

Very soon afterwards, there was an open quarrel between Germany and the Papacy. Prince Bismarck nominated the Cardinal Prince Hohenlohe as German ambassador at the Vatican. The appointment was variously viewed. The supporters of the Chancellor said that it was a proof of his liberality, and that he did not wish to show ill-will to the Catholics as a body. On the other hand, the Ultramontanes saw in the nomination a subtler purpose. Cardinal Hohenlohe was a Papist, but something more. He was a Liberal, a German Unionist, and an opponent of the Infallibility dogma. So it was held that Bismarck divined in such a prince of the Church a better instrument for counteracting Ultramontane intrigues, than any statesman chosen from the ranks of Protestantism. The Pope, however, refused to receive Prince Hohenlohe as German representative at his Court.

This led to a prolonged debate in the Reichstag, when, on the 14th of May, Prince Bismarck delivered an important speech. He said that the latest dogma as promulgated by the Holy See rendered it impossible to work in harmony with Rome. To restore peace among the religious denominations, it appeared necessary to seek a solution of the difficulties by enacting a law for the empire securing complete liberty of conscience. The rejection of an envoy by a government to whom it was proposed to accredit him was not a frequent occurrence. It was not a courteous proceeding, and it had never before happened to Prince Bismarck during a diplomatic career lasting over twenty-one years. It pained him the more, inasmuch as Prince Hohenlohe appeared fitted to bring about a conciliatory feeling. The regret he felt would not, however, justify him in manifesting irritation. Regard for the interests of the Catholic population of Germany, had determined him to nominate another envoy, however difficult it would be to find an equal to Cardinal Hohenlohe, and doubtful as he was of a substitute achieving good results. At a later stage of the discussion, Prince Bismarck declared emphatically that he should always reject any treaty with Rome in which the Papacy might claim that certain State laws should not be binding upon a portion of the subjects of the empire.

A number of deputies were for striking out of the estimates the cost of an envoy to the Pope, but the Chancellor's view was adopted and the charge sanctioned by a large majority.

The University of Strasburg was opened on the 1st of May with much ceremony. All Germany was profoundly interested in this matter, as it was expected that the University would greatly contribute to the revival of German sentiments in Alsace and Lorraine. As the conquered provinces were not yet ripe, however, for the introduction of the Federal Constitution in its entirety, the Government introduced a Bill proposing to suspend it until January 1st, 1874. The Bill was opposed by the Catholic party and the party of progress, but, being supported by all other sections of the House, it was passed by a large majority.

The Emperor William acted during this year as arbitrator in a dispute between Great Britain and the United States. The question arose out of the interpretation of a clause in the Washington treaty as to the American and Canadian boundaries, which involved the possession of the Island of San Juan, a territory somewhat larger than the Isle of Wight. The treaty provided that the boundary line should be continued to the middle of the channel which separates the continent from Vancouver's Island. The English reading of this gave San Juan to us, but the Americans maintained that the strait called De Haro, between San Juan and Vancouver, was really meant. By his award, the Emperor decided unreservedly in favour of the American claim.

One of the most momentous debates which had yet been held in the German Parliament took place on the 15th of

May. Several hundred petitions relating to the Jesuits were presented, some advocating their expulsion from the country, but the majority interceding on behalf of the Order. Bishop Monfang of Mayence opened the debate, defending the Jesuits, and he was supported by Herr Reichensperger, a member of the Supreme Court of Appeal at Berlin, and a cultured and accomplished historian. On the other side, the Government was urged to proceed against the Jesuits in the interests of peace by Privy Councillor Wagener, one of the leaders of the Conservative party; Prince Hohenlohe, late Bavarian Premier; Herr Fischer, Burgomaster of Augsburg, who like the Prince was a Roman Catholic; and the well-known Professor Gneist, of the University of Berlin. A report drawn up on the petitions stated that as a consequence of the pro-Papal tendencies until lately prevalent in the ministry, the number of convents had enormously increased. In 1864 there were only 69; in 1865 they had increased to 243; in 1866 to 481; and in 1869 to 826. The number of persons shut up in these institutions had risen from 976 in 1855 to something like 10,000 in 1869.

In accordance with a resolution of the House, the Government introduced a Bill placing the Society of Jesus under police supervision, and giving the Federal Council power to remove its members from any part of Germany where their presence should appear inconsistent with the public interest. Subsequently, as modified and adopted by a majority of the Federal Council, including all but the Polish and Ultramontane sections, the measure enacted that all convents and other establishments of the Order on German soil should be abolished; that the same veto should extend to all other orders and religious societies connected with the Jesuits, leaving the Government to determine the nature of such societies; and it conferred on the administrative authorities the right not literally of expelling German members of the Jesuit Order, but of assigning them localities where alone they might reside. Foreign members of the Order were to be expelled; and the authority for carrying the law into execution was vested in a committee of the Federal Council.

The Emperor William gave his sanction to the Act, and in consequence of these repeated collisions between the spiritual and temporal powers the following law was formally promulgated on the 4th of July :—' We, William, by the grace of God,

Emperor of Germany, King of Prussia, &c., in the name of the German Empire, with the assent of the Federal Council, and of the Parliament, ordain as follows: I. The Order of the Society of Jesus, as well as the monastic orders of Congregations affiliated to the said Society, are excluded from the territory of the German Empire. The creation of establishments by them is forbidden. Establishments of theirs at present existing shall be suppressed within a period to be settled by the Federal Council, but not later than six months. II. The members of the Order of the Society of Jesus, or of Orders and Congregations affiliated, may, if aliens, be expelled from the territory of the Confederation. If they are natives, their residence in certain districts, or certain places, may be forbidden or prescribed to them. III. The Federal Council will take the measures necessary for securing the execution of this law. In faith of which we have set our hand and seal imperial.'

The Pope and the Cardinals were exceedingly wroth at this action, though there is no doubt they would have taken similar steps themselves had the positions been reversed, for whenever they have had the power they have used it far more cruelly than Prussia for the suppression of religious opponents. Pius IX. employed extraordinary language in receiving an address from a German Ultramontane Society at Rome. ' Let us hold out,' he said, ' but let us hold out firmly united, and confiding in the justice of God Almighty. Who knows whether a little stone may not soon separate itself from a mountain top, and, coming down unexpectedly, smash the feet of the Colossus.' The allusions to the stone and the mountain were manifestly vague, but there were persons who interpreted them as referring to disloyal plots and intrigues.

A grand conference was held at Berlin early in September between the Emperors of Germany, Russia, and Austria. The gathering was a most brilliant one, and the fêtes splendid in the extreme. But all was not amusement, and the other European Powers were solicitous respecting this foregathering of powerful monarchs. While the potentates were discussing matters from their own points of view, the three Chancellors, Prince Bismarck, Prince Gortschakoff, and Count Andrassy, were likewise holding long and important interviews. But all designs, save the wish to bring the three

Sovereigns together, and so promote peace and good-will, were strongly repudiated. There were rumours of a Holy Alliance, and of a design to suppress all 'International' movements and the like. But whatever the objects of the meeting, France and the Pope were by no means pleased over it. The former Power saw its hopes of a foreign alliance against Germany indefinitely postponed, while the Vatican and the Ultramontanes were compelled to renounce the prospect of an ally and protector even in the chief of the House of Hapsburg, 'the born defender of the Catholic Church.' Prince Bismarck, in his reply to a deputation of the magistrates of Berlin—presenting him with the honorary diploma of citizenship—remarked that by means of the festive events of the last few days, confidence in the endurance of peace, which was nearly as valuable as peace itself, would be strengthened. The high persons who had met in Berlin would not leave with disappointed expectations. The meeting had not been called forth by aggressive intentions against any Power, or in any direction whatsoever. The amicable personal interview of the Emperors would strengthen the confidence of friends in a lasting peace, and clearly show to enemies the difficulties they would have to encounter in order to disturb that peace.

The Emperor William, after bidding farewell to his illustrious visitors, journeyed to Marienburg, the capital of West Prussia, to aid in celebrating the centenary of the first partition of Poland, when the province in question was restored to Prussia, of which it originally formed a part. A statue of Frederick the Great was to be erected to commemorate the event, and his successor now laid the foundation-stone of the memorial near the magnificent old castle of Marienburg. Even here the ruler of Germany came upon a thorn in the person of the recalcitrant Bishop of Ermeland, who wrote to the Emperor desiring to pay his respects to him in person at the centenary gathering. The Emperor, who is nothing if not frank, replied to the effect that he should be very glad to see the Bishop if he would retract the offensive expressions in his correspondence with the Ecclesiastical Department of State, and declare himself willing to obey the laws of the land to their fullest extent; but if not, well—he had better not go. The Bishop decided not to present himself before the Emperor.

The suppression of the Jesuits was regarded by some as an impolitic step, and it certainly threw the Roman Catholic Church into a militant attitude. A union of German Catholics was organized at Mayence, with the avowed object of supporting the Church in its conflict with the Empire. The members of the union met at Fulda in September, and issued a memorial stating their grievances. They explicitly asserted that canon laws were more binding than those enacted by the secular power; that the Church and not the State was rightfully supreme in ecclesiastical affairs, in education, and in marriage contracts; and they further upheld the episcopal right of excommunication.

When the Prussian Chambers reassembled in October, there was a desperate Parliamentary conflict in the Upper House over the New Districts Administration Bill. This was a government measure for remodelling the administration of the Six Provinces of East Prussia. It proposed to abolish the last remnant of feudal government surviving in the Prussian kingdom. Heretofore, in the counties to which the Bill referred, the magistrates and county assemblies—in whose functions it lay to make the roads, relieve the poor, and look after other matters of local interest—had been exclusively composed of the proprietors of land and estates, who also had the privilege of nominating to all the petty magistracies of their districts. It was now proposed to admit a large number of townspeople and villagers to the County Assemblies, where these classes had formerly scarcely been seen; to create honorary officials, to be elected by these assemblies, to perform the functions of the police on the larger estates, as well as in the villages; to bestow upon the villages the right of choosing their municipal officers, and of combining with neighbouring villages for the better management of local matters; and last, but not least, to empower the government officer at the head of the county—though he should remain a nominee of the Crown and retain the right of interfering with the proceedings of the new election officers and authorities—to officiate conjointly with a Board chosen by the County Assembly from the gentlemen of the district. These were great and important changes, practically vesting the right of self-government in the villages.

The Bill passed the Lower House, as might naturally be expected, but in the Upper it was thrown out. Although the

Emperor had himself intimated to Count Brühl, Vice-President of the Upper Chamber, that he desired and expected it to pass, the peers rejected the Government proposition by the enormous majority of 145 votes to 18. The feudal lords, whose long-standing but arbitrary rights were struck at by the Bill, were largely represented in the Upper Chamber, and they of course declined to vote for the extinction of their own power and influence. Representative institutions and local self-government were very obnoxious to them; and several speakers declared that to upset the rural life of the country was to introduce Republicanism at once into the nation. They held that the change was incompatible with the maintenance of the monarchy and the continued existence of the State. The vote in the Upper House brought on a constitutional crisis, and the Chambers were prorogued for twelve days.

Bismarck was resolved upon carrying the measure, for, although he had always been in sympathy with the aristocratic party, he held that this measure was absolutely essential to the more liberal requirements of a united Germany. Accordingly, when Parliament reopened, General von Roon reintroduced the Bill amended in the Upper House, and stated that the Government were fully resolved on carrying it by every constitutional means at its disposal, thus pointing to a creation of new peers if necessary. This step was eventually found to be requisite, and twenty-five new peers were created. The Emperor, it is stated, only consented with reluctance to a revolutionary step with which his feelings and principles through all his career as King of Prussia had been so little in accordance; but he felt that he must support his Chancellor in this matter.

In answer to a communication addressed to him by a highly esteemed Conservative member of the Lower House, His Majesty wrote a wise and timely letter on the subject. He reminded the Deputy that the Conservatives had looked forward to the speedy downfall of the State as an inevitable consequence of the agrarian and municipal reform of 1808, and he expressed his conviction that the time had arrived when the work begun in those early days must be resumed and to a certain extent completed. The Administration had become too complicated an engine to be conducted by professional officials alone; and the finances required to be lightened by the transfer of a portion of the public business to men not salaried by the State, and in a position to regard the honour of serving their country as their best reward. The Civil Service of Prussia was already 62,000 strong, and so badly paid that its members had a right to demand an increase of salary. As this demand could not any longer be refused, there was nothing left but to obviate the necessity of fresh offices being created as fast as had hitherto been done.

This was one of the most progressive deliverances the Emperor had yet made, and it caused great gratification, especially to the Liberals. It also turned a great many Conservative votes in the Upper House, and moderate counsels now prevailing, the measure was carried by 116 votes against 91.

Prince Bismarck, who had for some time back contemplated the step, retired after this victory from the Premiership of the Prussian Cabinet, and was succeeded by Count von Roon, the senior Minister of State. The Imperial Chancellor, however, still retained the department of Foreign Affairs in the Prussian Ministry.

A good many rumours set afloat at the close of 1872 to the effect that Bismarck's retirement from the Prussian Premiership was a triumph for the reactionary party, and that it signified a divergence of view between himself and the Emperor, were shown to be utterly unfounded on the first day of the New Year. The Sovereign wrote to his most trusty Chancellor a grateful letter, which was accompanied by the Order of the Black Eagle set in diamonds. Bismarck further tendered explanations in the Chamber of Deputies, denying that there were dissensions in the Ministry, and pointing out that the new Government was merely a continuation of his own.

Meanwhile the contest with Rome waxed hotter and hotter. The Pope issued a Christmas Allocution so fierce in spirit that it would have brought him within the law had he been amenable to its jurisdiction. Things reached such a pass, that on the 9th of January, 1873, Dr. Falck, the Minister for Education, brought in four very important Bills, dealing with both the State-recognised religions, the Protestant or Evangelical, and the Catholic. Their objects were to protect the freedom of individual persons ; to ensure the training of a German national in contradistinction from an Ultramontane clergy ; and to guard the rights and independence of the clergy themselves as against their ecclesiastical superiors.

Hitherto the Churches had been left free to govern themselves and to educate their own clergy. In the case of the Roman Catholics special seminaries had been instituted for the education of those destined for the priesthood from their youth upwards. All institutions of the kind now in existence were by the proposed law to be placed under rigorous State inspection, while it was forbidden to open any new ones. The State thus intended to take into its own hands the direct supervision of the education of the clergy; and candidates for the priesthood would be required to attend the State Gymnasia and Universities, so that a portion at least of their training might be received among the laity. Before they could enter the clerical ranks they must pass State examinations in philosophy, history, German literature, and the classical languages. The State claimed a right of supervision over clerical appointments, and heavy fines were instituted for making appointments which might be unconditionally revoked. Ecclesiastical discipline was dealt with, and the real purport of the measures was to substitute a national or German for a foreign or Ultramontane clergy. A supreme Royal Court was to sit at Berlin, and deal with cases involving ecclesiastical discipline. These Bills were discussed with much fervour and at great length, but ultimately all of them were passed by both Houses.

The German Diet opened on the 12th of March. In consequence of a report prepared by the Committee on Religious Orders, the German Federal Council decided to expel from the Empire the Monastic Orders of Redemptorists and Lazarists, and the Congregations of the Holy Ghost and the Sacred Heart. This decision gave rise to a warm debate in the Diet, when Prince Bismarck said that he confidently appealed to the judgment of history to pronounce whether he had been guilty of slandering the Ultramontane leaders when he designated them as antagonists, as enemies of the Empire, and as instigators and leaders of the plots against the Empire and the Imperial Government.

The Prussian Catholic bishops met at Fulda in April, and drew up a solemn protest against the new ecclesiastical laws. It was circulated amongst the clergy and the various dioceses, with the result that active resistance to the laws began to be offered. The State replied by instituting prosecutions, and the most distinguished of those against whom criminal proceedings were taken was Ledochowski, Arch-bishop of Posen, who had systematically made appointments to benefices in defiance of the laws. He was condemned to a fine of 200 thalers, or four months' imprisonment; but he still kept on the same course.

Parliament passed in June the third reading of the Bill for the introduction of the Imperial Constitution into Alsace-Lorraine from the 1st of January, 1874. From that date the annexed provinces would be ruled as an integral part of Germany, and be entitled to send their representatives to the Reichstag. There was one question with respect to which the Emperor was greatly chagrined by the policy of the Diet. A Bill was brought forward for altering the or-ganization of the national army; but when the House should have discussed it, the Deputies absented themselves. Even Bismarck shrank from rushing the Bill through under such circumstances, and the Emperor closed the session without its becoming law. A Press Bill, which contained several very stringent provisions, was also rejected by the Diet.

Several Royal and Imperial visits were exchanged this year. In April, the Emperor William went to St. Peters-burg, where he was sumptuously entertained; then the Shah of Persia and the King of Italy paid visits to Berlin, and between the Eastern monarch and the German Emperor a special treaty of friendship, commerce, and navigation was concluded. In October, the Emperor visited Vienna, where he had an enthusiastic reception. On the memorable anniversary of Sedan, the 2nd of September, the monument of Victory was unveiled by the Emperor William, on the Konigsplatz, Berlin. 'The column of Victory unveiled to-day,' observed His Majesty, in a speech delivered at the memorial banquet, 'is a proof to the present and future generations of what self-sacrifice and perseverance can accomplish. In conjunction with our faithful allies in the last glorious war, we strode from victory to victory by the grace and bountiful will of God, until we attained to the Unity of Germany in the establishment of a new Empire. I drink, therefore, in gratitude to my heroic people, my illustrious allies, and our glorious army.'

The conflict between the Government and the Ultramon-tanes continued all through the year, and in October great sensation was caused throughout Germany and all Europe by the publication of a correspondence between two august personages—the Pope and the Emperor William. Writing on the 7th of August, 1873, the Pope charged the German Government with aiming more and more at the destruction of Catholicism. But he had heard that the Emperor did not approve the harshness of the measures adopted by the Government, and if that were the case, the measures complained of could have no other effect than that of undermining His Majesty's own throne. Pio Nono added: 'I speak with frankness, for my banner is truth; I speak in order to fulfil one of my duties, which consists in telling the truth to all, even to those who are not Catholics; for every one who has been baptized belongs in some way or other, which to define more precisely would be here out of place—belongs, I say, to the Pope.'

The Emperor of Germany took some weeks to digest this extraordinary Epistle *from* the Romans, and on the 3rd of September despatched this masterly reply to the Pope:— 'I am glad that your Holiness has, as in former times, done me the honour to write to me. I rejoice the more at this, since an opportunity is thereby afforded me of correcting errors which, as appears from the contents of the letter of your Holiness of the 7th of August, must have occurred in the communications you have received relative to German affairs. If the reports which are made to your Holiness respecting German questions only stated the truth, it would not be possible for your Holiness to entertain the supposition that my Government enters upon a path which I do not approve. According to the constitution of my States, such a case cannot happen, since the laws and Government measures in Prussia require my consent as Sovereign. To my deep sorrow, a portion of my Catholic subjects have organized for the past two years a political party which endeavours to disturb, by intrigues hostile to the State, the religious peace which has existed in Prussia for centuries. Leading Catholic priests have unfortunately not only approved this movement, but joined in it to the extent of open revolt against existing laws.

'It will not have escaped the observation of your Holiness that similar indications manifest themselves at the present time in several European and some Transatlantic States. It is not my mission to investigate the causes by which the clergy and the faithful of one of the Christian denominations can be induced actively to assist the enemies of all law; but it certainly is my mission to protect internal peace, and preserve the authority of the laws in the States whose government has been entrusted to me by God. I am conscious that I owe hereafter an account of the accomplishment of this, my Kingly duty. I shall maintain order and law in my States against all attacks as long as God gives me the power; I am in duty bound to do it as a Christian monarch, even when to my sorrow I have to fulfil this royal duty against servants of a Church which I suppose acknowledges no less than the Evangelical Church that the commandment of obedience to secular authority is an emanation of the revealed will of God. Many of the priests in Prussia subject to your Holiness disown, to my regret, the Christian doctrine in this respect, and place my Government under the necessity, supported by the great majority of my loyal Catholic and Evangelical subjects, of extorting obedience to the law by worldly means.

'I willingly entertain the hope that your Holiness, upon being informed of the true position of affairs, will use your authority to put an end to the agitation carried on amid deplorable distortion of the truth, and abuse of priestly authority. The religion of Jesus Christ has, as I attest to your Holiness before God, nothing to do with these intrigues, any more than has truth, to whose banner, invoked by your Holiness, I unreservedly subscribe. There is one more expression in the letter of your Holiness which I cannot pass over without contradiction, although it is not based upon the previous information, but upon the belief of your Holiness—namely, the expression that every one who has received baptism belongs to the Pope. The Evangelical creed, which, as must be known to your Holiness, I, like my ancestors and the majority of my subjects, profess, does not permit us to accept in our relations to God any other mediator than our Lord Jesus Christ. This difference of belief does not prevent me from living in peace with those who do not share mine, and I offer your Holiness the expression of my personal devotion and esteem.'

There can be no question as to who had the best of it in this epistolary warfare. The Emperor won the engagement, and the press supported his views, at the same time vigorously attacking the Pope and his advisers. His German Majesty received congratulatory addresses from all quarters, and the Government was requested strenuously to maintain its course of action.

Amongst the numerous towns which sent up to the Emperor, Augsburg, in a remarkable address signed by Catholics and Protestants alike, expressed satisfaction and pride at the independent attitude of the nation's Sovereign. The Papal complaint that the Catholic religion was persecuted was declared to be a wanton perversion of the truth, and the Emperor was earnestly besought to continue to enforce the laws against the Ultramontanes.

As the Emperor's letter came opportunely just before the elections to the Prussian and Imperial Diets, it had the effect of deciding many waverers in favour of the policy of the Sovereign and the Premier, while another cause for this was the closeness of the relations between France and the Vatican. To the Prussian Diet there were returned as moderate Liberals—that is, those who were prepared to go all lengths with the Cabinet against the Papacy—178 members as compared with 116 in the previous Diet. Although the Ultramontanes gained some additional strength, yet as both the Liberals and moderate Conservatives might be expected to support the Ministry on most questions of Church policy, it was computed that the Cabinet could rely on a working majority of 311 in a House of 432 members. Prince Bismarck returned to the post of Prussian Premier just before the Diet opened on the 12th of November.

In the session now inaugurated another important measure, and one indicative of the signs of the times, was passed. This was a Bill sanctioning Civil marriage and Civil registration of births and deaths throughout the Prussian dominions. The Emperor held back for some time before giving his acquiescence to this measure; but he at length perceived that it was a natural corollary to the previous ecclesiastical legislation. Marriage had hitherto been a religious act, and it had become a subject of difficulty during the ecclesiastical crisis; the Ultramontane priests also declined to bury seceders in consecrated ground, and this had led in some cases to the interference of the police. The new proposals were adopted; and when the Act became law, it proved even a more sweeping measure than had been anticipated. In order to be recognised by the Civil authorities, all marriages, births, and deaths would henceforward have to be registered by the magistrate. The functions of the registrar were made obligatory, while those of the clergy were left optional.

On the 7th of December the Emperor, as King of Prussia, issued a very important decree intended to meet such cases as those of the recusant bishops. This decree enacted that throughout the Prussian dominions all Catholic bishops should, previous to receiving recognition from the State, take the following oath: 'I will be subject, true, obedient and devoted to His Majesty, carefully observe the laws of the State, and especially strive that the sentiments of honour and fidelity to the King, love of country, obedience to the laws, and all those virtues which denote at once the good subject and the Christian, shall be carefully cherished among the clergy and congregations entrusted to my episcopal guidance, and that I will not allow the clergy subject to me to teach or act in an opposing sense. In particular I promise to hold no communion or connexion within or without the country which may be dangerous to the public security.' The object of this new oath was to prevent co-operation with the Papal Court in any measures against Prussian policy; but it also abrogated the clause in the old oath by which bishops had declared their submission to the laws, but reserved to themselves all rights with regard to their spiritual obligations. There was to be no conflict in future between spiritual duties and the law.

Pius IX. became furious over the state of ecclesiastical affairs in Germany. In an Encyclical, he described the Old Catholics as 'wretched sons of perdition,' who had conspired against the Holy Ghost and the true successors of St. Peter, and he proceeded to excommunicate their newly-appointed head, Bishop Reinkens. But the Old Catholics, as in 'The Jackdaw of Rheims,' went on their way, 'not a penny the worse for this terrible curse.'

Two deaths of note occurred this year, which affected the Emperor not a little. King John of Saxony, a man of considerable culture, an able jurist, and a profound student of Dante, passed away in his seventy-second year. At one time his decease would have had more serious effects; but the existence of Saxony was now almost sunk in the German Empire. The King was succeeded by the Crown Prince,

Albert, who had greatly distinguished himself in the Franco-Prussian War. The second death was that of Elizabeth, Queen Dowager of Prussia, the widow of Frederick William IV. The Emperor felt the loss of his aged relative very keenly, for she had been a favourite with him. At the time of this melancholy occurrence, His Majesty himself was also somewhat seriously indisposed, but he was happily convalescent in the course of a few weeks.

The new year, 1874, was remarkable more for the energy and activity of the German Chancellor than for anything else. There was constant friction between himself and the Catholic party, and Prince Bismarck stood almost single-handed in the breach. Certainly, it was mainly his strong and overpowering personality which enabled him to gain his ends. The elections to the Imperial Diet, which took place early in the year, caused him some disappointment. The Centre or Ultramontane party increased in strength from sixty-two to about 100, so that altogether the opposition members numbered 170 as against some 400 supporters of the Government. The National Liberals rose from 116 to 150 members; the party of progress gained four new members; the Conservatives lost ground; and the Liberal National party disappeared entirely, being absorbed in the other sections.

Although both the Ultramontanes and the Social Democrats were opposed to the Chancellor's repressive ecclesiastical policy, it was supported as a necessity by nearly all the influential and liberal classes in Germany. Referring on one occasion to the ancient strife between Empire and Pope, when the latter was victorious, Bismarck had said, ' We will not go to Canossa; ' and he now took up the legislation with regard to the Catholics at the point at which it was left in 1873. It was necessary to supplement the Falck legislation by three additional Bills. The first simply explained certain terms which had been obscurely worded in the first laws, and had given rise to different interpretations in the law courts; but the second and third devised very practical measures for the administration of dioceses which might happen to be deprived of their bishops. The legislation was timely, for before many weeks had elapsed no fewer than four out of the twelve Roman Catholic bishops of the Prussian Kingdom came to a rupture with the Government.

Three of these dignitaries, Archbishop Ledochowski, the Archbishop of Cologne, and the Bishop of Treves were arrested and imprisoned for refusing to pay the fines imposed upon them for persistent contravention of the Falck Laws.

But as the incarceration of prelates could not continue for ever, and as it was necessary to adopt Imperial as well as Prussian legislation to meet the difficulty, a Bill was submitted to the Federal Council and the Reichstag, and passed during the spring session, to prevent the reassertion of their claims by offenders whose terms of imprisonment should be over. Such persons could be ordered by the administrative authorities of their several States to leave, or to take up their residence in certain districts. Should an offender still decline to conform to the law, the Government of his State should then be entitled to strip him of his right of citizenship, and to expel him from the territory of the German Empire. These provisions were to apply equally to persons who should have exercised the functions of an ecclesiastical office at variance with the law of the land, and had sentence pronounced against them for this offence by the proper court. The Imperial Diet passed this measure by the enormous majority of 257 votes to 95. Then came the Supplementary Falck Laws, which dealt with the question of appointments to vacant dioceses and parishes. It was decreed under certain conditions that Catholic congregations should be permitted to choose their own ministers, and thus to have a hand in the management of Church property. This appeared a very revolutionary change indeed to the Pope and the authorities of the Vatican.

The Imperial Parliament met in February, when a new Army Bill was brought forward. It was chiefly a systematic codification of the existing statutes, rendered necessary by the adoption of the Prussian laws in the minor States. A new scale of payment to the soldiers being adopted rendered necessary an additional sum of 14,000,000 thalers for the ensuing year. There were also other extras, which brought up the Military Budget to 113,000,000 thalers. The Bill placed the effective force of the army at 401,659 men in time of peace, and Count Moltke, in defending these measures, made some allusions to the prospect of peace or war as regarded foreign countries, which were eagerly commented upon throughout Europe. He pointed out that France had introduced compulsory service, lasting in all twenty years, instead of twelve as in Germany. The French Government was in a position to embody 1,200,000 men into the active, and 1,000,000 into the territorial army. After observing that Germany was pacifically disposed, but that the mildest of men might be dragged into a quarrel if he had a troublesome neighbour, Count Moltke said: 'If you wish for peace, be ready for war, and I believe that it is our duty, in the present condition of Europe, to declare either that we have no need of a strong army, or else to accord all that is necessary for maintaining it in full force.'

There was considerable difficulty with this Bill, which the Emperor strongly desired to see passed. He distinctly declined to accept certain compromises which were suggested, till at length Bismarck, foreseeing a complete deadlock, intervened. The Chancellor agreed to a suggestion made by Herr Bennigsen to the effect that the additional force required by the Government should be voted, but for seven years only and not for perpetuity. After much delay the Emperor at last yielded his assent to this, and the Bill was carried by a majority of eighty.

The affairs of Alsace-Lorraine next occupied the attention of the Diet. On the 16th of February, the Deputies for those provinces solemnly entered the House, two by two, and proceeded to deposit with the Speaker a motion to the effect that the Frankfort Treaty of Peace having been concluded without the sanction of the inhabitants of Alsace-Lorraine, the opinion of the latter should be taken on the subject. A lengthy debate ensued, and one of the Alsatian Deputies, while agreeing that Germany was entitled to a war indemnity from France, affirmed that the former had overstepped the limits by which a civilised nation ought to be bound in annexing Alsace-Lorraine. The Bishop of Strasburg, however, rose and said that he and his co-religionists in Alsace and Lorraine had no wish to question the validity of a treaty concluded between two of the great Powers of Europe. The motion was rejected by an overwhelming majority. Other antagonistic propositions were brought forward by the Alsatian Deputies, and at length, in consequence of their hostile attitude, the Government instructed the Alsatian authorities to avail themselves of the license allowed them under the statutes, of preventing the circulation in the province of such French journals as should advocate *revanche.*

Before the Imperial Diet was prorogued, a **Press Law** was passed, by which the police were to be deprived of the right of seizure previous to the condemnation of the indicted matter by the proper court of law. The clause declaring incitement to violate the laws a culpable offence was thrown out, as being too vaguely worded to appear safe. The practice of mentioning 'dummies' as responsible editors was by common consent heartily condemned, and was to be henceforth liable to a heavy fine. Alsace and Lorraine, in consequence of the attitude of the French press, were to be excepted from the operation of the law.

Prince Bismarck went to drink the waters at Kissingen in July, and while at that place he was the victim of an attempted assassination. His assailant was a young man named Kullmann, a journeyman cooper, ill-educated, and imbued with a fanatical hatred of the recent religious laws and their originator. At mid-day on the 13th, soon after the Chancellor had entered his carriage, and while he was in the act of saluting a person in the roadway, the latter drew a pistol from his pocket, and deliberately fired at the Prince. The bullet grazed the palm of the Chancellor's hand, just below the thumb. The coachman, fearing a second shot, struck the assassin across the face with the lash of his whip. The assailant then flung away the pistol and ran for his life. The Prince drove home perfectly calm and collected; but the wound in the hand caused him much pain for months afterwards. Kullmann was arrested after a desperate effort to escape. Bismarck visited him in prison and questioned him as to the reason for the crime. The culprit said his motives were revenge and hatred in consequence of the Ecclesiastical Laws. He did not appear to have any accomplices; but he had been incited to his reckless deed by the tone of the Ultramontane press and pulpit, and confessed that his immediate motive was what he had heard of the persecution of the Archbishop of Posen. Kullmann was sentenced to fourteen years' imprisonment.

Meanwhile, arrests of Roman Catholic priests for persistent infraction of the laws, and the sequestration of Church property, proceeded apace. In addition to the prelates previously named, Bishop Martin of Paderborn was arrested on

August 4. Declining to resign his see, he was prosecuted and deposed by the Government. Great manifestations of sympathy were shown him by the Westphalian Ultramontanes, and thirty ladies, including the Countess Nesselrode and the Countess von Merveldt, presented an address to him. The ladies were tried for this breach of the law, found guilty, and fined. Then came a demonstration of sympathy with these fair offenders from English Ultramontane ladies, including the Dowager Marchioness of Lothian and Lady Herbert of Lea, who went over to Münster to offer them their congratulations on ' suffering in the holy cause.' But the statesman with the iron hand went forward with his work.

The Emperor William opened the autumn session of the German Parliament on October 26. His Majesty said that important legislative labours awaited the Deputies. There were Bills forthcoming to secure unity of judicial procedure, and Bills for completing the Imperial military system. The most important of these, a measure for organising the *Landsturm*, was afterwards relegated to a committee. There was a Budget Bill for Alsace and Lorraine, and there were also measures, drawn up by the Federal Council, rendering Civil marriage obligatory throughout the Empire. A treaty establishing a postal union with Switzerland had been signed at Berne. His Majesty, in concluding his speech, spoke of the friendly relations of the Empire with foreign Powers, and said that the pacific intentions of his Government enabled it to disregard all unjust suspicions against its policy. This was an allusion to the action of certain French statesmen who, while their Government was professedly friendly with Germany, endeavoured to stir up the journals against her.

A very lively scene occurred in the Diet when the estimates came to be discussed for the Federal Council. The Chancellor —having been bitterly attacked by the Bavarian Clerical Deputy, Dr. Joerg— rose to reply, and replied to some purpose. After touching upon a recent intervention by Germany in Spain, as well as the relations she bore towards Russia, Prince Bismarck said: 'The preceding speaker alluded to the attempt on my life at Kissingen and designated Kullmann as a madman. He was not a madman. You don't want to have anything in common with Kullmann? That I comprehend ; but he clings tightly to your coat-tails nevertheless. I asked him myself, "Why did you wish to kill me, who had done nothing to you?" He replied, "On account of the Church Laws, and because you have insulted my fraction." I asked, "Which is your fraction?" And he answered, "The Centre fraction."' Here cheers and great tumult ensued. 'You may thrust Kullmann away,' cried the Prince, 'but he nevertheless belongs to you.'

This remark was received with thunders of applause by the Right and Left; but the Centre became wild with rage. 'Fie! fie!' they shouted, which is considered a very insulting expression in the German Parliament, and the President called the offending Deputies to order. Then Prince Bismarck added: 'I have no right to censure such exclamations as have been uttered by members on the second centre bench; but the expression *Pfui* (fie) is an expression of disgust and contempt. I am myself not a stranger to these feelings, but I am too polite to express them.' More uproar followed, with a passage at arms between Herr Windthorst and the Chancellor, after which the House broke up in the midst of bitter recriminations.

In consequence of the strained relations with the Vatican, the German Government resolved to suppress the post of envoy to the Pope. This led to another vehement debate, in the course of which the Catholic Deputies Joerg and Windthorst made a severe attack upon the foreign policy of Prince Bismarck. The Prince replied with equal energy, strongly censuring the Catholic party. The Chancellor's speech closed with these remarkable sentences: 'I am in possession of conclusive evidence proving that the war of 1870 was the combined work of Rome and France; that the Œcumenical Council was cut short on account of the war; and that very different votes would have been taken by the Council had the French been victorious. I know from the very best sources that the Emperor Napoleon was dragged into the war very much against his will by the Jesuitical influences rampant at his Court; that he strove hard to resist those influences; that in the eleventh hour he determined to maintain peace; that he stuck to this determination for half an hour; and that he was ultimately overpowered by persons representing Rome.' This speech was received with great satisfaction by a vast majority of the Deputies and the nation; and it is said that it produced a deeper and more lasting impression than any yet delivered by Prince Bismarck since the commencement of the conflict with the Church.

A great State trial drew the eyes of all Europe to Berlin towards the close of the year. The person implicated was a scion of the aristocracy, Count Harry von Arnim, who had formerly been an intimate friend of the German Chancellor. He had long been in the diplomatic service of Prussia, and had held posts of the highest distinction. Before the war of 1870 he was stationed at Rome, and after the conflict was appointed German ambassador at Paris. The Count was summoned from the French capital on the ground that he had not only openly expressed his dissent from the policy of Bismarck, but had even furnished to Austrian and Belgian journals articles attacking him. He was arrested on October 4, and further charged with having abstracted documents which he received in his official character as German ambassador in Paris.

The Count's trial began on the 9th of December in the City Court of Berlin. That tribunal found that on two heads of accusation—that of withholding papers acknowledged to be in his possession, and that of carrying off papers belonging to the Foreign Office—there was not evidence sufficient to make Count Arnim guilty on a criminal charge. But on the remaining count—that of taking with him from Paris to Carlsbad a series of despatches about ecclesiastical matters, which he said were not suited for the perusal of his successor at the Embassy—he was found guilty. The Court sentenced him to three months' imprisonment; but from this sentence both the Public Prosecutor and Count Arnim decided to appeal. The trial made it manifest that the Count had hoped, in concert with the Conservative and Catholic opponents of the Chancellor, to drive the latter from his high position, and to become his successor.

At this juncture, much to the dismay of the Court and the nation, Bismarck resigned the post of Chancellor. He probably took this step with the view of showing how dependent upon him Germany and Prussia were; and the trial had furnished additional evidence of his sagacity and powers of statesmanship. The immediate cause of his resignation was a vote of the Diet liberating one Majuncke, an

Ultramontane Deputy, who had been imprisoned for State offences. The Chancellor said he could not act if the Liberal party made common cause against him with his opponents. The Emperor absolutely declined to receive his resignation, however, and the Crown Prince paid him a special visit as a distinct mark of confidence. The Liberal party returned to their allegiance, and voted the Secret Service Fund of the Foreign Office as an emphatic mark of their confidence in the Chancellor. Thus, though hated by some of the Deputies, and the subject of plots against his life from without, the close of the year witnessed Bismarck stronger than ever, and more necessary to the Emperor and the State.

Progress was made with important legislation when the German Diet opened early in January, 1875. The Landsturm Bill was adopted by 198 against 54 votes. The effect of this new military measure was to extend the limits of liability for active service to all able-bodied Germans from between seventeen and forty-two years of age. The latter limit had previously been thirty-five years. The character of the Landsturm was also changed. It was now placed under the military law, and secured the protection which the law of nations confers in time of war upon organized armies in opposition to freeshooters. The Bill also facilitated the partial mobilization of the force. In the Landsturm the Diet created again the second ban King William gave up in 1860 under the more popular name connected with the days of the War of Independence. When the law came into operation, it was calculated that the disposable force of the German Empire would be raised to 2,800,000 men.

The Diet also passed a comprehensive measure extending the Civil registration of births, deaths, and marriages from Prussia to the whole Empire. This law made the services of the clergy superfluous in the three great domestic events of human life. Children could enter upon their career without having been baptized into any religious denomination whatsoever; marriages might be solemnized without the consent of the clergy, which was sometimes difficult to obtain in Catholic districts; and persons who had no recognised Christian belief or creed might be buried in consecrated ground. The bill also abolished clerical jurisdiction in suits for divorce, and it allowed Catholic priests, monks, and nuns to marry with impunity. Of course there was a great outcry in some quarters against what was termed 'godless' legislation.

The conflict between Empire and Papacy was again renewed with all its old bitterness. The Pope issued an Encyclical declaring the Falck Laws to be invalid and contrary to the Divine institution of the Church, and Bismarck replied by giving the Ultramontanes yet another stringent Falck measure. In March a Bill was brought before the Prussian Diet for withdrawing the State grants from Roman Catholic bishops. In justifying the action of the Government, Prince Bismarck said they were simply doing their duty in guarding the independence of the State and the nation against the oppression of Rome and the universal supremacy of the Order of Jesuits, and they were doing it with God for King and Fatherland. On the passing of the Bill, the Roman Catholic bishops presented a petition direct to the Emperor, attacking the ecclesiastical policy of the Chancellor. They appealed to the loyalty of the Catholics to the Prussian crown, and called upon his Majesty to deny his sanction to the proposed law. Again the bishops laid themselves open to an Imperial rebuff. Replying through his Ministers, the Emperor expressed astonishment and regret that the petitioners should assert it to be incompatible with Christian faith to comply with laws which in other States had been obeyed for centuries. The bishops were also told that they must have known that the measure to which they asked his Majesty to refuse his sanction could only have reached the Diet with his express consent. The grants would never have originally been made if the bishops and clergy had reserved to themselves the right to obey the laws of the State or not, as they thought fit, according to the Papal will. As to the confusion likely to be caused by the law, those prelates who in 1870, before the proclamation of the Vatican resolutions, saw that such confusion would arise from those resolutions, were reminded that by remaining true to the convictions they then expressed, they might have saved the Fatherland from the troubles which had since occurred.

But the priests went on remonstrating and ministers went on prosecuting, and the policy of the latter continued to gain ground. The States Grant Bill was triumphantly carried, and the Pope had himself to thank chiefly for this result.

His last Encyclical had been couched in tones so insulting to Germany that many Catholic Deputies, as well as members of the Upper House, openly condemned the conduct of the Vatican. It was remarked by one good Catholic that the Encyclical even exceeded in arrogance the dogma of infallibility, and that the Pope demanded in it a concession for a direct railway from Berlin to Canossa!

More ecclesiastical measures succeeded. One was passed for repealing articles 15, 16, and 18 of the Constitution. The first of these articles related to the independent administration of ecclesiastical affairs, and another to the unimpeded intercourse between religious associations and their superiors, while the other articles abolished the system by which appointments to clerical offices required the confirmation of the Government. The articles were obviously not in accordance with recent legislation, and therefore required to be repealed. The new Bill provided also that the legal position in the State of the Evangelical and Catholic Churches and other religious societies should be regulated in conformity with the new laws. Another Bill introduced struck at the alarming growth of Roman Catholic convents and religious establishments in Prussia. It was enacted that all religious orders and societies of the Catholic Church, having the character of Orders, should be excluded from the Prussian territory, and the establishment of branches of the same be prohibited, that existing branches should not be allowed to receive new members, and should be dissolved within six months, and that associations engaged in education might have the period within which they were to be dissolved extended to four years. This law was defended on several grounds, one being that the members of the various religious societies were passive instruments merely in the hands of their superiors, who were thereby empowered to destroy the basis of society, of the State, of the family, and of individual property. Bismarck was certainly fighting the battle with thoroughness, being convinced that he could not stop half-way in grappling with the evils which threatened the State.

Before the Prussian Diet closed it completed the work of district organization begun in a previous session. By an Act now carried through both Houses there was secured for Prussian citizens and corporations the right of appeal to independent judges, while the unity and impartiality of the proceedings was guaranteed through the institution of a supreme tribunal in Berlin. There would be a two-fold check upon arbitrary action on the part of the Government and its officials, through the prohibition of unlawful decrees, and through the superior judges, who would have power to rectify unlawful measures. The arbitrariness of bureaucratic action was thus rendered impossible under the new legislation.

As a pleasant contrast to heated debates in the Chambers, we find Berlin quite beside itself in May on the occasion of a visit by the Emperor of Russia to his Imperial uncle. The city was profusely decorated, and banquets and receptions were the order of the day. On the 11th a grand review was held at Potsdam, when upwards of 5000 men were drawn up in line in presence of the two Emperors, all the Princes and Princesses, the Grand Duke of Mecklenburg, and Field Marshals von Moltke and von Manteuffel. The Emperor William led the first regiment of the Guards, and the Emperor of Russia rode at the head of the Alexandra Regiment. As the review ended, the Emperor Alexander, placing himself again at the head of his regiment, ordered it, as a mark of homage, to present arms before the Emperor William, upon which that venerable potentate, overcome with emotion, pressed the hand of his Imperial guest. The two Sovereigns then embraced in presence of the thousands of assembled spectators, who burst into enthusiastic cheers. The Czar's visit closed on the 13th, when the Emperor William bade his nephew an affectionate farewell.

This meeting of Sovereigns was not without its political significance. There was a war scare on in Europe, in consequence of the friction between Germany and France and a closer approximation between Austria and Italy. The Czar and Great Britain were most desirous to preserve peace, and the former journeyed to Berlin with that object. In this he was successful, for, on receiving the Diplomatic Body just before leaving the Prussian capital, the Emperor Alexander told the representatives of the Powers that peace was ensured.

Several celebrations of deep interest to Germans took place in the summer and autumn. On the 18th of June, which was the second centenary anniversary of the battle of Fehrbellin, the foundation-stone of a monument to the

'Great Elector,' Frederick William, was laid by his namesake, the Imperial Crown Prince. 'May this stone,' said the Prince, 'which we to-day deposit in the soil, and the monument to be erected on this spot, be a witness to remote posterity of the sentiment which has always united my House and our people! The monument must remind us of a time when our State was still small and hardly known. By trust in God, and by always doing our duty towards our narrower and our larger country, we have now reached the point of having the destinies of Germany placed in our hands for the well-being and prosperity of the Fatherland.' Then, unsheathing his sword, the Prince exclaimed, 'With this feeling, I will call on you to cry, "Long live his Majesty the Emperor and King!"'

The Emperor himself was present at Detmold, on the 16th of August, when the heroic statue to Hermann, the first and ancient liberator of the German tribes, was unveiled. The monument had been thirty-seven years in building, and Ernst von Bandel, the sculptor, who had planned the work as a student, had grown grey while he executed it. The Emperor warmly grasped the artist by the hand, and congratulated him upon his success, and he was given a seat with the Princes and Princesses. At night bonfires were made, which vividly lit up the colossal and noble figure of Hermann, who, with uplifted sword, looked upon the battlefield of nineteen centuries ago. Nor was Baron Stein, the maker of modern Prussia, forgotten. A statue in his honour was subsequently erected on the Döhnhofsplatz in Berlin. The Emperor was unable to be present from indisposition, and Count von Moltke, who performed the ceremony, gave the signal for cheering by exclaiming, 'Long live his Majesty the Emperor!'

Returning to European questions, that there was now no danger of a rupture between Germany and Italy was proved by a visit which the Emperor William paid to King Victor Emmanuel at Milan in October. On several occasions during this visit, asseverations of close friendship were made. At a grand banquet given by the King to the Emperor on the 19th, the latter said, in reply to the toast of his health, which had been most warmly received, 'I am deeply moved by the reception I have met with on the part of your Majesty, and in this beautiful country. I know that the sympathy existing between Germany and Italy, and the personal relations of friendship so happily subsisting between us, will continue to be a guarantee for the preservation of the peace of Europe. I feel a pleasure in hoping that these relations will always remain the same, and it is with this wish I drink the health of your Majesty.'

In the autumn session of the German Diet the question was raised of a gradual European disarmament. Austria, France, and Italy had been sounded upon the subject. It was not intended to propose the dissolution of all standing armies, but merely to reduce the number of soldiers actually under arms, which, in proportion to the productive powers of the several countries, had attained a fearful height. Nothing definite was done in connection with the subject; but it was obvious that the German Parliament was in favour of military curtailment, inasmuch as it persistently refused to sanction any augmentation of the military estimates, notwithstanding the urgent remonstrances of the Minister of War. By way of showing the expensiveness of the British army, we may mention that while the total army and navy estimates of Germany were only £20,000,000 for 1,700,000 men, the estimates for the English army and navy were £24,800,000 for 535,000 men. Austria, too, had precisely the same number of men as England, and her expenditure was only £10,800,000. The whole of the armies of Europe, when on a war footing, numbered 9,333,000 men, with the prodigious annual cost of £136,804,000.

One of the most memorable incidents in 1876 was a visit which Queen Victoria paid to Germany. Her Majesty stopped at Coburg, where she had an interview with the Emperor William. The purpose of this visit was asserted to be the regulation of the succession to the throne of Saxe-Coburg, Prince Alfred (the Duke of Edinburgh) being prospective heir to the Duke, who had no children. While at Coburg, the Queen was also visited by the Crown Princess of Germany, with some of her children.

Prince Bismarck moved for a second time this year against Count Harry Arnim, who had evaded his previous sentence by leaving the country. He was now tried in connection with the publication of a pamphlet entitled *Pro Nihilo,* which created a great sensation, and which contained alleged false statements against the Emperor and his Government.

It further made known to the detriment of the State what was entrusted to the Count in official confidence. The Chancellor was more embittered than ever against his adversary. A more serious prosecution having now been instituted, the trial ended on October 12, when Count Arnim was found guilty by the High Court of State on the charges of betraying his country, offending the Emperor, and insulting Prince Bismarck and the Foreign Office. He was sentenced to five years' penal servitude—a terrible sentence to a man in the Count's position.

The German Parliament passed the Penal Code Amendment Bill this year, and finally completed the Judicial Law, by which considerable progress was made towards the desired end of national legal unity. Prince Bismarck also brought forward a daring proposition for the acquisition of all the German railways by the State; but it was so strongly opposed by the Southern States, that the bill founded upon his motion had to be restricted to Prussia alone.

The great event of the year 1877 was the Russo-Turkish war; but Germany was not involved in the conflict, and the year so far as she was concerned was one of comparative quietude and peace. The 1st of January being the seventieth anniversary of the beginning of the Emperor William's military career, his Majesty, in commemoration thereof, held a reception of the officers of the German army. The Crown Prince delivered an address to his Imperial father and Sovereign, and spoke of him as the type of all soldierly virtues, and the creator of the military organization which had consolidated Prussia and raised Germany to her former greatness. The German army was at once the defender of the Fatherland and guardian of freedom and unity. The organization introduced by the Emperor had enabled Prussia to fulfil its mission, and in the last terrible war it became the common property of the nation.

The Emperor, who was visibly moved, thus replied: 'If all the gentlemen, whose presence here to-day affords me especial pleasure, agree with the sentiments expressed by my son, I may esteem myself all the more happy, and I first tender you my thanks on that account. As I look back upon the day when I entered the army, I cannot but remember the state of affairs which then existed, and therefore from the moment when my father's hand led me into the army, and throughout my life, up to the pleasurable occasion afforded me to-day, my first thought has been to give humble thanks to the Arbiter of our destinies. My position has led to the greater part of my life being devoted to the army. My gratitude is consequently due to all those who have accompanied me in my military career and seconded my efforts. I always remember them with pleasure. I have to thank the valour, devotion, and constancy of the army for the position which I now occupy. From Fehrbellin to the last gloriously-ended war, the deeds of the Brandenburg-Prussian army are enrolled imperishably in the annals of the world's history. Prussia has become what she is chiefly through the army. I beg those who represent the army in my presence to-day to convey to all in the ranks my personal thanks, which they well merit, as I have been able to convince myself for a long time past of the sentiments and spirit by which the army is animated—a spirit which, in conjunction with that of the German troops, has been successful in creating a United Germany and a united army.'

As the Emperor's remark that his own position and that of Prussia were largely due to the army was perfectly true, it is of interest to note here the invention of the Krupp gun, which was perfected at this time. It was a formidable affair, as the French or any others who might attack Germany could easily find out for themselves. By this gun Herr Krupp completely revolutionised the whole system of fortification and siege operations. It had a fixed shield to prevent recoil, and in this lay its novelty and advantage. As there was no recoil, the gun remained steady, and no fresh aim was required. The result was that the guns could be fired very rapidly, and an experiment demonstrated that sixty shots could be fired in fifteen minutes.

The elections to the German Reichstag again proved less favourable to the Government. In the previous Parliament they had an absolute majority of 100, but now it was reduced to 80. The Ultramontanes lost considerably at the polling booths, while there was a considerable Conservative reaction, as well as a notable growth in the Socialist vote. During the session a Bill was passed transferring the right to legislate for Alsace-Lorraine from the German to the Alsace Parliament. The Reichstag also decided that the seat of the

Supreme Tribunal of Germany should be at Leipsic, and not at Berlin as desired by the Prussian Minister of Justice.

Great rejoicings throughout Germany marked the Emperor's 80th birthday, which occurred on the 22nd of March. From an early hour, as stated by the *Times'* correspondent in Berlin, congratulatory letters, bouquets, corn-flour wreaths, oak-leaf garlands, and other numerous gifts poured in at the Imperial Palace. Though there were many hundreds of written and telegraphic addresses, the Emperor opened them all with his own hand, and in many instances sent immediate telegraphic replies. By nine o'clock, all the windows of the Palace were adorned with birthday bouquets, and the Emperor now and then appeared behind the fragrant rampart to bow to the cheering multitude in the square. As usual on festive occasions, the ancient standard of the Holy Roman Empire floated over the Imperial Palace. The Crown Prince and Princess, with the Royal children, waited upon their beloved father and grandfather to offer him their congratulations. They were succeeded by the Princes and Princesses of the blood, and after these illustrious personages came the Court, the Ambassadors, Ministers, Generals, Envoys, and Federal and Parliamentary deputations.

The Emperor went to the old Palace at three o'clock, where the German Sovereigns, represented by the Grand Duke of Baden, the King of Saxony, the Grand Duke of Mecklenburg, and the Grand Duke of Saxe, were already assembled. His Majesty was presented with a huge oil painting, by Werner, commemorating King William's proclamation as German Emperor at Versailles on the 17th of January, 1871. In presenting this historical picture, which contains several hundred portraits, the King of Saxony said: 'The day on which your Majesty celebrates your eightieth birthday, in unimpaired vigour and health, has been selected by the German Sovereigns and Republics to express their joy at this happy event, and their attachment to your Imperial Majesty. This painting represents one of the most important occurrences in the history of Germany, and in the eventful life of your Imperial Majesty. It perpetuates the moment when your Majesty, complying with the expressed desire of the German Sovereigns and Republics, revived the Imperial dignity lost to our nation at a period of French usurpation. Your Majesty by this act sanctioned the result of our common struggles and victories. If we may add a wish, it is this: that your Majesty may reign in undisturbed peace for many years to come over the Empire re-established on the battlefield. May God grant it!'

There were few Germans, official or otherwise, who did not celebrate this auspicious event. The various sections of the German Parliament dined together in amity, and all the Ministers received. Divine Service was held in the churches, and addresses delivered in all public and private schools. Every city and town in the Empire had its congratulatory celebrations. The Emperor scarcely knew what to give Prince Bismarck on this occasion, but he bestowed upon him and his heirs the hereditary title of Pomeranian Master of the Hunt. Dr. Lauer, his Majesty's physician, was created a Privy Councillor and granted the title of Excellency, which the Emperor jocularly told him years before should be his if he made him an octogenarian. The most interesting of the numerous presents received by the Emperor were an engraving and a book, the former executed by Prince Henry, and the latter bound by Prince Waldemar, the younger sons of the Crown Prince. It is a custom with the dynasty that each of its Princes should learn a craft. The Emperor, for example, is a glazier, and the Crown Prince a compositor.

A few days after these rejoicings, there was another acute Chancellor crisis. Bismarck had had some difficulty with General Stosch, Chief of the Admiralty, and as the Prince was in ill-health, and had sustained more official friction than he could well bear, he tendered his resignation on the 1st of April, and asked for permission to retire immediately. A medical certificate was put in, showing that the Chancellor's continuance in office would be seriously prejudicial to his health, and might endanger his life. But the Emperor would not listen to Bismarck's resignation; he would grant him four months' leave of absence instead; and after much negotiation this settlement of the difficulty was agreed upon. The Prince retired until August; Herr Hofmann, President of the Imperial Chancery, took his place in the Department of Home Affairs; Herr von Bülow went to the Department of Foreign Affairs; and Herr Camphausen represented him in the Prussian Cabinet.

The Emperor William paid a visit to his new dominions of Alsace and Lorraine in May, arriving at Strasburg on the

1st. In reply to an address from the Alsace-Lorraine Committee, he urged the wisdom of resignation. The middle classes were very enthusiastic in their reception of his Majesty; but the upper and lower classes rather held aloof; nevertheless, the Kaiser expressed himself agreeably surprised at his cordial reception; and it was said that nothing to be compared with the festive celebration was ever witnessed in Strasburg under the French régime. No expense was spared to make the Emperor's visit successful, and every facility was afforded to the peasantry to come into the capital and enjoy themselves. The cathedral was splendidly illuminated. Metz refused to be pacified, however; the Town Council would vote no money for the Emperor's reception, and as the cathedral was injured by the German illuminations, a sullen feeling was created amongst the inhabitants.

The first week of the following September was called the 'Kaiser week,' as it was given up to celebrations and festivities at Dusseldorf, Darmstadt, Cologne, &c. On the 8th the Emperor arrived at Benrath Castle, the seat of the hereditary Prince of Hohenzollern, nine miles from Dusseldorf. On his way he visited the famous establishment of Krupp at Essen, where he witnessed the performances of the great hammer 'Fritz' on a mass of glowing metal weighing 37½ tons, which was to be the core of a thousand-pound cannon. An English correspondent wrote :—

'The Emperor attended the Sedan festival at Essen, dined at the villa of Herr Krupp, and afterwards conferred a decoration upon him. Monday was the day of the Kaiser parade, when all the world and his wife assembled at the inspection field, a wide stretch of sand about three miles north of the town. The Emperor and Empress, Crown Prince and Princess, with their eldest daughter, Princes Carl, Frederick Charles, and Albert, Field Marshals Moltke and Manteuffel, the Grand Dukes of Mecklenburg, Sachsen, Oldenburg, the Princes of Wied, Lippe, Schaumburg, &c., arrived at the field about ten o'clock. The Crown Princess was in the uniform of her Hussar regiment. There was a very large staff of foreign officers, from Great Britain, France, Austria, Italy, Russia, Sweden, and a dusky Major from Japan. Our own country sent the largest contingent, consisting of Lord Airey, the Duke of Manchester, Colonels Wilkinson, Graham, &c. The troops inspected consisted of the Seventh Army

Corps, eight regiments of infantry and one of rifles, the cuirassier regiment, two of Hussars, one of Lancers, and two batteries of field artillery, with a train battalion. They marched past first in companies, then in brigades, the artillery, according to German fashion, coming last. The marching of the infantry was said to be very good, and the cavalry seemed in excellent condition. Besides the regular troops, 18,000 in number, there were at least as many old soldiers on the field, with the flags and insignia of their Krieger-Vereine, who towards the close forgot all discipline and completely mobbed their old leader. During the week the Empress and Crown Prince have visited the studios of the principal artists, the picture galleries, and hospitals and public schools. And the army of regular troops was nothing in comparison with the invading host of enthusiastic Germans which has streamed into the town from every quarter. On the day of the Emperor's triumphal progress through the illuminated streets, it is reckoned that 300,000 strangers thronged the thoroughfares, and although trains were despatched in rapid succession throughout the night, daylight found thousands the next morning still in the streets. Such scenes were repeated below Cologne, then in Baden, and lastly at Darmstadt.'

Though eighty years of age, the Emperor was as vigorous as many men at half his age, and he relaxed few of his ordinary occupations and amusements. In the autumn he went upon his usual shooting excursion into Silesia. A contemporary observed that he ' usually arrives with the invited guests the evening before the *battue*, and proceeds to the hunting castle of Königswusterhausen, where, after supper, during which the finest horn-music from Berlin is always played, the whole company assembles as a smoking college, in the same hall in which it was held at the time of Frederick William I. This hall, in the second storey of the castle, is decorated with stags' horns, and stuffed boars' heads, being trophies of animals killed by the Emperor William. It contains the same peculiar chairs and the long oaken table which were in use there 170 years ago. There the merry company relate amusing hunting stories, drink beer out of old earthenware mugs, and smoke Turkish tobacco out of long Dutch clay-pipes till a late hour, just as it was in the days of Frederick William I.'

The Prussian Diet was considerably exercised in October and November owing to the non-fulfilment of the Government promises to complete the work of administrative reform throughout the provinces. Prince Bismarck had not returned to Berlin for the opening of the Diet, owing to differences with Ministers, it was believed, on certain Church questions. But several speakers of the Opposition declared that he never meant to carry out his promises in the former direction, and that administrative reform was a dead letter. The season closed leaving this and other matters, as well as the *personnel* of the Ministry, in a very unsatisfactory condition.

On the 1st of November there passed away Field Marshal Count Wrangel, in the ninety-fourth year of his age. He was the oldest soldier in the Prussian service, and was familiarly known as ' Papa Wrangel.' He was present in the commencement of his career at the battle of Leipsic, and his last military service was in 1864, when he commanded at the beginning of the second Danish campaign, and was created a Count. When very ill, the old hero declined to keep his bed; he would persist in lying on a sofa in full uniform, saying that a soldier must always hold himself in readiness to wait on his Sovereign, should he be summoned by him. It is such tough customers as Count Wrangel who are the strength of Prussia. The Emperor attended the old warrior's funeral obsequies in Berlin (though he was really buried at Stettin), following on foot a portion of the way. His participation in the procession was a very unusual mark of respect, as the etiquette is that Sovereigns should only follow Sovereigns or widows of Sovereigns.

Socialism had long caused the German Government deep anxiety and concern, and in 1878 it became necessary to take some active steps for its suppression. The immediate cause for this was an attempted assassination of the Emperor. While driving along Unter den Linden on the 11th of May, a man came up behind the carriage, and fired twice at the Emperor. The aged monarch was heard to exclaim, ' Is it possible that those shots are intended for me?' The assassin, who was now in the crowd, fired two more shots before he could be secured. He proved to be one Heinrich Max Hödel, a man of no importance, who had thought to foist himself into notoriety by his action. Hödel was brought to trial and executed. The German nation showed its joy over the

Emperor's escape by numberless addresses of congratulation, and amongst the most gratifying of foreign messages was one from Marshal Macmahon, President of the French Republic.

In consequence of the Hödel attempt, the Government introduced in the Reichstag an Anti-Socialist Bill of a very stringent character. It was strongly opposed by Bismarck's own friends, the National Liberals, Herr Von Bennigsen making a very effective onslaught upon it, and Dr. Lasker showing that, if passed, the Bill would either not work at all, or would have to be extended considerably beyond its present scope. The Government sustained a disastrous defeat, the bill being rejected by 251 to only 57 votes. The measure was withdrawn, and the Parliamentary session prematurely closed.

But Bismarck soon found plenty of ground for a war against the Socialists. On the 2nd of June, which was Sunday, a far more serious attack than Hödel's was made upon the Emperor. The details were thus given in a notification issued by the Berlin Prefect of Police: ' As the Emperor was passing through the street Unter den Linden, at about three o'clock in the afternoon, two shots were fired from the second floor of the house No. 18, Unter den Linden, and His Majesty was struck in several places. The assassin is Karl Edouard Nobiling, a doctor of philology and an agriculturist; he was born on April 10, 1848, at Kollno, near Birnbaum, has been living in Berlin during the last two years, and has resided at No. 18, Unter den Linden since the beginning of January last. Immediately after the deed was committed, the would-be assassin was seized, and is now under arrest. The two shots at the Emperor were fired by him from the window of a room on the second floor with a double-barrelled gun loaded with shot. On being arrested he inflicted severe wounds upon himself in the head, after first firing with a ready loaded revolver upon the persons who forced their way into his room. Nobiling confesses his crime, but absolutely refuses to make any statement as to the motives which induced him to commit it. The Emperor, according to a bulletin which has been issued, is wounded by about thirty small shot in the face, head, both arms, and the back.'

Unparalleled excitement prevailed in Berlin when the news spread from one quarter to another. The Emperor, who was alone, was driven back to the Palace and conveyed to bed, where a careful examination was made of his wounds. Some thirty grains of small shot were extracted, and then the operation was suspended, as the wounds caused the skin and muscles to swell. His Majesty was quite calm and composed throughout, and in the interval sent a message to the Shah of Persia regretting his inability to dine with him as previously arranged. It appears that Nobiling, who was a very young man, had been refused employment in the Ministry of Agriculture. He was a gentleman of a good military family, cultivated, and well to do, belonging to one of the darker Socialist sects. He died of his self-inflicted wounds. The Emperor gradually recovered, but during the time he was incapacitated the Crown Prince assumed the functions of Government, and discharged them during the Congress of Berlin, which was just about to assemble. When the Congress met to discuss the Eastern Question, England was represented by Lords Beaconsfield and Salisbury, and under the treaty which was concluded England acquired the island of Cyprus.

Prince Bismarck, in consequence of Nobiling's attempt upon the life of the Emperor, obtained the consent of the Federal Council to dissolve Parliament. The new elections were held on the 30th of July, and the supplementary elections on August 17th. Every effort was made to defeat the Socialists, and although they polled larger numbers they returned fewer members. The following were the final returns : 60 German Imperialists, 50 Conservatives, 97 National Liberals, 99 Ultramontanes, 25 Progressists, 15 Poles, 9 Guelphs, 9 Social Democrats, 3 South German Democrats, 4 Alsatian Autonomists, 6 Alsatian Protesters, 1 Dane, and 19 Independents, most of whom, however, were in sympathy with the Liberals. The Conservatives largely increased their strength as compared with the last Parliament, while the Liberals were greatly weakened ; and the Socialists only returned nine members instead of their previous twelve.

The Emperor's speech, which was read by deputy at the opening of the German Diet on the 9th of September, dealt chiefly with the attempts made upon His Majesty's life, and the Anti-Socialist bill prepared by the Government, which was shortly to be laid before the House. Hope was confidently expressed that the newly-elected Deputies would not refuse to grant the means of giving the peaceful development of the Empire the same security against attacks from within as it enjoyed against those from without; that the spread of the pernicious Socialist movement would be arrested; and that those who had been led away by it might be brought back to the right path. When the Anti-Socialist Bill was introduced on the 10th, Count Stolberg, as spokesman for the Government, admitted that the measure was one of great severity, but added that half measures would only do harm. The Ultramontane party opposed the bill, and recommended its reference to a select committee. Bebel, a Socialist member, delivered an able speech and denied that there was any connection between social democracy and the crimes of Hödel and Nobiling. Prince Bismarck vindicated himself from the reproach of having formerly courted the Socialists. Admitting his intimacy with Lassalle, he said that that prominent Socialist was deeply imbued with national and even with monarchical principles.

The bill was ultimately referred to a committee of 21 members. When the measure some time afterwards came back for its third reading it seemed to be in considerable danger. The Chancellor, however, flung himself into the breach, and asked the Deputies whether they were more afraid of him and of the Federal Government than of the Socialists; and he admitted that his aim went beyond the present measure, for he wished to unite parties in order to form a bulwark against all tempests to which the empire was exposed. The bill passed by 221 votes to 149. By this measure it was left to the authorities to decide what Socialist and Communist doctrines were, who Socialist and Communist writers were, and to take the most peremptory measures for their suppression. The bill came into force immediately, and four clubs in Berlin and a large number of publications were at once suppressed by the police. In other places it was as promptly and rigorously enforced.

The Emperor had so far recovered that on the 26th of September, together with the Empress and the Crown Prince, he attended the inauguration, at Cologne, of the monument to Frederick William III., the Emperor's father; it was under this sovereign that the Rhine province was added to Prussia in 1815. After an absence of three months from the capital, His Majesty returned to Berlin on the 5th of December. Shortly before his arrival, the Minister of State notified, under the Anti-Socialist Act, that for one year no person suspected of designs on the public safety would be permitted to reside in Berlin, Charlottenburg, Potsdam, or the neighbourhood; that the carrying of arms, except by soldiers or licensed persons, was prohibited; that no explosive projectiles might be sold or carried; and that 'permits' to carry arms would be granted only by the police. In resuming the reins of Government the Emperor issued an order publicly thanking the Crown Prince for the services he had rendered during six important months. Before the close of the year, 45 incriminated newspapers and 171 associations had been suppressed, and 150 books and pamphlets prohibited. The difficulties of another character with the Papacy had not been adjusted, it having been found impossible as yet to establish a *modus vivendi* between the Romish Church and the German Government.

A painful sensation was created throughout Germany by the terrible collision which occurred on the 31st of·May, between two German ironclads, the *Grosser Kurfürst* and the *König Wilhelm*. While advancing in two columns with another vessel up channel, the German squadron met two sailing vessels, to avoid which the *Grosser Kurfürst* had to give way, and consequently ported her helm. The *König Wilhelm*, which was steering parallel with the *Grosser Kurfürst*, endeavoured to pass one of the sailing vessels, but finding there was not time, put her helm hard-a-port, and came into collision with the *Grosser Kurfürst*, which, having resumed her original course, was now lying right across the bows of the *König Wilhelm*. The latter vessel struck the other between the main and mizen masts, and inflicted such injuries upon her that she sank in about eight minutes, with all on board. Every possible assistance was rendered in saving the men, but the boats on one side of the *Grosser Kurfürst* had been swept away, and those on the other side could not be got at. The Folkestone fishing fleet, which was passing, rendered valuable service, and saved between eighty and ninety lives. Out of a total crew of 497, however, only 216 were rescued, and three afterwards died from exhaustion. The *König Wilhelm* made into Portsmouth Harbour. The Emperor and all the members of the Imperial family were much moved on learning this disastrous news, and instituted minute inquiries into the catastrophe.

The Parliamentary history of the year 1879 was notable chiefly for two things—an announcement by Prince Bismarck of a startling change of political view, and the collapse of the National Liberal party. The Chancellor exhibited a spirit of opportunism in the foreign relations of Germany, and a spirit of reaction in home politics. Alarmed by the spread of Socialism and Rationalism, he resolved to abandon the National Liberal party, which had been largely his own creation, and under which he had ruled for ten years past. The time had now come when he must choose between his old supporters and the work—as he read it—of preserving and consolidating the interests of the Empire. Several incidents precipitated a declaration on the Chancellor's part of his new departure. The German Reichsrath unanimously refused permission to the Government to imprison two Socialist deputies who returned to Berlin after their expulsion; the clerical and Conservative press rejoiced over the disintegration of the National Liberal party; and three important members of the Government—Herr Hobrecht, Minister of Finance, Dr. Falck, Minister of Public Worship, and Herr Friedenthal, Minister of Agriculture, tendered their resignation. Bismarck's acceptance of these resignations was in itself significant, and on the 9th of July he openly announced his separation from the National Liberal party, and his adherence to the Clerical-Conservative coalition. The statement fell like a thunderbolt upon German and European Liberals, for it signified an abandonment of all progressive ideas affecting free trade, liberty of speech, education, liberty of the press, &c. Various reasons were given for this change of front, but Bismarck has been a statesman who could always look a long way ahead, and his real object now was to dissever himself from any political party and to stand alone, putting forward as his one end and aim the superiority of Germany as a whole. When the elections came on in October, the National Liberals were scattered as chaff before the wind, losing no fewer than one hundred seats, and amongst the rejected was their able leader, Dr. Lasker.

In the meantime the campaign against the Socialists was pushed vigorously forward. The measures of the Government were unquestionably hard and cruel in many instances, but they were successful—far more successful than Russia's repressive policy against Nihilism. It is said that when the Anti-Socialist Law finally passed, Bismarck chuckled and rubbed his hands, exclaiming, 'Now for the pig sticking.' By the end of 1879 there had already been issued 457 injunctions under the 'pig-sticking' law. Of these, 189 were to clubs and societies; 58 were to periodical publications, and 210 to non-periodical publications. The liberty of the press and of speech in Parliament were both curtailed.

The Government now abandoned the policy of free trade, for the Chancellor professed to be guided by the interests of the country and not by abstract principles. At least that was his boast. At the close of February, speaking in the debate on the Commercial Treaty with Austria, Bismarck said that the necessity for protecting home industries must be considered in every such engagement, although he was not altogether opposed to commercial treaties. But he frankly added that 'he had no wish to deny that he had changed his views in regard to commercial policy.' The Government in fact had reverted to the system of Protection. The Chancellor, having abandoned his old allies the Liberals, now relied upon the Agrarians, Protectionists, Ultramontanes and the Conservatives generally throughout Germany. Dr. Windthorst became a supporter of the Ministry, and an Ultramontane was elected Vice-President of the Reichstag. No wonder that the clericals exulted over these things, asserting that after all the man of 'blood and iron' had taken his first step towards Canossa. As the result of Bismarck's *volte-face* the Corn Duties were passed by 226 to 109, and a protective tariff and tariff law was passed in July, after a three months' debate, by 217 to 117 votes.

At the ensuing Prussian elections the Government secured a great victory. The Conservatives of all shades returned numbered 170, or more than double their previous strength; the Ultramontanes numbered 95, a gain of 6; National Liberals 97, a loss of 78; Liberals 17; Progressists 34, a loss of 34; Poles, 18; Danes, 2; Guelph, 1; Social Democrat, 1; and Christian Democrat, 1. As 217 was a majority of the whole House, the Conservatives only required the aid of fifty Ultramontane votes to command a working majority, and of this support they were practically assured. The Chancellor was again able to ride the storm, and to smile at the anger and opposition of those who cried, 'Away with him!' So far from going under, when confronted with apparently insuperable difficulties, 'he had reappeared on a higher vantage ground than ever, supported by the overwhelming majority of the German nation, and subsequently indefinitely reinforced by the moral and political support of the Austrian Empire.' The minister had forsaken the *Kulturkampf*, but not before it had struck its roots deeply into the German soil. This *Kulturkampf* 'was the resultant of the spontaneous development of both German Protestant, and Catholic education, fostered and cherished by all the German powers great and small, ever since the battle of Jena. It was this general educational impulse which led without bloodshed to the consolidation of Germany. It was no sudden creation of Prince Bismarck's: generations of German statesmen and German patriots had prepared the instrument to his hands.'

With regard to Germany's relations towards the Vatican, the accession of the new Pope Leo XIII. had been viewed with disfavour by the Ultramontanes but with complacency by the German Government. Under no circumstances would Bismarck relax his hostility to that party, which set at naught the supremacy of the civil authority, yet within proper limits he was far from being averse to the conclusion of a peace with Rome. But this was not yet in sight.

One of the most important measures adopted by the German Parliament was that for finally regulating the Government of Alsace-Lorraine. The question had given rise to several discussions, and the Emperor was desirous of bringing the matter to a conclusion. After his satisfactory visit to the conquered provinces, His Majesty had written that 'it confirmed him in the belief that the intelligent efforts of the Government and the growing confidence of the population would soon join Alsace and Lorraine with Germany in indissoluble bonds.' Prince Bismarck brought forward the expected regulation bill on the 15th of May. It was adopted almost in its entirety, and passed on June 23 by a unanimous vote of all parties, except that of the French section. It was duly signed by the Emperor, and an Imperial decree was issued ordering that the law should go into operation on October 1st. By this measure Alsace-

Lorraine remained an Imperial possession, and became virtually a federal state, of which the Emperor of Germany as such, and not in his capacity of King of Prussia, is the ruler. The Emperor appoints a Stadtholder, who resides in Strasburg, and may at any time be recalled. The Stadtholder does not exercise the functions of the Sovereign, but merely those which were hitherto exercised with regard to the Reichsland by the Imperial Chancellor and by the Lord-Lieutenant of Alsace-Lorraine. A ministry was to be constituted, and the State was to have a representative in the Federal Council, but no vote. General E. F. von Manteuffel was appointed first Stadtholder of the Reichsland.

The Emperor's speech from the throne at the opening of the Diet had made some references to the northern part of Schleswig. This had long been a vexed question, but a treaty between Austria and Prussia was now ratified which effected a settlement. Article V. of the treaty of Prague was altered to read—'His Majesty the Emperor of Austria transfers to His Majesty the King of Prussia all his rights to the Duchies Holstein and Schleswig acquired by the Peace of Vienna of October 30, 1864.' The provision that the Northern Districts of Schleswig should be ceded to Denmark if a vote of the people indicated their desire for this, was abolished. As the Emperor stated in his speech, his Government had failed in repeated attempts to settle the question with Denmark, and meanwhile the people affected by the promise were kept in uncertainty. The Schleswig-Holstein dispute was thus finally set at rest.

The German Government at this time paid great attention to its navy, and by the Samoan treaty and other measures showed its intention to protect, and possibly to promote, the extension of German commerce, now rapidly and legitimately extending along the sea-board of the world. One incident in connection with the navy which brought up mournful recollections was the court martial apppointed to inquire into the cause of the Folkestone disaster to the *Grosser Kurfürst*. Rear-Admiral Batsch was sentenced to imprisonment in a fortress for six months, and Captain Klauser to one month, while Captain Kühne was acquitted. Admiral Batsch was afterwards pardoned by the Emperor.

It is worthy of note that a universal Judicature Act was promulgated within three or four years of the Constitution of the German Empire. Other kingdoms and empires have failed to achieve such a vast legal reform in the course of centuries; but in 1879 the twenty-seven States of which Germany is composed, together with a variety of legally independent provinces, saw put into force a universal and compulsory Imperial Judicature Act. And during the session which witnessed the passing of this Act, a second very important measure was carried for the acquisition of all the railways, under certain conditions, by the State.

Many incidents of a personal interest, partly pleasurable and partly sad, occurred during the year in connection with the Emperor William and his family. On the 13th of March there was celebrated at Windsor the marriage of the Duke of Connaught with Princess Louise Marguerite of Prussia, daughter of Prince Frederick Charles. The Crown Prince represented the Emperor and Empress at the ceremony, which was attended by Her Majesty Queen Victoria and all the members of the Royal family. The 'Red Prince' gave his daughter away, the Prince of Wales produced the wedding-ring, and, after the nuptial knot had been tied, the Queen warmly embraced the bride.

Only a few days subsequent to this joyous ceremony there was mourning in the German Imperial Court. Prince Waldemar of Prussia, third son of the Crown Prince, and grandson of Queen Victoria, died on March 27 at Berlin, in his eleventh year, of heart disease. The attack began on March 24, when the symptoms were apparently those of a slight attack of diphtheria. No grave apprehensions were entertained until the night of the 26th, when the Prince suddenly became worse, and he died at half-past three on the following morning. The young Prince was a great favourite with his Imperial grandfather.

No little concern was caused by three several accidents which occurred to the Emperor himself during the year. On the 7th of March he was walking along a waxed floor in the palace at Berlin when he slipped down and slightly bruised himself. He passed a quiet night, and was able to transact business the next day. It subsequently transpired, however, that His Majesty lost consciousness for a few moments when he fell, and had to be assisted up by his attendants. The Emperor's medical advisers recommended him to spend a little time at Wiesbaden. On the 2nd of

June, while walking in the Babelsburg Palace, he again slipped, and in his fall injured the knee-cap. For a third time, as he was leaving the theatre at Berlin on the 21st of December, he slipped on the staircase, and in falling again injured his knee. Notwithstanding his advanced age, thanks to a splendid constitution, His Majesty soon recovered from his injuries.

The Emperor and Empress celebrated their golden wedding on the 11th of June, on which occasion they received the representatives of all the European Courts. Public rejoicings were general throughout the Empire, and large sums of money were collected for the endowment of charitable institutions in commemoration of the festival. Shortly before this event the Emperor had become a great-grandfather by the birth of the first child of the heir apparent to the Duchy of Saxe-Meiningen, who in 1878 was married to the eldest daughter of the Crown Prince of Prussia.

Two meetings of Imperial Sovereigns took place in 1879. In June the Emperor of Austria visited the Emperor William at Gastein. For some time back there had been rumours of a still closer *rapprochement* between the two empires, and it was now stated that the interview could only be taken to imply the strengthening of the bonds of amity between Germany and Austria. Russian journalists were at this juncture waging a very bitter controversy with the German press. The *St. Petersburg Gazette* even advised the Russian Government to 'leave the Bosphorus and the Danube for the present to their fate, and to tackle Prussia, the Imperial Chancellor having, in the matter of the Eastern question, wholly leaned to the side of the western Powers.'

Russian vituperation was seen to be groundless, however, in September, when the Emperors of Russia and Germany had an interview at Alexandrowa, in Poland. The cordial relations subsisting between the two monarchs were now still further cemented; and indeed for the moment no cloud was looming over the European horizon. Each Empire and State was busied with its normal duty of encouraging internal development and national progress.

CHAPTER XIV.

THE EMPEROR'S LATER YEARS.

EUROPE has seldom gone long without 'wars or rumours of wars.' There are in every State men who delight to fan the flame of international discord, either for individual or national purposes. It was natural, perhaps, that the great progress which Germany had made in the decade that ended with 1879, should have stirred feelings of jealousy amongst neighbouring Powers. Consequently, either Germany was always asserted to be contemplating mischief against other European States, or they were said to be conspiring against her.

Although, therefore, the year 1880 opened in quietude, it was not long before another Russian scare was exploited. The Northern Power was pointed to as the sole element of disturbance in Europe, and Prince Bismarck expressed his distrust of her. France was making advances to Russia, and to render these innocuous the German Chancellor cultivated cordial relations with the new Radical French Ministry. The massing of Russian troops in the Western provinces of the Czar's dominions, and the contemplated new fortifications, gave Germany some concern, so she gently sounded Austria as to whether this was the right thing to do. Then, too, France was rapidly perfecting her military organization, and the old saying of the great Napoleon was recalled, that Europe would be either Republican or Cossack within fifty years of his time. When Russia perceived that Bismarck was endeavouring to make friends elsewhere, great chagrin was expressed in St. Petersburg, where it had become an article of faith that Germany should adhere to her traditional policy of union with Russia. One thing was proved beyond question, that, whatever might be the cause, the Berlin Chancellor was now assiduously supporting the Austro-German alliance concluded in the previous year.

The scare passed over, but 'it's an ill wind that blows nobody any good.' The military party at Berlin scored largely by the false rumours, for they enabled the Government to bring forward with some success their new Army Bill. This measure, by far the most important of the year, was early laid before the Federal Council. It provided that from April 1, 1881, the infantry was to be formed into 503 battalions, the field artillery into 340 batteries, the foot artillery into 31 battalions, and the sappers and miners into 19. At the same time several new regiments were to be created— viz., 11 infantry, 1 field artillery regiment, of 8 batteries, 32 field batteries, 1 foot artillery, and 1 sapper regiment. The increase of the expenditure for the different German Governments was calculated as follows: for Prussia, 12,773,896 marks; for Saxony, 1,822,000 marks; for Wurtemburg, 547,242 marks; and for Bavaria, 2,170,104 marks, giving a total of upwards of 17,000,000 marks. For the building of barracks, magazines, &c., a gross sum of 26,713,216 marks was asked, of which Prussia would contribute 20,172,266 marks; Saxony, 3,220,400 marks: Wurtemberg, 428,050 marks; and Bavaria, 2,892,500 marks. The strength of the army in peace was to be fixed by the law from April 1, 1881, to March 31, 1888. The strength of the army had hitherto been 401,659, but the population of Germany having largely increased during the past seven years, the number of men under the imperial banners would be augmented in proportion.

The Bill came before the Reichsrath on the 1st of March, when General Von Kameke, the Minister of War, was charged to pilot it through the House. The General said that the Government regarded it as its duty to maintain the relative strength of the German Army. Germany's neighbours having considerably added to their military forces, there remained nothing but to follow suit. Germany was arming not for any immediate hostilities, but to maintain the balance of power. Count Moltke adduced arguments on similar lines in support of the bill. The Ultramontanes opposed the measure, but the National Liberals supported it, not to oblige the Government, but to ensure the safety of the country. The Bill was ultimately referred to a Committee of 21 members, and before this Committee General Von Kameke revealed the enormous strides made by France and Russia towards a complete arming of the population; and he depicted lugubriously the unsatisfactory condition of the German forces. The bill came back with an amendment to the effect that the number of supplementary reserves of the first class required to join in the military manœuvres should in time of peace be settled yearly with the Budget; but in cases of urgency all such might be called out by Imperial order at any time for a period not exceeding eight weeks. Other amendments were proposed in the Reichstag, but the Minister of War declined to modify his demands, and the military septennate was voted by 186 against 96. On the third reading an amendment was adopted exempting the Catholic and Protestant clergy from serving in the reserves, and the bill finally passed by 186 votes to 128.

Second only in importance to the Army Bill was a measure for the prolongation of the Anti-Socialist law of 1878. The committee appointed by the Reichstag to report on the bill decided, by ten votes against three, to prolong its operation until September 30, 1884, instead of 1886 as proposed by the Government. When the time for the second reading came on in the Chamber, the Socialists resolved upon a protracted struggle; but Ministers cut it short by passing a resolution combining the various Socialistic amendments. The second reading was carried, and the bill passed on May 4, by 191 to 94 votes. Herr Liebknecht delivered a powerful speech against it on the third reading, and taunted the Government with Cavour's well-known maxim, that any bunglers could govern under a state of siege.

Yet another resignation by Prince Bismarck of his office as Imperial Chancellor took place in April, in consequence of a vote come to in the Federal Council on the Imperial Stamp Duties Bill. Prussia, Bavaria, and Saxony had been outvoted by a combination of the smaller states under the leadership of Wurtemburg. The Emperor William, in a Cabinet order, whilst recognizing the difficulties of the Chancellor's position, declined to relieve him of his office, and called upon him to prepare proposals for bringing about a constitutional solution of such a conflict of duties as led to the recent resignation. On the 12th of May the German Federal Council adopted a resolution declaring receipts for post office orders and remittances liable to a stamp duty, thus reversing the previous vote which led to the resignation of Prince Bismarck.

With regard to Germany's relations to the Vatican and the Romish Church, no new laws were passed this year against the Catholics, but those on the Statute-book were enforced, gradually depriving the Ultramontanes in the Empire of their religious services, and punishing with rigour any attempt to supply their vacancies. Yet, though successful with his amendment of the Falck or May laws in this sense, Bismarck sustained several rebuffs during the session. Parliament rejected his proposed subvention to the Samoa Company—a project to revive by national funds the bankrupt house of Godeffroy, of Hamburg, which had once monopolized the South Sea Trade; and it also declined to allow the introduction of a tobacco monopoly, the Chancellor being unable to obtain the support of more than a third of the Reichstag for his project. But Bismarck was enabled to show that he was fully alive to the pecuniary interests of the community at large, by passing a bill for the regulation of usury abuses.

There was witnessed a disruption of the National Liberals during the recess, when Herr Lasker and a number of his friends formally seceded from the party. Shortly after this it was announced that Bismarck had been appointed Minister of Commerce. All kinds of rumours were afloat as the reasons for this step, but the first practical issue of it was the appointment by Royal decree of a committee of trade on agriculture, whose function it was to examine all economical questions, and to report on the needs of the country.

Towards the close of the year the *Judenhetze* movement, or persecution of the Jews, had passed into an advanced stage, and one which reflected scandalously upon Liberal Germany. In Berlin, the Orthodox clergy, under the leadership of Hofprediger Stöcker, had done their utmost to embitter public feeling against the Jewish race; and the movement was supported by the Ultramontane press, and even by the eminent historian Professor Von Treitschke. The main argument used in justification was .that the internal state of Germany, in view of its widespread Socialism and its external policy, produced a condition of things which rendered the preponderance of the Jewish element a source of danger. The census of 1871 showed that there were in Spain 6000 Jews, in Italy 40,000, in France and Great Britain 45,000 each, but in Germany 512,000. In Prussia alone the number had increased from 124,000 in 1816, to 340,000 in 1875. The Jews replied to the charges against them, that if they possessed more influence in Germany than elsewhere, it was because their mental capacities enabled them there to obtain more marked distinction than elsewhere.   Riots broke out in the autumn in the Prussian capital, occasionally caused by the Jews themselves, but more frequently by their Christian antagonists.   When the Prussian Chambers assembled in October, a petition was laid before the Landtag, praying that the movement of the Jewish population should be the subject of police reports; that only the lower places in the public service should be accessible to its members; and that restraints should be placed by the Government on the Jewish immigration.   No practical issue resulted from the debate, but the Government announced their determination not to permit the question of the civil rights of citizens of any religious denomination to be interfered with.

The Crown Prince represented his Imperial father on two very interesting occasions this year.   On the 20th of April he opened with much pomp at Berlin an International Fishery Exhibition, which proved to be most successful and encouraging; and on the 9th of the following month he inaugurated an exhibition of manufactures, agriculture, forestry, and the fine arts at Düsseldorf.   This was the largest exhibition of the kind ever held in Germany, and all the products were of exclusively German origin.

The foreign relations of Germany were, without exception, of a friendly character.   The Austrian alliance was especially strengthened during the year in consequence of a meeting of the two Emperors at Ischl on the 10th of August. Though the German Parliament frequently partook of the aspect of a bear-garden, nearly all parties were agreed upon one thing—that a close alliance with Austria was most profitable for the interests of Germany.

The Emperor William was the leading figure in a public ceremony in March, which must have called up many vivid recollections in his mind.   On the 11th of that month he unveiled a statue at Berlin to the memory of his brave and patriotic mother, the Queen Louisa, wife of King Frederick William III. of Prussia.   We have spoken of Queen Louisa in an earlier chapter of this work.   Besides the Emperor, there were present at the unveiling the Queen's two other surviving children, Prince Charles of Prussia and the Dowager Duchess of Mecklenburg-Schwerin.

Another celebration of great and unusual interest took place on the 15th of October, when Cologne Cathedral was formally consecrated and opened. It had taken more than six centuries to complete this work. The foundation-stone was laid on the 14th of August, 1248, and actual building commenced in 1257. A portion of the building was consecrated in 1322, but it was not until 1499 that the nave and aisles were covered with a temporary roof. In 1508 the stained glass windows were inserted, but the work was now suspended for many generations. It was resumed in 1823, and from that date to its completion £900,000 was expended upon the building, which cost altogether about £2,000,000. Cologne towers are the loftiest of any edifice in the world, being upwards of 500 feet in height, and exceeding by nearly 20 feet the spire of St. Nicholas Church at Hamburg, and by considerably more than that St. Peter's at Rome, Strasburg Cathedral, and the pyramid of Cheops. The Emperor William and the Empress, the Crown Prince and the Crown Princess, the King of Saxony, and several other German sovereigns were present at the opening of the cathedral, but the leaders of the Catholic party absented themselves.

The first session of the German Parliament in 1881 opened on the 15th of February. The Emperor's speech, which contained a direct appeal to working men, declared that the remedy for socialist excesses must be sought, not only in repression, but equally in a positive attempt to promote the welfare of the labouring classes. For this reason he hoped the working men's Accident Insurance Bill would be welcomed by the Parliament as a complement to the legislation against social democracy. In the same category he placed a bill to regulate the constitution of trade guilds by affording means for organizing the isolated powers of persons engaged in the same trade, thus raising their economic capacity and social and moral efficiency. The bill for providing biennial budgets would be again presented for the consideration of Parliament, as the allied governments were still suffering from difficulties inseparable from the simultaneous sitting of the Imperial and Provincial Parliaments. A stamp tax and a brewing tax were also announced. The Emperor viewed with great satisfaction the new financial policy of the empire, while the negotiations for treaties of commerce with neighbouring nations on the basis of the new customs policy were declared to be near a favourable termination. The relations with foreign nations were amicable and in consonance with the friendship which personally united the Emperor with neighbouring sovereigns.

The Government programme was severely handled by the Deputies. A custom, which had long been growing with Prince Bismarck, of treating political rather as personal questions, had greatly exasperated them, and they also entertained strong objections of a general kind to the legislation proposed. The principal Government bills were either rejected or considerably altered. The tax bills and the proposition to establish biennial budgets and biennial Parliaments were thrown out, and the bill providing for a working men's accident insurance was remodelled. The brewery tax bill was rejected, and the stamp tax bill completely transformed. To set against all these defeats, the Chancellor could only point to one triumph. The long-pending question of the entrance of Hamburg into the Zollverein was settled on June 15 by a majority of 106 to 46, the Hamburg Municipal council accepting the convention as drawn up by the Government.

The elections in October proved on the whole unfavourable to the Government. The Free Conservatives and Mixed Liberals lost largely, while the Secessional Liberals and Progressists gained to an equal extent. The new Parliament was thus constituted: Centre, or Clericals, 110; Progressists, 60; the Liberal Union or Secessionists, 48; the National Liberals, 45; the German Imperial party, 27; the Popularists or South German Democrats, 7; the German Conservatives, 50; Poles, 18; Alsace-Lorrainers, 15; Social Democrats, 13; and Independents or Savages, 4. The most prominent advocates of the Chancellor's new financial policy were rejected, as was also Herr Stöcker, the leader of the *Judenhetze*, notwithstanding the influence he possessed as chaplain to the Emperor.

When the Diet met, Bismarck had the amazing courage to bring out his old bills, which were promptly sat upon and extinguished by the Chamber. Nothing could more conclusively show the close relations between the Emperor and his Chancellor than a daring speech which the latter made in November. Herr Richter, in opening an attack upon Bismarck's financial schemes, said there was no conflict between the Reichstag and the Crown: the object of the conflict was not the Emperor, but his chief counsellor. Bismarck sprang up and gave a most emphatic statement of his views, proving that he set the Emperor high above the Parliament. The Emperor, he said, constituted a strong element in the German system of government, as was shown by the fact that under the reign of the present sovereign's brother the government of Prussia was carried on according to entirely different principles from those which had now been adopted. The Emperor William's personal share in the Government was such an active one that he would not allow himself to be prohibited from speaking to his people before the elections. As for himself, he completely represented the Emperor's policy. Germany was not to be governed after the English fashion. The conduct of affairs was in the hands of the Emperor, whose responsible adviser was the Chancellor, and he would continue to be so. In another speech the Prince observed that he considered the Government a better guarantee for the union of Germany than the Reichstag, which caused him many difficulties and greatly increased those already in existence. These bold views were clearly against the supremacy of the people in their own concerns. Bismarck merely looked upon Parliament as a body whose duty it was to register the acts framed by the Government with the sanction of the Emperor; but the House remained firm and declined to endorse the Chancellor's policy at command.

In foreign affairs Germany was now unquestionably the leading European State. Nothing of importance was done by other Powers without her being thought of or consulted. The Emperor William met the Emperor Francis Joseph in August, and the Emperor of Russia at Dantzic in September; this latter meeting caused considerable comment, but the interview was merely one for the renewal of the good feeling hitherto existing between the two empires. In his speech from the throne on November 17 the Emperor of Germany declared that the meetings at Gastein and Dantzic were the expression of the close personal and political relations between the sovereigns and their empires. 'The confidence thus existing between the three imperial courts was a trustworthy guarantee of peace, which was the identical aim of their policy.'

The rising against the Jews became very serious in the provinces of Pomerania and West Prussia, and in the city of Berlin. The agitation in the capital was led by many prominent men, chief amongst whom was the Court Chaplain Stöcker. The students of the University of Berlin were also most rancorous in their hostility. Professor Virchow was amongst the few distinguished Germans who denounced the agitation. Petitions against the Jews poured into the German Parliament; but at length the movement attained to such a pitch of virulence that the Government were obliged to take energetic measures to abate the excitement and arrest the agitation.

The marriage of the prospective heir to the German crown was celebrated with great pomp on the 27th of February, 1881, in the Royal Schloss at Berlin. The bridegroom was Frederick William Victor Albert, eldest son of the Crown Prince of Prussia and of Germany, grandson of the Emperor William and of Queen Victoria, nephew in the fifth degree of Frederick the Great, and twenty-fifth lineal descendant of the valorous Conrad, cadet of Hohenzollern. The bride was Augusta Victoria, daughter of Duke Frederick of Schleswig-Holstein. Germany regarded it as particularly happy that the daughter of the dispossessed Duke of Schleswig-Holstein should thus become the future Empress of Germany.

Great sensation was caused early in January, 1882, by the introduction of the royal prerogative into the constitutional questions upon which Bismarck and the German Diet were at variance. The Emperor, as King of Prussia, issued a manifesto which made short work of the ideas of the Constitutionalists—that Bismarck was sheltering himself behind his master, and that the King reigned but did not rule. The royal rescript declared that the Prussian Constitution of 1850 transferred a portion of the law-giving powers to the Legislature, but left the King the full power of initiation and approval. The policy of the Government was the King's policy, although it must be represented by his ministers; his royal acts were his own, although the countersigning minister became responsible for them to the laws and the country. They expressed his will and pleasure, and should not be spoken of as emanating from the ministry but from the King himself. ‘It is my will,’ said his Majesty, ‘that both in Prussia and in the legislative bodies of the empire, there may be no doubt left as to my own constitutional right, and that of my successors, to personally conduct the policy of my Government; and that the theory shall always be gainsaid that the inviolability of the King, which has always existed in Prussia, or the necessity of a responsible counter signature of my Government acts, deprives them of the character of royal and independent decisions.'

But the real sting of the rescript was in its tail. In the concluding paragraph the King stated, or was made to state, that while he had no wish to restrict the freedom of elections, he would expect all officials to hold aloof from opposing Government candidates. It was actually added that 'the duty which, in their oaths of office, they swore to perform, extends to supporting the policy of the Government even at elections.' The rescript greatly discomposed the Deputies, some of whom imagined it to portend a *coup d' état.* But Bismarck affirmed in the House that the publication of the manifesto did not mean any further restriction of the liberties of the people.

Ecclesiastical legislation was a feature of the session, and it revealed a desire on Bismarck's part to come to a better understanding with the Vatican. Dr. Windthorst brought forward a motion for the repeal of the law prohibiting the exercise of ecclesiastical functions without the authority of the Government. Though opposed by the Conservatives and National Liberals, the resolution was carried by a large majority. The Government remained neutral, owing, it was said, to their wish to secure the support of the Centre for a new Ecclesiastical Bill. By this bill the Government was to be empowered to restore to their sees the deposed bishops, and to dispense with the decrees which prevented foreign priests from exercising ecclesiastical functions in Prussia. When the bill was brought forward, on the motion of Dr. Windthorst, who said the *Kulturkampf* was now dead, it was referred to a committee. Coming back from thence, it ultimately passed without the clauses compelling Roman Catholic bishops to notify each appointment of a clergyman in their respective dioceses to the secular authorities. This was a great concession to the Clerical party, and it was followed by the passing of a grant of 90,000 marks for the revival of a Prussian Mission at the Vatican. These were substantial departures from the Chancellor's old policy.

Amongst the measures brought forward in the German Parliament was the Tobacco Monopoly Bill, which was described in the Emperor's speech as a measure of indirect taxation for increasing the revenue of the Empire. Had it passed, however, it would have had a much wider scope, as it must have vastly increased the power of the Imperial Government at the expense of the local governments of the various states forming the Empire. The Clericals opposed this tobacco monopoly, and so did the Socialists. Though the latter were in favour of State monopolies, they thought the landed interest should be taxed first. During the debate on the second reading, Prince Bismarck denied the allegation that the scheme would injure the interests of the workmen employed in the tobacco trade; and he was of opinion that the interests of the working classes had been sacrificed to the Moloch of Free Trade, far more than they ever could be by the proposed monopoly. 'You may ask me,' he concluded, 'why I do not resign if you do not adopt this bill. My reply is that I remain out of personal consideration for the Emperor. When I saw him lying in his blood after Nobiling's attempt, I made a vow that I would never resign without his consent. The welfare of the country must mainly rest upon the dynasty, which will preserve the military and political unity of the Empire, and carry us through any difficulties which may fall on the country through the atrophy of faction.' Nearly every speaker of eminence in the House condemned the bill, which had previously been rejected by a special committee by 21 votes to 3. The House now rejected the first article of the bill by 276 to 43 votes; but being willing to unite with the Chancellor in all measures necessary for the preservation of the Empire, that portion of the committee's report which expressed a want of confidence in the Chancellor's financial plans was rejected, and that directed specifically against the Tobacco Monopoly Bill only adopted by 155 to 150 votes.

In the elections to the Diet which took place in October the Government were victorious. The Old Conservatives and the Free Conservatives gained seventeen seats, while the National Liberals lost eighteen. The Conservatives and Ultramontanes together had a considerable majority over all other sections in the new Prussian Parliament. The German

Chancellor's foreign policy during 1882 was conceived in the interests of peace. This was aided by the death of Gambetta and the removal of Bismarck's rival, Count Beust, from the Austro-Hungarian embassy at Paris, which diminished the probabilities of a French war of revenge. Desirous of avoiding all European complications, the Berlin Chancellor opposed the idea of an Anglo-French occupation of Egypt, which he feared might lead to a conflict like that which followed the Austro-Prussian occupation of Schleswig-Holstein.

The Emperor William and Prince Bismarck were extremely disappointed that the Reichstag made no progress with the Socialist laws in the session of 1883. Accordingly, on the 14th of April, His Majesty returned to the subject, and issued another rescript. He declared that he deemed it one of the first of his duties as Emperor to address his care and attention to the improvement of the condition of the labouring class, and again urged the Reichstag to grant a biennial budget, out of consideration for his declining years, in order that the autumn session might be devoted to the plans of social reform which he had at heart, and the hope be fulfilled before his death of the development and realization throughout the Empire of the reforms begun by his father in the beginning of the century. The Emperor expressed his conviction that since the issue of the anti-socialist law, legislation should not be confined to police and penal measures, but should seek to remedy or alleviate the cause of evils combated in the penal code. He was gratified by the success of the first of his endeavours, in the remission of the two lowest grades of the class tax in Prussia, and hoped to see the accident insurance bill (presented in an amended form), with the supplementary project of sick funds under corporative administration, embodied in laws before the separation of the Reichstag. The attention of Parliament could then be devoted in the ensuing winter session to a further proposal to provide for the maintenance of superannuated and invalided labourers.

But it was a case of piping unto the Deputies, and they would not dance. Although the Chancellor threw the whole weight of his restless energy into the legislative struggle, the indignant Liberal majority referred the propositions to the budget committee, which was practically shelving them. The only thing they did before separating in June was to vote the biennial budget, but as the fiscal year had ended it was not difficult to console themselves for this slight infraction of constitutional principle.

The Socialist question was undoubtedly a matter of grave difficulty in Germany. Bismarck had thrown over the National Liberal party, by whose aid he had accomplished the unity of the Empire, and in order to gain other allies he had been obliged to make great concessions. His legislation for the labouring classes, his conciliation of the Vatican, and the amendment of the Falck laws, were all steps taken with the view of securing Ultramontane support for his Imperial financial policy, and for his measures for the nationalization of the Prussian railroads. It was necessary to pass some measures for the relief of the working classes, or they would revolt against the military system, and rush into still greater socialist excesses. The accident and sickness insurance bill—which proposed that the Government should insure the workpeople, and the employers and communes provide the premiums—was passed in almost its original shape.

Some notable public changes now occurred. General von Kameke, the War Minister, retired owing to a difference with the Emperor. The Progressist deputies insisted that there should be no augmentation of military pensions unless the officers were made subject to direct taxation like civilians. Von Kameke was willing to accept this compromise, but the Emperor declined to listen to it. Baron von Stosch, the minister for the navy, retired because of a quarrel with the Chancellor, and the Emperor perpetuated an old anomaly by insisting upon a military man being appointed to the direction of the navy. Herr von Bennigsen, leader of the National Liberal party, unable longer to endure the overbearing conduct of Bismarck, resigned his seats in the Reichstag and Prussian Landtag, and retired from political life. The other great Liberal leader, Lasker, had already retired.

The Prussian Chamber passed a bill relaxing the Ecclesiastical May Laws. Although it fell short of the demands of the Vatican, it yielded so much that Bismarck was taunted with having made the pilgrimage to Canossa after all. This Relief Act enabled bishops to perform episcopal acts even out of their own dioceses, and to appoint vicars, chaplains, etc., in vacant parishes. The celebration of mass by priests not authorized by the Government was no longer a criminal offence, and the right of appeal to the Minister of Public Worship was granted.

Germany concluded a commercial treaty with Spain, and also a copyright treaty with France. Her general relations with the latter Power required careful management, but the Chancellor was equal to the occasion. The attendance of King Alfonso of Spain, and King Milan of Servia, besides the King of Saxony, the Crown Prince of Portugal, and the Prince of Wales, as the guests of the Emperor William at the autumn manœuvres in September, was among the indications of the supreme influence of Bismarck, and the success of his peace policy in Europe.

An imposing ceremony, in which the Emperor William was the central figure, took place early in the summer. On the 9th of June, accompanied by his son, the Crown Prince, and other members of his family, he laid the foundation stone of the new Houses of Parliament in Berlin. Prince Bismarck, the Secretaries of State, and other high officials, as well as many eminent political personages, attended the ceremony, which was of the most brilliant character.

The Emperor unveiled the great national monument on the Niederwald, near Rudesheim, on the 28th of September. Eighty thousand persons were present at the celebration. The monument, which overlooks the Rhine, was erected in commemoration of the victories over the French in 1870–71. It consists of a colossal statue, said to be an idealized portrait of the artist's daughter, and representing Germania as a woman in a girdle-bound robe, her left hand resting on the hilt of a drawn sword, and her right holding a laurel-wreathed Imperial crown. The bronze figure alone is about thirty-six feet in height, and with the pedestal and socket, measures about eighty feet. The artist was Johannes Schilling, of Dresden, and the founder of the statue, Von Miller of Munich. The total cost of the monument was estimated at 1,196,000 marks, part of which was raised by public subscription, and the rest from a Parliamentary grant.

The National Liberal party, which had been disorganized

by the retirement of its leader, Herr Von Bennigsen, called a Convention at Berlin on the 18th of May, 1884. It was largely attended, and unanimously adopted a declaration, asserting the loyalty of the National Liberals to the Emperor, and their resolve to maintain, unimpaired, the constitutional rights of the representatives of the people, and pledging them to support the Accidents Insurance Bill and Anti-Socialist Bill. The Secessionists from the National Liberals, however, now united with the Progressists, and the combined party styled itself the 'German Liberals.' Its political programme was of the most advanced character, and it was strongly hostile to the Government, while the National Liberal party adhered to its former policy of promoting the unity and progress of the Empire by maintaining a conciliatory attitude towards Prince Bismarck, notwithstanding his anti-Liberal tendencies. The Chancellor assumed a friendly tone towards the latter party, but on several occasions vehemently attacked that of the new Liberals. He affirmed his conviction that it had no future, and declared that he would fight against it to his last breath, such being his duty to his country and his Emperor. Bismarck's language was largely justified when the elections to the sixth German Parliament came on. The New Liberals sustained a disastrous defeat, their numbers falling from 104 to 63. But a further noteworthy feature of the elections was the great advance of the Socialists from 10 to 24 members. The Socialist vote generally had enormously increased. The Conservatives and National Liberals also gained considerably.

Two Government bills, dealing with Socialism, were brought forward in the German Parliament early in 1884. The first provided for the prolongation of the law against Socialism for another two years, September 1884–86. The reasons assigned for this measure were, the continuance of the Socialist movement and its danger, as shown by recent criminal attacks on life and property in Germany and other civilized States; the good effects produced by the law; and the fact that the fears expressed that its powers might be abused had proved unfounded. The Chancellor spoke earnestly in favour of the bill, and as he also held out a threat of dissolution, the Government gained an unexpected victory, the bill passing by 189 to 157 votes.

The second measure designed against the Socialists was the Explosives Bill. It was brought forward in consequence of a diabolical attempt made upon the life of the Emperor at the unveiling of the Niederwald monument in the previous September. The knowledge of this attempt did not transpire until some time afterwards. The leader of the conspiracy in connection with this atrocious crime was a compositor named Reinsdorf. At the trial, which took place at Leipsic, Reinsdorf defended himself with much ability, and in an eloquent speech garnished with classical quotations, he argued in favour of the confiscation of private property, and the abolition of central Government. Reinsdorf's chief accomplices were Küchler, another compositor, and Rupsch, a journeyman saddler. The latter confessed, while in prison, that he had, at Reinsdorf's instigation, placed a stone bottle containing dynamite in a drain running across the road by which the Emperor was to pass; but that he did not light the match, as he had intended from the first to frustrate the plan. The judges disbelieved his story, however, and sentenced Reinsdorf, Küchler, and Rupsch to death. Two other prisoners were sentenced to ten years' penal servitude, while three more were acquitted. It was scarcely surprising after this Anarchist revelation that the Government should introduce their Explosives Bill, or that the Reichstag should quickly pass it, as it did, on the 15th of May. The measure provided that the manufacture, sale, and possession of explosives, as well as their importation from abroad, should only be permitted if authorized by the police, and that the following offences should be punishable by penal servitude: 1. Wilfully endangering, by means of explosives, life, person, or property, or ordering explosives with such intent, or under circumstances affording no proof of its having been intended that they should be employed for legal purposes. 2. Inciting to the commission of the above crimes by delivering speeches before popular assemblages, by placarding notices, or by publishing pamphlets. It was further enacted that when the crimes above mentioned should have fatal consequences, they should be followed by the death punishment.

A new Prussian States Council was established in June with the Crown Prince as President and Bismarck as Vice-

President. It consisted of 71 members, 12 of whom were landed proprietors, 6 merchants and manufacturers, 4 clerics, and 4 communal officials, the rest of the members being appointed by the King. The Council was to devote itself chiefly to matters of legislation, and was to have a consultative character.

Prince Bismarck met with several serious reverses in Parliament. Although Government opposed a motion for the payment of the Deputies, it was carried by 180 to 99. Herr Windthorst's bill for the repeal of the law empowering the Government to expel priests who had been guilty of illegal conduct was also carried, notwithstanding the Chancellor's urgent remonstrances. It passed its first and second reading by a majority of 217 to 93. A third defeat took place on the proposal to pay a salary of 20,000 marks for a second Director at the Foreign Office, which was rejected by 141 to 119 votes. This decision, however, was strongly condemned by the country, and the personal animus in it led to a strong reaction in favour of Bismarck.

The Chancellor again turned his attention to colonial settlements, with a view of providing new markets for the products of German industry, and opening a vent for the superfluous energy which was too often spent in mischievous agitation. The question of protection to German subjects on the Congo and at Angra Pequena, gave rise to a long diplomatic correspondence between Germany and England, but at length Prince Bismarck made it clear that his Government had a right to protect German subjects at Angra Pequena. Steps were accordingly taken to define the exact rights of Great Britain and Germany respectively on the Congo. As usual, Bismarck, who was now generally known as the 'honest broker' of Berlin, came in for the largest slice of the cake. Great Britain welcomed Germany as a neighbour in the district of Cape Colony, and as a further step in German colonization a convention was concluded between Germany and the Transvaal.

The Emperor William received a pacific mission from Russia this year, and there was another meeting between the Austrian and German Emperors at Ischl. The two Sovereigns subsequently held a conference, in September, with the Emperor of Russia at Skirnievice, in Poland. A formal alliance was concluded between the three Emperors, and one of its chief features was an agreement to maintain the *status quo* in Europe.

Prince Bismarck entered upon his seventieth year on the 1st of April, and he took this opportunity of announcing that he intended to resign the Presidency of the Prussian Ministry, and the Portfolios of Foreign Affairs and Commerce in the Cabinet, retaining only the post of Imperial Chancellor. He had long been taking too much work upon himself, and his health at times appeared greatly shattered. On the ensuing 1st of September, being the thirteenth anniversary of Sedan, the Emperor conferred upon his Chancellor the highest military order in his gift. His Majesty, in presenting the order, thus spoke of Bismarck as a soldier :—

'To-day's anniversary, which recalls one of the most prominent events in the period of twenty-two years during which we have worked together, also reminds me that on this day, as well as during two wars, you stood by my side, not only as a highly-proved man of counsel, but also as a soldier, and that there is in Prussia an Order for Merit which you do not yet possess. It is true this Order has a special military meaning, but, nevertheless, you ought to have had it long ago, for truly at many a grievous time you have shown the highest courage of the soldier, and you have also thoroughly and completely proved at my side in two campaigns that, apart from everything else, you have the fullest claim to conspicuous military distinction. I will, therefore, now make up for what I have hitherto neglected, by conferring on you the accompanying *Ordre pour le Mérite*, and that, too, with oaken leaves, in token that you ought to have had it long ago, and that you have repeatedly deserved it. Knowing, as I do, how much you are imbued with the spirit of a soldier, I hope it will gratify you to receive this Order, which several of your ancestors proudly wore ; as I, for my part, derive satisfaction from thus bestowing this well-merited soldier's reward on the man whom God in His gracious providence has placed at my side, and who has done such great things for the Fatherland. I shall, indeed, be most heartily glad to see you in the future wearing the *Ordre pour le Mérite.*'

The expulsion of the Poles from Prussian territory led to a good deal of ill-feeling between Germany and Austria and

Russia. When the latter Powers complained and asked for information, the former replied that the matter was one which concerned the internal affairs of Prussia only. The edict issued by the Government ordered all Poles who were not Prussian subjects to be expelled from the country, and this edict was carried out with great severity. The total number of persons banished exceeded 34,700, the majority of whom were Russian subjects. Most of them found a refuge in Austria, but others emigrated to America. No charge of disloyalty or conspiracy was made against them, neither were the poorest of them paupers. The edict was especially hard upon those thrifty workmen who had for years been members of mutual relief societies, and who had paid the necessary premiums to secure a provision in old age. They now lost their savings and were turned adrift to begin life anew. The question was discussed in the Prussian Diet on the 6th of May, 1885, when the Home Minister, Herr von Puttkamer, affirmed that the measure was dictated by State necessity, and that the Government could not tolerate the presence in Prussia of large numbers of Poles who were not Prussian subjects any more than it could that of Danes in Schleswig-Holstein or of Frenchmen in Alsace-Lorraine. The Polish element in the population had been growing largely in excess of that of the German, and the edict was necessary for the political security of the State and the maintenance of German nationality and German culture. The Minister's explanations were deemed very unsatisfactory, though no practical issue was raised upon them.

At a later date, however, the subject came up again in the German Parliament, when the Imperial Government was requested to take steps to check the expulsion of Poles from the country. Prince Bismarck opposed to this a declaration from the throne which caused great excitement. The Chancellor was extremely wroth at the supposition that the Imperial Government could be called in to redress wrongs alleged to be committed by Prussia within her own territories. 'There exists,' he said, 'no Government in the Empire entitled, under the control of the Reichstag, to claim supervision, as this interpellation endeavours to do, of the exercise of the rights of Sovereignty enjoyed by the individual States of the Confederation, in so far as the right to exercise such supervision has not been conceded to the Empire.' The Emperor-King was therefore compelled to express to the Reichstag his conviction that 'the view adopted by the majority of deputies in supporting the interpellation in question is at variance with the German constitution,' and in case of any endeavour being made to carry the same into effect, he would 'maintain and defend against such endeavour the rights of each of the Federal Governments, as recited in the Treaty of Confederation.' Bismarck concluded by entirely denying the competence of the German Parliament to call the Kings of Prussia and Bavaria, or the Grand Dukes of Baden and Hesse, to account for the way in which they exercised their Sovereign rights within their own particular dominions. He then strode from the Chamber, followed by the other members of the Federal Council.

A debate on the question of Sunday labour gave Prince Bismarck the opportunity of delivering a singular speech, in which he ventilated his views upon the English Sabbath. The Ultramontanes and the Socialists having brought forward in the Reichstag a Bill for the prohibition of Sunday labour, the Chancellor strongly opposed the scheme on economical and political grounds, and also in the interest of working-men themselves. Workmen who would thereby lose 14 per cent. of their wages would certainly be against such a measure, he said, which would also diminish by one-seventh the production of the country, and inflict a heavy loss on the manufacturers. Moreover, a Sunday spent in pleasure was likely to be followed by a Monday spent in drink. The industrial prosperity of England and the United States was due to other causes than the Sunday holiday.

'England,' continued the Prince, 'would not enjoy so great an industrial superiority over Germany if her coal fields and her iron mines were not in close proximity to each other, and if she had not enjoyed the blessings of civilization long before Germany did. Even in the time of Shakspeare, about 300 years ago, there was a degree of prosperity, culture, and literary development in England far above what we possessed at that time in Germany. The Thirty Years' War had a retrograde effect on Germany more than on any other nation; and I cannot admit that Englishmen are better Christians than the Germans. If the keeping of the Sunday had not been from time immemorial an English custom, I doubt very much if any Government or Parliament would now be strong enough to make it compulsory. For my part, the English Sunday has always produced an unpleasant impression upon me; I was glad when it was over, and judging by the way the Sunday was passed in England, I think Englishmen were so too. Here in our villages we are glad to see the people enjoying themselves in their Sunday best, and we thank God that we are not under the compulsion of the English Sunday. Some forty years I went to England for the first time, and I was so glad to land, after a bad passage, that I whistled a tune. "Please don't do that," said a fellow-passenger. "Why not?" I inquired. "Because it is Sunday!"'

There were some truths and some fallacies in this speech, but it was effectual in shelving the Bill, which was put off for inquiries. When the information sought for was forthcoming it was very largely antagonistic to the proposal.

Two important financial measures became law in Prussia during the year. One provided for a graduated income-tax. There were seventeen different rates of the tax, commencing with a rate of about $3\frac{1}{2}d$. in the pound for incomes of from £80 to £90, and ending with a rate of $7\frac{1}{2}d$. in the pound for incomes of over £500 a year. Besides the usual allowances, relief was provided to the extent of half the rate originally imposed in special circumstances, such as continued illness or misfortune. The second law was one relating to exchange duties. The fixed stamp introduced by the law of July, 1881, had not proved very productive, and the large profits of speculators on the various exchanges had remained untaxed. By the new law, purchases of stock, shares, foreign bank-notes, &c., were to be subject to a duty of one-tenth per cent., and purchases of goods at the various exchanges, if not produced by one of the contracting parties, were to be taxed at the rate of one-fifth per cent.

The Brunswick succession caused some excitement in 1885, the Duke of Cumberland, only son of the King of Hanover, claiming the throne. As the Duke had long been at the head of the anti-Prussian party in Hanover, however, the Federal Council decided against him, and the Brunswick Diet unanimously elected Prince Albrecht regent.

The important post of Governor of Alsace-Lorraine became vacant by the death of Field Marshal von Manteuffel. The Marshal had ruled benevolently and yet despotically, with the object of making Alsace-Lorraine the most German of German States. But he signally failed, and fifteen years of German rule had produced only distrust and discontent. The new Governor appointed was Prince Hohenlohe-Schillingfürst, German Ambassador in Paris, who had for nearly a quarter of a century taken a prominent part in German politics.

Prince Bismarck was once more occupied with important colonial questions. The Congo Conference concluded its labours in the month of February; and it was decided that freedom of commerce should be established in the basin and mouths of the Congo, on the whole coast line between the Colony of Gaboon and the province of Angola, and in the countries between the Congo basin and the Indian Ocean— subject, however, to the assent of their rulers. But difficulties next arose between Germany and England, with regard to the German acquisitions in the Cameroons and New Guinea. After a long correspondence between the Foreign Minister of Germany and the English Colonial Minister, these differences, together with others arising out of German Protectorates in various quarters, were satisfactorily adjusted. On the whole, German relations with Great Britain, and also with France, were of a pacific character. A serious dispute, however, arose between Germany and Spain out of the establishment of a German Protectorate over the Caroline Islands. Spain had claimed the suzerainty of these islands since the seventeenth century, but she had never been in actual possession of the territories. Germany now repudiated her claim, hoisted her own flag upon one of the islands, and placed all the group between the equator and 11 degrees north and 164 degrees east of Greenwich under German protection. Spain protested, and Bismarck—feeling for once that he was wrong—agreed to submit the matter to the Pope. The result was that by a protocol ultimately signed by the German and Spanish Governments, the Caroline Islands were left under the Sovereignty of Spain, while to Germany was granted the right of forming agricultural colonies in the islands, and she also obtained possession of certain coaling and naval stations. With regard to the Eastern Questions, both Asiatic and European, the German Chancellor still threw his influence into the scale of peace.

The celebration of Prince Bismarck's seventieth birthday, which occurred on the 1st of April, 1885, was also the celebration of his fiftieth year of public life. The double event excited great enthusiasm through all Germany. Many valuable presents were made to him, but the most important was the gift of the purchase deeds of the ancestral estates of Schönhausen, which had been sold by the family when in difficulties, and were now repurchased for £150,000, raised by subscriptions throughout the Fatherland. Among the congratulations received by the Prince were an autograph letter from the Emperor of Germany, telegrams from the Emperors of Russia and Austria, the Kings of Saxony, Bavaria, Sweden, Roumania, Siam, Wurtemburg, and Belgium, as well as 2100 letters and 3500 telegrams from various sources.

The Emperor William, accompanied by the Crown Prince and other members of his family, went to the Chancellor's residence, and, affectionately embracing him with tears in his eyes, presented him with a reduced copy of Von Werner's famous painting of the ' Proclamation of the Empire at Versailles.' The Emperor's letter, referred to above, ran as follows :—

'My dear Prince,—The German people having shown a warm desire to testify to you, on the occasion of your seventieth birthday, that the recollection of all you have done for the greatness of the Fatherland lives in so many grateful hearts, I, too, feel strongly impelled to tell you how deeply gratified I am that such a feeling of thankfulness and veneration for you moves the nation. I am rejoiced at this, for you have most richly earned the recognition, and my heart is warmed at seeing such sentiments manifested in so great a measure ; for it dignifies the nation in the present, and strengthens our hopes of its future, when it shows appreciation of the true and the great, and when it celebrates and honours its most meritorious men. To me, and to my house, it is an especial pleasure to take part in such a festival ; and by the accompanying picture, we wish to convey to you with what feelings of grateful recollection we do this, seeing that it calls to mind one of the greatest moments in the history of the House of Hohenzollern—one which can never be thought of without at the same time recalling your merits.

' You, my dear Prince, know how I shall always be animated towards you with feelings of the fullest confidence, of the most sincere affection, and the warmest gratitude. But, in saying this, I tell you nothing which I have not often enough already repeated to you, and methinks that this painting will enable your latest descendants to realise that your Kaiser and King, as well as his house, were well conscious of what they had to thank you for. With these sentiments and feelings, which will last beyond the grave, I end these lines. —Your grateful, faithful, and devoted Kaiser and King, WILHELM.'

In addition to the fame which Bismarck had acquired, one would think that even a less kingly appreciation than this would have kept him at his post many times when he was tempted to retire to his Pomeranian estates.

The Prussian Parliament met in January, 1886, and almost immediately the Polish question was again raised. A motion approving the action of the Government was introduced by the National Liberals and Conservatives, by way of reply to the previous hostile interpellation of the Ultramontanes. Prince Bismarck, in an able speech lasting more than two hours, placed the whole question on the basis of international policy. He contended that the action of the Prussian Government towards the Poles since 1815 had been an uninterrupted series of blunders, culminating in the philanthropic ideas of 1848. The Polish rising in 1830 first opened the eyes of the Prussian authorities to the true aspect of the question. Frederick William IV. hoped to win over the Poles by conciliation, but he was rudely awakened from his dream by the insurrections of 1846 and 1848. The concession of certain constitutional privileges since had only increased the disaffection of the Poles, and accentuated their aversion to their German rulers.

The Chancellor unfolded a plan for the acquisition of such Polish estates as might become free. He proposed to farm them out to Germans, provided that they pledged themselves to remain German, and, above all things, to marry German wives. The estates would be allotted on leases, but the tenants would become proprietors of the soil in from twenty-five to fifty years. Polish soldiers and officials would at the same time be given an opportunity of availing themselves of the advantages of German civilization by being

posted for service in provinces far away from their homes.
Bismarck then concluded with the following peroration, which
created great excitement in the House: 'Gentlemen, the
future is not wholly free from apprehensions. It is not
foreign dangers that menace us, but it is impossible to work
with such a majority as that in the Reichstag. We must aim
at becoming stronger: we must show that we stand not on
feet of clay, but of iron. We must find a means of becoming
independent of the obstruction of the majority of the Reichstag. I do not advocate such a step, but, if the Fatherland
should be endangered, I should not hesitate to propose to
the Emperor the necessary measures. The minister who
will not risk his head to save the Fatherland, even against
the will of the majority, is a coward. I will not allow the
achievements of our army to perish by internal discord,
which I will find the means of counteracting.' This was a
bold speech, and it was followed by another in which the
Chancellor compared the position of the Poles in Germany
to that of the Parnellites in England. After protests from
the Poles, the Radicals, and the Centre party, the policy of
the Prussian Government was approved by 234 votes, the
Opposition minority having previously left the House. Bills
were subsequently brought in and carried through, granting
100,000,000 marks to the Government for German colonization in Polish districts and for transferring to the State the
supervision in such districts of popular education.

As a counter-move against Democratic Socialism the
Chancellor introduced into the German Parliament the
Spirit Monopoly Bill and the Socialist Bill. The Radicals
opposed the former bill because it strove to bring about an
aristocratic socialism instead of that which was in favour
with the working classes. Bismarck, in supporting the
measure, let fall some ominous expressions. 'We do not
know what may happen in France,' he said. 'We hope that
peace will not be endangered for a long time, but, even at
the risk of losing my reputation as a diplomatist and a
statesman, I must confess that in the spring of 1870 I did
not foresee or fear the war which came a few months
later. If any such danger should again threaten us, I want
Germany to be at the height of her power. We have had
peace for fifteen years, but the nation is not yet fully prepared, and I hasten on these reforms in order that the

Empire may really stand fast if war should come to test our firmness.' The House was not to be played upon through fear, however, and the Bill was rejected by 181 to 3 votes only. The second measure proposed to prolong the Socialist Law for five years. It was strongly attacked by Herr Bebel, who declared that the incessant pressure of the ruling classes was finally driving the lower orders to use force in self-defence. It was so in Belgium, and, if similar conditions existed in Germany, he would be the first to adopt similar measures to counteract them. Prince Bismarck replied in severe terms. He affirmed that Bebel's words contained a direct threat to assassinate the German Emperor if certain conditions existed in Germany, as to which he and his fellow-socialists were to decide whether they justified such assassination. After a good deal of recrimination the Continuance Laws against the Socialists were passed by a majority of 169 to 137, but they were only to continue for two years instead of five as proposed by the Government.

Great excitement was caused in June by the news that King Louis II. of Bavaria had become insane, and that, while suffering from mental derangement, he had committed suicide in the Lake of Starnberg, dragging down with him to a watery grave his physician and attendant, Dr. Gudden. King Louis was popular with the lower classes, but his mania for building palaces and his refusal to perform the Royal functions had caused great embarrassment to his ministers. As the King's brother, Prince Otto, was also suffering from mental derangement, the Regency was assumed by Prince Luitpold, uncle of the late sovereign. Prince Luitpold was a supporter of the new *régime* in Germany, and was opposed to all Ultramontane measures, though a strong Catholic himself. The Emperor William at once accepted the Regent, whose mother, by the way, was a niece of Queen Louisa, the mother of the German Emperor.

The difficulties with Rome, which for four years had caused great friction in Germany, were satisfactorily adjusted in May of this year. A revision of the May Laws was carried by a majority of 260 to 108. Neither Bismarck nor the Pope could claim a complete triumph in regard to this legislation, for, although the Chancellor made considerable concessions, he by no means surrendered the control of the Roman Catholic Church in Prussia, while the Vatican had been obliged also greatly to abate its demands. Shortly before the Bill was introduced in the Prussian Parliament, the Pope had said in reply to an address from a party of German Catholics: 'I believe that you may now look with confidence to the future. The Emperor William has assured me of his kind sentiments and of his determination to meet the wishes of his Catholic subjects.' Practically this new legislation abrogated all the provisions of the May Laws except that which gave the State control over the ecclesiastical appointments of the Roman Catholic Church in Prussia. This provision was conceded by the Pope—whom Bismarck described as 'a wise, moderate, and pacific gentleman'—in return for the abandonment by the Prussian Government of various checks, such as those relating to State examinations of candidates for the priesthood, which had been described by the Chancellor as almost worthless, but which were regarded as very important at the Vatican.

Germany over sea still continued to be a matter of much concern with Prince Bismarck. His colonial policy was vigorous and adventurous, though he caused it to be known that the German flag would only go where German trade had already penetrated. Nevertheless, the naval expenditure greatly increased, for in addition to keeping ships at the six existing trans-oceanic naval stations, the German Government held in constant readiness a flying squadron, so as to be prepared for all emergencies. Other evidences of colonial enterprise were the founding of a seminary of Oriental languages in connection with the University of Berlin, and the grant of a Government subsidy to a line of German mail-steamers to Eastern Asia, with a branch service to Australia.

An agreement was concluded between Prince Bismarck and Baron Courcel, the French Ambassador, as to the possessions of Germany and France respectively on the West Coast of Africa. Germany ceded to France all her rights of sovereignty or protectorate over the territories of the Campo River; while France, on her part, recognized the German protectorate over the Togo country, and withdrew the claims arising from her relations with King Mensa to the territory of Porto Seguro. She further recognized the protectorate of Germany over Little Popo, and in both territories the French and German settlers were to be treated alike. With respect to the South Seas, Germany engaged not to do anything to prevent the occupation by France of islands in the immediate vicinity of the Society Islands or of the New Hebrides. Great Britain and Germany also came to an agreement as to the boundaries of their respective possessions in the Western Pacific, and a further settlement was concluded between the two Powers of the difficulties which had arisen on the West Coast of Africa. A convention was likewise concluded between Germany and Portugal as to South Western and Central Africa.

European relations, however, became seriously strained. France had completed her powerful armaments, Russia was assuming a threatening attitude, and Austria had grown lukewarm in her demeanour towards Germany. All this, of course, meant the fanning of the war spirit in Germany. Prince Bismarck decided to prepare for all eventualities by an increase of the German army. A Bill was accordingly brought forward in the Reichstag for raising the peace strength of the army—which stood at 427,274 men—by about 40,000 men, and for strengthening the artillery by twenty-four new batteries : the augmentation to take effect from the beginning of the ensuing financial year, namely April 1, 1887. The existing Septennate, which fixed the peace strength of the army, did not expire until 1888 ; but the Government represented that, although its relations with Foreign Powers were friendly, it was necessary—in view of the recent augmentation of the armies of Russia and France—to establish an increased peace strength of the German army before the expiration of the Septennate. The Bill was opposed by the Liberals and the Centre, on the ground that there was no urgent necessity for it, but Count Moltke declared that Europe was ‘ bristling with arms,’ and that the rejection of the measure would ‘ involve a very serious responsibility—perhaps the misery of a hostile invasion.’ The Count's speech made a profound impression, and the Bill was unanimously referred to a committee. This committee offered to grant the Crown 450,000 men for three years, instead of 468,000 for seven years ; but the Government refused to accept any compromise, and the debate was consequently adjourned *sine die*.

Prince Bismarck now sought to achieve his ends by

diplomacy, and was once more successful. The Emperor William, in a letter to the Czar, appealed to him to help in maintaining peace at least during the few years remaining to him (the German Emperor); and Austria was given to understand that if she interfered with Russian policy in Bulgaria she would receive no countenance from Germany. Shortly afterwards the European horizon became more peaceful.

The year 1886 was a very busy one for the Emperor William personally, though he was now nearly completing his ninth decade. On the 3rd of January, the twenty-fifth anniversary of his accession to the throne of Prussia was celebrated with cordial feelings through the whole of Germany. At Berlin, this Silver Jubilee of his rule was observed with more public demonstrations than had been the aged Emperor's desire. He was borne onward, however, by the current of the people's will. In the Chapel of the Royal Schloss there was a brief religious ceremony, attended by the Emperor and Empress, his Majesty's sister, the Dowager Duchess of Mecklenburg-Schwerin, the Crown Prince and Princess, with other members of the Royal Family, Prince Bismarck, Count Moltke, and other notabilities, the Foreign Ambassadors and their wives, &c. The ceremony, which was very short, only lasted for half an hour. The religious service consisted mainly of the deeply pious 'Now thank we all our God,' most effectively performed by a military band, and of a sermon by the chief Court preacher, Dr. Kögel, which partook of a politico-historical character.

The illustrious company then withdrew to the adjacent White Saloon, or Throne Room, where their Majesties received the congratulations of all those assembled. The ladies of the Diplomatic Corps first began to file past and to do obeisance. 'The Empress sat out this tedious ceremony to the end,' wrote an English correspondent, 'but the Kaiser stood the whole time without even wincing, and without so much even as changing from one foot to the other. The Emperor gives his hand to most of the Ambassadresses of the great Powers, and has a kindly word to say to each. With the profound courtesies of these diplomatic dames he seems chivalrously pleased. But when, at the head of their husbands, Prince Bismarck paces up to the throne, the Emperor is very visibly affected. The Chancellor stoops low to press his lips to the hand of his beloved Kaiser, and the latter returns the compliment by embracing his mighty and devoted servant, and kissing him on either cheek. That was an incident which few who saw it will ever forget. But our attention is for the moment diverted from it by the Russian Ambassador, who now approaches the throne, and, after making what seems to be a little set speech, quietly presents to the Emperor a sealed missive, which doubtless contains the personal congratulations of his lord and master the Czar, with, perchance, a brotherly assurance that peace and order in the East of Europe are now secured, so far as the policy of his particular Government is concerned. After this the Emperor gives his hand to Baron de Courcel, as if to express his pleasure at the friendly relations between the Empire and the French Republic, and then his Majesty beckons the approach of Sir Edward Malet, with whom he speaks a few words, as also of Lord Wolseley, to whom he flatteringly extends his hand. This honour is not accorded to all, and a long string of various dignitaries flows past without receiving any special mark of Imperial favour. But the continuity of this mutely reverencing stream is at last broken again, when Moltke glides up with a grave but courtly grace. To him the Emperor makes haste to give his hand, which Moltke, like Bismarck, would fain press to his lips; but his Majesty, with unmistakeable emotion, assumes himself the burden of gratitude, and embraces the great strategist in the same manner as he honoured his Chancellor. And again in the Throne Room there was a suppressed murmur of admiration of the mighty deeds which were recalled by this touching attachment of the Kaiser to the men who had done such great things for him and his House.'

The Emperor was busily engaged all day, and in the evening attended the opera. The house rang with 'Hochs!' when he took his seat, and also on his departure after the performance. The way to the Palace was blocked with a dense and cheering multitude; and Unter den Linden and the other main thoroughfares of Berlin were brilliantly illuminated.

In the Prussian capital, on the 10th of June, the Emperor William unveiled the equestrian statue of his brother, Frederick William IV., which has been placed in front of the

National Gallery. The ceremony was imposing. but essentially military in character. All the garrison regiments of Berlin were represented, and the principal State dignitaries were present. The Emperor and the members of his family occupied a pavilion which had been erected opposite the statue. In unveiling the memorial the Emperor saluted it thrice, and the troops presented arms. A Royal salute was then fired, and all the bells of the city pealed forth. At the foot of the statue was the simple inscription, 'To the memory of King Frederick William IV. King William.'

The centenary of the death of Frederick the Great was celebrated on the 17th of August at Berlin, and in the chief cities of the Empire. But the most interesting public ceremonial was that at Potsdam, the cradle of the Prussian Army. The garrison church of the town, where the great Frederick still reposes, was hung with hundreds of conquered flags and standards. The Emperor William, surrounded by all the members of his family, his Generals, his Ministers, and deputations from the Potsdam regiments, attended service in the chapel. At its conclusion the Emperor rose, and, approaching the open vault containing the remains of his distinguished ancestor, deposited a large wreath of laurels on the coffin, his example being followed by the Crown Prince and the other members of the Imperial House. All the troops then defiled before the Emperor in the Castle Garden, his Majesty himself giving the words of command, and thrice, too, he saluted with his sword when the Crown Prince led past him the 1st Foot Guards, wearing the conical brass head-gear of Frederick's time. Next followed the most characteristic incident of the centenary. The Emperor drove off to Sans-Souci, and spent several minutes of silent and solitary devotion in the room where his heroic ancestor breathed his last a hundred years before, and within little more than a decade of his Majesty's own birth. What surprising events had intervened between the reigns of the two Prussian kings !

Alsace-Lorraine, under its new Governor, Prince Hohenlohe, took a completely new departure in the year 1886. Although previously it had been bitterly hostile to the German rule, at the municipal elections of July the German party carried most of their candidates. At Metz their numbers in the Council were increased from four to twelve, and at Strasburg the 'protest' party could only elect nine members out of thirty-six. When the Emperor William visited Strasburg for the army manœuvres in September he was extremely well received. His Majesty reviewed 38,000 men on the Polygon outside the city, and the people were apparently much gratified by the Imperial visit, as well as strongly impressed by the martial bearing and admirable skill of the troops. The Emperor, on receiving the principal dignitaries of the city, assured the Bishop that he had offered his hand to help to restore religious peace to Germany, and he trusted the clergy would support him in that difficult task. He also expressed great satisfaction to the Burgomaster at the result of the recent municipal elections. His Majesty added that the people of Strasburg were quite as loyal as in the older provinces; and he saw with great pleasure that—though he had acceded with much hesitation to Prince Hohenlohe's urgent wish for the re-establishment of the Strasburg municipality—his misgivings had proved totally groundless.

We have seen that the Emperor William was present at the formal opening of Cologne Cathedral, and an interesting incident which has recently occurred in connection with the Cathedral and the German Kaiser may be recalled here. A bell weighing nearly twenty-seven tons, the clapper itself being three quarters of a ton, has been placed in position in the Cathedral. The inauguration ceremony was carried out amidst great pomp, a solemn religious service forming part of the proceedings. The bell was constructed from twenty-two cannons taken from the French in the war of 1870–71, and presented by the Emperor for that purpose. It bears an inscription recording that 'William, the most august Emperor of the Germans and King of the Prussians, mindful of the heavenly help granted to him whereby he conducted the late French war to a prosperous issue, and restored the German Empire, caused cannons taken from the French to be devoted to founding a bell to be hung in the wonderful Cathedral then approaching completion.' A likeness of St. Peter, the name-patron of the Church, is on the one side, beneath which is a quatrain in the style of the medieval concerts, praying that as devout hearts rise heavenward at hearing the sound of the bell, so may the door-keeper of heaven open wide the gates of the celestial mansion. On the opposite side is an inscription in German, the English of which runs as follows :—

> 'I am called the Emperor's bell;
> I proclaim the Emperor's honour;
> On the holy watch-tower I am placed.
> I pray for the German Empire,
> That peace and protection
> God may ever grant to it.'

This biographical and historical record cannot more fitly close than by some references to the ninetieth anniversary of the Emperor William's birth. Such an event is rare if not unparalleled in the history of sovereigns, and the celebrations which accompanied it were of a remarkable character. Not only Germany, but Germans all the world over, honoured the event by the most enthusiastic demonstrations of loyalty. In Berlin, of course, the greatest interest naturally centred ; and amongst those who journeyed thither to present their congratulations to the Emperor in person, were the Prince of Wales, the Crown Prince of Austria, the King and Queen of Saxony, the King and Queen of Roumania, the Crown Princes of Denmark and Sweden, representatives of the Czar, the King of Italy, and other sovereigns, while even the far East rendered its tribute in the person of Prince Komatsu of Japan. The whole of this memorable day, March 22, 1887, was given up to commemorative processions, services, and banquets ; and the accounts furnished by the correspondents of English journals in the Prussian capitals show that the celebration was truly unique. Although the Kaiser had not gone to bed till past midnight, he was up and dressed at eight o'clock. The first to congratulate His Majesty, as in many years past, were his two faithful valets. When Engel, the keeper of the wardrobe, addressed his Imperial master, the Emperor replied, 'It has been God's will that I should live to see this day. It was a favour I could scarcely hope for, but if it be God's will, I may, perhaps, even live to see one more birthday.' All the royal servants received as keepsakes a medal with an inscription and the dates, '1797, 22nd March, 1887.' At half-past nine the Empress made her affectionate congratulations, and conducted her husband to a room in which quite a legion of birthday presents had been arranged. The whole palace wore the aspect of a flower garden ; and indeed all day long magnificent floral offerings continued to arrive from all parts of the Empire.

When the Emperor appeared at the window of the Palace at ten o'clock, cries of 'Long live the Kaiser!' rent the air, and these were carried onwards and repeated by thousands who were not fortunate enough to see him, till the distant streets were filled with a hoarse roar, and the whole city seemed to ring with acclamations. Immediately in front of the Palace the loyal cries were repeated with renewed vigour every time the aged monarch showed himself, while as far as eye could reach the air was alive with fluttering handkerchiefs. Dressed in his parade uniform, with broad silver epaulettes and scarlet facings, the Emperor looked exceedingly well. No sign of tremulousness was apparent in the hand which he constantly waved in salutation to his subjects, and his figure was firm and upright.

The distinguished visitors were received in the Emperor's apartments on the first floor of the palace, which were fragrant with exotics and spring flowers from the north and south of Europe. The Emperor's birthday table was in a room adjoining the reception chamber, and it groaned beneath its burden of mementoes, presented by the members of the Kaiser's family. Amongst these welcome offerings was a portrait of the Emperor's great-grandson, a noble and beautiful boy. There was also amongst other presents a General's sash, after the exact pattern of the sashes worn by Frederick the Great. Of presents by foreigners, one very tastefully arranged basket, sent by six little English girls at school in Berlin, attracted much attention. The Christian names of the girls were written on the cards, with the words, 'To the dear Emperor,' and the following humane wish, 'Please make your people be kind to the poor horses that drag the bricks about.'

Though the Emperor was strong and well the reception was very wisely not prolonged too much. It was a touching sight, and one rendered doubly interesting and memorable by the fact that the Kaiser profited by the opportunity to announce the formal betrothal of his grandson, Prince Henry, the Crown Prince's sailor son, to the Prince's cousin, Princess Irene of Hesse, granddaughter of Queen Victoria. Congratulations were, under the happy circumstances, of course given to the young pair, who were now looking out upon life, as their patriarchal grandparent looked back upon it. The Empress Augusta, though somewhat infirm, kept up bravely through the presentation ceremony, and leaned upon the arm of her grandson, Prince William, whose charming young wife led up her little sons to present their congratulations to their Imperial great-grandsire. As for the Emperor, he actively threaded his way about among the guests; and 'the gaiety of his manner, the erectness of his gait, and the elasticity with which he stooped to kiss a lady's hand at parting, must all have tended to make his visitors doubt the fact that he had already lived a score of years beyond the Psalmist's allotted span of threescore years and ten.'

The various Royal personages excited much interest as they were driven up to the Palace. 'Perhaps the greatest excitement was associated with the approach of Prince William. His Royal Highness rode in a State coach, splendidly decorated in green and gold, of the unwieldy shape of a century ago. Silver crowns surmounted the roof, and the six splendid Pomeranian browns that drew it were caparisoned in silver and pale blue. The German Crown Prince and the Princess Royal, with their two daughters, rode in a carriage and six, with liveries of purple, blue, and silver. Volleys of cheers greeted the appearance of this carriage. The Crown Princess was enveloped in an ermine cloak, and smiled, with evident satisfaction, at the warmth with which they were welcomed. The Prince of Wales, who drove up in a splendid carriage and six, was heartily cheered by the people. The manner in which the Queen of Roumania was greeted was also most enthusiastic, and when she bowed her acknowledgments in her own peculiarly graceful manner, the cheers were redoubled. It seemed as if the people were not only welcoming the Queen, but Carmen Sylvia, the poetess.

'The reception was over, but the people still remained behind. They were rewarded for their patience, for a sudden stir among the people, succeeded by loud "Hochs!" showed that something important was happening. A plain carriage and pair drove slowly up, in which was seated Prince Bismarck. A similar movement again ran through the crowd, and Count Von Moltke appeared in a small open carriage, drawn by two spirited bays. They entered the

Palace within a few minutes of each other, and when the Emperor appeared at the window they could be seen on each side of him in the background; Prince Bismarck on his right, and Count Moltke on his left hand. It was a thrilling moment when these three men, who have accomplished so much for the Empire in common, showed themselves side by side. It is impossible to know what they said; but it is easy to imagine the thoughts which filled their hearts. As the great statesman and general drove away shortly afterwards there were signs of deep emotion on their faces.'

Wherever the stranger turned in the Prussian capital on this memorable day, he saw nothing but patriotic crowds: the shops were filled with patriotic mottoes; patriotic banners hung from the outward walls; in 'the theatres, at night, the patriotic plays and prologues elicited the chief interest. Portraits and busts of the Emperor, surrounded by wreaths, were to be seen everywhere; and above all the tumult of the day resounded the cheers for the nonagenarian monarch. Berlin had never witnessed such a scene; even the triumphal entry of the victorious German army in 1871 could not vie with it in enthusiasm. For days the rejoicings were maintained with an interest that never tired or grew faint.

The celebration was more than a mere personal one—it was the apotheosis of the German nation. The central figure of the Emperor represented its strength, its grandeur, and its powers of endurance. German unity was at last complete in all its far-reaching and magnificent development; and could the spirit of Stein have looked down upon the scene, and contemplated the vast work which had been achieved, that master mind would have been abundantly satisfied.

CHAPTER XV.

PERSONAL CHARACTERISTICS.

THE interest attaching to the great historical figures of the world is not all concentrated upon their public relations. Men are anxious to know something about the man as well as the ruler, nor is this curiosity injurious or unworthy. It is a matter which sensibly affects the meanest to know how the greatest wears that humanity which is common to both. How a monarch lives, what he does, and what are his traits of character, are points upon which we are all glad to learn something; for the same nature and passions are given to us all. Shakspeare has beautifully shown how the peasant and the king are one in the sight of Him who fashioned men in the same mould.

The German Emperor has always set before himself a high ideal of conduct and morals. In accordance with one of the family statutes of the Hohenzollerns, every member of that House, before confirmation, is required to draw up and submit to his or her parents, sponsors, and religious instructors, a profession of faith, which shall demonstrate to those responsible for the moral training of the candidates, whether their vows have been duly kept and their duties and obligations fulfilled. Such a statement Prince William composed, at the age of eighteen, when preparing for confirmation, and the document was 'equally remarkable for its pure doctrinal orthodoxy, devotional feeling, and vigorous literary style.' But in addition to this, the Prince drew up a supplementary manifesto, which he entitled 'Life Principles.' Of this manifesto—which sets in a clear light the manly and robust moral character of the Prince—the following free translation has been published:—

' With a thankful heart I acknowledge God's great beneficence in permitting that I should be born in an exalted station, because thereby I am better enabled to educate my soul and heart, and am put in possession of copious means wherewith to build up worthiness in myself. I rejoice in this station—not on account of the distinction it confers upon me amongst men, nor on account of the enjoyments it places at my disposal, but because it enables me to achieve more than others. In humility I rejoice in my station, and am far from believing that God has intended, in this respect, to put me at an advantage over my fellow-men. I am equally far from considering myself better than anybody else on account of my exalted station. My Princely rank shall always serve to remind me of the greater obligations it imposes upon me, of the greater efforts it requires me to make, and of the greater temptations to which it exposes me.

' I will never forget that a Prince is a man—before God, only a man—having his origin, as well as all the weaknesses and wants of human nature, in common with the humblest of the people ; that the laws prescribed for general observance are also binding upon him ; and that he, like all the rest, will one day be judged for his behaviour. For all good things that may fall to my share, I will look up gratefully to God ; and in all misfortunes that may befall me, I will submit myself to God, in the firm conviction that He will always do what is best for me. I know what, as man and Prince alike, my duty is to true honour. I will never seek honour to myself in things illusory. My capacities belong to the world and to my Fatherland. I will therefore work unintermittently within the circle of activity prescribed to me, make the best use of my time, and do as much good as it may be in my power to do.

' I will maintain and keep alive within me a sincere and hearty good will towards all men, even the most insignificant—for they are all my brethren. I will not domineer over anybody in virtue of my princely dignity, nor bring to bear upon any one the pressure of my princely prestige. When compelled to require any service at the hands of others, I will do so in a courteous and friendly manner, endeavouring, as far as in me lies, to render the fulfilment of their duties easy to them. But, in accordance with my own duty, I will do all I can to destroy the works of hypocrisy and malignity, to bring to scorn whatever is wicked and shameful, and to visit crime with its due measure of punishment ; no feelings of compassion shall hinder me therefrom. I will, however, be careful not to condemn the guiltless ; on the contrary, for me it shall ever be a labour of love to defend the innocent.

' To the utmost of my ability I will be a helper and advocate of those unfortunates who may seek my aid, or of whose mishaps I may be informed—especially of widows, orphans, aged people, men who have faithfully served the State, and those whom such men may have left behind them in poverty. Never will I forget the good that has been done to me by my fellow-men. Throughout my whole life I will continue to value those who have rendered me service.

' For the King, my father, I entertain a respectful and tender affection. To live in such sort that I may be a joy to him will be my utmost endeavour. I yield the most punctilious obedience to his commands. And I entirely submit myself to the laws and constitution of the State. I will perform my service-duties with absolute exactitude, and whilst assiduously keeping my subordinates to their duty, will treat them amicably and kindly.'

Few Princes of eighteen, or indeed men of any other age or station, have ever drawn up such a moral code for their guidance as this. What is much more noble, however, and more to the purpose, the Emperor has throughout his long career conscientiously endeavoured to fulfil its obligations. The sterling uprightness of his character found another strong verification in a memorandum which, as King of Prussia, he drew up and caused to be appended to an ordinance respecting officers' courts of honour. Many are the anecdotes told illustrative of the high value which the Emperor attaches to duty, but one very simple incident must suffice. A distinguished personage was once in conversation with His Majesty when the guards came by. The Kaiser was most particular to fasten the top button of his uniform before showing himself to the soldiers, whereat the visitor marvelled greatly. He asked the Emperor why he should stand so much upon ceremony with men who saw him almost daily face to face. The Emperor replied, 'That is not the question at all: as the head of the Army, I am bound to show my soldiers an irreproachable example in the way of *tenue*. They have never seen me with my coat unbuttoned, and I do not intend that they ever shall. For, let me tell you, it is the one button left unbuttoned that is the ruin of an army!' The French paid dearly for this perfect soldierly form and preparedness on the part of the Germans during the war of 1870–71.

The Emperor has always cared more for the substance of a thing than the appearance. This holds true in great things as well as in little. A good example was furnished at the time when he accepted the Imperial dignity. Those Sovereigns who were great sticklers for forms and ceremonies represented to His Majesty that only his Coronation was wanting to set the seal upon the New Empire and himself as Emperor. The Kaiser heard all they had to urge, and then replied: 'I am very much obliged to you for attaching so much importance to my Coronation as

German Emperor, although I do not share your views in that particular direction. However, if the German people make a point of it, I am quite ready to be crowned whenever and wherever the nation may please, provided the needful insignia are placed at my disposal for the ceremony. Personally, I experience no desire to be crowned, and nothing is farther from my intention than to spend a single penny of my private means upon regalia. In a word, if Germany wants her Kaiser crowned, let her pay for his crown ; I certainly will not. Crowned or not crowned, I am what the voice of the nation has by acclamation pronounced me to be, and shall remain so, please God, as long as I live!' The sovereigns are still waiting for the Imperial Coronation.

The uniform kindness of heart and forgiving disposition of the Kaiser are proverbial. It is said that in the past, the exercise of these qualities has sometimes been called for even in his relations with the Empress. Her Majesty is reported to have tried occasionally the fine and chivalrous temper of her husband, who is fourteen years her senior. The Emperor is a soldier, frank, open-hearted, and now and then somewhat impatient of the mere *convenances* of society ; but the Empress Augusta has little sympathy with military habits or the military life. She is a *dilettante* in literature, science, and the arts ; and she is reputed to have sometimes attempted to thwart the schemes of Bismarck, but in vain. Nevertheless, the Emperor's devotion to her has always been conspicuous, and his thoughts have gone out first to his wife when he has been fighting for the cause of Germany on the battlefield.

When at Ems the Emperor has always delighted to mingle with ordinary folk and enter into conversation with them. He has borne his ninety summers lightly, and exhibited a freshness and energy which men two-thirds his age might envy. Under the colonnade at Ems, on the occasion of his last visit, His Majesty entered into conversation with a number of ladies and gentlemen. Then he visited the goldsmiths' shops, and made large purchases, joking with the jewellers meanwhile. In one shop he took up an ornament, and when the jeweller pointed out what a fine piece of work it was, he remarked in reply, 'Yes, and it will be a fine price, no doubt. If you find a purchaser,

I shall congratulate you.' 'I know who might buy it, your Majesty.' 'Who, then?' 'Your Majesty, yourself.' 'Can't be.' The Emperor is very partial to seals, of which he has a valuable collection. He now asked the price of one which pleased him. 'It costs a thousand marks, your Majesty.' 'That is too dear.' 'Your Majesty will recollect that in the year 1882, you bought one that cost fifteen hundred marks.' The Emperor immediately remembered the fact, and replied, 'Yes, you are right; but the handle was much larger.' As the Kaiser was walking in the colonnade, he observed a young cadet, and beckoning to him to come near, said, 'What do you mean to be, my son?' 'A Field-Marshal, your Majesty.' The Emperor laughed, and remarked to his companions, 'He knows how to answer.' Like a venerable father, he wandered hither and thither, with a friendly word for many of his subjects, and kind greetings for all. By his desire, some thirty officers and soldiers who were staying at Ems for the sake of the waters took up their station before the Emperor's lodging. His Majesty came among them, and kindly inquiring after their circumstances, and the cause of their stay at Ems, wished each separately a speedy recovery. This paternal interest in his subjects has done much to strengthen their affection for him.

In his habits of life the Kaiser is extremely simple. When at home in the Palace at Berlin, he breakfasts every morning at half-past seven, invariably using coffee, with a large allowance of milk, and bread without butter. Should the weather permit, he takes walking exercise daily before luncheon, which is served at one o'clock. Boiled crab is a favourite dish at this meal, and is partaken of with great relish. Between luncheon and dinner, affairs of State are attended to for at least two hours, and sometimes longer. Then he rests until it is time to dress for dinner. The fixed hour for this is four o'clock. Every morning the chief cook submits the bill of fare for approval. It usually consists of five courses. The Kaiser has a decided preference for plain food. He is liberal in the use of fruit, and drinks mineral water procured from a natural spring. A cup of tea, without bread or cake, is the only refreshment he takes between dinner and bedtime. He makes a point of resting for half an hour after breakfast and luncheon, and an hour after dinner. When there are guests invited to dinner they meet him in an ante-chamber, where a quarter of an hour is spent in chatting. He then leads the way to the dining-room. The invitations are always sent out at an early hour, and the seats discussed with the Court-Marshal. When there are no guests the Emperor dines with the Empress, and the cook takes orders from her.

In summer, while at Gastein or some other watering-place, the Emperor goes to the bath-room at half-past seven o'clock in the morning. He breakfasts at eight, and walks at ten, accompanied by a personal adjutant and special attendant. Luncheon is served at eleven o'clock, and between twelve and three he confers with the officers of the civil and military cabinets, who are in waiting. Dinner is served at four: it consists of soup, fish, boiled beef, two *entrées*, dessert, and fruit. All the members of the Imperial suite attend. At six o'clock he takes a carriage ride, makes a social call, and chats for an hour or longer. He is never out of bed later than ten o'clock. The Emperor takes considerable interest in sanitary science, and is very particular in the matter of air and ventilation. Riding to hounds has always been one of his favourite amusements; and he is a splendid figure on horseback. It is not too much to say that such a simple life as is here sketched out, with its accompanying wise and wholesome regimen, would do much to prolong many an existence which is now cut short by luxury and indulgence.

Some other traits of the Emperor may be mentioned. His firmness is well-known; whenever he has made up his mind as to what is right to be done, his will is inflexible, and nothing would move him from his purpose. Constancy might well be his motto—constancy in friendship, in truth, and in religion. He can, moreover, be very generous, as his personal treatment of the dispossessed King of Hanover testified; the Emperor Napoleon also well knew this fact. He is humane too, and has always entered upon war with great reluctance. Bismarck, who upon this point is well qualified to speak, has said that there could not be a more humane man than his Imperial master. Strangely enough for one who has been concerned in so many wars, His Majesty is a lover of peace, and has repeatedly smoothed over difficulties which might easily have led to European conflicts. More than once he has declared that the blood of Germans shall only be shed to protect the honour and interests of the Fatherland. The Emperor's sincere and unaffected piety we have already had occasion to refer to in the course of this work. In all the great crises of his life, he has been strangely moved and influenced by it; but his faith has been of a robust nature, weakened by none of the grosser elements of superstition.

It seems strange that one who has been equally noble, both as a man and as a sovereign, should have been a mark for the assassin's bullet. This very point was the subject of an interesting conversation between Prince Bismarck and General Grant shortly after Dr. Nobiling's attempt. The ex-President of the United States happened to be in Berlin at the time. General Grant having expressed his horror at the crime, and made an allusion to the Kaiser's venerable years, Bismarck replied with much emotion: 'Here you have an old man, one of the best men on earth, and yet they try to take his life. There never was a man of simpler, more magnanimous, and more humane character than the Emperor. He is totally different from those who are born to such a high position, or at least from many of them. You know that persons of his rank, princes by birth, are inclined to look upon themselves as something wholly different from other men, attaching but little value to the feelings and wishes of others. But the Emperor, on the contrary, is a man in all things. He has never in his life wronged any one, nor hurt any one's feelings, nor acted with severity. He is one of those men whose kindly disposition wins all hearts; and he is always occupied with, and mindful of, the happiness and welfare of his subjects, and of those about him. It is impossible to imagine a finer, nobler, more amiable, and beneficent type of a nobleman, with all the high qualities of a sovereign and the virtues of a man. I should have thought that the Emperor could have passed through all his dominions alone without danger; and now they seek to kill him.'

The Chancellor further said: 'In certain respects the Kaiser resembles his ancestor Frederick William, the father of Frederick the Great; inasmuch as the old King had the same homely sort of character—lived simply and retired, and led a true family life, possessing all republican virtues.

And so it is with our Kaiser, who is in all things so republican, that even the most incarnate democrat would admire him if his judgment were impartial.' General Grant observed that he did not see why a person who committed such a crime as Nobiling's, which not only imperilled the life of an aged sovereign, but filled the world with horror, should not be visited with the severest punishment. To this Bismarck responded: 'That is precisely my view; and my conviction on this head is so strong, that (among other reasons) I resigned the reins of power in Alsace so as not to have to exercise mercy in cases of capital punishment. It was impossible for me to force my conscience. Well, now, look at this aged nobleman, this Emperor of ours, whose subjects sought to murder him—such is his largeness of heart, that he never will confirm a sentence of death. It is impossible to imagine anything more unique—a monarch, whose clemency, so to speak, has abolished capital punish-ment, becoming himself on that very account the victim of a murder, or an attempt to murder! That is a fact; but in this respect I cannot agree with the Emperor; and in Alsace, where I as Chancellor had to countersign acts of mercy, I always inwardly rebelled against doing so. In Prussia that is the business of the Minister of Justice, but in Alsace it fell to me. I feel, as the French say, that we owe justice something, and that in the case of crimes like this they must be severely punished.' Grant and Bismarck were at one in thinking that such criminals should be destroyed, but the Emperor invariably leaned to mercy's side.

There seemed every probability that the Imperial family of Germany would continue to enjoy for some time unbroken peace and happiness, when the Crown Prince was suddenly struck down by a painful malady towards the close of 1887. On the advice of his medical men he left Berlin for San Remo, and there, under the assiduous attentions of Sir Morell Mackenzie and certain German specialists, he partially recovered, and went through the operation of tracheo-tomy, which was successfully performed. For several days afterwards he was in a precarious condition, but ultimately recovered much of his strength, owing to his vigorous constitution.

Early in March 1888, however, the Emperor himself was

stricken with illness, and the fact that he was unable to take his usual stand at the windows of the Palace at Berlin, and watch the march past of the troops, was regarded as an unfavourable omen. An official bulletin made known that His Majesty was suffering from a general cold, combined with an affection of the mucous membrane of the throat and an irritation of the eyelids. Then he became troubled by acute abdominal pains, and in consequence of loss of appetite suffered a marked loss of strength. On the 7th it was seen that he was in a critical condition ; but, although very weak, he recovered from a prolonged torpor, and the following day took food, and conversed rationally with the Empress and with his grandson Prince William. The same afternoon, nevertheless, it was felt that the end was near. The aged monarch was full of fortitude, and joined fervently in the prayers offered up by the Court Chaplain. He then took leave of everybody, his mind being perfectly clear, and his ideas quite consecutive. When requested to guard his remaining strength, the Kaiser said, ' No ; I feel I have not much more time to live—I prefer to say all I wish to say.' At six o'clock he took the Communion, and shortly afterwards a false report was spread in Berlin that the Emperor was dead.

His Majesty passed a much better night than had been expected. During the succeeding day, Thursday, he conversed with Prince Bismarck, thanking him for his services. He also welcomed his daughter the Grand Duchess of Baden, and spoke of his absent son the Crown Prince. ' About half-past five o'clock a paroxysm of extreme weakness supervened, and many of the attendants believed that all was over. But the Emperor suddenly rallied, and looking round, recognised the members of his family. He asked for Count Moltke, and then called Prince William to come close to him, and talked with them for a long time. He began by speaking of the Army and of Prussia ; then referred to the alliances into which Germany had entered, and to the possible wars of the future with neighbouring peoples, to whose military institutions he had, he said, of late given special attention. His soldiers and reminiscences of the wars in which he had taken part formed a portion of this extraordinary discourse, which was broken now and again by a return of the delirium. Several familiar names passed the aged Emperor's lips during this conversation, which was, however, all on one side, and lasted until about ten o'clock on Thursday night.' He now appeared to sleep for four hours, but at two o'clock on Friday morning, the 9th, it was noticed that a serious change had taken place. The members of the Imperial family were again summoned at three o'clock. The Emperor recognised those nearest and dearest to him, but the remaining hours of his life were passed in a semi-conscious state, yet without suffering; and at half-past eight o'clock he entered calmly, and without a struggle, upon his eternal rest.

It is stated that in the course of conversation with Prince William at his bedside, the Emperor wanderingly remarked, 'Thou must treat the Emperor of Russia with consideration, for that will only redound to our good;' and then afterwards, laying his hand on Bismarck's shoulder, His Majesty said, 'Thou hast done that well.' When Dr. Kögel, the Court Chaplain, repeated to the Emperor the words of the Psalmist—'Yea, though I walk through the valley of the shadow of death, I will fear no evil: for Thou art with me ; Thy rod and Thy staff they comfort me'—the Emperor observed, 'That is beautiful (Das ist schön).' The preacher then quoted from the Gospel of St. John the sentence, 'In the world ye shall have tribulation; but be of good cheer, I have overcome the world.' But the Emperor did not reply to this. His last words are said to be those with which he replied to a question from his daughter, the Grand Duchess of Baden, as to whether he was tired and would like to rest. 'I have no time at present to be tired,' responded His Majesty. 'Sometimes, when his thoughts were wandering, the dying Monarch would think of his afflicted son and successor far away on the Mediterranean shore, and murmur, 'Fritz, lieber Fritz.' When the Emperor, uttering a gentle sigh, had yielded up his spirit, the illustrious mourners around the simple camp-bed knelt down and kissed his folded hands.'

The following more extended details of the last hours of the Emperor are reported to be from one who never left the bedroom :—'From eleven o'clock the Emperor did not sleep, but lay in a half-unconscious condition. The doctors tried all in their power to arouse him, and at length succeeded.

His Majesty did not suffer at all, and was quite conscious; but his strength decreased so rapidly that the doctors saw that the end was approaching. At intervals the Emperor spoke a few words to the Grand Duchess of Baden and the Princess William, but in such a weak voice that he could scarcely be understood. Towards six in the morning he became unconscious, and was not able to recognize anybody. The Empress was led away before this, and the Grand Duchess of Baden was so overcome that she, too, had to leave the death-bed. Suppressed sobs resounded through the room. Prince William stood the whole time at the bedside, and never took his eyes off his grandfather. All at once the Emperor moved his arms, as if trying to raise himself. His chest heaved, and with a deep sigh he fell back on the pillow, and all was over. All present kissed his hand, and the Court Chaplain blessed him. No death struggle made his last moments painful. As he lay on the historical iron bed which had been his companion in all phases of his career, the expression of peace on his countenance was a true reflex of what his life had been during the last eighteen years.'

The following is another account:—' Yesterday evening, when the Emperor awoke from his heavy swoon, the Court Chaplain, Dr. Kögel, offered up a prayer, which consisted mostly of selections from the Bible. The Emperor interrupted him frequently with the words " That's right " and " Good." When the Grand Duchess of Baden asked him if he had heard the words of the clergyman, he said " Yes." After the Emperor had partaken of a little food he seemed very talkative, and spoke with Prince William, probably renewing a conversation which he had had with him within the last few days. He spoke in a clear voice about the political situation and the military arrangements of Germany. He mentioned that the reforms he had carried out in the army had been copied in France. He talked about Russia, and expressed a strong opinion that it would not come to a war with that country. The Emperor spoke in the most friendly terms about the Austro-German relations, but it is not certain whether he was conscious or wandering in his mind. The Grand Duchess of Baden begged him not to tire himself with too much talking. He answered, " I have no time to be tired." After a while, however, he fell asleep again, and awoke about eight o'clock. He then left his bed, dressed and undressed himself, not allowing anybody to help him. After this he lay down again, and passed several quiet hours. During the night he asked for some champagne, which was given him. Towards four o'clock he became weaker, and Prince Bismarck, Count Moltke, and the Court Chaplain, Dr. Kögel, were again sent for. The two former left the Palace towards seven o'clock. The whole Imperial family were present when the Emperor died. The Duke of Ratibor, Count Otto Stollberg, and Count Wernigerode, who is Minister of the Household, were also in attendance. Just before His Majesty breathed his last, the Court Chaplain gave the Benediction, and, when all was over, said a prayer. The Empress and all the members of the Imperial family then approached the bed, and each kissed the hand of the departed Monarch. The officers on duty and the servants afterwards entered the chamber, but the doctors only left it at ten. In the meanwhile all the Ministers of State arrived at the Palace, and offered their condolences to the Empress.'

His Majesty is reported to have said shortly before his death, adopting the usual familiar way in German of speaking of one's relations or intimate friends, and which we might perhaps render into English thus :—'Once more I should like to embrace Fritz, my Fritz,' referring, of course, to the Crown Prince.

In the sitting of the Reichstag, Prince Bismarck announced the death of the Emperor. The Chancellor was overcome by his emotion, and had to make long pauses to suppress his tears. In the course of his address he said :—' During the last days of his life I received from our late august master, as a confirmation of the power of work which only left him with his life, the signature which lies before me, and which empowers me to close the Reichstag at the usual time after its labours are concluded, that is to say, about to-day or to-morrow. I requested the Emperor to sign only with his initials. His Majesty replied that he believed himself to be still able to write his name in full. In consequence, this historical document, the last signature of His

Majesty, lies before me. Under the existing circumstances, I assume that it would be in accordance with the wish of the Reichstag, as well as of the Federal Governments, if the Reichstag were not to separate just now, but remain in Session until after the arrival of His Majesty the Emperor. I therefore do not make any use of the Imperial authorization beyond depositing it in the archives as an historical document, and requesting the President to facilitate the adoption of resolutions in accordance with the feeling and conviction of the Reichstag. It is not for me, standing in this official place, to give expression to the personal feelings with which the decease of my master, the departure of the first German Emperor from our midst, fills me. This is, in fact, not necessary, for the feelings which animate me live in the hearts of every German. But there is one thing which, I think, I ought not to conceal from you—it does not concern my emotions, but my experiences—the fact that, amid the sore visitations with which the Ruler just departed from us lived to see his House afflicted, there were two circumstances which filled him with satisfaction and comfort. One of them was that the sufferings of his only son and successor, our present Sovereign lord, have elicited throughout the world, not only in Germany, but, one might say, in every part of the earth—I have had to-day a telegram of this kind from New York—a sympathy which shows the confidence which the dynasty of the German Imperial House has acquired among all nations. This is a legacy which the Emperor's long reign bequeaths to the German people. The confidence which the dynasty has won will be transferred to the nation, despite all efforts to the contrary. The second fact in which His Majesty found solace in many a hard trial was this—that the Emperor could look back, with a satisfaction which glorified and illumined the evening of his life, to the fulfilment of his chief life-task—the foundation and consolidation of the nationality of the people to which he, as a German Prince, belonged.'

After a few heartfelt words from the President von Wedell in honour of the Emperor William, Prince Bismarck descended the steps from the benches of the Bundesrath and approached Count Moltke, who had heard his words, and with whom he most cordially shook hands. They were joined by the Duke of Ratibor and Minister von Puttkamer, and when they separated, Prince Bismarck handed the historical document to the President, who showed it to the Deputies.

Messages of condolence were received by the Imperial family from all the leading Sovereigns of Europe, from the French President, and from Germans in all parts of the world. At the English Court, in London, and throughout the whole of Great Britain, the mournful intelligence of the Emperor's death was received with profound regret and sympathy.

The Crown Prince was now proclaimed the new German and Prussian ruler, under the title of Frederick III.

The official *Reichsanzeiger* published the following telegram, which the Emperor Frederick sent to the Imperial Chancellor from San Remo:—

'In the moment of deepest sorrow for the home-going of His Majesty the Emperor and King, my beloved father, I express to you and to the Ministers of State my thanks for the devotion and fidelity with which you all served him, and count upon the assistance of all of you in the heavy task laid upon me. I leave for Berlin on the morning of the 10th.

(Signed)   'FRIEDRICH.'

This was followed by an Imperial decree to the Ministers of State concerning the *Landestrauer*, or national mourning. It says:—'Regarding the mourning hitherto customary, we will make no decree, but leave it to each German to express his sorrow for the departure of such a monarch, and to determine the duration of the restriction of public amusements as seems fittest to himself.'

The Emperor Frederick and the Empress Victoria left San Remo for Berlin on the 10th of March.

Now that the Emperor William is numbered with his fathers, we are able to reflect upon the wonderful fact how the mightiest of all the European States, in this the most active and advanced era in the world's history, was ruled, and ruled admirably, by a nonagenarian monarch. He only succeeded to the throne of Prussia at sixty-four years of age, a period when most men begin to 'shuffle off' this mortal coil.' Yet he lived for more than a quarter of a century

after his accession, and such a quarter of a century as has
rarely been seen in the annals of any nation or people. Vast
upheavals took place during its course, and the map of
Europe was several times reconstructed, always to the greater
glory and advantage of Prussia and the German race. Nothing
more surprising in the way of territorial and historical
changes could well be conceived. The life of the German
Kaiser spanned the whole momentous period from Jena to
Sedan.

The life of the Emperor William was the rampart of the
peace of Europe. No other agent was so powerful in ensuring
tranquillity. Fortunately, his successor, though not wielding
the same powerful personal sway in Europe, is distinguished
for the same pacific tendencies; and it would require very
strong provocation indeed to compel him to draw the sword.
Germany is a salutary interposing force between Austria
and Russia, and exercises a modifying influence upon both
those Powers. So long as the alliance between Germany
and her Imperial neighbours last, there will be no war. Of
course, it needs but a slight thing to kindle the war-flame
in Europe; but when so many Powers are armed to the
teeth and ready for war, the responsibility is all the greater for
the individual Power which casts the match into the powder.
This is the one paramount restraining consideration.

What will be the future of Germany now that the Emperor
William is dead? That is a question which no doubt
frequently agitated the mind of the late Kaiser, as it is one
which must now cause the deepest solicitude to his Chancellor. It cannot be forgotten that all the co-makers of
Germany—and not alone the late Emperor—have, like their
Imperial master, been growing old together. 'Sufficient
unto the day is the evil thereof,' is a good maxim for individuals, but newly-formed Empires and States are to a great
extent compelled to forecast the future. Time only can prove
whether the new and younger race, which now begins to succeed to the Imperial inheritance in Germany, will be able to
maintain it intact, and to deepen and strengthen the foundations of the Empire. The veterans of 1870 are passing away;
who will take their place? Such is the problem of the future.
Meanwhile, the venerable Emperor William has gone to that
'bourne from whence no traveller returns,' and the eyes of

the whole civilized world, which followed him with kindly and wondering interest in the flesh, can do so no longer. Viewed in its relations to the German race and the German Empire, his career was great and glorious beyond that of any contemporary sovereign ; and, notwithstanding the imperfections which cling to all of human mould, when history comes to delineate his character, it will depict him as a man amongst men, a king amongst kings, and a true father to his people.

APPENDIX.

STATISTICS OF THE GERMAN EMPIRE.

It will be of value, as well as interest, to add here certain facts and statistics concerning the Constitution, population, finances, &c., of the German Empire. This information is gleaned from recent official returns.

The confederated States known as the German Empire, were formally united under the Emperor William on May 4, 1871, when the constitution of the German Empire replaced the articles of confederation between the North German States, and the treaties by which the Grand Duchies of Baden and Hesse, and the kingdoms of Bavaria and Würtemburg, entered the League during the Franco-Prussian War. The Sovereign powers of the Empire are vested in the Prussian Crown and the Federal Council (Bundesrath), but the concurrence of the Reichstag (Parliament) is necessary to the exercise of certain functions. The Reichstag is elected by universal suffrage. It has certain rights of control over the acts of the Government. For example, to declare war (if not merely defensive) the Emperor must have the consent of the Federal Council, in which body, conjointly with the Reichstag, are vested the legislative functions of the Empire. The Federal Council represents the individual States, and the Reichstag the entire nation. The Federal Council consists of sixty-two members, who are appointed by the governments of the individual States for each session, while the members of the Reichstag, 397 in number, are elected by universal suffrage, under the ballot, for a term of three years. The Chancellor of the Empire (Prince Bismarck) presides over the Bundesrath, or Federal Council, and he has also the right to interpose in the deliberations of the Reichstag. The Emperor calls both bodies together annually. All Imperial laws must be voted by a majority in both Houses, and the Emperor's assent, with the counter-signature of the Chancellor, are necessary to give them effect. Prussia and the other States, in addition to their joint Imperial relations, have of course a separate Constitution, Parliament, and Ministry of their own.

The area of Germany is 211,149 square miles. The census of December 1, 1880, gave the total population of the Empire at 45,234,061, of whom 22,185,433 were males, and 23,048,628 females. The number of foreigners scattered throughout Germany was only 275,856, of whom 117,547 were born in Austria-Hungary, 28,244 in Switzerland, 23,593 in Denmark, 17,772 in the Netherlands, 17,393 in France, 15,107 in Russia, 11,155 in Great Britain and Ireland, 10,326 in the United States, and the remainder in various other countries. By December, 1885, the number of foreigners in Germany had made no perceptible increase, being then only 276,057. According to an enumeration of the population of the Empire with reference to professions and employments, made on June 5, 1882, the inhabitants of the Empire were thus distributed:— Those engaged in agriculture, stock-raising, and gardening, 18,838,653; forestry, hunting, and fishing, 384,593; mining industry and works of construction, 16,054,291; commerce and transportation, 4,529,780; labour for hire and domestic service, 938,143; public service, ecclesiastical, and liberal professions, 2,223,184; and those without profession or employment, 2,245,257. As compared with the year 1871, the number of those engaged in agriculture had increased enormously, whilst those engaged in personal and domestic service had decreased in like proportion. The latest census of the German Empire, taken on December 1, 1885, gives the total area of the twenty-five States of the Empire at 211,149 English square miles (as stated above) and the total population at 46,852,680.

At the time of the census of 1880, the population was thus divided as regards religious belief: Evangelical, 28,318,592; Catholic, 16,229,290; other Christians, 93,894; Jewish, 561,612; and those unassigned, 30,673. The Protestant element thus embraced 62·6 per cent. of the entire population.

In 1881 there were 47,720 emigrants who renounced German nationality, as compared with 28,780 in 1880. With every year since 1880, the number of emigrants from the German Empire has been very great. In 1881 the total number of emigrants reached 210,547; in 1882 it was 193,687; in 1883, 166,119; in 1884, 143,586; and in 1885, 103,642. The total emigration from 1820 to the end of 1882 was nearly 4,000,000, of which number about 3,250,000 emigrated to the United States.

The population of German cities containing upwards of 100,000 inhabitants in 1880 was as follows: Berlin, 1,122,330; Hamburg, 285,859 (with suburbs 410,127); Breslau, 272,912; Munich, 230,023; Dresden, 220,818; Leipsic, 149,081; Cologne, 144,772; Königsberg, 140,909; Frankfort-on-the-Main, 136,819 (including faubourgs, 164,697); Hanover, 122,843 (with Linden, 145,227); Stuttgart, 117,303; Bremen, 112,458; Dantzic, 108,551; and Strasburg, 104,471.

Education is compulsory throughout all the German States, and the elementary schools are supported by the Communes. It appeared from the returns of 1878, that all recruits of the army could read and write, though in Bavaria, and some other parts of South Germany, there was a small percentage whose education generally was backward. The Empire, however, will contrast favourably with other European States in the matter of education. In the universities of Munich, Münster, Freiburg, and Wurtzburg, Roman Catholic theology is taught, and in Bonn, Breslau, and Tübingen, both Catholic and Protestant; all the other universities are of an exclusively Protestant character. In addition to students for degrees, there are non-matriculated students, who in Berlin always number considerably more than a thousand annually.

With regard to the financial condition of the Empire, the Budget for the year 1884–5—which was voted July 2, 1883—estimated the yield of the customs duties at 196,450,000 marks, the mark being equal to one shilling in English money. The excise duty on sugar was estimated at 46,865,000 marks; on salt, 37,262,600 marks; on tobacco, 13,940,920 marks; on spirits, 35,925,900 marks; on malt, 15,791,000 marks; the net receipts of posts and telegraphs, 25,832,193 marks; of railroads, 16,690,600 marks; stamp duties, 19,436,680 marks; receipts of the invalid funds, 28,665,120 marks; and surplus of the budget of 1882–83, 15,825,000 marks. The extraordinary receipts were estimated as follows: From construction fund for fortifications, 10,400,000 marks; for Parliament-house, 2,000,000; from loan for extraordinary purposes, 22,192,720—making a total of 34,592,720 marks. The above sums, together with receipts from minor sources amounting to 83,702,768 marks—to be provided by the matricular quota shares of the States—made up a total budget of 590,819,344 marks. This amount was to be appropriated as follows: Current expenditure, 544,327,866 marks; extraordinary expenditure, 46,491,478 marks. The military administration absorbed no less than 339,872,490 marks of the current, and 26,762,678 of the extraordinary expenditure.

The German Budget for the year 1887–88 presented an estimated revenue and expenditure of 746,888,121 marks, the permanent expenditure being placed at 627,351,430 marks, and the non-recurring at 119,536,691 marks. The total estimated expenditure showed an increase of 53,554,816 marks over that of the previous year; and to meet the extraordinary expenditure of 1887–88 a loan of 66,000,000 marks would be necessary.

The various loans authorized by the Reichstag, and the dates of the laws authorizing them, were as follows: June 14, 1877, 77,731,321 marks; June 14, 1878, 97,484,865 marks; March 13, 1879, 68,021,071 marks; October 13, 1880, 37,627,203 marks; April 5 and December 12, 1881, 64,912,885 marks; February 15, 1882, 29,674,405 marks; and July 2, 1883, 18,192,720 marks. Of the amount authorized prior to April 1, 1882, there had been issued at that date 319,239,000 marks. The value of the bank-notes of the Empire in circulation at the same date was 153,164,210 marks.

On October 1, 1886, the total funded debt was estimated to amount to 460,000,000 marks; and there was in addition an unfunded debt amounting to 137,527,800 marks. As a set-off against the debt of the Empire, there existed the following invested funds: the fund for invalids, 514,360,717 marks; the fortification fund, 30,950,600 marks; fund for Parliament buildings, 20,996,400 marks; and a war treasure fund, 120,000,000 marks.

Touching the commerce of the Empire, the total value of the imports in 1881 was 2,961,000,000 marks; and the total exports 2,974,000,000 marks. The imports of cereals were 372,000,000, and the exports 96,000,000 marks; the imports of fermented liquors, 43,000,000, and the exports 75,500,000; imports of live animals and animal products 330,000,000, and exports 186,000,000. The exports of manufactured products were nearly 90,000,000 marks more than in 1880. In 1885 the total German imports amounted in value to 2,989,969,000 marks, and the total exports to 2,915,257,000 marks. The strength of the German merchant marine on January 1, 1882, was as follows: Ordinary vessels, 4,509; tonnage, 1,194,407; crews, 39,109; steamers, 458; tonnage, 251,648; crews, 9,516.

The iron industry, as investigated by the Iron and Steel Manufacturers' Association of Germany, gave some very remarkable results, which followed upon the introduction of protective duties. In January, 1879, 325 private firms and joint-stock companies employed 153,979 hands, and paid in wages 9,333,396 marks monthly; in January, 1883, they gave employment to 206,150 labourers, an increase of 33·9 per cent., and paid in wages 14,754,350 marks monthly—an increase of 57·2 per cent. These statistics, however, were compiled by a protective body, and they might be susceptible of modification now.

The strength of the German Army on the peace footing, 1886–7, is as follows: Officers, 18,143; rank and file, 427,274;

horses, 81,773 ; guns, 1,374. The war strength of the army is (as regards rank and file), more than treble this number, being raised to 35,427 officers, 1,500,000 men, 312,731 horses, and 2,500 guns. If to these figures be added the Landsturm and the one-year volunteers, the total war-strength of trained soldiers would be about 2,650,000 ; while with the addition of those not trained, on account of not being up to the standard at the time of drilling, the total available force of all classes would be 5,670,000. Every German is liable to service, and no substitution is allowed. The strength of the German Navy on April 1, 1886, was as follows: Number of vessels, 98 ; guns, 554 ; indicated horse-power, 162,405 ; crews, 17,472.

In all parts of Germany, except the Mecklenburg States, complete free trade in land has been established, and all personal and material burdens removed that would interfere with the operation of this principle. In the West German States, small estates and peasant proprietorship are the rule, but in the North large estates prevail. The land is very serviceable, for of the whole area of Germany 94 per cent. is classed as productive, and only 6 per cent. as unproductive. On the 5th of June, 1882, there were no fewer than 5,276,344 separate agricultural enclosures, each cultivated by one household. Corn crops, and hay and grass are the principal growths, though there is also a considerable produce from the vineyards. Forestry is an industry of great importance. The value of domestic animals in 1883 was 5,944,511,000 marks—horses and cattle furnishing more than three-fourths of the whole. The iron industry in Germany is a large one. In 1883 there were 335 works in operation, producing finished iron ; besides 75 steel works ; and a total of nearly 200,000 men were employed in the iron trades. With regard to shipping, on January 1, 1886, Germany had engaged in the foreign trade, 4,135 vessels ; and on January 1, 1883, she had 18,372 ships engaged in the river, canal, and coast trade of the Empire, 2,460 of which had a tonnage of 150 and upwards.

The railways of the Empire completed and open for public traffic in 1886 had a total length of 23,535 English miles ; of these lines 20,407 miles belonged to and were worked by the State, 422 miles were owned by private companies but were worked by the State, and the remainder were owned and worked by private companies. In a short time, however, all the railways will be absorbed by the State.

The telegraphic and postal services of Germany have made great strides. In the year 1885 the total number of telegraphic despatches was 19,131,225, of which 13,622,250 were inland,

and the remainder international. The length of telegraph lines in the Empire at the end of 1885 was 51,537 miles, and of telegraph wires 184,380 miles. The Imperial Post Office carried, in 1885, 815,689,030 letters, 243,871,890 post-cards, 19,117,000 patterns, 224,382,000 stamped wrappers, 524,473,250 newspapers, and 176,353,000 registered packets and money orders, &c., of the value of 18,296,431,600 marks. The total receipts from the post office and telegraphic services amounted in 1884–85 to 193,607,130 marks, and the total expenditure to 168,976,045 marks. The number of post offices was 17,452, with 13,413 telegraphic stations at the end of 1885, and 93,845 persons employed.

Germany extended her Empire in 1884 by taking under her protection certain portions of the West Coast of Africa. By a treaty concluded in 1886 the German East Africa Company acquired still further rights over territory exceeding in area 100,000 square miles. Other territories annexed in 1885 were Kaiser Wilhelm's Land, New Guinea, 70,300 square miles in extent, the New Britain and other islands, now known as the Bismarck Archipelago, embracing an area of 18,150 square miles; and, in 1886, three islands in the Solomon Group, to the east of Bismarck Archipelago, with an area of 6,000 square miles.

THE END.